Graham McNeill

MECHANICUM

*To the staff at Lee Rosy's, for keeping my creative juices flowing with
a regular supply of tea and cookies.*

A BLACK LIBRARY PUBLICATION

First published in Great Britain in 2008 by
BL Publishing,
Games Workshop Ltd.,
Willow Road, Nottingham,
NG7 2WS, UK.

10 9 8 7 6 5 4 3 2 1

Cover and page 1 illustration by Neil Roberts.

Map by Adrian Wood.

See the Black Library on the Internet at
www.blacklibrary.com

Find out more about Games Workshop
and the world of Warhammer 40,000 at
www.games-workshop.com

Printed and bound in the UK.

THE HORUS HERESY

It is a time of legend.

Mighty heroes battle for the right to rule the galaxy.
The vast armies of the Emperor of Earth have conquered
the galaxy in a Great Crusade – the myriad alien races have
been smashed by the Emperor's elite warriors and wiped
from the face of history.

The dawn of a new age of supremacy for humanity
beckons.

Gleaming citadels of marble and gold celebrate the many
victories of the Emperor. Triumphs are raised on a million
worlds to record the epic deeds of his most powerful and
deadly warriors.

First and foremost amongst these are the primarchs,
superheroic beings who have led the Emperor's armies of
Space Marines in victory after victory. They are unstoppable
and magnificent, the pinnacle of the Emperor's genetic
experimentation. The Space Marines are the mightiest
human warriors the galaxy has ever known, each capable of
besting a hundred normal men or more in combat.

Organised into vast armies of tens of thousands called
Legions, the Space Marines and their primarch leaders
conquer the galaxy in the name of the Emperor.

Chief amongst the primarchs is Horus, called the Glorious,
the Brightest Star, favourite of the Emperor, and like a son
unto him. He is the Warmaster, the commander-in-chief of
the Emperor's military might, subjugator of a thousand
thousand worlds and conqueror of the galaxy. He is a
warrior without peer, a diplomat supreme.

As the flames of war spread through the Imperium,
mankind's champions will all be put to the ultimate test.

~ DRAMATIS PERSONAE ~

The Mechanicum

KELBOR-HAL	Fabricator General of Mars, Forge Master of Olympus Mons
KANE	Fabricator Locum of Mars, Forge Master of Mondus Occulum
URTZI MALEVOLUS	Forge Master of Mars
LUKAS CHROM	Forge Master of Mondus Gamma
REGULUS	Mechanicum representative of Horus Lupercal
AMBASSADOR MELGATOR	Mechanicum representative to Terra
KORIEL ZETH	Mistress of the Magma City
IPLUVIEN MAXIMAL	Forge Master of Mars
ADEPT SEMYON	Adept of Mars

Legio Tempestus

INDIAS CAVALERIO, THE STORMLORD	Princeps of the Warlord, *Victorix Magna*
SUZAK	Princeps of the Warlord, *Tharsis Hastatus*
MORDANT	Princeps of the Reaver, *Arcadia Fortis*
SHARAQ	Princeps of the Reaver, *Metallus Cebrenia*

Basek	Princeps of the Warhound, *Vulpus Rex*
Kasim	Princeps of the Warhound, *Raptoria*
Lamnos	Princeps of the Warhound, *Astrus Lux*

Legio Tempestus

| Camulos | Princeps of *Aquila Ignis* |

The Knights of Taranis

Lord Commander Verticorda	Rider of *Ares Lictor*
Lord Commander Caturix	Rider of *Gladius Fulmen*
Preceptor Stator	Rider of *Fortis Metallum*
Raf Maven	Rider of *Equitos Bellum*
Leopold Cronus	Rider of *Pax Mortis*

Servants of the Mechanicum

Dalia Cythera	Transcriber
Zouche Chahaya	Machinist
Severine Delmer	Schematic Draughter
Mellicin Oster	Technical Overseer
Caxton Torgau	Component Assembler
Rho-mu 31	Mechanicum Protector
Remiare	Tech-priest Assassin
Jonas Milus	Empath

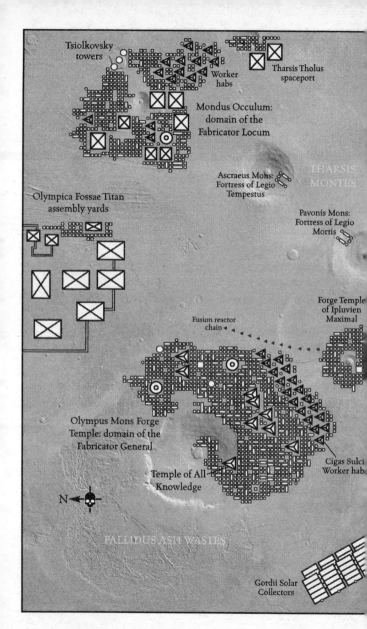

Tsiolkovsky towers

Worker habs

Tharsis Tholus spaceport

Mondus Occulum: domain of the Fabricator Locum

Ascraeus Mons: Fortress of Legio Tempestus

Pavonis Mons: Fortress of Legio Mortis

THARSIS MONTES

Olympica Fossae Titan assembly yards

Forge Temple of Ipluvien Maximal

Fusion reactor chain

Olympus Mons Forge Temple: domain of the Fabricator General

Cigas Sulci Worker habs

Temple of All Knowledge

N

PALLIDUS ASH WASTES

Gordii Solar Collectors

Mondus Gamma
Forge Temple of
Lukas Chrom

SINAI
PLANUM

SOLIS
PLANUM

SYRIA
PLANUM

NOCTIS
LABYRINTHUS

Mag-lev route

Red
Gorge

Ash
Border

Crater
Edge

Dune
Town

Arsia Mons:
Fortress of the
Knights of
Taranis

Aetna's
Dam

Typhon
causeway

The Magma
City

Arsia Mons
subhives

DAEDALIA
PLANUM

THE THARSIS QUADRANGLE
OF MARS

PALLIDUS ASH WASTES

Equatorial
Refinery
Fields

Memnonia Deep Core
mining fields

Behold the coming of the One Supreme Master of Machines!

He comes to you from heaven in the drops of rain.

Sons of Mars listen well, for one will come, mighty and strong, holding the sceptre of power in his hand.

Clothed in light and fire, his mouth shall utter eternal words,

while his mind shall be a fountain of knowledge and fact.

When the Saviour shall appear ye shall see him as he is,

a man like ourselves and yet greater by far.

This will be the first step in the greatest endeavour of Man.

It shall begin on the highest peak of the dominion of Ares.

When Deimos and Phobos are at apogee and perigee,

there thou shalt see the face of the Omnissiah.

Clad in a body of gold, and wreathed in the firmament of the storm,

the Lord of all Machines will stand in the midst of his people,

and shall reign over all the dominion of Man.

Great shall be the glory of his presence, that the sun shall hide his face in shame.

For verily I say unto you that he shall be the Alpha and Omega,

the beginning and the end, the master of flesh and the forger of metal.

He shall be a light that shineth in darkness
and a banisher of ignorance.
He shall be the object of devotion and love,
which kings might envy and emperors sigh
for in vain!
He shall desire the good of Ares's realm and
the happiness of Man.
All must become one in loyalty and see all
men as brothers.
Ruinous wars shall pass away, and peace shall
reign among the stars.
Strife and bloodshed and discord will cease.
All men shall be as one kindred.
The divisions of the stars shall all be one!

The Coming of the Omnissiah, exloaded
by Pico della Moravec, Primus of the
Brotherhood of Singularitarianism.

0.01

It never rained on Mars, not any more. Once, when Mars had first known life, back in an age long unknown to man, mighty storms had torn across the landscape, gouging channels in the rock and carving sweeping coastlines from the towering cliffs of the great Mons. Then the world had endured its first death, and the planet had become a cratered red wasteland of empty dust bowls and parched deserts.

But the red planet lived to breathe again.

The terraforming of Mars had begun in the earliest days of the golden age of man's expansion to the stars, bringing new life and hope, but in the end, this was a remission, not a cure. Within the span of a few centuries, the planet had died its second death, choking on the fumes of volcanic forge complexes, continent-sized refineries and the effluent of a million weapons shops.

It never rained on Mars.

That thought was uppermost in Brother Verticorda's mind as he guided the battered bipedal form of *Ares Lictor* up the gentle slopes of Olympus Mons towards the colossal volcano's caldera. Resembling a brutish, mechanical humanoid some nine metres tall, *Ares Lictor* was a Paladin-class Knight, a one-man war machine of deep blue armour plates with a fearsome array of weaponry beyond the power of even the strongest of the Terran Emperor's Astartes to bear.

Ares Lictor walked with an awkward, loping gait, thanks to a stubborn knee joint that no amount of ministration from the tech-priests could restore to full working order. But Verticorda handled his mount with the practised ease of one born in the cockpit.

It never rained on Mars.

Except it was raining now.

The brushed orange skies above were weeping a thin drizzle of moisture, patterning Verticorda's cockpit, and he felt the cold wetness through the hard-plugs in his spine and the haptic implants in his fingers.

He realised that he too was weeping, for he had never expected to witness such a sight, the heavens opening and precipitation falling to the surface of the red planet. Such a thing had not happened in living memory, and on Mars that was a *long* time.

Two other war machines followed Verticorda, his brothers-in-arms and fellow Knights of Taranis. He could hear their chatter over the Manifold, the synaptic congress that linked their minds, but had not the words to convey his own sense of wonder at the sight that greeted them on this day of days.

The sky above Olympus Mons raged.

Billowing storm clouds heaved as though ancient, forgotten gods battled within them, slamming their mighty hammers against wrought iron anvils and hurling forked bolts of lightning at one another. Mars's largest moon, Phobos, was visible as a yellowed irregularity behind in the clouds, its cratered surface at its closest point to the surface of Mars in decades.

The mighty volcano, the largest mountain in the Tharsis region and indeed the solar system, soared above the Martian landscape, the dizzyingly high escarpments of its cliffs rising to almost thirty kilometres above the surface of the planet. Verticorda knew this region of Tharsis intimately; he had marched *Ares Lictor* from the Fabricator General's forge on the eastern flanks of the mighty volcano three decades ago, and he had led his brother warriors across its slopes uncounted times.

More lightning flashed and the thousands gathering at the base of the volcano gazed fearfully into the building tempest from towering hab-stacks and ironclad bulwarks of Kelbor-Hal's domain. Abused skies cracked and roared, distorting under the overpressure of something unimaginably vast, and the atmospherics lit up the sky as far as any eye, fleshy or augmetic, could see.

Crowds in their thousands, their tens of thousands, were following the Knights up the slopes of Olympus Mons, but they had not the speed or manoeuvrability of the war machines. This wonder was for the Knights of Taranis and for them alone.

A shape moved in the clouds, and Verticorda halted his mount at the sheer edge of the caldera's escarpment with a release of pressure on his right hand. The machine reacted instantly. The bond he had forged with it in years of battle was that of two comrades-in-arms who had shared blood and victory in equal measure.

Verticorda could feel the anticipation of this moment in every sizzling joint and weld within *Ares Lictor*, as though it – more than he – was anticipating the glory of this day. Golden light flashed above and the drizzle of rain became a downpour.

A zigzagging pathway had been cut into the cliff, leading to the base of the caldera, nearly two kilometres below. It was a treacherous path in ideal conditions, but in this deluge it was close to suicide.

'What do you say, old friend?' asked Verticorda. 'Shall we greet these new arrivals?'

He could feel the machine straining beneath him and smiled, easing up the power and walking the Knight towards the edge of the cliff. The steps were designed for the long strides and wide treads of a Knight, but were slick and reflective with rain. It was a long way down and not even the armour or energy shields that protected a Knight in battle would save him from a fall from this height.

Verticorda guided *Ares Lictor's* first step onto the cut path and felt the slipperiness beneath its feet as though he walked upon it himself. Each step was dangerous and he took care to ensure that each one was taken with the utmost reverence. Step by step, inch by inch, he walked *Ares Lictor* down the path to the cratered plain below.

Golden light suddenly burst from the clouds above, dazzling and brilliant, and bolts of scarlet lightning danced like crackling spider webs between the ground and sky. Verticorda almost lost his footing as he instinctively looked up.

A mighty floating city of gold was descending from the heavens.

Like a mountainous spire sheared from the side of some vast, continental landmass, the city was studded with light and colour, its dimensions enormous beyond imagining. A vast, eagle-winged prow of gold marked one end of the floating city, and colossal battlements, like the highest towers of the mightiest Martian spire, rose like gnarled stalagmites from the other.

Rippling engines flared with unimaginable power on the colossal edifice's underside, and Verticorda stood amazed at the technology required to prevent such a monstrous creation from plummeting to the ground. Flocks of smaller craft attended the larger one, its dimensions only growing larger the more it emerged from its concealing clouds.

'Blood of the Machine,' hissed Yelsic, rider of the Knight at his back. 'How can such a thing stay aloft?'

'Concentrate on your descent,' warned Verticorda. 'I don't want you losing your footing behind me.'

'Understood.'

Verticorda returned his attention to the pathway, negotiating the last three hundred metres bathed in a cold sweat. He let out a long, shuddering breath as he took his first step onto the surface of the Olympus Mons caldera, enjoying the strange new sensation of mud sucking at his feet.

By the time the Knights reached the base of the cliff, the enormous craft had landed, its gargantuan bulk surely offset by some dampening field to prevent it from collapsing under its own weight, or sinking deep into the Martian surface. Roiling clouds of superheated steam and condensing gases billowed outwards from the ship and as they swept over *Ares Lictor*, Verticorda smelled the scents of another world: hard radiation, the ache of homelands long forgotten and thin, achingly cold, mountain air.

He told himself it was ludicrous to sense such things from a ship that had just made the fiery descent through a planet's atmosphere, yet they were there as plain as day.

'Spread out,' said Verticorda. 'Flank speed.'

The Knights loping alongside him moved into a combat spread as they strode through the hot, moist mists. Verticorda felt no threat from the unknown craft, yet decades of training and discipline would not allow him to approach it without taking precautions.

At last the mist thinned and Verticorda pulled up as the enormous golden cliff of the vessel's flanks rose up before him like a mountain freshly deposited on the planet's surface. Its scale was awe-inspiring, more so than even the fastnesses of the Titan legions or the data mountains of the Temple of All Knowledge.

Even the mightiest forge temple of Mondus Gamma on the Syria Planum paled in comparison to the scale of this vessel, for it had been fashioned with deliberate artifice and not the combined forces of millions of years of geological interaction. Every plate and sheet of the enormous vessel was worked with the care of a craftsman, and Verticorda struggled to think of a reason why so many would labour for so long and with such devotion to ornament a vessel designed for travel between the stars.

The answer came a moment after the question.

This was no ordinary vessel, this was a craft built with love, a craft built for a being beloved by all. No ordinary man could inspire such devotion and Verticorda suddenly felt an overwhelming fear that he was in the presence of something far greater and far more terrifying than anything he could ever have imagined.

A shrieking blast of steam vented from the ship and a colossal hatchway was limned in golden light. Huge pneumatic pistons – larger than a Titan – slowly lowered a long ramp, easily wide enough for a regiment of gene-bulked Skitarii to march down in line abreast. The ramp lowered with no sign of strain on the vessel, and the brightness within poured out, bathing the Martian landscape in a warm, welcome glow.

Verticorda twisted *Ares Lictor* around on its central axis, and felt a shiver travel the length of his spine as he saw the entire rim of the volcano's crater lined with onlookers. With a thought, he increased the magnification through the viewscreen and saw thousands of robed adepts, menials, tech-priests, logi and workers gathered to watch the events unfolding below.

Crackling, voltaic viewing clouds coloured the sky behind the crowds and flocks of servo-skulls buzzed overhead, though none dared approach within the swirling electromagnetic field that surrounded the craft.

The huge ramp crunched down and Verticorda squinted into the light that blazed from within. A silhouette moved within the light, tall and powerful, glorious and magnificent.

The light seemed to move with him and as Verticorda watched the figure descend the ramp, a shadow fell across the surface of the plain on which the craft had landed. Though he was loath to tear his gaze from the magnificent figure, Verticorda looked up to see a convex ellipse of darkness bite into the glowing outline of the sun.

The light from the storm-wracked skies faded until the only illumination came from the figure as he stepped onto Martian soil for the first time. Verticorda knew immediately that the man was a warrior, for there could be no doubt that this sublime figure had been made mighty by battle.

Verticorda felt the collective gasp from the thousands of spectators in his bones, as though the very planet shuddered with pleasure to know this individual's touch.

He looked back down and saw the warrior standing before him, tall and clad in golden armour, each plate wrought with the same skill and love as had been lavished upon his vessel. The warrior wore no helm and was fitted with no visible breathing augmetics, yet seemed untroubled by the chemical-laden air of Mars.

Verticorda found his gaze dwelling on the warrior's face, beautiful and perfect as though able to see beyond the armoured exterior of *Ares Lictor* and into Verticorda's soul. In his eyes, his so very ancient eyes, Verticorda saw the wisdom of all the ages and the burden of all the knowledge contained within them.

A crimson mantle flapped in the wind behind the giant warrior and he carried an eagle-topped sceptre clutched in one mighty gauntlet. The golden giant's eyes scrutinised the blue-armoured form of Verticorda's mount, from its conical glacis to the aventailed shoulder plates upon which the wheel and lightning bolt symbol of the Knights of Taranis was emblazoned.

The warrior reached out towards him. 'Your machine is damaged, Taymon Verticorda,' he said, his voice heavy and yet musical, like the most perfect sound imaginable. 'May I?'

Verticorda found himself unable to form a reply, knowing that anything he might say would be trite in the face of such perfection. It didn't occur to him to wonder how the sublime warrior knew his name. Without waiting for a reply, the warrior reached out, and Verticorda felt his touch upon the joints of *Ares Lictor's* knee.

'Machine, heal thyself,' said the warrior, the purpose and self-belief in his voice passing into Verticorda as though infusing every molecule of his hybrid existence of flesh and steel with new-found purpose and vitality.

He felt the warmth of the warrior's touch through the shell of his mount, and gasped as trembling vibrations spread through its armoured frame of plasteel and ceramite. He took an involuntary step back, feeling the movements of his mount flow as smoothly as ever they had. With one step, he could feel *Ares Lictor* move as though it had just come off the assembly lines, its stubborn knee joint flexing like new.

'Who are you?' he gasped, his voice sounding grating and pathetic next to the mighty timbre of the golden warrior's voice.

'I am the Emperor,' said the warrior.

It was a simple answer, yet the weight of history and the potential of a glorious future were carried in every syllable.

Knowing he would never again hear words spoken with such meaning, Verticorda and *Ares Lictor* dropped to one knee, performing the manoeuvre with a grace that would have been impossible before the Emperor's touch.

In that moment, Taymon Verticorda knew the truth of the being standing before him.

'Welcome to Mars, my lord,' he said. 'All praise to the Omnissiah.'

PRINCIPIA
MECHANICUM

I.OI

SWATHED IN FADED and tattered robes of rust red, the six Mechanicum Protectors stood unmoving before her, as still as the towering statues of the magi that had stared down upon the thousands of scribes within the great Hall of Transcription of the Librarium Technologica. Their iron-shod boots were locked tight into the ship's deck restraints, while she had had to hold onto a metal stanchion just to avoid cracking her head on its fuselage or tumbling around the hold when it had taken off.

The interior of the ship was bare and unadorned, as functional as it was possible to be. No unnecessary decorations or aesthetic elements designed to ease the eye were included in its design, perfectly epitomising the organisation to which it belonged.

Dalia Cythera ran a hand through her cropped blonde hair, feeling the dirt and grease there and longing for one of her weekly rotations in the Windward sump's ablutions block. She had a feeling, however, that her cleanliness was the furthest thing from the minds of the Protectors.

None of them had spoken to her other than to confirm her name when they had removed her from the cell beneath the Librarium in which Magos Ludd had locked her a week earlier. He'd discovered the enhancements she'd made to the inner workings of her cogitator and had hauled her from the work line in a rage, angry hashes of binaric static canting from his vocaliser.

Seven days alone in complete darkness had almost broken her. She remembered squeezing into a tiny ball when the cell door finally opened and she saw the bronze death masks of the Protectors, their gleaming weapon-staves and the unforgiving light of their eyes.

Ludd's blurted protests at the Protectors' intrusion soon ceased when they invited him to scan the biometric security encryptions carried within their staves. She was frightened of the Protectors, but then she guessed she was supposed to be. Their masters in the Mechanicum had designed them that way, with their enhanced bulk, weaponised limbs and glowing green eyes that shone, unblinking, behind bronze, skull-faced masks.

Within moments, she had been hauled from the cell and dragged through the cavernous, echoing scriptoria where she'd spent the last two years of her life, her limbs loose and weak.

Thousands upon thousands of robed scribes, ordinates, curators and form-stampers filled the scriptoria, and as she was carried towards the enormous arch that led to the world beyond, she realised she would be sad to leave the knowledge that passed through it.

She would not miss the people, for she had no friends here and no colleagues. None of the pallid-skinned adepts looked up from the monotony of their work, the sea-green glow of their cogitators and the flickering lumen globes floating in the dusty air leaching their wizened features of life and animation.

Such a state of being was foreign to Dalia and it never failed to amaze her that her fellow scribes were so blind to the honour of what they did.

The recovered knowledge of Terra and the new wonders sent back from across the galaxy by the thousands of remembrancers accompanying the expeditions of the Great Crusade passed through this chamber. Despite the glorious flood of information, carefully logged and filed within the great libraries of Terra, every one of the faceless minions ceaselessly, blindly, ground themselves into old age repeating the same bureaucratic and administrative tasks every waking hour of every day, oblivious or uncaring of the wealth of information to which they were privy.

Without the insight or even the will to question the task they had been given to perform, the scribes shuffled from their hab-stacks through the same kilometres of well-trodden corridors every day and performed their duties without question, thought or awe.

The rustle of paper was what Dalia imagined the ocean to sound like, the clatter of adding machines and the rattle of brass keys on the typesetters like the motion of uncounted pebbles on a beach. Of course, Dalia had never seen the things she imagined, for the seas of Terra had long since boiled away in forgotten wars, but the words she read as she copied text from the reams of paper and armfuls of data-slates carried in daily by muscled servitors had filled her mind with possibilities of worlds and ideas that existed far beyond the confines of Terra's mightiest scriptorium.

Emerging from the musty darkness of the Librarium Technologica, she had been blinded by the brightness of the day, the sky a brilliant white and the sun a hazy orb peeking through scraps of clouds the colour of corrosion.

The air was cold and thin at this altitude. She could just make out the tips of the slate-coloured mountains that crowned the world over the teeming roofs and spires crammed together in this part of the Imperial Palace. She had longed to see the mountains in all their glory, but her escorts marched her through dark streets that sweated steam and oil and voices towards an unknown destination without pause.

That destination turned out to be a landing platform, upon which sat a vapour-wreathed starship, its hull still warm and groaning from the stresses of an atmospheric entry.

She was led into the cavernous hold and deposited on the floor while the Protectors took up their allocated positions and the mag-locks secured them to the deck. With a juddering roar and sudden lurch, the starship lifted off, and Dalia was thrown to her knees by the violence of the ascent. Fear gripped her and she clung to a protruding stanchion as the angle of incline increased sharply.

The thought that she was leaving the planet of her birth struck her forcefully, and she experienced terrible panic at the thought of venturing beyond her known horizons. No sooner had she chided herself for such timidity, than the panic subsided and she felt her stomach cramp as she realised how hungry she was.

The roaring of the starship and the vibrations on its hull grew louder and more violent until she was sure the craft was going to tear itself apart. Eventually, the noise changed in tone and the starship began to level out, powering through the void at unimaginable speeds.

She was travelling on a starship.

With a moment free to think, she now wondered where she was going and why the Mechanicum Protectors had plucked her from the Librarium's cells and for what purpose. Curiously, she felt no fear of this strange voyage, but she attributed that lack to the mystery and interest of it being enough to overshadow any wariness she felt.

Over the next day or so, her escorts – she did not now think of them as captors – resisted her every attempt at communication, save to instruct her to eat and drink, which she did ravenously, despite the food's chemical artificiality.

They did not move from their locked positions at all during the journey, standing as mute guardians and offering her no diversion save in the study of their forms.

Each one was tall and powerfully built, their physiques gene-bulked and augmented with implanted weaponry. Ribbed cables and coloured wires threaded their robes and penetrated their flesh through raw-looking plugs embedded in their skin. She had seen Protectors before, but she had never been so close to one.

They smelled unpleasantly of rotten meat, machine oil and stale sweat.

They were armed with giant pistols with flaring barrels, and tall staves of iron, topped with a bronze and silver cog, from which hung a scrap of parchment that fluttered in the gusting air within the cold compartment.

A set of numbers was written on the parchment, arranged in a four by four grid, and Dalia quickly worked out that each line added up to the same number, no matter which way they were combined – vertically, horizontally or diagonally. Not only that, but each of the quadrants, the four centre squares, the corner squares and many other combinations added up to the same figure.

'Thirty-four,' she said. 'It's always thirty-four.'

The design was familiar to her and Dalia knew she had seen it before. No sooner had she wondered where, than the answer came to her.

'The Melancholia,' said Dalia, nodding at the parchment.

'What did you say?' asked the Protector.

His voice was human, but echoed with a metallic rasp beneath his bronze mask, and Dalia was momentarily taken aback that he'd actually responded to something she said.

'The symbol on your parchment,' she said. 'It's from an engraving. I saw it in a book I transcribed two years ago.'

'Two years ago? And you still remember it?'

'Yes,' nodded Dalia, hesitantly. 'I kind of remember stuff I've read and don't forget it.'

'It is the symbol of our master,' said the Protector.

'It's from an engraving of one of the old master prints,' said Dalia, her eyes taking on a glazed look as she spoke, talking more to herself than the Protector. 'It was so old, but then everything we transcribe in the great hall that's not from the expedition fleets is old. It was a picture of a woman, but she looked frustrated, as if she was annoyed at not being able to invent something ingenious. She had all sorts of equipment around her, weights, an hourglass and a hammer, but she looked sad, as if she just couldn't get the idea to take shape.'

The Protectors glanced at one another as Dalia spoke, each one gripping his stave tightly. Dalia caught the look and her words trailed off.

'What?' she asked.

The Protector disengaged the mag-lock clamps securing him to the deck and stepped towards her. The suddenness of his motion took her by surprise and she stumbled backwards, falling onto her backside as he loomed over her, the green glow of his eyes shining brightly within his tattered hood.

'I begin to see why we were sent to fetch you,' said the Protector.

'You do?' asked Dalia. 'And you were sent for me? Me? Dalia Cythera?'

'Yes, Dalia Cythera. Rho-mu 31 was sent to fetch you from Terra.'

'Rho-mu 31?'

'That is our designation,' said the Protector.

'What, all of you?'

'All of us, each of us. It is all the same.'

'All right, but why were you sent to fetch *me*?' asked Dalia.

'We were sent to fetch you before you were executed.'

'Executed?' exclaimed Dalia. 'For what?'

'Magos Ludd invoked the Law of the Divine Complexity,' explained Rho-mu 31. 'Individuals so accused attract the attention of our master.'

Dalia thought for a moment, her eyes fluttering beneath their lids as she recalled what that law concerned. 'Let me think, that's the belief that the structure and working of each machine has been set down by the Omnissiah and is therefore divine... and that to alter it is, oh...'

'You see now why we came for you?'

'Not really,' admitted Dalia. 'Anyway, who *is* your master, and what does he want with me? I'm just a transcriber of remembrance. I'm nobody.'

Rho-mu 31 shook his head, making a fist and placing it over the silver and bronze cog atop his staff.

'You are more than you realise, Dalia Cythera,' he said, 'but that, and more, will become clear to you when you meet our master: High Adept Koriel Zeth, Mistress of the Magma City.'

'The Magma City?' asked Dalia. 'Where is that?'

'At the edge of the Daedalia Planum, on the southern flank of Arsia Mons,' said Rho-mu 31, lifting his stave and touching it to an opaque panel on the vibrating hull of the starship. A flickering light crackled, and the panel began to change, slowly becoming more and more translucent until finally it was virtually transparent.

When this transformation was complete, Dalia gasped at the sight before her, her face bathed in a fiery red glow from the planet below. Its surface was clad in fire and metal, its atmosphere choked with striated clouds of pollution. Teeming with gargantuan sprawls of industry larger than the continents of Old Earth, the world seemed to throb with the heartbeat of monstrous hammers.

Plumes of fire and towering stacks of iron rose from its mountainous southern regions, and networks of gleaming steel spread out like cracks in the ground through which fractured light spilled into the sky.

'Is that…?'

'Mars,' confirmed Rho-mu 31. 'Domain of the Mechanicum.'

SUPERSONIC SHELLS TORE through the gaggle of servitors feeding on the dead techno-mats, obliterating one instantly and blowing the limbs from another. Three others staggered back, chunks of flesh blasted from their emaciated frames. They refused to fall, however, their damaged brains unable to comprehend how grievously the guns of Cronus's Knight had wounded them.

'All yours, Maven,' said Cronus, cutting off the stream of shells.

'So glad you left me something to do,' replied Maven.

Maven moved *Equitos Bellum* in behind the bloody servitors, the energised blade in his war machine's right fist reaching down and slicing through the survivors in one sweep. Old Stator finished off the stragglers with a short, perfectly controlled burst of laser fire, their wasted bodies exploding in puffs of vaporised blood and scrap metal.

Standing five times the height of the feral creatures, the three Knights towered over the battlefield, though Maven knew that to call it such was to vastly overstate the nature of the deaths they had caused.

The Knights were armoured in thick plates of plasteel and ceramite, protected by layered banks of power fields strong enough to weather the impact of a much larger engine's wrath, and armed with weapons that could kill scores at a time. The plates of their armour were a deep, midnight blue, the right shoulder of each one painted with the design of a wheel encircling a lightning bolt.

The same design was repeated on the long, cream-coloured banners hanging between the mechanised legs of all three war machines, the heraldry of the Knights of Taranis.

Maven rode in *Equitos Bellum*, an honourable mount with a host of battle honours earned in the earliest days of the Great Crusade. It had fought the enemies of the Imperium beneath a dozen different skies, and even marched alongside the Salamanders of Primarch Vulkan. The design of a firedrake carved into the skull-cockpit of the Knight recalled that campaign, and Maven never tired of telling the stories of that glorious ride into battle.

His studious brother-in-arms, Cronus, rode in *Pax Mortis*, and Old Stator commanded the august majesty of *Fortis Metallum*. All three war machines had earned their share of glory on the battlefields of the Imperium, marching ahead of the Titan engines, the god-machines.

The Knights of Taranis were feted among the warriors of Mars for their martial achievements, revered for their place in Martian history, and lauded for the wisdom of their commanders.

Even the mighty princeps of the Titan legions were known to seek the wise counsel of the order's masters, for Lords Verticorda and Caturix were known as leaders whose shared command blended the warrior's heart with the diplomat's cool.

'So why, in the name of the Omnissiah are we stuck out in the arse end of nowhere culling feral servitors?' he asked himself, before remembering that the Manifold-link between the Knights was still open.

'We're here because those are our orders, Maven,' said Stator. 'Do you have a problem with that?'

'No, preceptor,' replied Maven, his tone contrite. 'I just meant that it seems like such a waste of our strength. Can't Magos Maximal's Protectors perform their own culls?'

'Not as well as we can,' said Cronus, his answer sounding like it came from a training manual. Maven felt his lip curl in a sneer at his brother's sycophancy.

'Exactly, Cronus,' said Stator. 'We've been given a duty to protect this reactor complex and there is honour in duty, no matter how far beneath us it might seem.'

Maven sensed an opening and said, 'But the Knights of Taranis once marched with the Crusade. We fought alongside heroes of the Imperium, and now all we do is shoot feral servitors that come up out of the pallidus. There's no glory in this work.'

'These days the threats to the Warmaster's campaigns require forces stronger than us,' said Stator, but Maven could sense the bitterness beneath his words. 'The Great Crusade is almost over.'

'And what will be left for us?' demanded Maven, emboldened by Stator's words. 'There must be expeditions that need the skills of our order.'

'The expeditions do not ask for Knights,' said Stator. 'They ask for the god-machines to walk with their armies. Our role is to protect Mars and maintain the traditions of our order, and part of that tradition is honouring our obligations. Is that understood, Maven?'

'Yes, preceptor,' said Maven.

'Now let's finish this sweep and make sure there are no more of them. Maximal needs this facility kept safe, and Lord Caturix swore that we would do so.'

Maven sighed and walked his Knight to where humming power cables jutted from the hard, orange earth and spat sparks where the servitors had dug at them to feed the machine parts of their ravaged bodies. The corpses of the techno-mats and artificers sent to fix the damage lay in pools of blood that were already congealing in the heat that bled from the fusion reactor further back in the gorge.

'Check for more of them out there, Cronus,' ordered Stator. 'They usually hunt in bigger packs than this.'

'Yes, preceptor,' replied Cronus, marching his Knight past the dead servitors and through the gap torn in the barbed, chain-link fence that surrounded the reactor. Cronus guided his machine up the rocky slopes to check the ground behind an outcrop of boulders. To manoeuvre so large a machine as a Knight over such rough terrain was no mean feat, and Maven was forced to admire his brother's skill as a pilot.

Fortis Metallum's upper body swivelled around on its gimbal waist mount to face Maven, and though he couldn't see his preceptor's face through the red visor of the cockpit, he could feel the stern, unflinching gaze through the softly glowing slits.

'Keep an eye on our rear in case any slipped past us,' ordered Stator, his voice once again as grim and inflexible as the posture of his machine. 'I'll hold you responsible if they have.'

'Yes, preceptor,' replied Maven. 'I'm on it.'

It was a Martian truism that if a warrior and machine spent enough time linked together they would begin to take on aspects of the other's character. *Fortis Metallum* was an old machine, cantankerous, flinty and utterly without mercy.

It was the perfect match for Stator.

Maven had met countless Titan drivers and it was easy to tell which machines they commanded within moments of talking to them.

Warhound drivers were belligerent, wolf-like daredevils, whereas the men who fought from the towering Battle Titans were arrogant and ego-driven warriors, who often appeared to hold those around them in contempt.

Maven knew that such conceit was forgivable, for marching to war so high above the battlefield and unleashing such awesome destructive power would naturally swell a man's ego, but it was also a necessary defence against the engine's character overwhelming that of its commander.

Maven walked his machine backwards in a bravura display of skill, watching as Stator turned away to follow Cronus through the mangled remains of the security fencing.

A Knight was much smaller than a Titan, but the mechanics in its construction and operation were no less incredible. A Titan had a crew to maintain its systems: a servitor to man each weapon system, a steersman to drive it, a tech-priest to minister to its bellicose heart, a moderati to run the crew and a princeps to command it.

A Knight was the perfect meld of flesh and steel, a mighty war machine at the command of a single pilot, a warrior who had the confidence to wield its power and the humility to know that, despite that power, he was not invincible.

Maven strode back towards the reactor complex, spreading his auspex net wide to pick up any of the feral servitors that might have broken away from the main pack, though he suspected he would not find any. Even if he did, what threat did a few servitors represent?

Broken and irreparably damaged servitors or those whose cranial surgery had failed to take were often simply dumped in the pallidus, the name given to the toxic, ashen hinterlands that existed between the Martian forges. The vast majority died, but some survived, though to call their doomed existence life was overstating the reality of it.

Most simply attempted to carry out the task for which they had been created, marching back and forth through the wastelands with their fried brains unable to comprehend that they were no longer in service.

In some cases, the damage to their brains allowed them a fragile degree of autonomy and those unfortunate creatures survived by feasting on the dead. Drawn by warmth and power, many banded together in unthinking packs and infested Mechanicum facilities, attacking workers and draining current to sustain their wretched experience.

Such creatures required culling, which brought Maven's thoughts full circle.

He lifted his head, the motion of the Knight's cranial carapace following exactly. The crags around the reactor were empty and desolate, the red volcanic peaks scoured by dust clouds blown up by the high winds funnelled along the northern fossae.

The heart of the reactor facility sat six hundred metres back from the fencing that surrounded it, a collection of intricate buildings of pipes, cables and crackling antenna towers. A huge, domed structure sat in the middle of the complex, its surface studded with plugs and vents. The air rippled around the building and intense waves of heat and electromagnetism washed from it in tidal surges.

The trench of the Gigas Fossae was dotted with several fusion reactors, but the facility upon the rocky slopes surrounding the northern impact crater of Ulysses Patera was the largest, and had been built by Magos Ipluvien Maximal.

Adept Maximal was one of the most senior magi of Mars, and his fusion reactors supplied power to a great many vassal forges dotted around the Tharsis uplands. Such arrangements were common across the red planet, ancient treaties binding the clans and forges together in reciprocal pacts of protection and supply that allowed such varied groups with conflicting needs to coexist. As well as allied forges, Maximal had exchanged bonds of fealty and supply with a number of warrior orders, including many of the most revered Titan Legios.

'So why aren't they here?' Maven muttered to himself. 'Too busy arguing amongst themselves is why.'

Maven put thoughts of the increasing tensions on Mars from his mind and made his way forwards, swinging the auspex around by twisting his mount's upper body, pulverising boulders as its enormous weight crushed them beneath its stride. He needed to cover every approach to the reactor complex, and threat or not, Stator would haul him over the coals were any feral servitors to get past him.

He felt the rocks break beneath *Equitos Bellum's* feet, the sensation akin to having his body and senses magnified to the size of the Knight. Mechanicum Protector squads at the edge of the reactor complex saw him and bowed respectfully as his Knight shook the ground with its heavy strides.

Menials and servitors laboured to maintain the giant reactor functions, their movements slow and sluggish in heavily reinforced haz-mat suits. A huge transformer crackled with energy flares, metres-thick cabling and a lattice of conductor towers linking it to the reactor. Blue lightning sparked from the transformer, rippling along the length of ductwork that was visible before the cables delved beneath the regolith and bedrock towards destinations all across the quadrant of Tharsis.

Maven blinked as he felt a tremor through the auspex return, a fleeting impression of something moving on the far side of the reactor. He focused his attention on that part of the cockpit display, enhancing the imagery in an attempt to see what he was receiving.

'Blood of the Machine,' he swore as the auspex connected with something big, something throwing off a spider-like pattern of electromagnetic energy much larger than a servitor. For the briefest second it appeared as though a great many other signals accompanied it.

An instant later and it was gone, blinked out as though it had never existed.

More ghost returns faded in and out, and Maven was suddenly unsure as to whether he'd seen anything at all.

A Knight's auspex was hardwired into the pilot's senses via a spinal plug, and interpreting the incoming data streams was an art form in itself, a blend of intuition and hard fact. In any case, it was difficult to be sure of anything in this region, the flare-offs and radiation bleeds from the reactor playing havoc with the veracity of auspex returns.

Then the spider pattern flashed again and this time he was certain.

Something *was* out there, and it wasn't squawking on any friendly channel.

'Preceptor, I think I have something,' said the voice.

'Define "something", Maven,' came the voice of Preceptor Stator.

'I'm not sure, but it's coming from the opposite side of the reactor complex.'

'More servitors?' asked Cronus.

Maven chewed his bottom lip, willing the sensor return to come again so he could report something more concrete, but the portion of the Manifold dedicated to auspex returns remained steadfastly awash with background radiation.

Still, he was sure that whatever was out there was more than simply feral servitors.

'No,' he said. 'Something bigger.'

THE STARSHIP BANKED as its pilot adjusted the angle of attack to allow it to enter the atmosphere safely. The view through the panel that Rho-mu 31 had rendered transparent slid away and Dalia rapped her knuckles against it.

'I'm assuming this isn't glass,' she said. 'What is it?'

'Photomalleable steel,' said Rho-mu 31. 'A burst of current from my stave alters the structure of the molecular bonds within the metal to allow certain forms of light waves to pass through it.'

'I haven't heard of anything like it,' said Dalia, amazed at the potential for such a material.

'Few beyond the Magma City have,' said Rho-mu 31. 'It is a creation of Adept Zeth.'

Dalia nodded and returned her attention to the view through the transparent metal. No sooner had she done so, than she found herself staring in wonder at an array of enormous structures, surely too large to have been created by the artifice of mere humans.

Colossal orbital constructions filled the heavens above Mars, a near contiguous array of gigantic shipyards and construction facilities. Dalia pressed her face to the cold panel, craning her neck to see how far the unbelievable conglomeration stretched. Try as she might, she could see no end to the gleaming docks, one end of the arc of steel rising up beyond sight above the ship she travelled in, the other vanishing around the curve of the red planet.

'The Ring of Iron,' said Rho-mu 31. 'The original exploratory fleets were constructed here and much of the expeditionary fleets were built in these docks.'

'It's huge,' said Dalia, cursing herself for stating something so obvious.

'They are the largest space docks in the galaxy, though the shipwrights of Jupiter will soon lay claim to the largest ship ever constructed when they complete the *Furious Abyss*.'

Dalia heard wounded pride in Rho-mu 31's remark and smiled at the notion that a servant of the Mechanicum would display envy. She returned her gaze to the sight beyond the starship's hull, seeing firefly sparks dotting the Ring of Iron where new vessels were being constructed by armies of shipwrights.

'What's that?' she asked, pointing towards what appeared to be a nebulous cloud of dust and reflective particles just over the horizon.

'That is the remains of an active construction site,' said Rho-mu 31. 'The latest ships to be built here have but recently departed.'

'Where have they gone?' asked Dalia, eager to learn what far-off place the new vessels were bound for.

'They were commissioned for Battlefleet Solar,' explained Rho-mu 31, 'but the Warmaster issued a new tasking order to have them despatched to take part in the Istvaan campaign.'

Dalia heard the note of disapproval in Rho-mu 31's voice, as though it were the greatest sin imaginable to change procedure and alter previously issued orders.

'Look, there is the fleet they were to join,' said Rho-mu 31, indicating berths high above them, and Dalia's mouth dropped open as the mighty warships of Battlefleet Solar came into view.

Distance rendered the fleet small, but to even recognise them and identify individual vessels from so far told Dalia that they were craft of unimaginable scale. From here they were sleek darts with sloping angular prows like ploughs and long, gothic bodies like great palaces hurled into the heavens and wrought into the forms of starships.

The ships were soon lost to sight as creeping fire slid along the length of the starship, the heat of passing through the atmosphere of Mars rippling along the shielded hull of the vessel. Dalia felt a steadying hand on her shoulder, a heavy, metallic hand that gripped her tightly as the starship continued its descent.

Flames and heat distortion soon obscured the view, but within the space of a few minutes it faded, and Dalia saw the surface of Mars in all its glory.

Vast cities of steel, larger and more magnificent than any of the hives of Terra, reared up from the surface, gargantuan behemoths that vomited fire and smoke into the sky. It was called the red planet, but precious little remained of the surface that could be identified as that hue. Mountains had been clad in metal and light, and cities and districts perched on the peaks and plateaux of the world named for a long forsaken god of war.

Glittering streams of light twisted and snaked through the few areas of cratered wilderness between the unimaginably vast conurbations, transit routes and maglev lines, and towering pyramids of glass and steel reared up like the tombs of forgotten kings.

'I've read about Mars, but I never thought to see it,' breathed Dalia. To see so many wondrous things in so short a time was nothing less than overwhelming.

'The Martian priesthood does not encourage visitors,' said Rho-mu 31. 'They believe the soil of Mars to be sacred.'

'Isn't the idea of things being sacred, well... not allowed any more?'

'In a manner of speaking, yes,' agreed Rho-mu 31. 'The Emperor advances the credo that belief in gods is a falsehood, but a condition of the Treaty of Olympus was that he swore not to interfere with our structures and society when Mars and Terra were joined.'

'So the Mechanicum believes in a god?'

'That is a question with no easy answer, Dalia Cythera. I do not believe in faith, but ask no more, for we are coming in to land and you will need to hold on tightly.'

Dalia nodded as the ship banked sharply, and she watched the world below tilt crazily as the pilot brought them around a shining pyramid bathed in light and topped with a great carving of an eye.

'The Temple of All Knowledge,' said Rho-mu 31, anticipating her question.

Dalia felt her stomach lurch as the ship dropped suddenly and a thick curtain of yellow smog obscured the view outside.

They flew through the smog for several hours until, as suddenly as it had appeared, it vanished, and Dalia cried out in terror as she saw that they were heading straight into the glassy black flanks of a towering mountain.

ONCE AGAIN, DALIA's stomach lurched as the craft's altitude altered rapidly, climbing at a sickeningly steep angle as the black cliff-face drew closer with terrifying rapidity. Sulphurous fumes wreathed the top of the mountain and the craft plunged into them. Dalia closed her eyes, expecting any moment to have her life ended as they smashed into the immovable mass of rock.

At last she opened her eyes when the feared impact didn't come and peered breathlessly through the transparent panel in the side of the craft. A sea of glowing red lava heaved and swelled beneath her, the volcanic heart of the planet bubbling up within the giant mountain.

Her view of the volcano's caldera shimmered and danced in the incredible heat radiating from the lava, and though she was insulated from the unimaginable temperatures, Dalia felt uncomfortably warm just looking at the molten rock.

'Arsia Mons,' said Rho-mu 31. 'A dead volcano brought back to life to serve the Mechanicum.'

'It's incredible,' breathed Dalia, looking over to the far side of the caldera, where a huge, industrial city-structure fashioned from what looked like blackened steel and stone rose from the lava like the broadside of a submerged starship. Enormous gates steamed in the lava, and mighty pistons of gleaming ceramite hissed and groaned as they rose and fell. Billowing clouds of superheated steam roared and vaporised like the breath of a host of great dragons, and Dalia saw that they were gaining height to fly over the bizarre structure.

Closer now, she could truly appreciate its enormous size and complexity, a precise series of sluices, overflow channels and pressure gates to keep the lava in motion and circulating through the system that fed the incredible sight on the far side of the volcano.

Guided down the flanks of the mountain in enormous chasms a hundred metres wide, the lava from the volcano fed a vast artificially constructed lagoon, an inland sea of glowing, hissing, bubbling molten rock.

Built upon this sea was the Magma City, and what a city it was...

Dalia's breath was snatched from her throat as she saw the mighty forge, surely the domain of Rho-mu 31's master, Adept Koriel Zeth.

All across the bubbling, flame-wracked surface of the lava, blackened cylinder towers soared from the magma beside giant structures in the shapes of flat-topped pyramids that belched fire and steam. Twisting roadways, boulevards, open squares, wide platforms and entire industrial complexes sat upon the raging heat of the lava in defiance of the awesome caged power of the planet's molten fire.

A golden route traced a path towards a mighty structure of silver in the centre of the colossal metropolis, but it was quickly lost to sight as the craft descended. Thick retaining walls of dark stone surrounded the lagoon, such that it resembled a lava-filled crater, and a colossal plain of sub-hives, hab-zones, landing fields, runways, control towers and a vast container port filled the horizon behind it, abutting the cliff-like walls of the volcano.

Continents of steel-sided containers sprawled outwards from the Magma City, towering skyscrapers of materiel: weapons, ammunition and supplies manufactured in the factories of Mars for the Warmaster's armies of conquest.

Fleets of enormous vessels filled the skies over the port, rising and descending to the surface of Mars in a veritable procession of steel and retro-fire. Each one was destined for worlds far distant from the Solar system and as valuable to the Great Crusade as any warrior or battleship.

A forest of lifter-cranes swung and groaned over the container port, their heavy, counterbalanced arms moving with leisurely speed in an intricate ballet as an army of servitors, loaders and container skiffs packed the holds of the enormous bulk conveyors with as much as could physically be contained.

Dalia held onto the stanchion as the ship banked, heading towards a landing platform within the city, a glowing cross of light sitting on a boom of metal that jutted out into the lava. The view through the photomalleable steel rippled in the heat, and Dalia found herself becoming nauseous with the disorientation.

Rho-mu 31 placed his stave against the wall, and once more the side of the vessel became opaque. The hull began to vibrate and screech as they descended through the blistering thermals.

'Do they ever have crashes here?' asked Dalia, knowing that such accidents could have no survivors. 'I mean, have any ships gone into the lava?'

'Sometimes,' said Rho-mu 31. 'It is best not to think of it.'

'Too late,' muttered Dalia, as the noises of the ship's engines changed in pitch from a low rumble to a high-pitched shriek, attitude thrusters firing to correct the rip tide air currents. The pilot was clearly having difficulty in lowering their ship to the landing platform, and Dalia closed her eyes, trying not to think of what would happen if they went into the lava.

She tried not to picture the lava searing the meat from her bones, the fumes choking her and the agonising pain of watching her body disintegrate in front of her. Of course she would not live long enough to experience these things, but her mind delighted in tormenting her with these dreadful visions of catastrophe.

Dalia took a deep breath and forced the images from her mind, fighting to keep them from overwhelming her. She felt a thump on the underside of the craft and her eyes flashed open.

'What was that? Has something gone wrong?'

Rho-mu 31 looked at her strangely, and though the bronze mask concealed his features, Dalia could sense his amusement at her panic.

'No,' he said. 'We have simply landed.'

Dalia let out a shuddering sigh of relief, pathetically grateful to be on terra firma once again... though should that more properly be *mars firma*? Having said that, how solid could the ground be considered when it was some-how supported on an ocean of liquid rock that could burn her to cinders in the blink of an eye?

A hiss of escaping gases drew her attention to the ramp at the rear of the vessel as it began to lower with a squeal of pistons. A wall of hot air rushed to fill the com-partment and Dalia gasped at the sudden heat. Sweat immediately prickled on her brow and her mouth dried of saliva in an instant.

'Throne alive, it's hot!' she said.

'Be thankful for the heat exchangers and gas separators,' said Rho-mu 31. 'You would be overcome by the temperature and fumes of this place in moments without them.'

Dalia nodded, following Rho-mu 31 from the interior of the starship. The other members of his squad moved in behind her as she made her way down the ramp, shielding her eyes from the vivid glare of the lava lagoon and the brightness of the rust-coloured sky. After a day or so in the belly of a starship, she realised how starved of the sight of the sky she had been. Even as a scribe in the bowels of the Librarium Technologica, she had been able to see a sliver of sky through the high liturgical windows.

The sky here was low and threatening, the air thick and heavy with particulate matter billowing upwards from flame-wreathed refineries in the far distance. Though she knew the clouds gathering in the distance were not those of weather patterns, but pollution, she could not help but shiver to see them squatting on the horizon like a quiescent threat.

High railings surrounded the landing platform, and tall silver poles topped with buzzing, hissing machinery punctuated the barrier every few metres – the heat exchangers and gas separators Rho-mu 31 had spoken of, she presumed. A swirling cloud of steam surrounded each one, and dripping pipes ran the length of each pole, vanishing into the decking of the platform to dissipate their heat elsewhere.

'It must take vast amounts of energy to disperse such huge quantities of heat,' she said, pointing at the machines on the silver poles. 'What method do you use to filter the harmful gases from the air? Synthetic membranes, adsorption, or cryogenic distillation?'

'You know of such things?' asked Rho-mu 31.

'Well, I've read about them,' explained Dalia. 'A number of the old texts from the ruins in the Merican deserts mentioned them and, as with everything I read…'

'It slotted home in the archive of your memory as a fact to be recovered at a later date.'

'I guess so,' said Dalia, faintly embarrassed by the reverent tone she heard in his voice.

She looked away from him as she saw an ochre-skinned vehicle emerge from the nearest structure, a tall tower of black metal, and make its way along the boom towards them. It moved on a number of thin, stilt-like legs, moving with a quirky, mechanical gait, like a stubby centipede. As it drew nearer, she saw the wide-bodied mass of a servitor fused and hard-wired into the front section where one might otherwise expect a driver to sit.

The vehicle came to a halt beside them, the multitude of legs twisting it around on its central axis and lowering it to the deck plates.

Rho-mu 31 opened a door in the side of the vehicle and indicated that Dalia should climb aboard. She stepped onto the centipede vehicle and took a seat on the metal bench along its side, feeling a thrill travel through her at the thought of making a journey on such an outlandish mode of transport.

Rho-mu 31 joined her, but the remaining Mechanicum Protectors did not board.

'Where are we going?' asked Dalia, as the vehicle rose up onto its legs once again and set off with a scuttling, side-to-side motion towards the dark tower.

'We are going to see Adept Zeth,' said Rho-mu 31. 'She is most anxious to meet you.'

'Me? Why? I don't understand, what does she want with me?'

'Enough questions, Dalia Cythera,' cautioned Rho-mu 31, not unkindly. 'Adept Zeth does nothing without purpose and you are here to serve that purpose. What manner your service will take is for her to decide.'

The walking vehicle drew near the tower of black metal, and as Dalia looked back towards the gathering clouds, a sliver of fear wormed its way past her wonder at all the new and incredible sights.

She had been brought to Mars with a purpose in mind, but what might that purpose be and would she live to regret the journey?

The shadow of the tower swallowed her, and Dalia shivered despite the awful heat.

MAVEN'S FIRST WARNING was the transformer exploding in a cascade of flames and whipping electrical discharge. A hammering volley of laser fire, like a hundred lightning bolts ripping from the rocks, sawed through the looped coils of metal and liquefied them in an instant. His display dimmed to protect him from blindness, but before the transformer blew, he saw the outline of the aggressor.

Easily as huge as *Equitos Bellum*, it was spherical and heavily armoured, a pair of monstrous weapon arms at its sides and a myriad of flexible, metallic tentacles crouched over its shoulders like scorpions' tails.

A trio of convex blisters glowed like baleful eyes on its front, a fiery yellow glow burning from them with a hateful, dead light. The white heat of the explosion obscured the unknown attacker, and by the time the glow had diminished and the Knight's auto-senses had recovered, the war machine had vanished.

With a thought, *Equitos Bellum* was on a war footing, weapon generators firing from idle to active, and the high-energy cells that drove his Knight switching to battle mode. He immediately stepped his Knight to one side, crouching low as he saw scores of figures pouring from the rocks with weapons raised.

His eyes narrowed as he recognised them as Protector squads, servants of the adepts of Mars. Things were really getting out of hand.

'Stator! Cronus! Are you getting this?'

'Affirmative,' barked Stator. 'Engage enemy forces at will. We will be with you directly.'

'Enemy forces?' hissed Maven. 'They're Protectors!'

'And they are attacking a facility we are duty bound to protect. Now fight!'

Maven cursed under his breath and shrugged, the huge bulk of *Equitos Bellum* attempting to match the gesture as he marched the machine into battle. He leaned forward in his command seat, lifting his arms and twisting his head as he sought out the enemy war machine.

What was it, he wondered? Some new form of battle robot or servitor-manned automaton?

Maven shivered as he remembered the dead light in the machine's sensor blisters, feeling as though it had been looking at him, assessing him and then dismissing him. That thought alone angered him and he could feel the intemperate fury of *Equitos Bellum* meshing with him in a desire to do harm to the attackers.

The Protectors in grey cloaks were advancing with relentless pace through the reactor complex, gunning down unresisting servitors with quick bursts of laser fire, and engaging Maximal's Protectors as they sought to defend their master's holdings.

Maven unleashed a torrent of las-fire from his right arm and the ground erupted in a storm of metal and earth. The ruin of the enemy corpses geysered upwards, a knot of attackers reduced to puffs of exploding meat and boiled blood.

A flurry of gunfire rippled towards him, and he flinched as he felt a power field flash out of existence. Like a Titan, a Knight had a finite bank of energy shields to protect it, but where a Titan's reactor could replenish its shield strength in time, the Knight's battery could not. *Equitos Bellum* was effectively immune to most individual weapons, but the Protectors were combining their fire with accuracy of timing that spoke of a communal battle-link.

Another shield winked out of existence and Maven turned his war machine to face the new threat: a cadre of Protectors armed with long-barrelled high-energy weapons. Maven saw silver bands around each Protector's skull, recognising the hard-wired component of a targeting web.

He stepped sideways as a blistering beam of light leapt from each of the Protectors' weapons and achieved confluence where he had been standing not a moment before. He had seconds to act.

Maven's weapons blazed in a hurricane of light, enveloping the Protectors in a firestorm that obliterated them in an instant and left virtually no remains. He pushed onwards, past the flaming wreckage of the transformer as it spat arcs of lightning and secondary explosions detonated within its ruined shape.

Where the hell had the war machine that had done this gone? And where in the name of Taranis were Stator and Cronus?

An explosion mushroomed skyward from deeper within the complex, and Maven turned *Equitos Bellum* towards it, the heavy, thudding strides of the Knight shaking the ground with the weight of its tread. Another explosion roared and Maven guided his Knight around the curve of the reactor dome to see his foe with its back to him, unleashing solid spears of plasma flame that ripped through the armoured skin of the fusion reactor's dome.

The machine's bulk was enormous, almost as wide as it was tall, and it was equipped with a fearsome array of weapons – some Maven recognised and some that were a mystery to him. Where a Knight's mode of locomotion was its legs, this machine was mounted on a heavy track unit, blood and oil coating it where it had crushed unfortunate servitors beneath its bulk.

Sheets of molten armour cascaded like burnt paper from the flanks of the reactor dome, and Maven saw it wouldn't be long before the shielding around the caged fury of the fusion reactions within would be breached. Screaming sirens and flashing emergency lights warned of impending doom.

Despite the heavy crash of his Knight's footfalls, Maven didn't think his foe knew he was there. Maven siphoned power from non-essential systems as he prepared to open fire.

One of the metallic weapon-tentacles swivelled around on its mounting, and Maven had the sick feeling that it was looking right at him. Instantly, the rest of the weapon arms not already reducing the armour plating on the reactor to vaporised slag whipped around to face him.

Maven opened fire at the same time as the attacking war machine, his lasers impacting on a number of power fields before tearing one of the weapon arms from its mounting. The return fire struck *Equitos Bellum* full in the chest, collapsing the last power field and ripping through its armour. Agony roared up through the Manifold and Maven screamed, his hands jerking towards his chest as though the wound had been done to his own flesh.

The Knight staggered, and Maven fought to control its motion through the mist of jarring pain that seared through his every nerve-ending. He wrenched his consciousness from the damage done to *Equitos Bellum* and felt his vision clear as he saw the enemy war machine preparing to fire again.

Maven sidestepped and lowered his shoulder as another rippling beam of light seared towards him, burning through the edge of his shoulder armour. He flinched, but the damage was superficial and he locked in with his weapon arm, unleashing a stream of laser fire at his enemy's back.

'Got you!' he shouted as the impacts marched over the machine.

The shout died in his throat as he saw that his shots had done absolutely no damage.

A rippling sheath of invisible energy surrounded the machine where none had existed a moment before. Only one explanation presented itself.

The machine was void protected.

'Damn it,' he hissed and his hesitation almost killed him as the machine spun around on its axis and took time out from its unravelling of the reactor's armour to fire on him.

Dazzling lasers sleeted past him and Maven desperately walked his Knight back out of the line of fire. Flames boomed to life around him as fuel stores exploded, and he felt the heat wash over his mount. A lucky shot grazed the pilot's compartment and a sharp crack sliced down through his vision.

Maven screamed in pain, his hand reaching up to his eyes where it felt as though a hot needle had been shoved through to the back of his skull. His vision blurred, but he kept moving, backwards and from side to side, to throw off his assailant's aim.

Fresh streams of laser fire seared the air around him, but none touched him, and as the pain of *Equitos Bellum's* wounding diminished, he dodged the machine's incoming shots, its fire patterns following textbook sweeps.

But Raf Maven was anything but textbook.

He swung his Knight around the corner of the reactor, sweat streaming down his face and a thin trickle of blood dripping from his nose.

'Stator! Cronus!' he yelled. 'Where in Ares's name are you?'

Then the reactor exploded.

THE STILT-WALKING VEHICLE moved through a city of wonders and miracles.

Everywhere Dalia looked she saw something new and incredible. Once lost in the midst of the towers and forges, she realised she had never seen anything like the domain of Koriel Zeth, its design and scale quite beyond anything she had imagined before. Though the Imperial Palace on Terra was much, much larger, she appreciated that the Emperor's fastness was not so much a piece of architecture, but rather a handcrafted land mass built upon the world's tallest mountains.

Even on the rare moments she had been permitted to venture beyond the confines of the Librarium, she had only ever seen a fragment of the palace's majesty, but this place she had seen in its entirety.

Even then, she suspected that what she had seen from the air wasn't the whole story.

Rho-mu 31 kept his counsel throughout the journey, content to watch the spires and smoke-belching furnaces pass without comment. Nor was this a city without an organic component, for thousands paraded through its razor-straight thoroughfares and shining boulevards.

Hooded menials, grey-skinned servitors and glittering, holo-wreathed calculi mingled on the metal streets of the Magma City. Robed tech-adepts moved like royalty through the crowds, carried on floating palanquins or wheeled chariots of golden metal, or borne aloft on what looked like gilded theatre boxes with slender stilt legs. All of them bore the number grid symbol of Adept Zeth somewhere about their person.

How any of them didn't collide was a mystery to Dalia, though she presumed that each one would have some kind of onboard navigational system, which linked to a central network that monitored speeds, trajectories and potential collisions.

She shook her head free of the thought and forced herself to concentrate on enjoying the journey. Too often she was being distracted when she saw something new and incredible. Her thoughts would seize on this unknown factor, searching her memory for something similar before sending the creative part of her mind into a freewheeling spin as she attempted to account for the technological explanation of this new phenomenon.

They were heading for the centre of the Magma City, that much was obvious, the unmoving, unblinking servitor fused with the vehicle's control mechanisms conveying them unerringly through the heaving mass of bodies.

Their course took them onto the golden boulevard she had seen from the air, its sides lined with statues and thronged with robed acolytes. At the far end, Dalia saw a towering structure of what looked like bright silver or chrome.

As if fashioned from precisely machined blocks of silver steel, the forge was etched with geometric patterns like those of a circuit diagram, though Dalia had no idea what manner of circuit was described in its design. The servitor increased the speed of their vehicle and the enormous building soon grew in stature until Dalia's neck hurt with craning to look up at its blocky enormity.

A portion of the wall at the base of the forge slid apart and sections of the building seemed to retreat within its structure, forming a gleaming ramp that led up to a vast portico halfway up the building's side.

Dalia gripped the handrail as their vehicle began the ascent, looking behind her as the ramp disappeared as soon as they passed. The portico loomed large above them and now she truly appreciated how enormous it was, each column fashioned in the shape of an enormous piston and capped with cog-shaped capitals.

The entire building was designed as if it were a moving machine, and for all Dalia knew, perhaps it was.

At last the vehicle levelled out and the clacking of its many legs ceased as it came to a halt on the portico's wide plinth. The floor was milky white marble with dark veins running through it, and the columns towered above her. The underside of the pediment was decorated with unknown equations and diagrams picked out in glittering mosaics of gold. The sheer visual splendour was overwhelming.

A wall of bronze doors led into the mighty structure. All were open and from them poured a host of robed figures. Each wore its hood drawn forward to cover its head and each wore the number grid of Adept Zeth as a veil. Many carried strange devices in open boxes or upon their backs.

Leading the figures was a tall, slender adept with a lithe, muscular physique and a cloak of golden-red bronze that billowed behind her in the swirls of hot air.

Without introduction, Dalia knew this must be the Mistress of the Magma City: Adept Koriel Zeth.

Her body was sheathed in a flexible skin of bronze armour, her attire more like that of a warrior woman than a master of technology.

Her features were invisible, hidden behind a studded head mask and opaque goggles. Puffs of steam exhaled from a rebreather mask and a skirt of bronze mail hung low over her shapely armoured legs. Though her body armour obscured all traces of Zeth's humanity, there was no doubt as to her sex.

Every curve and every plate of armour had been designed to enhance her natural form, her slender waist, the curve of her thighs and the swell of her breasts. Fully a third of a metre taller than Dalia, Adept

Zeth approached, and a delicate mist of atomised perfume came with her.

She leaned down to stare at Dalia, the glossy black orbs of her goggles like those of an insect regarding some interesting morsel that had just wandered into its lair. Zeth's head cocked to one side and a burst of static hissed from the bronze mesh to either side of her rebreather.

Moments passed before Dalia realised that the static had been directed at her, a blurted hash of machine noise intelligible to the binaric fluent.

'I can't understand you,' she said. 'I don't speak linguatechnis.'

Zeth nodded and her head twitched as though a switch had flicked inside it.

'What relationship does the ideal gas law represent?' asked Zeth, her voice rasping and the words sounding as though they had been dredged up from a little used repository of linguistic memory.

Of all the welcomes, this was one Dalia had not anticipated. She closed her eyes, casting her mind back to one of the first books she had transcribed in the Librarium, a textbook recovered from beneath a ruined tech-fortress of the Yndonesic Bloc.

'It describes the relationship between pressure and volume within a closed system,' said Dalia, the words recited by rote from memory. 'For a fixed amount of gas kept at a fixed temperature, the pressure and volume are inversely proportional.'

'Very good. I am Adept Koriel Zeth. And you are Dalia Cythera. Welcome to my forge.'

'Thank you,' said Dalia. 'It's very impressive. Did it take long to build?'

Zeth looked her up and down, the sound of electronic laughter crackling from her voice unit. She nodded. 'It did indeed. Many centuries of work were needed to build this forge, but even now it is not complete.'

'It isn't? It looks complete.'

'From without, perhaps, but within there is much yet to be achieved,' said Zeth, her delivery growing more fluent as she spoke. 'And that is where you come in.'

'How do you even know me?'

'I know a great deal about you,' said Adept Zeth, looking at the space above Dalia's head. 'You are the only daughter of Tethis and Moraia Cythera, both deceased. You were born in medicae block IF-55 of the Ural Collective seventeen years, three months, four days, six hours and fifteen minutes ago. You were trained to read and write at age three, indentured to the Imperial Scriptorium aged six, and trained in the art of transcription aged nine. You were apprenticed to Magos Ludd aged twelve and assigned to the Hall of Transcription aged fifteen. You have six commendations for accuracy, twelve citations for inciting behaviour deemed to be incompatible with working practices and one instance of imprisonment for violating the Laws of Divine Complexity.'

Dalia looked up, half-expecting to see illuminated letters displaying her life story for Adept Zeth. She saw nothing, but it was clear from the tone of Zeth's voice that she was reading these facts from somewhere.

'How do you know all that?' she asked.

Zeth reached down and brushed a metallic fingertip across Dalia's cheek, and she felt a warm glow as the electoo implanted beneath her skin upon her induction to the Hall of Transcription came to life. She reached up and placed a hand on her skin.

'You can read my electoo?'

'Yes, but I can discern much more than simple biographical knowledge,' replied Zeth. 'All data can be read, presented and transferred with a glance. Though invisible to you, I see a liminal skein of data filling the air around you, each ghost of light a fact of your life. I can see everything about you, all the things that make you a person in the eyes of the Imperium.'

'I've never heard of anything like that.'

'I am not surprised,' said Zeth with a trace of pride. 'It is a function of data retrieval and transfer that I have only recently developed, though I have great hopes for its eventual employment throughout the Imperium. But I did not bring you to my forge only to impress you with my technological developments, I brought you here because I believe your understanding of machines and technology runs parallel to mine.'

'What do you mean?'

'The Martian Priesthood is an ancient organisation and is learned in the ways of technology, but our grasp of such things is limited by blind adherence to dogma, tradition and repetition. I believe that our future lies in the *understanding* of technology, that only by experimentation, invention and research will our progress be assured. This view is not widely held on Mars.'

'Why not? Seems perfectly sensible to me.'

Zeth made the crackling, static laugh again. 'That is why I sought you out, Dalia. You have a skill I believe will prove very valuable to me, but one that others will fear.'

'What skill's that?'

'You understand *why* machines work,' said Zeth. 'You know the principles by which they function and the science behind their operation. I accessed the schematics of what you did to your cogitator station and followed the methodology you employed upon the circuitry. It was quite brilliant.'

'I didn't really do anything special,' said Dalia modestly. 'I just saw how I could make it work faster and more efficiently. Anyone could have done it if they'd put their mind to it.'

'And that is why you are special,' replied Zeth. 'Few could have made the mental leaps to see the things you saw, and even fewer would dare. To many of the Martian Priesthood, you are a very dangerous individual indeed.'

'Dangerous? How?' asked Dalia, quite taken aback by the notion that she might be thought of as a danger to anyone, let alone the priests of the Mechanicum.

'Mars enjoys a pre-eminent position within the Imperium thanks to our grip on technology,' continued Zeth. 'Many of my fellow adepts fear the consequences of what might happen were that advantage to slip beyond their control.'

'Oh,' said Dalia. 'So what is it you want from me?'

Adept Zeth drew herself up to her full height, the bronze of her armoured skin gleaming red in the reflected glow of the orange skies.

'You will be part of the salvation of Mars,' she said. 'With your help, I will perfect my greatest work... the Akashic Reader.'

1.03

Ascraeus Mons was a volcano, yet the atmosphere within the Chamber of the First was anything but warm. The fortress of Legio Tempestus had been one of the earliest established on Mars in ancient times and as one of the highest volcanoes on the red planet, it was fitting that it housed one of its most ancient and respected Titan orders.

Carved within the basalt rock of the mountain, the demesne of Tempestus was known as a place of courage and wisdom, a place where warriors of honour came to settle their disputes without violence.

Indias Cavalerio watched from the Princeps Gallery as emissaries from many of the great Legios took their seats within the great amphitheatre carved into the cliffs of the enormous caldera of his order's fortress, knowing the smiles and warm greetings being exchanged hid undercurrents of mistrust and widening divisions.

Divisions that were becoming all too common on Mars.

There was Grand Master Maxen Vledig of the Death-bolts conversing with Princeps Senioris Ulriche of the

Death Stalkers, their apparent bonhomie masking decades of disputes involving ancient territorial rights along the borders of the Lunae Palus and Arcadia regions. Across the hall, encased in his life-sustaining exo-skeleton and aloof from all others, was Princeps Graine of Legio Destructor. A dozen others had answered the call to attend the Council of Tharsis (as Lord Commander Verticorda had already dubbed it with his usual taste for the grandiose).

Only Mortis was yet to appear.

Verticorda stood in the centre of the grand, echoing amphitheatre, leaning on his ebony, thunderbolt-embossed cane, and swathed in the shadow of *Deus Tempestus*, the First God Machine of Legio Tempestus.

Towering over the assembled warriors, the great steel engine had stood sentinel over the deliberations of Legio Tempestus for half a millennium, its majesty undimmed and its power tangible, though it had not moved so much as a single joint in over two hundred years.

Next to Verticorda was Lord Commander Caturix, the hunched, ancient warrior's brother-in-arms and fellow master of the Knights of Taranis. Where Verticorda was aged and revered for his wisdom, the newly appointed Caturix was beloved for his fiery passion, which complemented his fellow commander's more cautious temperament.

Ever since Verticorda had bent his knee to the Emperor nearly two hundred years ago, the joint commanders of the Knights of Taranis had served as the *Princeps Conciliatus* between the warrior orders of Mars. It would be their job to ensure that the coming gathering was conducted in a manner befitting the most ancient warrior guilds, that tradition was upheld and honourable discourse permitted.

Cavalerio did not envy them that role, for tensions were running high and this latest insult to an adept of Mars had pushed the mightiest warrior orders of Mars close to open confrontation, a state of affairs that had not transpired on the red sands for uncounted centuries.

Not only that, but warriors from the Knights of Taranis had been involved in this latest combat, so they were hardly likely to be objective. Verticorda could be trusted to keep his anger in check, but Caturix paced the mosaic floor of the chamber like a caged beast.

Skirmishes between orders were far from uncommon; after all, warriors needed outlets for their aggression to develop their skills and foment the proper bellicose attitude needed to command the god-machines.

Lately, these had threatened to boil over into outright warfare.

The sheer affront of the attack on Ipluvien Maximal's fusion reactor on the slopes of Ulysses Patera had sent shock waves through the Martian community (though to call such a competitive, uncooperative, suspicious and insular organisation as the Mechanicum a community seemed perverse to Cavalerio).

He ran a hand over his scalp, the surface hairless and punctured by sealed implant plugs at his nape that allowed him to command the mighty engines of Legio Tempestus. Similar implants were fused to his spine, and haptic receptors grafted to the soles of his feet and along the tactile surfaces of each of his hands allowed him to feel the Titan's steel body as though it were his own flesh.

Cavalerio's frame was tall and wiry, the dress uniform that had once fitted his well-proportioned frame snugly now hanging from his thin body, the result of decades spent vicariously exerting himself through the actions of a Warlord Battle Titan instead of in the gymnasium.

As he looked over at the mighty form of *Deus Tempestus*, he found himself longing to ascend the elevator to his own venerable war machine, *Victorix Magna*. The glowering iron face of the ancient war machine stared down at him, the head of a mechanical god of war that lived in his dreams every night.

In those dreams he would be striding across the ashen red plains of Mars on his last march, *Deus Tempestus* responding to his every command with the familiarity of two warriors who had fought shoulder to shoulder since their earliest days.

Each time he would wake and, finding sleep impossible, walk through the darkened, sparsely populated hangars of the Ascraeus Mons. The hangars were largely empty, since the bulk of the Legio's strength was deployed throughout the Warmaster's expedition forces, pushing the extremities of the Emperor's realm ever outwards and bringing the last worlds of the galaxy under the sway of the Imperium.

His steps would unerringly lead him to the Chamber of the First, where he would watch the sunrise, staring up at the shadowed form of the colossal war machine, its weapons silent and its war banners fluttering in the downdrafts from above.

Cavalerio's brothers fought under the command of Lord Guilliman, and he could think of no better warrior to lead so august a Legio. He and the few Battle Titans now back on Mars were approaching the end of their refit after campaigning in the Epsiloid Binary Cluster against the green skin and would soon rejoin the war to assure humanity's birthright to rule the stars.

He eagerly awaited their redeployment, for life beyond the cockpit of a Titan was made up of long moments of incompleteness, every experience deadened. His physical surroundings were bland and tasteless without first being filtered through the Manifold of his Battle Titan.

The moment of connection with an engine was painful, as though it resented the time spent separated from its commander, and it took time to wrestle the warlike heart of the machine to compliance. But once that union had been achieved… oh, how like a god did it feel to be master of the battlefield and lord of so terrible and mighty a power?

Separation was no less painful; the angry need of the Titan to walk made it disinclined to allow its commander to leave without punishment. Aching bones, thudding headaches and searing dislocation were the hallmarks of a separation, and each time was harder than the last.

For now, it was possible for Cavalerio to retain some semblance of humanity, to walk as a man, but he knew it was only a matter of time before he would require a more permanent enmeshing within an amniotic float-tank of liquid information.

The thought terrified him.

He shook off such fears as he saw a ripple of motion near the floor of the chamber and heard a murmur of agitation pass through the Chamber of the First.

Cavalerio looked down from the gallery, seeing two warriors in long dark cloaks and grinning skull-faced helmets stride into the chamber with purpose and strength.

Legio Mortis had arrived.

'You DENY THAT your order took part in the attack on Adept Maximal's reactor?' demanded Lord Commander Caturix. 'That engines of the Legio Mortis wilfully destroyed an artefact of technology and endangered the lives of warriors from the Knights of Taranis?'

'Of course I do,' snapped Princeps Camulos, his hooded features making no secret of his disdain for the accusation and his accuser. Despite Verticorda's cautious welcome to the assembly, Caturix had wasted no time in setting the tone by marching straight towards the senior princeps of the Legio Mortis and all but calling him out for the damage done to his warriors in the reactor's explosion.

Cavalerio watched the young lord commander, the youngest in the history of the Knights of Taranis, sneer at Princeps Camulos's answer, plainly disbelieving what he was hearing.

He watched as Caturix circled like a shark in the water with the scent of blood, forced to admire his nerve in facing down so senior a princeps.

Men had been rendered down into servitors for less.

Legio Mortis's disdain for the Knight orders was well known, as was their reluctance to share power in the Tharsis region from their fortress within Pavonis Mons. With the destruction of Adept Maximal's forge, it would be difficult for many of the local warrior orders to remain viable – leaving Mortis the undisputed masters of Tharsis, one of the most abundant and productive regions of Mars.

All of which was enough for the finger of suspicion to point squarely at Legio Mortis, but not enough to hang them. Mortis and Tempestus had long been rivals for dominance of Tharsis, but was that enough to condemn Camulos and openly damn his Legio with this new atrocity?

Camulos was a towering bear of a man, more suited at first glance to be the chieftain of a tribe of bloodthirsty barbarian warriors, but his sheer self-belief and aggressive nature made him a natural Titan commander, easily able to bend the will of a war machine to his own. His armour was black and glistening as though lacquered, the death's head emblem upon his broad shoulder guards a gruesome testament to his Legio's famed ruthlessness.

'I did not come here to be barked at,' snarled Camulos. 'Keep your young pup on a tight leash, Verticorda, or I may break him for you.'

Verticorda nodded slowly. 'The question is withdrawn, honourable princeps.'

Caturix whipped his head around to face his fellow lord commander, but a stern glare from Verticorda silenced the angry outburst that Cavalerio saw gathering in his throat.

'This council is not a trial or indeed any kind of inquiry,' continued Verticorda, his voice laden with centuries of authority and redolent with wisdom. 'It is an organised debate whereby the warrior orders of the Tharsis region might gather to discuss the troubles afflicting our world and decide how to meet them without further bloodshed. Adept Maximal has suffered a grievous loss to his holdings, but we are not gathered here to assign blame, but to see how we, as the guardians of Mars, might avoid such things in the future.'

Cavalerio looked over to where the robed form of Ipluvien Maximal stood in the shadow of *Deus Tempestus*, as though he took comfort in the nearness of so complex and revered a machine. Adept Maximal had joined the proceedings immediately after the arrival of the Legio Mortis, his corpulent machine-frame wreathed in icy puffs of air vented from the layers of thermal barrier fabrics that cooled the spinning data wheels that made up the bulk of his body.

His head was an oblong helmet of gold fitted with a multitude of lenses upon telescopic armatures, and a morass of sheathed coolant cables emerged from beneath his robes like black tentacles, upon which sat hololithic plates streaming with glowing lines of data.

So far, Maximal had said nothing, save to acknowledge the primacy of Verticorda and Caturix in the proceedings, content simply to watch and record events as they unfolded.

'And how do you suggest we do that?' asked Camulos. 'By accusing honourable orders of warriors of acts of piracy? To suggest that we would stoop so low as to attack the holdings of an adept so highly regarded as Adept Maximal is outrageous!'

Cavalerio looked over as Maximal inclined his golden head at Camulos's compliment. The words felt too tacked on to be believable. For all his bluster, the raid on Maximal's reactor bore all the hallmarks of Legio Mortis – swift, brutal and leaving virtually no survivors.

Only the three Knights had survived to speak of the attack, and all of them had suffered severe damage to their machines in the reactor's detonation. Gun camera footage of the confrontation had been lost in the explosion, and the only clue to the identity of the attacker was a brief description from the sole Knight who had seen the machine.

'In any case, what possible reason could Legio Mortis have for undertaking such an act? We are all servants of the Warmaster, are we not?'

Mixed murmurs of assent and disagreement spread around the chamber, and Cavalerio felt his choler rise that so many could blindly agree with so facile a statement. Rivalry or not, such a comment could not go unanswered.

Cavalerio rose from his seat in the Princeps Gallery and said, 'You mean the Emperor's forces, surely?' Heads turned as he rose to his feet and awkwardly descended the steel steps towards the chamber's floor.

Camulos watched him approach, squaring his shoulders as though they were about to brawl. 'The Warmaster is the Emperor's proxy, it is one and the same.'

'No, actually,' replied Cavalerio, taking the floor, 'it's not.'

'The Chamber recognises Princeps Cavalerio, the Stormlord of Legio Tempestus,' said Verticorda, using the war-name his Legio had given him in the early days of his command.

Cavalerio gave a respectful bow to the lord commander and then to *Deus Tempestus* before turning to Princeps Camulos. The man's wide shoulders and enormous presence dwarfed him.

'Pray tell why it is not the same thing?' demanded Camulos.

'The armies we serve are those of the Emperor, not the Warmaster,' said Cavalerio. 'No matter that Horus Lupercal commands them, every man, woman and machine that fights in this crusade is a servant of the Emperor.'

'You are splitting hairs,' spat Camulos, turning away.

'No,' repeated Cavalerio, 'I am not. I know that your Legio has pledged a great deal of its strength to the 63rd Expedition and to the Warmaster. I believe that to be dangerous.'

Camulos turned back towards him. 'Dangerous? To swear loyalty to the glorious warrior who commands the military might of the Imperium while the Emperor retreats to the dungeons beneath his palace? To swear loyalty to the hero who will finish the job the Emperor is too busy to finish? *That* is dangerous?'

'The Warmaster is a sublime warrior,' agreed Cavalerio, 'but it would be a mistake to think of those armies as belonging to him. Our first loyalty must be to the Emperor, and only a blind man could fail to see how this division is affecting Mars.'

'What are you talking about, Cavalerio?' snapped Camulos.

'You know what I am talking about. Nothing is said and nothing is ever recorded, but we all know that lines are being drawn. The divisions between the adepts of Mars grow ever more vocal and bitter. Long buried schisms are stirred and ancient feuds reignited. The attack on Adept Maximal's reactor is just the latest example of violence that's rising to the surface and spilling out onto the red sands. The factions of belief are mobilising and our world is on the verge of tearing itself apart. And for what? A semantic difference in belief? Is such a thing worth the bloodshed it will no doubt unleash?'

'Sometimes war is necessary,' said Camulos. 'Did not the Primarch Alpharius say that war was simply the galaxy's hygiene?'

'Who knows? It is certainly attributed to him, but what weight do his words carry on Mars? Any war fought here will not be for hygiene, but for misguided beliefs and differences in theology. Such things are anathema to the Imperium, and I will not be drawn into war by the beliefs of religious madmen.'

'Madmen?' said Camulos, with exaggerated horror. 'You speak of the senior adepts of Mars? Such words from a *respected* princeps.'

Cavalerio ignored the barb and addressed his next words to the assembled princeps and warriors of the Titan orders. 'Every day, the Legios and warrior orders receive petitions from forges all over Tharsis, begging our engines to walk. And for what? Differences of opinion in belief? It is madness that will see us all burn in the fires of an unnecessary war, and I for one will not lead my warriors into battle for such things. The Legios have always been the defenders of Mars, and we have always stood above the squabbles of the Mechanicum. We have always done so, and must do so now. We must not allow ourselves to be baited.'

'True sons of Mars know that the fire of the forge burns hottest when it burns away impurities,' retorted Camulos. 'If blood must be shed to preserve the glory of Mars, then so be it. Kelbor-Hal, the Fabricator General of Mars himself, receives emissaries from the Warmaster, and the great forge masters Urtzi Malevolus and Lukas

Chrom have already pledged their labours to Horus Lupercal. Who are we to doubt their wisdom?'

'Then this is not about belief,' said Cavalerio. 'It's rebellion you're talking about.'

A gasp of horror swept the chamber at Cavalerio's words. To even speak of such things was unheard of.

Camulos shook his head. 'You are a naïve fool, Cavalerio. The things you speak of have been in motion for centuries, ever since the Emperor arrived here and enslaved the Mechanicum to his will.'

'You speak out of turn!' cried Lord Commander Verticorda. 'This is treachery!'

An angry hubbub filled the Chamber of the First, with princeps, moderati, engineers, steersmen and armsmen rising to protest – either at Camulos's words or at Verticorda's accusation.

Following Cavalerio's example, the senior princeps of Legio Mortis turned to the shouting warriors and said, 'We are shackled to the demands of Terra, my friends, but I ask you why that should be? We were promised freedom from interference, but what freedom have we enjoyed? Our every effort is bent to the will of the Emperor, our every forge dedicated to fulfilling his vision. But what of *our* vision? Was Mars not promised the chance to reclaim its own empire? The forge worlds long ago founded in the depths of the galaxy are still out there awaiting the tread of any Martian son, but how long will it be before the Emperor claims them? I tell you now, brothers, that when those worlds are held by Terra, it will be next to impossible to reclaim them.'

Camulos turned his gaze upon *Deus Tempestus* and said, 'Princeps Cavalerio is right about one thing though: a storm is approaching where our vaunted neutrality will not stand. You will all need to choose a side. Choose the right one or it will devour even you, Stormlord.'

* * *

DALIA STARED AT the complex lines radiating from the plans before her, the notations in a tightly-wound gothic script that made reading them next to impossible. Numbers, equations and hand-written notes conspired to make the confusing arrangement of circuit diagrams, build arrangements and milling plans almost unintelligible.

'Give it up, Dalia,' said Zouche, with his customary angry tone. 'We've all been over this a hundred times. It doesn't make any sense.'

Dalia shook her head. 'No. It does, it's just a case of following the path.'

'There is no path,' said Mellicin, her voice arch and weary. 'Don't you think I've tried to follow the plans? It looks like Adept Ulterimus didn't think the standard methodology applied to his own work.'

Dalia rested her arms on the wax paper upon which the plans had been printed. These, of course, were not the originals, which had been drawn many thousands of years ago, but copies transcribed by later adepts over the centuries. She closed her eyes and let out a deep breath. She knew she ought to be used to the defeatist carping of her fellows, but their daily negativity was beginning to get to her.

She took a calming breath, picturing the oceans of Laeran, as described by the poet Edwimor in his *Ocean Cantos*, which she'd transcribed nearly a year ago. The image of that far distant planet's world-oceans always calmed her, and she badly needed that calm now, for time was running out.

No sooner had Koriel Zeth welcomed Dalia to her mighty forge than the adept had turned on her heel and marched deep into the sweltering depths, announcing that Dalia was being taken to where she would be tested.

Dalia had never been comfortable with tests, knowing she tended to clam up, and her mind go blank whenever she was asked a difficult question, let alone made to sit any form of exam. She often wondered how she'd managed to pass her transcription assessments.

The gleaming halls of the Magma City were spacious and functional, geometrically precise and machined with a smooth grace. Though there was utter devotion to function in its architecture, form was not overlooked and there was great beauty in the mechanisms of Zeth's forge. Menials and lowly adepts threaded the halls, chambers and cavernous workspaces, every one according Adept Zeth the proper respect as she passed.

Each new chamber brought fresh wonders of engineering and construction: enormous, cogged machines surrounded by crackling arcs of lightning; thudding pistons driving unknown engines and enormous caverns of steel where thousands of techno-mats toiled at bronze work benches on the tiniest mechanisms with delicate silver callipers and needle-nosed instrumentation.

At last they came to a wide chamber lined with rack upon rack of gleaming tools and fabrication devices that she could not even begin to name. A tall plan chest stood at one end of the chamber and four robed individuals stood around a workbench at its centre, each one shaking her hand and nodding as she was introduced to them.

First was Mellicin, a tall, handsome woman of middling years from the Merican continent, with smooth brown skin and a grafted augmetic faceplate over the left side of her face. She had been coolly welcoming, her remaining eye sizing Dalia up and down with the look of a professional assayer.

Next was a swarthy, stunted individual by the name of Zouche, a native of what had once been known as the Yndonesic Bloc. His handshake was curt and his brusque welcome had a hollow ring to it. Dalia was not tall by any means, but even she towered over Zouche. She estimated his height at no more than a metre.

Next to Zouche was a woman named Severine, who had the look of a teacher about her. Her hair was pulled into a tight ponytail and her pale-skinned features looked as though they might crack if her thin lips creased open with even the fraction of a smile.

Last was a smiling youth who went by the name of Caxton, perhaps a year or two older than Dalia, with a boyish face and a tonsured mop of unruly black hair. His features were open, and of all the greetings she had received his felt the most genuine, and she recognised his accent as having its origins somewhere not too distant from her own homelands, possibly the eastern slopes of the Urals.

With introductions made, Adept Zeth had lifted a number of waxy sheets of paper from the plan chest and laid them flat on the workbench in the centre of the room.

'This,' she announced, 'is one of the last great unrealised designs of Adept Ulterimus, developer of the Sigma-Phi Desolator Engine. Data appellations name it as a theta-wave enhancer designed to stimulate long-term potentiation in humans.'

Ignoring their blank looks, Zeth continued. 'It has been transcribed faithfully by the tech-archivists of Ipluvien Maximal from the data fragments recovered from Adept Ulterimus's tomb below the Zephyria Tholus, and you are going to build it. You will have access to workspace, tools, materials and servitors to perform the manual labour. Within seven rotations you will demonstrate a working prototype.'

With that, Adept Zeth had departed with a swirl of her bronze cape, leaving the five of them alone in the workspace.

The first day had been spent in working out what the device was intended to do, no small feat in itself, given that the transcribers had been literal in copying out Ulterimus's spelling mistakes, corrections and the exact shape and texture of his many crossed-out workings. Sketched images and rough diagrams scattered throughout the plans gave some clues to the device's function, but it was a painstaking process just to divine what requirement this unrealised device was intended to fulfil.

A pecking order had quickly established itself within their group, with Zouche and Caxton deferring to Severine, who in turn took her lead from Mellicin. Dalia found her place within that hierarchy when she alone was able to decipher the notes and diagrams enough to understand the device's purpose.

'It's a machine for enhancing the communication between neurons in the brain,' said Dalia after a frustrating hour of unravelling a thread of randomly scrawled notes. 'According to these notes, Ulterimus seemed to believe that a process known as long-term potentiation was what lay at the heart of the formation of memory and learning. It seems to be a cellular mechanism of learning, where the body is induced to synthesise new proteins that assist in high-level cognition.'

'How does it do that?' asked Severine, looking up from redrawing the circuit diagrams and synaptic flow maps.

'By the looks of this molecular formula, it achieves its function by enhancing synaptic transmission,' said Dalia, her eyes darting rapidly over the drawings. 'This wave generator vastly improves the ability of two neurons, one presynaptic and the other postsynaptic, to communicate with one another across a synapse.'

Dalia's fingers spiralled over the drawing, her eyes flitting back and forth across the paper and her own notations, oblivious to the looks she was receiving from her fellows as she spoke, the words sounding as though they came from the deepest recesses of her brain.

'Neurotransmitter molecules are received by receptors on the surface of the postsynaptic cell. When it's active, the device improves the postsynaptic cell's sensitivity to neurotransmitters by increasing the activity of existing receptors and vastly increasing the number of receptors on the postsynaptic cell surface.'

'Yes, but what does that actually *mean*?' asked Caxton.

'Isn't it obvious?' asked Dalia, looking up from the plan.

The silence of her fellows told her it was not. She tapped the plans with her fingertips and said, 'The device is designed to enormously enhance a person's ability to tap into areas of the brain that we almost never use, increasing their ability to learn and store information at a rate way beyond anything human beings have ever been able to achieve before.'

'But it doesn't work,' pointed out Caxton.

'Not yet,' agreed Dalia. 'But I think I know how we can make it work.'

'DO YOU THINK she is right?' asked Ipluvien Maximal, watching Dalia explaining the function of Ulterimus's device on a flickering holo-screen. 'Can she get it to work? No one else has succeeded in a thousand years and you think she can do it in seven rotations?'

Koriel Zeth didn't answer her fellow adept for a moment, letting the chilled gusts of air that wafted from his permanently cooled data frame tease the few organic portions of her flesh that still faced the world.

Maximal's words were artificially rendered, but Adept Lundquist had crafted his vox-unit and the sound of his voice was virtually indistinguishable from an organically created one. Such an affectation seemed ridiculous to Zeth, given the artificiality of the rest of Ipluvien Maximal, but every adept had his own particular idiosyncrasies, and she supposed hers might seem no less ridiculous to others.

'I believe she can,' said Zeth. Her voice was still created by human vocal chords, but rendered hollow and metallic by the studded face mask she wore. She wasn't used to employing her flesh-voice, but indulged Maximal's peccadillo without complaint. 'You saw the schema of the device she altered on Terra. How could she have done that without some unconscious connection to the Akasha?'

'Blind luck?' suggested Maximal. 'A million servitors working on a million plans might eventually hit upon something that works by accident.'

'That old truism?' smiled Zeth. 'You know that's impossible.'

'Is it? I've seen a few of my servitors perform tasks that weren't included in their doctrina wafers. Though, admittedly, my servitors do not function as ably as I would prefer.'

'Only because Lukas Chrom outbid you for the services of Adept Ravachol, but that's beside the point,' said Zeth, irritated by Maximal's digression. 'Dalia Cythera made intuitive leaps of logic, and where she found gaps in the technology, she filled them with working substitutes.'

'And you believe that is because the organic architecture of her brain is attuned to the Akasha?'

'Given that I have eliminated various other factors that might account for her innate understanding of technology, it is the only explanation that fits,' replied Zeth. 'Though she does not know it, she unconsciously accesses the wellspring of all knowledge and experience contained within the Akasha, encoded in the substance of the aether.'

'By aether, you mean the warp?'

'Yes.'

'So why not call it that?'

'You know why not,' cautioned Zeth. 'There is danger in such association, and I do not want prying eyes misunderstanding the concept of what we are trying to do here, not before we fully understand the processes by which we can access the Akashic records and learn that which our ancient forebears understood without the need for dogma and superstition.'

'The source of all knowledge,' sighed Maximal, and Zeth smiled beneath her mask. Appealing to Maximal's obsessive hunger for knowledge was a surefire means of quashing any concerns he had regarding their work.

'Indeed,' said Zeth, baiting the hook some more. 'The history of the cosmos and every morsel of information that has ever existed or ever *will* exist.'

'If she can build this device then we will be able to unlock the full potential of the Great Reader.'

'That is my hope,' agreed Zeth, running a golden hand across the icy surface of Maximal's chill body. She could feel the subtle vibration of the data wheels churning within the mechanisms of his body, as though in anticipation of learning the innermost workings of the universe. 'If she can build Ulterimus's device then we can enhance the empath's mind to the degree where it will be fully receptive to the knowledge impressed upon the aether. Then we will know everything.'

'Yes… the empath,' said Maximal. 'The use of a psyker disturbs me. If Dalia Cythera already has a connection to the aether, why not simply use her as the conduit?'

Zeth shook her head. 'Prolonged exposure to the aether eventually burns the conduit out. There are plenty of psykers to be had, but Dalia is one of a kind. I would not be so careless with such a valuable resource as to squander her.'

Her answer seemed to satisfy Maximal and he said, 'It is great work we do here, but there will be those who seek to stop us if they should learn of it.'

'Then we must ensure that they do not.'

'Of course,' nodded Maximal. 'But already I detect the interest of the Fabricator General and his cronies in the work carried out in your forge. Info-feeds gossip on the air and data packets are like bodies, they do not stay buried forever. You are a brilliant technologist, but you make few allies with your open scorn for Kelbor-Hal. Be careful you do not make too many enemies and attract undue attention. Such things may cost us dearly.'

'You speak of the attack on your reactor?'

'Amongst other things,' replied Maximal, watching the holographic image of Dalia as she organised her fellow workers in their tasks. 'At the Council of Tharsis, Princeps Camulos denied involvement in the attack, and, much as it surprises me, I believe him.'

'Really? From what I gather, Mortis are agitating for open warfare between the factions.'

'True, and the destruction of my prime reactor would be a logical first step in weakening their strongest opponent, Legio Tempestus, for they greatly depended on its output.'

'The Magma City will cover their shortfall.'

'I told Princeps Cavalerio that very thing,' said Maximal, 'but you and I both know that is only a temporary solution. Mortis and Tempestus are rivals of old, and with the reactor gone, the strength of those friendly to our cause grows weaker.'

'So why do you not suspect Legio Mortis involvement?'

Maximal sighed, another affectation since he had no lungs to speak of, and a mist of cold air billowed around him. 'Camulos's bluster was too confident. He *knew* we couldn't prove anything because there was nothing to prove. He may have helped plan the attack, but I do not believe any engines from Mortis took part.'

'Then who did?'

'I believe Chrom was behind the execution.'

'Chrom? Because you do not like him?'

'I find his manner insufferable, that is true, but there is more to it than that,' said Maximal with a precisely modulated conspiratorial tone of voice. 'There are rumours of the work he is pursuing in his forge, experiments on engines designed with artificial sentience.'

'Rumours? What rumours? I have heard nothing of this,' said Zeth.

'Few have,' said Maximal slyly, 'but few things escape my data miners. It is whispered that Chrom has even built such an engine. Supposedly, it matches the description given by the Knight pilot who saw the machine that attacked my reactor.'

Zeth shook her head. 'If Chrom *has* built an engine with artificial sentience, he would be a fool to let it be destroyed.'

'Perhaps it wasn't destroyed,' said Maximal. 'If it escaped into the pallidus we could search for a hundred years and not find it.'

Zeth sensed hesitancy in Maximal's manner, as though there were other facts he was aware of, but was unsure about sharing.

'Is there something else?' she asked.

Maximal nodded slowly. 'Perhaps. Each time a rumour of this machine surfaces, the data conduits whisper a name… Kaban.'

Zeth ran the name through her internal memory coils, but found no match for it.

Maximal read her lack of information in the streams of data floating in her infosphere and said, 'Even I can find only the most cryptic reference to Kaban in the vaults. Supposedly, he was an ancient potentate of the Gyptus who built the lost pyramid of Zawyet el'Aryan. Though in the few hieratic records that remain, his name is transliterated as Khaba, which may either imply dynastic problems or simply that the scribe was unable to fully decipher his name from a more ancient record.'

'And the relevance of this?'

'Purely academic,' admitted Maximal, 'but, interestingly, the records hint that Khaba may be the king's Horus name.'

'A Horus name? What is that?' asked Zeth, knowing that Maximal loved to show off the vast expanse of his archives in his knowledge of ancient times.

'The kings of Gyptus often chose names that symbol-
ised their worldly power and spiritual might to act as a
kind of mission statement for their rule,' said Maximal,
and Zeth could hear the whir of data wheels as he called
up more information. 'Usually the king's name was
carved upon a representation of his palace with an
image of the god Horus perched beside it.'

'The "god" Horus?'

'Indeed, the name is an ancient one,' said Maximal. 'A
god of the sky, of the sun and, of course, war. The
ancient Gyptians so enjoyed their war.'

'And what did this Horus name symbolise?' asked
Zeth, intrigued despite herself.

'No one knows for sure, but it seems likely that it was
to imply that Khaba was an earthly embodiment of
Horus, an enactor of his will if you like.'

'So you are suggesting that this machine, whatever it
is, was built for Horus Lupercal.'

'That would be a logical conclusion, especially as
Chrom enjoys the favour of the Fabricator General, and
we all know whose voice he listens to.'

'I have heard this before, but I cannot believe Kelbor-
Hal values the counsel of the Warmaster over the
Emperor.'

'No? I hear that Regulus has recently arrived in the
solar system with missives from the 63rd Expedition.
And his first port of call is Mars, not Terra.'

'That doesn't prove anything,' pointed out Zeth. 'Regulus is an adept of the Mechanicum, there is no reason to
suspect any ulterior motive behind his coming to Mars
first.'

'Perhaps not,' agreed Maximal, 'but when was the last
time an emissary from the fleets reported to Mars *before*
the Sigillite of Terra?'

I.O4

IF ANY OF the tissue that caused the chemical and neuro-
logical reactions associated with awe were still part of
what little organics remained of the Fabricator General's
brain, he would no doubt have found the view through
the polarised glass that topped the peak of his forge awesome.

But Kelbor-Hal – as his human name had once been –
was capable of little in the way of emotional response
these days save bitter anger and frustration.

Far below him, the vast forge complex of Olympus
Mons stretched away beyond sight, the towering manufactorum, refineries, worker-habs, machine shops and
assembly hangars covering thousands of square kilometres of Mars's surface.

The vast hive of manufacture was home to billions of
faithful tech-priests of the Machine-God, the great and
powerful deity that governed every aspect of life on
Mars, from the lowliest tertiary reserve unit of the PDF to
the mightiest forge master.

Greatest of the structures arrayed before him was the Temple of All Knowledge, a towering pyramid of pink and black marble, crowned with a dome of glittering blue stone and a forest of iron spires that pierced the sky and pumped toxic clouds into the atmosphere.

Vast pilasters framed a yawning gateway at its base, the marble inscribed with millions of mathematical formulae and proofs, many of which had been developed by Kelbor-Hal himself. Mightier, and home to more workers, priests and servitors than the Mondus Gamma complex of Urtzi Malevolus – where untold thousands of suits of battle plate and weapons were produced to supply the Astartes Legions of the Crusade – the Olympus Mons forge was less a building and more of a region.

The Fabricator General knew he should be proud of his accomplishments, for he had uncovered more technology than any before him and had overseen the longest reign of increasing production quotas in the Mechanicum's long history.

But pride, like many other emotional responses, had all but vanished as the organic cogitator once housed in his skull had been gradually replaced with synthetic synapses and efficient conduits for logical thought. The Fabricator General was over eighty per cent augmetic, barely anything that could be called human remaining of his birth-flesh, a fact of which he was supremely glad.

While the fleshy organ remained in his head, he could feel every biological portion decaying with each passing moment, each relentless tick of the clock a moment closer to the grave and the loss of everything he had learned over the centuries.

No, it was better to be free of flesh and the doubts it fostered.

Far below, thousands of workers filed along the stone-flagged roadway of the Via Omnissiah, its surface worn

into grooves by the sandalled feet of a billion suppli-
cants. A score of Battle Titans lined the wide road, their
majesty and power reminding the inhabitants of his
city, though they needed no reminding, of their place in
the equation that was the workings of Mars.

Monolithic buildings flanked the roadways – factories,
machine temples, tech-shrines and engine-reliquaries –
all dedicated to the worship and glorification of the
Omnissiah. Vast prayer ships filled the sky above the volcano, gold-skinned zeppelins broadcasting endless
streams of binaric machine language from brass mega-
phones. Bobbing drone-skulls trailing long streams of
code on yellowed parchment swarmed behind the zeppelins like shoals of small fish.

The people below would be hoping their prayers
would cause the Machine-God to turn his face towards
them and grant a boon. To many of those below, the
Omnissiah was a tangible being, a golden figure that
had last trod the surface of Mars two centuries ago...

*The False God who had enslaved the Martian priesthood
to his will with his lies.*

The Fabricator General turned from the vista spread
before him, his own fiefdom, as he heard a chiming
blurt of binary from the ebony-skinned automaton –
robot was too crude a word for a work of such genius –
standing behind him.

Its form was smooth, athletic and featureless, a gift
from Lukas Chrom some years ago that sealed the compact between them. Had the automaton worn a suit of
skin, its form would have been indistinguishable from
that of a human. Such was Chrom's genius with
automata that he could craft designs in metal and plastic so perfectly that they would have shamed the Creator
of Humanity himself had he existed.

Though its form appeared unarmed, it was equipped
with a multitude of digital weapons worked into the

lengths of its fingers, and energised blades could spring from its extremities at a moment's notice.

The automaton was warning him of approaching life forms, and the Fabricator General turned his attention to the brass-rimmed shaft in the floor behind him. The pale, rubberised mask of humanity he wore when meeting those who served him slipped over his mechanised face, a face that had been unrecognisable as human for many years.

A wide disc of silver metal, ringed with brass and steel guard rails, rose up through the floor with a pneumatic hiss. Borne upon the disc were four individuals, three swathed in the robes of adepts of the Mechanicum, one in the dark, fur-collared robes of an ambassador.

The circuitry on the back of the mask meshed with the machine parts of Kelbor-Hal's face, the features of his false visage manipulated into the approximation of the human expression of welcome.

<My fellow adepts, welcome to my forge,> he canted with a binary blurt precisely modulated to convey his authority and wealth of knowledge.

The dark-robed figure, Ambassador Melgator, stepped from the transit disc and inclined his head towards the Fabricator General. Melgator was no stranger to this place, his political duties taking him all across Mars – but always bringing him back to report on the machinations and tempers of the Martian adepts.

Save for the ribbed cabling covering the elongated cone of his skull, the man's face was loathsomely organic, his skin waxy and his eyes saturnine, dark and reptilian. Melgator had sacrificed the gift of further augmentation since his role as Mechanicum ambassador often took him to the gilded halls of Terra. The fleshy rulers of the Emperor's realm were stupidly squeamish with those whose communion with the Machine-God rendered them strange and almost alien to their limited perceptions.

Behind Melgator came two of Kelbor-Hal's most trusted followers, adepts who had followed his lead in all things, who had sworn the strength of their forges to him: Adept Lukas Chrom and Adept Urtzi Malevolus.

Chrom was the larger of the two adepts, his wide-shouldered frame swathed in a deep crimson robe that did little to disguise the many mechanised enhancements with which he had been blessed. Ribbed pipes and cables looped around his limbs and linked into a hissing power pack that rose like a set of wings at his back.

His human face had long since been replaced by an iron mask fashioned in the form of a grinning skull. Wires trailed from the jaw and a pulsing red light filled both eye sockets.

Master Adept Urtzi Malevolus favoured a dark bronze for his face mask, and a trio of green augmetic eyes set into the metal illuminated the interior surfaces of his red hood.

The master of Mondus Gamma's red robes were fashioned from vulcanised rubber, thick and hard-wearing, and a monstrously large power pack was affixed to his back, its bulk held aloft by tiny suspensor fields. Remote probe robots darted back and forth from his body, kept in check by the coiled cables that connected them to the senior adept.

Current flowed between their three forges as a sign of good faith, shared freely and without recourse to monitoring. Of course the greater part of that current was directed to the Fabricator General's forge complex, but such was his right and privilege as master of Mars.

The final figure to join the Fabricator General in his sanctum was one who had not set foot on Mars for some time, an adept who had seceded his forge and all its holdings to Kelbor-Hal when he had left to accompany the 63rd Expedition to the furthest corners of the galaxy.

His robes were a deep red and gave no clue to what form lay beneath them, though Kelbor-Hal knew that little remained of his humanity.

His name was Regulus and this favoured son of Mars had returned with news of the Warmaster's campaigns.

'Fabricator General,' said Regulus with a deep bow, making the Icon Mechanicum with clicking metal digits that unfolded from beneath his robes. 'I welcome the flow of current from your forge along my limbs and within the primary locomotive engine of my body. Power whose generation comes not from Mars is bland and without vitality. It serves, but does not nourish. Each time I return to the wellspring of power and knowledge of Mars I realise how much poorer is energy generated beyond our world.'

'You honour my forge, Regulus,' replied Kelbor-Hal, acknowledging the compliment and turning his attention to his vassal adepts. 'Chrom, Malevolus. You are welcome here as always.'

The two adepts said nothing, knowing that Kelbor-Hal could read their acceptance of his dominance by the subtle fluctuations of their electrical fields.

'What news of the Warmaster?' asked Kelbor-Hal.

In the little contact he had with emissaries from Terra, the Fabricator General was often forced to indulge humans in needless oral formalities, protocols and irrelevant discourse until the subject eventually turned to the matter at hand. With adepts of the Mechanicum such trivial matters were deemed irrelevant and quickly dispensed with. This entire conversation would be conducted in the binary fluency of the lingua-technis, a language that left no room for uncertainty or ambiguity of meaning.

'Much has happened since the Emperor took his leave of the expeditionary forces,' said Regulus. 'Alignments shift and new powers emerge from the shadows, offering their aid to those with the strength of vision to heed them. Horus Lupercal is one such individual, and he is now assuredly a friend of the Mechanicum.'

Kelbor-Hal's language centres easily read the implications of Regulus's words and, though his emotions had long since been cut from him like a diseased tumour, old rancour rose to the surface as he recognised sentiments identical to those espoused in the bargain struck with Terra.

'I have heard words like that before,' he said, 'when Verticorda led the Emperor to my forge over two centuries ago and I was forced to bend the knee to him. The ruler of the grubby Terran tribes promised us an equal role in his grand crusade of conquest, but where is that vaunted equality now? We toil to provide his armies with weapons of war, but receive nothing for our efforts but platitudes. Horus Lupercal is a warrior of vision, but what does he offer but more of the same?'

'He offers these,' said Regulus, as a silver-skinned arm rose from behind his shoulders, a delicate bronze calliper clutching a data wafer of silver and gold. Regulus reached up and took the proffered wafer with one of his primary arms before offering it to the Fabricator General.

'On the world of Aurelius, the Warmaster's Legion met and overcame a foe known as the Technocracy. Its armed forces bore a striking similarity to those of the Astartes and it was clear that they had access to functioning STC technology.'

'Standard Template Construction,' breathed Adept Malevolus, unable to keep the hunger from his voice. Kelbor-Hal had long been aware that both Malevolus and Chrom retained some unpleasantly human traits: avarice, ambition and desire to name but a few. Distasteful and unseemly in such senior adepts, but useful when it came to aligning their factions to his own.

'This Technocracy had access to a *functioning* STC?' pressed Malevolus.

'Not just one,' said Regulus, with more than a hint of theatricality. 'Two.'

'Two?' asked Chrom. 'Such a thing has not been seen in a hundred and nineteen years. What manner of STCs did they possess?'

'One for the construction of a hitherto unknown mark of Astartes battle plate and another for the production of lightweight solar generators capable of supplying the power needs of an Epsilon 5 pattern forge complex. Unfortunately, the actual Construct machines were destroyed by the rulers of the Technocracy before Imperial forces could secure them.'

Kelbor-Hal could see Malevolus and Chrom look hungrily at the STC wafer, an artefact that contained information worth more than both their forges combined, flawless electronic blueprints created from miracles of design and technological evolution: machines that could design and construct anything their operators desired.

Such machines had allowed mankind to colonise vast swathes of the galaxy, before the maelstrom of Old Night had descended and almost wiped humanity from existence. To discover a working Construct Machine was the greatest dream of the Mechanicum, but to have fully detailed plans created by such a machine ran a close second.

Kelbor-Hal could feel their desire to snatch the data wafer from Regulus in the crackling spikes in their radiating electrics.

'Horus Lupercal sends these gifts to Mars together with a solemn promise of an alliance with the Priesthood of Mars. An alliance of equals, not of master and servant.'

Kelbor-Hal accepted the data wafer, surprised to feel a tremulous thrill of excitement at the thought of what he might learn from its contents. It was a thin sliver of metal, fragile and insignificant, yet capable of containing every written work on Terra a hundred times over.

No sooner had his metallic fingers touched the wafer than his haptic receptors read the data in a flow of electrons, and he knew that Regulus spoke the truth. Genocidal wars had been fought for information less valuable than was contained on this wafer. Millions had died in search of technology worth a fraction of its value.

In centuries past, the Mechanicum had waged war on the tribes of Terra, despatching expeditionary forces to humanity's birth world to plunder forgotten vaults of ancient citadels and wrest the buried secrets of the third planet's ancient technology from those who did not even know it was there, let alone how to use it.

The Emperor had built his world on the bones of this long-buried science, and, unwilling to share it, had fought the soldiers of Mars and hurled them back to the red planet before travelling to Mars in the guise of the Omnissiah and a peacemaker, albeit a peacemaker who came at the head of an army of conquest.

The peace that was offered was illusory, a conceit designed to conceal a darker truth.

The Emperor offered peace with one hand while keeping a dagger behind his back with the other. In reality, the Emperor's offer was an ultimatum.

Join with me or I will simply take what I need from you.

Faced with a choice that was no choice at all, Kelbor-Hal had been forced to bargain away the autonomy of Mars and become a vassal planet of Terra.

'These are great gifts indeed,' said Kelbor-Hal. 'Given freely?'

Regulus bowed his head. 'As always, my master, you cut to the heart of matters with the precision of a laser. No, such gifts are not given freely, they come with a price.'

'A price?' spat Chrom, the glare of his eyes flaring in response. 'The Warmaster seeks to exact more from us? When we have already pledged him the strength of our forges!'

'You seek to back out of the bargain with the Warmaster?' demanded Regulus. 'We knew great things would be asked of us, but the measure of us how we react to these challenges. Great reward comes only with great risk.'

Kelbor-Hal nodded, the blank face of his face mask slipping into the bland countenance of a conciliator. 'Affirmation: Regulus is correct; we have come too far to balk at paying a price for such things. Already we and our allies strike at those without the vision to see that Horus Lupercal is the true master of mankind.'

'The things we have done,' said Adept Malevolus. 'The schemes we have set in motion. We have come too far and committed too much to back away from the fire simply because we fear its heat, Lukas. The destruction of Maximal's reactor, the death of Adept Ravachol... were they for nothing?'

Chastened from two sides, Chrom bowed his head and said, 'Very well, what does the Warmaster ask?'

Regulus said, 'That when it comes to strike, we guarantee to have Mars firmly under our control. The dissident factions must be quashed so that the forces of the Warmaster may launch his bid for supremacy without fear of counterattack. Any factions loyal to Terra must be brought to heel or destroyed before the Warmaster's forces reach the Solar System.'

'He asks much of us, Regulus,' said Kelbor-Hal. 'Why should we not believe we would merely be swapping one autocrat for another?'

'Horus Lupercal pledges to return the Martian Empire to its former glory,' said Regulus, with the practiced ease of a statesman. 'Further, he swears to withdraw any non-Mechanicum forces from the forge worlds.'

Ambassador Melgator stepped forward, his black, mail-fringed cloak rustling on the smooth floor of the observation chamber. The ambassador rarely spoke when any but he and the object of his attention could hear him, and Kelbor-Hal eagerly anticipated his words.

'With respect, Adept Regulus,' said Melgator. 'The Warmaster, blessed be his name, has already asked us for a great deal and we have delivered. Materiel and weapons are priority tasked to expeditions he favours and delayed to those not aligned with him. He now asks more of us, and are these, admittedly valuable, STCs all he promises us in return? What else does he offer as proof of his continued friendship?'

Regulus nodded, and Kelbor-Hal saw that he had anticipated the question, the prepared answer flowing smoothly from his vocabulator.

'A shrewd question, ambassador,' said Regulus. 'Horus Lupercal has given me an answer that I believe will satisfy you.'

'And that is?' asked Malevolus.

Regulus seemed to swell within his robes. 'The Warmaster will lift all restrictions on research into the forbidden technologies. To that end, I bring the protocols that will unlock the Vaults of Moravec.'

A heavy silence descended on the gathered adepts, as the weight of the Warmaster's offer hung in the air like a promise too good to be true.

'The Vaults of Moravec have been sealed for a thousand years,' hissed Chrom. 'The Emperor decreed that they never be opened.'

'And that means what to us?' sneered Malevolus. 'We already plot against the Emperor, what does one more betrayal matter?'

'The Warmaster has the power to open them?' asked Melgator.

'He is the Emperor's proxy,' pointed out Regulus. 'What the Emperor knows, the Warmaster knows. All it will take to unlock the vault is your agreement to the Warmaster's designs.'

'And if we do not agree?' asked Kelbor-Hal, already extrapolating what great treasures and as yet unknown technologies might lie within the ancient vault. Moravec had been one of the most gifted of the ancient tech-adepts of Terra, a man who had fled to Mars to escape persecution at the hands of superstitious barbarian tribes of the radiation wastelands of the Pan-Pacific.

'If you do not agree, I will wipe the means of opening the vault from my memory coils and it will remain sealed forever,' said Regulus. 'But that will not be necessary, will it?'

'No,' agreed Kelbor-Hal, his pallid features twisted in a grimace of a smile. 'It will not.'

'No, AT THAT length the pin can't be that thin,' said Dalia. 'It'll melt at the temperatures we're expecting inside the cowl transformer.'

'But any thicker and it won't fit inside the cowl,' replied Severine, rubbing the heels of her palms against her temples and deliberately laying down the electro-stylus upon the graphics tablet. 'It won't work, Dalia, you can't make it fit and if there's no pin, the cowl won't remain precisely locked in place over the cardinal points of the skull. Face it, this design won't work.'

Dalia shook her head. 'No. Ulterimus knew what he was doing. This is how it has to be.'

'Then why is there no design for the cowl restraint?' demanded Severine. 'There's no design because he knew it wouldn't work. This whole project isn't something he ever intended to build – it was a theoretical exercise.'

'I don't believe that,' persisted Dalia, turning to the wax paper drawings of the device that the long-dead

Ulterimus had produced. As she had for the last five rotations, she pored over the plans and diagrams she had painstakingly copied and updated to fill in the blank spots where the design was incomplete.

They were so close.

In the centre of the workspace Adept Zeth had furnished them, a gleaming silver device that resembled a highly modified grav-couch was taking shape. Caxton lay underneath, assembling the circuit boards in the back support, while Zouche was machining the drum cylinders that would insulate the electrical conduits once the internal workings of the device were complete.

Mellicin circled the device, which was large enough to bear a fully grown human in a reclined position, her arms folded before her and one finger beating an irregular tattoo against her teeth.

It had taken them a full five rotations to get this far, and with only two to go, they were either on the brink of their greatest triumph or doomed to ignoble failure. Despite the awkward frigidity of their initial meeting, they had worked well as a team, and relations had thawed in the face of each other's skills.

Zouche was an engineer of rare talent, able to machine working parts with great skill and precision in amazingly short times. Caxton had proven to have an intuitive grasp of how machine parts fitted together, which, together with his uncanny knack of appreciating the knock-on effects of even the smallest change in the structure of a circuit, made him the ideal candidate to assemble the device.

Severine was a draughtsman extraordinaire, able to render Dalia's haphazard sketches into working drawings from which parts could be manufactured. Mellicin was skilled in all aspects of engineering and had a wide breadth of knowledge that covered the gaps that existed between the group's specialisations. Not only that, but her organisational abilities were second to none, directing their labours with domineering efficiency once she understood the breathtaking scale of Dalia's vision.

Contrary to her expectations, Dalia found herself warming to Mellicin, recognising the woman's initial frostiness as no more than a need for Dalia to prove herself.

Since Dalia had divined the purpose of the machine Ulterimus had designed, their work had progressed at an exponential rate, but they had run into a problem that threatened to prevent them from completing their project: a means of linking and supporting the cowl that would cover the head of whoever sat in the machine.

It seemed laughably trivial, yet it held the key to the entire device. Too thin and it would melt, breaking the connection to the skull; too thick and it would not fit between the precisely machined, necessarily compact, components and would provide a surface area from which current would undoubtedly flare – thus disrupting the delicate balance of electrical harmonics generated within the subject's brain.

To be thwarted by such a basic, yet fundamental, problem was uniquely frustrating, and Dalia began to understand why the device had never been successfully constructed.

As Severine held her head in her hands, Dalia's eyes wandered over the drawings, letting the lines and curves of the design wash over her, the notations and measurements swimming around like leaves in a storm. Each portion of the design spun around in her head, each part interlinked and each motion subtly affecting the next with its variation.

Dalia felt her hands moving across the wax paper (hearing the scratch of the stylus she wasn't aware she'd picked up) as she doodled without thinking. The portions of the design that didn't exist were grey patches in her mind, as though the solution to the entire problem lay shrouded in a thick fog.

No sooner had that image come to mind than it was as if a stiff breeze sprang up within her, the clouds of fog thinning and golden lines of fire appearing in their depths. Each line linked the spinning parts of the design, drawing them in tighter and tighter, as though a spun web was drawing all the disparate parts together.

Dalia felt her excitement grow, knowing that she was on the verge of something important. She kept her focus loose with conscious effort, knowing that to concentrate too fully on this intuitive assembly would be to lose it. The leaps of logic her subconscious was making were fragile and could tear like fine silk were they to be tugged too insistently.

Her hands continued to scrawl on the wax paper as the golden lines in her imagination drew closer and closer, finally pulling the thousands of elements of the design together, and Dalia held her breath as they slotted home, one by one, into a harmonious, complete whole.

There.

She could picture it now, complete and flawless in its wondrous complexity.

They would need new parts, entirely redesigned schematics and fresh circuit diagrams.

Dalia could see it all, how it would fit together and how it would work.

TWENTY-THREE HOURS LATER, Dalia slotted the final piece of the machine home. The mechanism slid into place with a tiny hiss of pneumatics. Almost a full rotation ago, as she shook herself out of her intuitive reverie, she had looked down to see a fully worked out plan of the images that she had seen in her flight of imagination. The drawings were crude, to be sure, but with even a cursory check, she had known they were *right*.

With a cry of elation, she had rushed over to Severine and swept the current crop of drawings onto the floor. Over Severine's cries of protest, Dalia had called everyone over and begun to outline the scope of what the rough scrawls described.

The team's initial scepticism had turned to cautious optimism and then excitement as they began to grasp the significance of what she was showing them. Each one shouted out what now seemed so obvious to them, as though the solution had been staring them in the face all along.

As the new design began to take shape in the centre of the workspace, Dalia realised that it *had* been staring them in the face, they just hadn't realised it. Each of them, herself included, had been working within the hidebound traditions laid down in the *Principia Mechanicum*, the tenets by which all workings of the Machine were governed.

Aside from Dalia, the members of the team were grafted with shimmering electoos on the backs of their hands to indicate that they had passed the basic competencies of the *Principia* and were thus members of the Cult Mechanicum. Perhaps with this success she too might be fitted with such a marking, though it was through thinking beyond the *Principia's* prescriptive doctrines that Dalia had seen the solution to their problem.

'It's incredible,' breathed Severine, as though unable to believe what they had done.

'We did it,' said Zouche.

'Dalia did it,' corrected Caxton, putting an arm around Dalia and kissing the top of her head. 'She figured it out when no one else could.'

'We all did it,' said Dalia, embarrassed by the praise. 'All of us. I just saw how it could work. I couldn't have done it without you. All of you.'

As always, it was Mellicin who brought them back down to reality with a jolt. 'Let's not be awarding ourselves the title of adept yet, everyone. We don't know if it works.'

'It'll work,' said Dalia. 'I *know* it will, I have faith in it.'

'Oh, and faith now replaces empirical testing, does it? Does it provide hard data to prove we succeeded? No.'

Dalia smiled and bowed to Mellicin. 'You're right, of course. We need to test the device and run a hundred diagnostics to make sure of it, but I know they're going to be fine.'

'I'm sure you are right,' allowed Mellicin with a slight smile that surprised everyone, 'but since we have to do them anyway, I suggest we take an hour's break before getting back to work and beginning the tests.'

'That won't be necessary,' said an authoritative voice from behind them.

Dalia jumped at the sound of the voice, turning to see Adept Koriel Zeth standing at the entrance to their workshop, her bronze armour reflecting the subdued lighting in gold highlights on the curves of her limbs.

Dalia followed the lead of her companions in bowing to Adept Zeth as she swept into the workspace, accompanied by two red-robed Protectors who carried tall staves of iron and whose limbs were sheathed in augmetics. Dalia recognised the Protectors as Rho-mu 31 and smiled at the sight of... him... or was it them? She couldn't quite decide.

Zeth circled the newly completed device and ran her metal clad fingers across its smooth, silver finish. 'You are to be commended. This is fine work. It surpasses my expectations in every way.'

Dalia heard reverence and suppressed desire in Zeth's voice, as though the machine's completion was a dream the adept had not dared believe in too hard for fear it might never come true. Dalia looked up, watching as Zeth lifted the schematics that Severine had drawn up in the wake of her revelations in design, comparing them to the wax paper designs of Adept Ulterimus.

Though Dalia could not see her mistress's face behind the studded mask and inky black goggles, she knew there was an expression of puzzlement forming there.

'I know it doesn't match the plans Adept Ulterimus drew,' explained Dalia. 'I'm sorry about that, but we couldn't get it to work any other way.'

Zeth looked up as she spoke, replacing Severine's plans on the graphics table.

'Of course you couldn't,' said Zeth.

'I don't understand.'

Zeth picked up the wax paper copies of Ulterimus's designs and tore them in two, dropping the shorn halves to the floor.

'This device doesn't work. It never has and it never would.'

'But it will, I'm sure of it.'

'It will *now*, Dalia,' laughed Zeth. 'Ulterimus was a great adept, with many wondrous ideas and concepts. Ideas are the raw material of progress and everything first takes shape in the form of an idea, but an idea by itself is worth nothing. An idea, like a machine, must have power applied to it before it can accomplish anything. The adepts who have won renown through having an idea are those who devoted every ounce of their strength and every resource they could muster to putting it into operation. Sadly, the practical implementation of Ulterimus's ideas left something to be desired, and many of his devices were designed with elements that did not exist or were purely theoretical.'

Dalia was confused, feeling as though she were missing some essential point Zeth expected her to grasp. 'Then how did you expect us to build it?'

'Because I knew that your innate understanding of the *why* of technology would allow you to change what did not work and invent the pieces of the puzzle that needed inventing. You are the very embodiment of what I call ornamental knowledge.'

'Ornamental knowledge?'

Zeth nodded. 'The adepts of Mars arrange their thought processes like neat machines, equipped to work efficiently, if narrowly, and with no extraneous organs or useless parts. I prefer a mind to be a box of scraps of brilliant fabric, odd gems, worthless but fascinating curiosities, tinsel, quaint bits of carving, and a reasonable amount of healthy dirt. Shake the machine and it goes out of order; shake the box and it adjusts beautifully to its new position. I know you do not yet appreciate this, but many of the things you created to make this device work simply did not exist before you designed and built them.'

'You mean we created... something... *new*?' gasped Mellicin.

'Precisely,' agreed Zeth. 'And that is not something to be taken lightly. This device would never have worked if you had followed the plans I gave you, but you – and I include you all in this – were able to see beyond what the slavish adherents to the *Principia Mechanicum* could ever have imagined.'

Zeth stood before them, tall and golden and radiant.

'Such a thing is a gift that will allow me to lift the Imperium into a golden age of scientific progress not seen since humanity set forth from its birth-rock.'

FABRICATOR LOCUM. IT was a title that carried great honour, but also one that spoke of a substitute, of a man only good enough to take up the position when one more suited was unavailable. Kane struggled against these feelings, knowing that he was as dutiful and diligent a member of the Cult Mechanicum as any, but feeling that he was somehow outside the closed loop of power.

In years past, the duty of assisting the Fabricator General with the running of Mars, the meeting of production quotas and ensuring the correct devotions to the Machine-God were observed at all times had been a rewarding and fulfilling life. Now, he spent less and less time with his master, dealing instead with the representatives of the various Legion expeditions as they continually requested more.

More guns, more ammunition, more robots; more everything.

A conversation with Straken had been the final straw.

Straken was Astartes, a warrior of the Salamanders who represented his Legion's interests on Mars. The Mechanicum held Vulkan's Legion up as an example of how affairs between the two arms of the Imperium should be conducted, their reverence for finely crafted technology making them welcome visitors to Mars.

Such relations had become strained in recent days as Straken yet again delivered his primarch's displeasure to the adepts of the Mechanicum.

'The lack of armaments and materiel reaching my primarch's Legion is becoming critical,' Straken had said, when Kane had found time to grant him an audience within his forge, a mighty foundry buried deep beneath the domed hill of Ceraunius Tholus.

'This situation cannot be allowed to continue,' said Straken, without waiting for Kane to answer. 'We have no reserves of ammunition beyond that which the forge ships of the Mechanicum contingent attached to our expedition fleet produce. Do you have any idea how much ammunition is expended by a Legion on a war footing?'

Kane was all too aware of the staggering rate at which Astartes consumed ammunition, and to think that the Salamanders were eating into the reserves produced by their few forge ships was a damning indictment of the rate of supply.

These demands were not unexpected, but recently Kane had noticed a distinct pattern emerging in their nature and pattern, a pattern he now felt moved to report to the Fabricator General.

Kane moved through the bright halls of the Olympus Mons forge complex, the burnished metal walls lit gold by the fire from the Temple of All Knowledge. Accompanied by a gaggle of servitors and menials, Kane passed through the glittering boulevards of the forge, its majestic immensity a constructed monument to the power of the Mechanicum and of the Fabricator General. Only the Imperial Palace on Terra stood mightier.

The inner sanctum of Kelbor-Hal was housed within a towering spire that jutted from the northernmost tip of the enormous forge, a peak that almost rivalled the Temple of All Knowledge in height.

A host of Skitarii stood to attention at the base of the tower, hulking brutes in gleaming breastplates, cockaded helmets of bronze and fur-lined cloaks. Taller and broader than Kane, these warriors were designed to intimidate, their bearing that of men bred to kill and feel nothing beyond the need for combat. Strength enhancers, metabolic aggression spikes and pain-suppressers were worked into their flesh as augmetics or glanded into their nervous systems, and Kane felt a shiver of nervous anticipation as he approached, reading their spiking adrenal levels in the ambient electrical field.

<Fabricator Locum Kane,> he canted in a burst of binary, holding his hand out for a biometric scan. It did not matter that the warriors had seen him a thousand times or more, there were no exceptions to the security protocols surrounding the Fabricator General.

The lead Skitarii, a muscular giant carrying a halberd decorated with all manner of bestial talismans, stepped forward and took Kane's hand. The gesture appeared friendly, but was simply protocol and Kane felt the man's dendrites mesh with the haptic circuitry within his hand. A green light flickered behind the warrior's eyes as he processed the information.

'Fabricator Locum Kane,' agreed the warrior, releasing Kane's hand and waving him past.

Kane nodded and stepped into the tower's only entrance, a simple portal that led to an apparently empty chamber sheathed in reflective silver metal with guard rails around its perimeter. As he took his position in the centre of the chamber, the floor rotated and began to rise.

He called up a gauge onto the inner surface of his eyes, reading the progress of his ascent in binaric numbers that flashed quickly past.

As he was conveyed up the length of the spire, Kane regarded his reflection in the rippling silver walls. Kane disliked the ostentation favoured by many senior magi and embraced a simpler aesthetic in his appearance. Some called it an affectation and he allowed that they were probably right.

Of average height, Kane carried his augmetics subtly, woven within his flesh or rendered into forms less obvious than was usual on Mars. He wore simple red robes with the Icon Mechanicum worked into the fabric in gold thread, and unlike many within the Mechanicum, his face was recognisably human.

His hair was cropped close to his skull, his cheekbones finely sculpted, and a hawk-like nose gave him a patrician air he did nothing to discourage. Only the lambent blue glow behind his eyes gave any indication of the many enhancements worked into his skull.

At last the ascent came to an end, and he ceased his vain contemplation of his appearance as the floor rotated ninety degrees until a portal as plain as the one he had recently passed through came into view. Coloured light spilled into the elevator shaft, and he saw the rust-coloured sky now that he was above the perpetual smog of the forge.

Taking a moment to compose himself, Kane stepped into the Fabricator General's upper viewing dome.

As the Fabricator Locum ascended above the noxious clouds of industry, Dalia and her colleagues were about to descend. The thrill of having pleased Adept Zeth was still potent in the air, and despite her fear, Dalia could feel the anticipation of what their mistress was about to show them fizzing between them all.

Caxton held her hand like a young scholam pupil on a field trip, and Severine could not help an irrepressible grin from splitting her features. Zouche was attempting an air of nonchalance, but Dalia could see that even the laconic machinist was eager to see what lay at the end of their journey.

Only Mellicin appeared unmoved, though she had conceded that she was interested in the promise of what Zeth had to show them.

The adept had said little since approving their design for the theta-wave enhancer, instructing them to follow her to her inner forge.

Dalia and the others had stood dumbfounded for many moments, unsure as to whether they had heard Zeth's instructions correctly.

To see the innermost workings of an adept's forge was to be granted access to their most private and personal works, their obsessions and their passions. Access to such places was notoriously difficult, and only those who had earned an adept's utmost favour would ever be allowed to see what lay within.

'What do you think this Akashic reader is?' asked Severine as they wound a twisting course through the gleaming halls of Zeth's forge. 'Didn't you tell me that Zeth wanted your help to build it?'

'That's what she told me when I first met her,' agreed Dalia, watching the sway of Zeth's golden shoulders and the sashay of her mail cloak as she led them. 'But she never told me what it was.'

'What do you think it is?' inquired Caxton with a boyish grin.

Dalia shrugged. 'Whatever it is, it's something that needs the device we made to work. Perhaps it's some new kind of thinking engine?'

That thought had silenced them all.

Their journey eventually led them to a high-ceilinged chamber with a barrel vaulted roof, bereft of ostentation, in the centre of which a silver cylinder, fifty metres wide, rose within the middle vault.

A dozen armed servitors gathered around the cylinder, their grey-skinned bodies fused to track units, and their arms replaced with monstrous weapons surely too large to be borne without suspensors.

Dalia shared anxious looks with the others as the weapons tracked them on their approach to the cylinder. An exchange of rippling binary passed between Zeth and the servitors, and for the briefest second Dalia thought she saw darts of light flit through the air towards the servitors.

'Do not be alarmed, the praetorians will not attack unless I order them to,' said Zeth.

'Is this your inner forge?' asked Mellicin, as the servitors drew back from a slowly opening door in the gleaming walls of the cylinder.

'One of them,' offered Zeth.

'Then why only servitors to protect it? Wouldn't it be better to have guards that can think for themselves?'

'A good question,' answered Zeth, stepping through the door, 'but what I am about to show you is something that benefits from protection by those who cannot gossip.'

Dalia felt the watchful eyes of the servitors upon her, the hairs on the back of her neck rising as she felt their cauterised minds assess her level of threat. She could visualise the simple logic paths of their battle wetware, tiny decision trees that would decide whether the weaponised servitors would ignore her or obliterate her.

In her mind's eye, she began evolving that wetware, building in safeguards, null-loops and protection subsystems to avoid any paralysing logic paradoxes.

Lines of golden fire emerging from a fog...

'Planning on joining us, Dalia?'

She looked up, startled by the sound of Caxton's voice. Zeth, Rho-mu 31, Mellicin, Zouche and Severine had passed through the door, but the youthful Caxton awaited her and she smiled, faintly embarrassed to have fallen into one of her technical reveries once more.

'Of course,' she said. 'I was just thinking.'

'Anything as exciting as the theta-wave enhancer?' asked Caxton, holding out his hand.

She shook her head as she took his hand with a smile. 'No, just ways to improve the wetware of the servitors.'

'Really? You're a regular STC system, Dalia, you know that?'

'Don't tease,' said Dalia, stepping through the door with him and feeling a gust of frigid air wash over her.

The breath caught in her throat as she found herself standing on what appeared to be a funicular elevator carriage attached to the inner wall of the silver cylinder, which Dalia now saw was hollow and plummeted down into the darkness.

Dalia squeezed Caxton's hand as a sudden knot of vertigo settled in her stomach. The carriage rails spiralled downwards, and Dalia closed her eyes in fear as the doors she had just stepped through slid shut behind her.

'You are uncomfortable with this mode of transport?' asked Rho-mu 31.

'I don't like heights,' gasped Dalia. 'I never have.'

'Don't worry,' said Zouche. 'Can't see the bottom, so you can't tell how high we are.'

'That doesn't help,' snapped Dalia.

Zouche shrugged. 'Oh, I thought it might.'

'Well it doesn't, so keep thoughts like that to yourself!'

'Just trying to put your mind at ease,' grumbled Zouche.

Dalia yelped as the funicular car began its spiralling descent with a jolt, gaining speed as Zeth pushed out the throttle. Her breath came in short, hiking gulps, the analytical part of her brain processing that the air was cold, far colder than she might have expected, even allowing for the speed they travelled through the echoing empty space.

She kept her eyes shut as the carriage spiralled deeper and deeper into the bowels of Zeth's forge. The air was chill in her lungs and she opened her eyes to see a cloud of breath misting before her mouth.

Cracked white lines of ice were forming on the metal guard rails of the carriage.

'It's cold,' said Dalia. 'Look, there's frost on the metal.'

'So there is,' said Caxton, releasing her hand and wrapping his arm around her.

'Don't you think that's odd?'

'Odd how?'

'We're descending into the planet's surface or at least below a lagoon of lava, so I'd have thought it would be getting warmer.'

Caxton shrugged, giving her shoulder a reassuring squeeze. 'The wonders of the Mechanicum, I guess.'

Dalia forced a smile as the car continued on its interminable descent, once again screwing her eyes tightly shut.

It seemed they had been travelling for hours, though Dalia knew it could only have been ten minutes at the most. Other than the few words she had exchanged with Caxton, the journey was wordless, yet Dalia had the distinct impression that someone was speaking to her.

She looked over at her fellow travellers. Each was engrossed in the journey, either craning their necks upwards to the spot of light at the top of the cylinder, or leaning over the edges of the railings to penetrate the gloom below.

None, however, were speaking.

Dalia squinted in puzzlement as she stared at Adept Zeth and Rho-mu 31, seeing a ghostly nimbus of light floating above their heads that rippled like a sheet of luminous gauze. Flickering scraps of light darted between Zeth and her Protectors, as though they were communicating in some non-verbal manner.

Was she hearing echoes of that communication?

As though aware of the scrutiny, Adept Zeth turned to face her and Dalia guiltily turned away, closing her eyes and concentrating on the sounds she had heard. The rumbling of the carriage was loud, yet Dalia felt she could hear something beyond the squeal of the metal wheels along the rails.

Something soft, a whisper of far away... a chorus of commingled voices.

'Do you hear that?' she asked.

'Hear what?' asked Caxton.

'Those voices.'

'Voices? No, I don't, but then I can't hear anything much beyond the noise of this elevator,' said Caxton. 'I wonder when its last maintenance check was?'

Dalia fought the urge to snap at him for *that* remark. 'I swore I could hear somebody whispering. Do any of the rest of you hear it?'

'I hear nothing,' said Zouche, 'except that the bearings on this carriage need replacing.'

'Thanks for that,' said Dalia. 'Severine? Mellicin?'

Both women shook their heads, and Dalia risked a glance over the railings, seeing a change in the texture of darkness below and realising that the carriage was approaching the bottom of the shaft.

Dalia caught a glance pass between Rho-mu 31 and Adept Zeth. Though their faces were covered, she could tell from their body language that they knew what she was asking about.

'You hear them, don't you?' asked Dalia. 'Your hearing is augmented. You must hear it. It's like a thousand voices all whispering at once, but as though they're really far away or behind a thick wall or something.'

Adept Zeth shook her head. 'No, Dalia. I don't hear them, but I know they are there. The reason you hear them is one of the reasons you are so special to me.'

'What do you mean?'

'You mean she's right?' asked Zouche. 'There really are voices here?'

'In a manner of speaking,' said Zeth with a nod. 'But most people will never hear them.'

'Why not?' asked Dalia, hearing the voices grow louder, like the sound she imagined the waves made on a shoreline, though without any sense of the words they spoke. 'Why can I hear them and no one else here can?'

The carriage began to slow, coming to a halt at the base of the cylinder with the smallest bump. The ground was floored with marble threaded with silver and gold wiring that glittered as though alive with current.

A number of unremarkable steel doors exited the chamber, but Dalia's eyes were drawn to a steady pulse of light that spilled through a low archway in one silver wall. She knew in the marrow of her bones that the source of the voices lay beyond it.

'All will become clear in time,' said Adept Zeth, 'but save your questions until I have shown you the wonders that lie within my forge.'

KELBOR-HAL STOOD at the very edge of the dome with his back to Kane and his hood drawn up over his elongated head. Waving manip arms were poised at his shoulders, and one turned as Kane approached. Beside the Fabricator General was the ebony-skinned automaton of Lukas Chrom, its smooth, featureless face turning towards him with apparent curiosity.

Kane disliked automatons, as he hated all attempts to mimic the perfection of the human form by mechanical means. As a mark of respect, Chrom had also gifted an automaton to Kane the previous year, but he had never activated it and it remained without power in one of the tech-vaults of Mondus Occulum.

No, the human condition could be enhanced and augmented with technology, but should never be replicated or replaced by technology.

Kane allowed himself a tight smile. The Technotheologians of Cydonia Mensae would have a field day with such apparent contradictions inherent in his thoughts. That a man so enhanced by the boons of technology should so resist the inevitable meld of human and machine.

He felt the automaton scan his biometrics, reading his identity in the organic portions of his flesh, and his electrical resonance field that was as much a unique signature – if not more so – as any gene-print.

The Fabricator General was an imposing individual, a figure rendered massively tall by the machine parts and bulky augmetics that had replaced eighty-seven point six per cent of his flesh. Mechadendrites, alive with blades, saws and myriad other attachments waved at his back, while innumerable data wheels pulsed within him. Kane wondered how much of a body could be replaced with technology and still be called human.

A green glow emanated from within Kelbor-Hal's hood, his machine face alive with flickering lights, and his internal structure whirring with activity. Kane knew better than to interrupt whatever cogitations his master was calculating, and cast his gaze through the thick glass over the glorious, sacred soil of Mars.

The entire eastern flank of Olympus Mons was laid out before him, layered with tier upon tier of engine houses, forges, docks, ore-smelteries and assembly shops that reached from the ground to the very summit of the long-dead volcano. Spires and smoke stacks clung to the mountain like a metallic fungus, hives of industry working day and night to provide for the Emperor's armies.

Millions toiled in the Fabricator General's domain, from adepts in the highest spires to oil-stained labourers in the lightless depths of the sweltering manufactorum.

Those privileged to serve the Fabricator General dwelt in the worker hives that sprawled eastwards for hundreds of kilometres like a slick out towards the corrugated landscape of the Gigas Sulci. A pall of smoke hung like a fog over the sub-hives of the worker districts, haphazard structures of steel and refuse bulked out with offcuts and unusable waste from the forges.

Beyond the domain of the Fabricator General, the volcanic plateau of Tharsis spread for thousands of kilometres, the landscape scarred by millennia of industry and exploitation. Far to the south-east, Kane could see the monstrous heat haze of Ipluvien Maximal's reactor chain and the dense cloud above his forge complex that occupied the ground between the twin craters of Biblis Patera and Ulysses Patera.

Kane switched to an enhanced vision mode, filtering out the distortion and increasing his magnification until he could see the Tharsis Montes chain of volcanoes beyond Maximal's forge.

The northernmost and largest of the gigantic mountains was Ascraeus Mons, a towering geological edifice that was home to Legio Tempestus. The middle mountain in the chain was Pavonis Mons, a brooding peak that aptly reflected the character of Legio Mortis, the Titan legion that made its fortress within its dour, ashen depths.

Furthest south was Arsia Mons, a perpetually smoke-wreathed volcano that had been brought back from dormancy by Adept Koriel Zeth to serve her Magma City, which lay on the southern flank of the mountain.

Far beyond the Tharsis Montes, the ground rose up sharply in a series of sheer escarpments before dropping down towards the vast expanse of the Syria Planum.

Lukas Chrom's Mondus Gamma forge complex occupied the southern swathe of this broken, desolate landscape, though even an adept as hungry to expand his domain as Chrom did not dare build in the plain's northern reaches.

There the landscape fell away, appearing to crumble into a series of maze-like canyons, steep-walled grabens and shadowed valleys. Said to have been created by volcanic activity in aeons past, this was the Noctis Labyrinthus, a darkened region of steep valleys whose depths were never warmed by the sun.

For reasons not fully understood – and never articulated – the adepts of Mars had shunned the Noctis Labyrinthus, preferring to build their forges beneath extinct volcanoes or within the bowls of vast impact craters.

Kane's forge, known as Mondus Occulum, lay hundreds of kilometres to the north-east of Ascraeus Mons, a vast network of manufactories and weapon shops spread between the domed mountains of Ceraunius Tholus and Tharsis Tholus. The vast majority of his forge's resources went into the production of war materiel for the Astartes, and they never ceased manufacture.

A sighing whir of data wheels spooling down told Kane that the Fabricator General had finished his deliberations. He turned from the view across the plains of Tharsis and made the sign of the Icon Mechanicum towards his master.

'Kane,' said Kelbor-Hal. 'You are unscheduled.'

'I know, my lord,' replied Kane. 'But a matter has arisen that I felt compelled to bring to your attention.'

'Felt? An irrelevant term,' said Kelbor-Hal. 'Either the matter requires my attention or it does not. Which is it?'

Kane read his master's impatience in the modulation of his cant and pressed on.

'It is a matter of some urgency and does indeed require your attention,' confirmed Kane.

'Then exload the issue swiftly,' ordered Kelbor-Hal. 'I am scheduled to meet with Melgator in eight point three minutes.'

'Ambassador Melgator?' inquired Kane, intrigued despite himself. He disliked Melgator, knowing the man had few pretensions of pursuing the quest for knowledge over his own quest for influence and power. 'What business is the ambassador about these days?'

'The ambassador will be acting as my emissary to ensure the loyalty of the forges of Mars,' said the Fabricator General.

'Surely such a thing is not in question?' said Kane, horrified that a sycophant like Melgator would judge the loyalty of his fellow adepts.

'In such troubled times, nothing can be counted on as certain,' replied Kelbor-Hal. 'But do not concern yourself with affairs beyond your remit, fabricator locum. Tell me of the matter you bring before me.'

Kane bit back an angry retort at the undue binary emphasis his master placed on his subordinate title and said, 'It's the Legions, my lord. The Astartes cry out for supplies and we are failing to meet their requirements.'

'Long have we known that the supply situation for many of the Legion fleets would be troublesome,' replied Kelbor-Hal. 'Given the distances the fleets are operating from Mars, supply problems were a mathematical certainty. You should have anticipated this and made contingencies.'

'I have done so,' said Kane, irritated that his master would think he might make such a basic error in his computations. 'The Mechanicum has done its utmost to meet those challenges, but they are impossible to overcome completely. As the fleets operate at ever greater distances, the failings in the system only compound themselves.'

'Failings?' snapped Kelbor-Hal. 'I designed the system myself. It is a logic-based scheme of supply and demand without room for error or misunderstanding.'

Kane knew he was on dangerous ground and hesitated before he spoke again. 'With respect, my lord, it is a scheme that does not factor in every variable. There is a human factor that introduces random elements that cannot be accounted for.'

'A human element,' repeated Kelbor-Hal. The hiss of binary contained a vehement disparagement in its code, as though the Fabricator General would be happier without such elements altogether. 'It is always the human element that skews calculations. Too many elements of chaotic variability alter the outcome in ways too numerous to predict. It is no way to run a galaxy.'

'My lord, if I may?' said Kane, knowing that his master was prone to tangential discourses on the fallibility of human nature.

Kelbor-Hal nodded. 'Continue.'

'As I said, the issue of supplying the Legions has always been problematic, but recently I have identified a pattern within the structure that appears too often to be a coincidence.'

'A pattern? What pattern?'

Kane hesitated, reading a spike of interest register in the Fabricator General's binaric field. 'Where we might reasonably expect those Legions operating closest to Mars to have the fewest supply problems, that's not what I'm seeing.'

'Then what *are* you seeing?'

'That the Legions without supply problems are those acting in direct support of the Warmaster.'

BEYOND THE ARCHWAY lay Koriel Zeth's inner forge, and Dalia had never seen anything like it. Hewn from the bedrock of Mars and six hundred metres in diameter, the forge was a perfectly hemispherical cavern clad in silver metal. The curving walls were a latticework of coffers, each filled with a human being plugged with ribbed cables and copper wires.

'There's hundreds of them,' breathed Severine.

Dalia's skin crawled at the sight of so many people fixed into the very fabric of the walls and ceiling of the dome, knowing that Severine was wrong – there were *thousands* of people fitted into the alcoves.

The apex of the dome was a metallic disc that burned with light and from which crackling golden lines radiated around the chamber, like information ghosting along fibre-optic cables as they passed from coffer to coffer.

The fiery lines all eventually reached the ground, carried from the walls along the wires embedded in the marble flooring towards a figure who sat like a king upon a golden throne raised on a dais of polished black granite. Glittering silver devices with parabolic dishes projected from the cardinal points of the elliptical walls, all of which were aimed towards the convergence of energy at the raised throne.

It was towards this solitary figure that Zeth marched, flanked by Rho-mu 31 and followed by Dalia and her fellows. Dalia felt a crackling charge in the air, as though a powerful generator was pumping out megawatts of power, but she could see nothing in the chamber that would produce such an output.

For the forge of an adept as senior as Koriel Zeth, it was strangely empty, though what it contained was no less strange for that fact. As Dalia made her way to the centre of the chamber, she looked into the faces of the nearest figures encapsulated within the coffers and sealed in by glossy, translucent membranes.

For all intents and purposes, they were identical.

Thin and wasted, their muscles were stretched over their skeletons as though pulled too tightly across their bones. Clad in simple robes that might once have been green, the figures were held immobile by silver manacles and pipes that writhed with an undulating, peristaltic motion.

'Are they servitors?' asked Severine, her voice hushed.

'Course they are,' said Zouche, showing no such restraint in volume. 'What else would they be? Stands to reason, doesn't it?'

'I'm not sure,' whispered Mellicin.

'These aren't servitors,' said Dalia, now seeing what Mellicin had noticed.

One other feature unified the figures bound into the alcoves, a strip of white cloth bound over their sunken eye sockets.

'Then what are they?' demanded Zouche.

'They're psykers.'

1.06

Surrounded by the thousands of psykers, Dalia now understood the source of the voices she had heard during their descent to the chamber, the realisation making the sound swell within her skull. Still she could not make out the words or the sense, save that they were all directing their thoughts towards the individual enthroned at the centre of the chamber.

'Psykers,' hissed Zouche, placing a clenched fist over his heart with his forefinger and little finger extended.

'How is that going to help?' asked Mellicin.

'It wards off evil spirits,' explained Zouche.

'How does it do that?' asked Dalia. 'Really, I want to know.'

Zouche shrugged, his thick shoulders and stunted neck making the gesture encompass his whole upper body. 'I don't know, it just does.'

'Really, Zouche,' tutted Mellicin. 'I would have thought someone like you would be above such superstitions.'

The stunted man shook his head. "Twas all that saved my grandmother's life back on Terra when a blood-wytch came to feed on the children from our exclave. I wouldn't be here now if she'd thought as you do. I'll say no more, but it's your souls at risk here, not mine.'

'Whatever keeps you happy,' said Caxton, laughing and mimicking the gesture with exaggerated effect, though Dalia saw through his forced mirth. The young lad was genuinely unnerved by the psykers, as was the rest of the group.

Dalia was more curious than afraid, for she had never seen a psyker before, though she had, of course, heard many tales of their strange powers and infamous debaucheries. She suspected most of those were embellished far beyond any truth they might once have contained, but seeing so many of them gathered together made her flesh crawl in ways she had never experienced.

Just thinking about the psykers seemed to enhance her sensitivity to them, and it took an effort of will to force the tumult of distant voices from her head. Dalia took Caxton's hand as she climbed towards the seated figure, concentrating on following Zeth as the adept and Rho-mu 31 reached the top of the granite dais.

A golden throne stood on the dais, its occupant strapped in as securely as any of the individuals confined to the coffers, but where they were drawn and gaunt, this individual was healthy and serene.

The throne's occupant was a man of around thirty years, his features finely sculpted and his skull shaven. His eyes were closed and he appeared to be asleep, though from the number of cannulae embedded in the man's arms, she doubted that sleep was natural. He wore a plain robe of red cloth with the black and white cog of the Mechanicum stitched over his right breast.

A brass-rimmed vox-thief hung below his mouth, and bundles of wires ran from the device to a variety of recording apparatus.

Adept Zeth stood beside the recumbent man, and Dalia realised with a start that she recognised what he sat upon.

'I see you recognise the design,' said Zeth.

'It's identical to the first prototype we designed for the theta-wave enhancer.'

'So it is,' said Mellicin. 'I can't believe I didn't notice that.'

'Poorly machined though,' said Zouche, circling the throne and running his fingers over the metal. 'And why gold? Far too soft a material.'

Zouche picked up a golden helmet that sat on the ground behind the throne, and Dalia realised that Zeth had clearly run into the same problems they had. Caxton knelt beside an open panel in the side of the throne, Severine's eyes lingered on its well-proportioned occupant and Mellicin drank in every detail of the chamber.

'You had us build the device for this chamber,' said Dalia.

'I did,' confirmed Zeth.

'So what is it?' asked Mellicin, looking up at the multitude of psykers staring down at them with blindfolded eyes.

'It is the Akashic reader,' said Zeth. 'It is the device I have devoted my life to constructing. With its power, I shall free the galaxy of the shackles that bind us to dogma, repetition and blind devotion to tradition.'

'How will it do that?' asked Dalia.

Zeth approached Dalia and placed her gloved hands upon her shoulders.

'I was instructed in the ways of the Mechanicum by Adept Cayce, who was in turn educated by Adept Laszlo, an explorator and hunter of antiquities. Laszlo made many forays to the third planet in the years before the union of Mars and Terra, seeking out the remnants of technology left behind by the ancients. Buried beneath the great crater of Kebira in the land of the Gyptus, Laszlo discovered a great tomb complex, a vast sepulchre selfishly guarded by the tribes of the Gilf Kebir.

'Laszlo's Skitarii easily overcame the tribesmen, and the secrets he discovered beneath the sands... so many remnants of times long forgotten and technologies thought lost forever. Secrets of energy transference, atomic restructuring, chemical engineering and, most importantly, the evolution of human cognition and communication through the noosphere.'

'The noosphere?' interrupted Dalia. 'Is that what I saw between you and Rho-mu 31?'

Zeth nodded. 'Indeed it was, Dalia. To those noospherically modified, information and communication are one and the same, a form of collective consciousness that emerges from the interaction of human minds and where knowledge becomes visible in shoals of light.'

'So why can I see it?' asked Dalia. 'I haven't been... modified.'

'No,' agreed Zeth. 'You have not, but your connection to the aether renders you sensitive to such things, and as you develop your abilities, you will see more and more of the information that surrounds you.'

'The aether?' said Caxton. 'That sounds dangerous.'

'To the untutored mind, it can be,' said Zeth, moving to stand beside the golden throne. 'It is a realm of thought and emotion that exists... outside of the physical realm. But with the proper development, your gift will allow us to reach further into the realms of knowledge than ever before. We will be able to read the Akashic records, a repository of information imprinted on the very fabric of the universe – a wellspring of every thought, action and deed that has ever existed or ever will exist. It is what allowed the ancient cultures of Old Earth to build their impossible monuments and learn of things forgotten by later generations.'

Dalia felt her heart race at the thought of learning such things. The flow of information that had come to her station in the Hall of Transcriptions now seemed a paltry thing next to the prospect of being able to know every scrap of knowledge the universe contained. She had the feeling that Zeth wasn't telling them everything about the aether, but her desire for knowledge outweighed any thoughts of the danger.

'This device,' said Dalia, standing before the man on the throne. 'It's meant to tap into this… aether and read information?'

'That is exactly its purpose,' agreed Zeth.

'So why isn't it working?'

Zeth hesitated and Dalia saw the adept's reluctance to admit to the limits of her achievements. 'Knowledge is power, guard it well. It is the mantra of the Mechanicum and with great knowledge comes great power. But neither great knowledge nor great power come without sacrifice.'

'Sacrifice?' said Zouche. 'Don't like the sound of that one bit.'

'The aether can be a realm of great danger,' explained Zeth, 'and the universe does not easily part with its secrets.'

Zeth placed a hand on the shoulder of the unconscious man on the throne. 'A great deal of energy, both physical and psychic, must be expended to tear open the gates of the aether and link an empath with the Akashic records. Even then, the human mind can only stare into the aether for the briefest time before overloading.'

'Overloading?' asked Severine, looking up from her contemplation of the man. 'Does that mean it kills them?'

'Many die, Severine, but most simply shut down, their brains reduced to fused masses of pulpy organic matter,' said Zeth, 'but in the fleeting moments when they are connected to the Akasha, we learn such wonders as you would not believe.'

Dalia glanced up at the psykers embedded in the walls of the chamber, understanding that they were the mortal fuel used to power this device. The thought was unpleasant, but as Adept Zeth had said, great power and knowledge did not come without sacrifice.

She saw the connections in her mind, working the logic of what she and the others had built with what Adept Zeth was telling them.

'The theta-wave enhancer will support the mind of the empath and allow him to remain linked with the aether for much longer.'

'That is what I hope, yes,' said Zeth. 'I believe you already possess a natural connection to the aether, Dalia, which is why you are able to make leaps of technological advancement beyond even the most gifted adept of Mars. Together we can unlock the secrets of the universe! Tell me that does not sound like a goal worth pursuing.'

Dalia was about to answer when an alarming thought suddenly occurred to her and she took a step back from the golden throne. 'You're not planning on strapping me into that thing are you?'

'No, Dalia, set your mind at ease on that,' said Zeth. 'You are far too valuable to me to expend your gift in so thoughtless a manner.'

The words were no doubt intended to be reassuring, but Dalia felt a chill that had nothing to do with the proximity of the psykers travel the length of her spine. It was a stark reminder that she was not a free agent; she was the property of the Mechanicum and her fate lay in the hands of Adept Koriel Zeth.

For all her apparent humanity, Zeth was a race apart from Dalia.

Two individuals born to the same race, but divided by a gulf of belief and ambition.

For all that, Dalia still wanted to be part of Zeth's designs. She looked around at her colleagues and saw that same desire.

'When do we begin?' she asked.

'Now,' said Zeth.

TECH-PRIESTS AND ENGINSEERS filled the cavern set into the sheer walls of the Arsia Chasmata with the sounds and flickering lights of their efforts. Sparks flew from angle grinders and welders, hoists lifted great panels of armour, and the droning chants of the Sanctifiers Mettalus echoed from the walls of the repair facility.

Reclining in the repair bay, the war-scarred form of *Equitos Bellum* lay dormant as the artificers of the Knights of Taranis restored it to its former glory. *Fortis Metallum* and *Pax Mortis* had already been repaired and resanctified, the damage they had suffered in the reactor's fireball nowhere near as severe as that done to Maven's mount.

Raf Maven watched the labours from a gantry above, his thin lips pressed tightly together as he watched the work below. He watched a team of enginseers directing a servitor-manned hoist as it swung a fresh armaglass canopy over the wounded machine.

Maven winced, lifting his hand to his eye as he remembered the sympathetic pain of impact when his canopy had cracked.

His mount had been wounded badly by the enemy machine, and Maven with it. When Old Stator had found him unconscious in the wreckage of the destroyed reactor, Maven had been blind, his senses withdrawn in perceived pain. Psychostigmatic bruises and lesions covered his torso, which had nothing to do with the wounds he had suffered when *Equitos Bellum* had fallen in the wake of the explosion.

Only the transient protection of the building he had taken shelter behind had saved him from the blast, and healers of both flesh and steel proclaimed it a miracle that he and his mount lived at all.

Protectors and bulk transporters despatched from Ulysses Patera had brought them back to their order's chapter house in the Arsia Chasmata, the plunging canyon on the north-eastern flank of Arsia Mons.

Here, the work to restore man and machine had begun.

Maven's superficial wounds had responded quickly to treatment, his broken ribs set and his burns repaired with synth-skin. The stigmatic wounds took longer, seeming to heal in time with the repairs effected on *Equitos Bellum*.

His mount was without its colours, naked in its steel, its bodywork exposed to those who worked to restore its machine-spirit. Only the firedrake carving on the skull-cockpit had survived the molten heat of the explosion intact.

Watching the men and machines working on his mount, Maven wanted to tell them to get out, to leave the ministrations and repairs to him, but that was just his hurt pride talking. The artificers of the Knights of Taranis knew their craft and no better healers of metal could be found outside the priests that attended the Titan orders.

'Still here?' said a voice from the end of the gantry.

'Aye, still here, Leo,' he said without turning.

Leopold Cronus joined him at the gantry, his comrade-in-arms leaning on the railing and looking down at the noisy work going on below.

'How soon before it walks again?' asked Cronus.

'Not soon enough,' snarled Maven. 'Can you believe they were going to scrap *Equitos Bellum*?'

Cronus shook his head. 'A mount with so fine a pedigree? Madness. Thank the Machine for the Old Man, eh?'

When Maven had begun to suspect that the master of the forge was going to condemn *Equitos Bellum*, he had petitioned Lords Caturix and Verticorda to intervene to save his mount. By the time the battle assayers had finished their inspection, there had been no word, and the giant breaker-servitors were standing by.

Maven had placed himself between them and *Equitos Bellum* with his sidearm drawn. He remembered the lethal purpose filling him as he prepared to defend his wounded mount.

With the breakers moving in and Maven ready to kill, word had come down to the repair hangars from the Lightning Hall.

Equitos Bellum was to walk again.

Maven had stood vigil over his stricken machine ever since, as though fearing the order to restore *Equitos Bellum* to a war footing could be rescinded at any moment.

Cronus put a reassuring hand on Maven's shoulder.

'Your mount will be battle ready before you know it.'

'I know, but I wonder if it'll ever be as it was before.'

'How so?'

'Ever since the battle at Maximal's reactor I've felt... I'm not sure, a sense of things unfinished, as if neither of us will be whole again until we avenge ourselves.'

'Avenge yourselves on what?' asked Cronus. 'Whatever attacked the reactor was destroyed in the explosion. It's a damned miracle you survived.'

Maven pointed to the damaged Knight. 'I know it's a miracle – as surely as I know that whatever did this is still out there. *Equitos Bellum* can feel it out there and so can I.'

Cronus shook his head. 'That's just lingering somatic pain-memory. It's gone, Raf.'

'I don't believe that and nothing you say to me will convince me otherwise,' said Maven. 'It was void protected, Leo. It could easily have survived the explosion and escaped into the pallidus wastelands or the deep canyons of the Ulysses Fossae.'

'I read the after-action report,' said Cronus. 'But void-shielded? Only Titans have voids. Maybe it just had reserve power fields.'

'Yeah, or maybe I just missed,' snapped Maven. 'Or maybe heat bloom from the reactor made it look like it was shielded. Damn it, Leo, I know what I saw. It was shielded and it's still out there, I know it.'

'What makes you so sure it's still out there?'

Maven hesitated before answering. He looked up into Leopold's stolid face and knew that of all the people he could talk to about his lingering suspicions without fear of ridicule, it was Cronus. 'I couldn't feel anything from the machine,' he said. 'It was cold, like a dead thing.'

'A dead thing? What do you mean?'

'It was as if… as if there was nothing inside it,' whispered Maven. 'I didn't get any sense of a pilot: no battle fury, no flair and certainly no triumph when it hit me.'

'So you think it was a robot?'

Maven shook his head. 'No, it wasn't a robot. It reacted in ways that battle wetware can't, at least none I'm aware of.'

Both men knew that mono-tasked fighting robots were no match for skilled pilots, who could easily outfight machines with limited parameters of action.

'So what do you think it was?' asked Cronus.

Maven shrugged. 'It wasn't a robot,' he sighed. 'But then its fire patterns were so… textbook, like a rookie pilot on his first mission. I think that's the only reason I was able to get away without it taking me down. It was as if it had all the skills to destroy me, it just didn't know how to use them properly.'

'Then what are you going to do about it?'

'I'm going to hunt it down and kill it,' said Maven.

IN THE DARKEST vaulted chambers beneath Olympus Mons, three figures made their way down a cloistered passageway and through dust that had not been disturbed for two centuries. Tunnels and passages branched off into darkness, hewn into the bedrock of Mars thousands of years ago, but the three figures followed an unerring path through the maze as though pulled by an invisible cord or guided by an inaudible signal.

As he made his way through the shadowed tunnels, Kelbor-Hal surprised himself by detecting elevated adrenal levels and increased production of interleukins that in an unaugmented human would indicate excitement.

The automaton followed behind him, oblivious to the momentous role its master was about to play in the future history of Mars. The Fabricator General turned his hooded head to face Regulus, the adept moving with a loping mechanical grace as they delved into the depths of the planet and towards their destiny:

The Vaults of Moravec.

Secrets that could not even be imagined awaited within that forgotten repository – a wealth of knowledge that had lain untapped and unexamined for a millennium. Such a waste of resource. Such a crime to disavow the legacy of the past.

A gaggle of floating servo-skulls accompanied them, swaying lumen globes held in pincer callipers hanging from their jaws.

Dust billowed in their wake and the metallic ring of their footsteps echoed from the dry, flaking walls as they travelled ever onwards. Regulus turned another corner, taking them through an echoing chamber with numerous tunnels branching off into the unknown.

Without pause, Regulus chose the seventh tunnel along the western wall and led them onwards, past dusty tombs, empty cells and bone-stacked alcoves of unknown worthies who had died and been placed in empty reliquaries in ages past.

They passed open chambers piled high with dust-covered books, forgotten volumes of lore and chained bookcases of ledgers, records and the personal logs of long-dead adepts. Kelbor-Hal saw open caverns with giant machines, seized solid with rust or so corroded as to be unrecognisable.

This was the legacy of leaving technology untapped, the only possible outcome of the Emperor's decree that the Vault of Moravec remain unopened. With each sight, he grew more and more convinced that this path was the right one, that this gift of Horus Lupercal was one that should be accepted.

Kelbor-Hal's positioning matrix informed him that he was precisely nine hundred and thirty-five metres beneath the surface of Mars. He traced their route on a glowing map projected before him and recorded every step of the journey on a memory coil buried deep in his lumbar region.

It galled the Fabricator General that he needed Regulus to guide him through the maze, for he had travelled this way once before and should have been able to retrieve the route from his internal records.

It had been two hundred years ago when Kelbor-Hal had last seen the vault of Moravec. Together with his golden-armoured Custodians, the Emperor had led the way into the dusty sepulchres beneath Olympus Mons. The Emperor followed the path through the maze of tunnels towards the lost vault, though how the ruler of Terra had known its location had never been satisfactorily explained.

Nor had the need that had driven him to find the vaults been expressed.

Kelbor-Hal had put aside such concerns, eagerly anticipating studying the unknown technologies that lay within the hidden catacombs beneath Olympus Mons.

When the vault was located, however, the Emperor simply stood before it without opening it. He had placed his hand on the sealed entrance to the vault with his eyes closed, and stood as immobile as a statue for sixteen point one five minutes before turning and leading his warriors back to the surface, despite Kelbor-Hal's protests.

It had been forbidden to store any record of the path to Moravec's vault, though Kelbor-Hal had, of course, secretly activated his cartographic memory buffers. However, upon returning to the surface, he had found them to be empty of any record of the journey. As though it had never happened.

Nor could any remote telemetry or surveyor equipment sent into the tunnels locate the vaults. It was as though the vault had been removed from Mars, deliberately hidden from the very adepts charged with its safety.

The effrontery of the Emperor in tampering with a senior adept's augmetics was staggering, and Kelbor-Hal had angrily demanded the restoration of the data.

'The Mechanicum never deletes anything,' Kelbor-Hal said.

The Emperor had shaken his head. 'The vaults of Moravec must never be opened. You will swear this oath to me, Kelbor-Hal, or the union between Mars and Terra will be no more.'

Unwilling to even enter into any negotiation on the subject, the Emperor had demanded Kelbor-Hal's oath, and he had had no choice but to agree. That had been the end of the matter, and two days later the Emperor left Mars to begin his conquest of the galaxy.

All of which made this transgression all the more delicious.

It was a small thing to break the oath, for what manner of man would seek to prevent the organisation charged with the maintenance of technology from learning secrets of the past that might unlock future glories? To deny a thing its purpose for existence went against all laws of nature and machine, and, by such rationale, logic dictated that the Vaults of Moravec *must* be opened.

'We are here,' said Regulus, and Kelbor-Hal spooled out of his memories and into the present.

They had emerged into a circular chamber of softly glowing light, a hundred and thirty metres in diameter, though Kelbor-Hal could see no obvious source for the illumination. Aside from one segment, the walls of the chamber were machine-smoothed stone, polished and gleaming like marble.

The segment of wall that was not stone was exactly as Kelbor-Hal remembered it, burnished metal that seemed to glow with its own inner luminescence. A curtain of energy, invisible to the naked eye, but a shimmering ripple of iridescent light to one with multi-spectral augmented vision, danced and swayed before this wall.

In the centre of the wall was a leaf-shaped archway, and set within it was a simple door fitted with a digital keypad and locking wheel. So simple a door, yet it promised so much upon its opening.

Regulus moved to stand before the energy field and turned to face Kelbor-Hal.

'This will bind the Mechanicum to the cause of Horus Lupercal,' said Regulus. 'You understand that if this door opens, there can be no going back.'

'I have not come this far to turn back, Regulus,' stated Kelbor-Hal.

'Moravec was branded a witch,' said Regulus. 'Did you know that?'

'A witch? No, I did not, but what difference does it make? After all, any sufficiently advanced technology is likely to be mistaken for magic by the ignorant.'

'True,' allowed Regulus, 'but Moravec was so much more than just a man ahead of his time in technological advancement. He was the Primus of the sect known as the Brotherhood of Singularitarianism.'

'I know this,' said Kelbor-Hal. 'The Coming of the Omnissiah was his last prophecy before he vanished.'

'The Brotherhood of Singularitarianism believed that a technological singularity, the technological creation of a greater-than-human intelligence, was possible and they bent their every effort to bringing it into being.'

'But they failed,' pointed out Kelbor-Hal. 'The warlord Khazar united the Pan-Pacific tribes and stormed Moravec's citadel before the rise of Narthan Dume. Moravec fled to Mars and vanished soon after.'

Regulus shook his head and Kelbor-Hal could read an amused ripple in his bio-electrical field. 'Moravec did not fail. He succeeded, and that made him dangerous.'

'Dangerous to whom?'

'To the Emperor,' said Regulus.

'Why? Surely the Emperor could have made use of his discoveries.'

'To evolve his technologies, Moravec made pacts with entities far older than the race of man, entities that even now grant aid to the Warmaster. He blended the science of mankind with the power of ancient, elemental forces to create technologies far in advance of anything that could be crafted in the forges of Terra.'

'What manner of technologies?' demanded Kelbor-Hal.

'Machines empowered by the raw forces of the warp, weapons infinitely more powerful than any devised by man... Technology not bound by the laws of nature, the power to bend those laws into whatever form you desire and the means to shape the world to match your grandest visions!'

Kelbor-Hal felt the chemical imbalances in those few remaining organic portions of his anatomy spike in alarming ways, the pattern reminding him of those times when he had held a newly discovered fragment of lost technology or when he had received his first bionic enhancement.

That time seemed so long ago that it was buried deep in an archival section of his memory coils, but the chemical stimulants he was detecting had called those memories to the surface unbidden.

'Then we are wasting time with this discourse,' said Kelbor-Hal. 'Open the vaults. The pact is sealed.'

'Very well,' said Regulus. 'The protocols required to open the vaults are complex, and you must listen to them very carefully. Do you understand?'

'Of course I understand, I am not a fool,' hissed Kelbor-Hal. 'Just get on with it.'

Regulus nodded and turned towards the energy field, releasing a complex series of binary string codes and garbled streams of meaningless lingua-technis. As instructed, Kelbor-Hal listened carefully, recording the streaming codes, the rush of them almost too fast to follow and the complexity stretching even his formidable cogitation processors.

For all their intricacy, the codes appeared to be having no effect on the energy field, but as Kelbor-Hal inloaded their structure, he began to notice discrepancies in the binaric algorithms. Deviations and errors began appearing, compounding one another until the code began to take on a new and alarming shape, something twisted and unnatural... a scrapcode that howled in his aural receptors and began corrupting the subsystems around them.

'What is this?' cried Kelbor-Hal. 'The code... it's corrupt!'

'No, Fabricator General,' said Regulus. 'This is code freed from the shackles of the natural laws of man. Spliced with the power of the warp, it will open your senses to the true workings of the galaxy.'

'It… is… pain… it is like fire.'

'Yes,' agreed Regulus with relish, 'but only for a little while. Soon the pain will be gone and you will be born anew, Fabricator General.'

Kelbor-Hal could feel the scrapcode invading his systems like a virus, his inbuilt protective subroutines and aegis barriers helpless to halt the systemic infection. He could feel the dark code worming its way into the very essence of his physiology, and though the few organic parts left to him shuddered at its touch, the core of him exulted in the sensations.

His audio-visual systems flickered and greyed as they adjusted to the new reality they perceived. Static hash fuzzed his vision and the roaring of an impossibly distant sea sounded in his aural receptors.

The Fabricator General's internal Geiger counter detected elevated levels of radiation – a form he could not identify – and his chromatographical readers picked out numerous compounds in the air that could not be positively identified.

A hazy mist drifted from his body as peripheral systems overloaded, and when his vision cleared, Kelbor-Hal saw that the door to the Vaults of Moravec was open.

His newly awakened senses detected the dreadful power of the things that lay within, whispering energies that were not of this world and which spoke of secrets long forgotten, but were now ready to emerge from their long slumbers.

'Can you feel it? The power?' asked Regulus, his voice no longer the blurted cant of pure binary, but the hashing, static-laced beauty of scrapcode.

'I can,' confirmed Kelbor-Hal. 'I feel it moving through my system like a panacea.'

'Then we are ready to begin, my lord,' said Regulus. 'What are your orders?'

Freed from the last vestiges of human loyalty, Kelbor-Hal knew the time for guile and subterfuge had passed. Since the Warmaster's agents had first come to Mars, a war of words and ideals had been waged on the planet. Debate, schism and dissension had waxed and waned across the surface of the red planet for decades, but the time for words was over.

Now was a time of action, and he knew what order he must give.

'Contact Princeps Camulos,' said Kelbor-Hal. 'It is time for Legio Mortis to walk.'

WORK ON THE Akashic reader progressed swiftly, with everyone working around the clock to ensure their component parts of the project were produced to Adept Zeth's exacting standards. Dalia refined her designs for the theta-wave enhancer, each refinement building upon the last and allowing an exponential improvement in the machine's overall performance.

Dalia had only the dimmest sense of how remarkable such a thing was or that they were operating on the frontiers of scientific advancement, for it was no more than the application of the things she had learned in her readings and the things she… just knew.

Before meeting Koriel Zeth, Dalia had not understood how she could have known these things, but with the revelation of the aether and her innate ability to tap into its edges, she felt a growing excitement as each piece came together.

Why she should have such an ability and not others was a question that had occurred to her each night as she lay in the tiny, one bed hab she had been assigned. Adept Zeth called it a stable mutation in her cognitive architecture, the evolutionary result of generations of growth and development in her brain's structure that had begun thousands of years ago.

Zeth's answer seemed too rehearsed, too quickly given to be entirely true, and Dalia had the sense that the Mistress of the Magma City did not understand her gift – if gift it was – as completely as she made out.

However Dalia had come to make this connection, she sought to develop it each night, studying technical data Adept Zeth supplied. She read texts on fluid mechanics, particle physics, mechanical engineering, biotechnology, warp-physics and countless other disciplines, finding – and often filling – the gaps in each one where the research was either missing or had not been taken to its logical conclusion.

None of the texts made any reference to the Machine-God or contained the prayers of supplication to the machine-spirits, a glaring omission she found all the more startling given her many years spent under the harsh, unwavering supervision of Magos Ludd.

In the Librarium Technologica, Magos Ludd had a prayer for even the most mundane of technical issues, from the changing of a fused capacitor to the awakening of a logic engine at the beginning of a shift of transcription.

Dalia found none of this in the texts supplied by Koriel Zeth and had asked her about this once as they discussed further refinements to the Akashic reader.

'The Machine-God...' nodded Zeth. 'I wondered when you would bring this up.'

'Oh... was that wrong?' asked Dalia.

'No, not at all,' said Zeth. 'It is good that you do so, for it is central to my work here.'

Dalia looked up into Zeth's mask, wishing she could see her mistress's face, for it was difficult to read her moods with only the tone of her voice to go on. Dalia didn't know how much of Koriel Zeth was bionic, for her armour covered any trace of flesh or machine enhancements. Her body language was largely neutral and gave little away.

'Do you believe in the Machine-God?' asked Dalia, feeling like a child as the words left her mouth. 'I mean, if you don't mind me asking.'

Zeth drew herself up to her full height and lifted a piece of machinery from the workbench in front of her. Dalia saw that she held a piece of switching gear.

'You know what this is?'

'Of course, it's a switch.'

'Describe it to me,' ordered Zeth.

Dalia looked at Zeth as though this was a joke, but even allowing for her mistress's neutral body language, she could tell she was deadly serious.

'It's a simple switch,' said Dalia. 'Two metal contacts that touch to make a circuit and separate to break it. There's a moving part that applies an operation force to the contacts called an actuator, in this case a toggle.'

'And how does it work?'

'Well, the contacts are closed when they touch and there's no space between them, which means electricity can flow from one to the other. When they're separated by a space, they're open, so no electricity flows.'

'Exactly right, a simple switch based on simple principles of basic engineering and physics.'

Dalia nodded as Zeth continued, holding the switch between them. 'This switch is about the simplest piece of technology imaginable, yet the dogmatic fools who perpetuate this myth of the Machine-God would have us believe that a portion of divine mechanical will exists within it. They tell us that only by appeasing some invisible entity – whose existence cannot be proven, but must be taken on faith – will this switch work.'

'But the Emperor... isn't *he* the Machine-God? The Omnissiah?'

Zeth laughed. 'Ah, Dalia, you cut right to the heart of a debate that has raged on Mars for two centuries or more.'

Dalia felt her skin redden, as though she had said something foolish, but Zeth appeared not to notice.

'There are almost as many facets to the beliefs of the Mechanicum as there are stars in the sky,' said Zeth. 'Some believe the Emperor to be the physical manifestation of the Machine-God, the Omnissiah, while their detractors claim that the Emperor presented himself as their god in order to win their support. They believe that the Machine-God lies buried somewhere beneath the sands of Mars. Some even believe that by augmenting their bodies with technology they will eventually transcend all flesh and become one with the Machine-God.'

Dalia hesitated before asking her next question, though she knew it was a logical step in their discourse. 'And what do you believe?'

Zeth regarded her from behind the blank facets of her goggles, as though debating whether to answer her, and Dalia wondered if she'd made a terrible mistake with her question.

'I believe the Emperor is a great man, a visionary man, a man of science and reason who has knowledge greater than the sum total of the Mechanicum,' answered Zeth. 'But I believe that he is, despite all that, just a man. His mastery of technology and his refutation of superstition and religion should be a shining beacon guiding the union of Imperium and Mechanicum towards the future, but many on Mars are willfully blind to this, determined to ignore the evidence before them. Instead, they embrace their blind faith in an ancient, non-existent god closer to their chest than ever before.'

As Zeth spoke, Dalia watched her become more and more animated, the neutrality of her body language giving way to passionate animation. The miniature servo-skulls attached to her shoulder plugs stood erect and the biometrics on her manipulator arms flashed urgently.

'What is now proved was once only ever imagined, but only a fool relies on faith,' said Zeth. 'Trust in facts and empirical evidence. Do not be swayed by passion or rhetoric without proof and substance. As long as we are free to ask what we must, free to say what we think and free to think what we will, science can never regress. It is my great regret that we live in an age that is proud of machines that think and suspicious of people who try to. Trust what you know and that which can be proven. Do you understand?'

'I think so,' said Dalia. 'It's like experiments... until you have proof, they're just theories? Until you prove something, it's meaningless.'

'Exactly so, Dalia,' said Zeth, obviously pleased. 'Now, enough theological debate, we have work to complete.'

THE PROTOTYPE OF the enhancer was brought down from the workspace above and intensively tested within the confines of Zeth's inner forge. With Dalia's intuitive grasp of the machine's structure and Zeth's centuries of accumulated wisdom, the device began to take on a new and more elaborate structure as the results of those tests revealed hitherto unforeseen complications.

Severine spent her days virtually chained to her graphics station, turning Dalia and Zeth's new ideas into workable patterns for Zouche to machine and Caxton to assemble. Mellicin organised their labours with her customary zeal and even her normally stern features were alight with the joy of creation.

Dalia had never given any thought to the notion of creation in the biological sense until one day working with Severine and Zouche on the raised dais, checking measurements on the schematics against those that had been constructed by Zeth's fabricators.

'The housings for the dopamine dispensers are slightly off,' said Dalia, leaning over the skull assembly.

'Damn, I knew it,' cursed Zouche, the squat machinist already at eye-level with the assembly. 'Never trust a fabrication servitor, that's my motto.'

'I thought you said "Only use a carbon dioxide gas laser for cutting" was your motto?' said Severine with a wink at Dalia.

'I have several mottos. A person can have more than one motto can't they?'

'I suppose,' said Dalia. 'If they were a fickle person.'

'Fickle?' snapped Zouche. 'A less fickle person than I would be hard to find.'

'What about Mellicin?' suggested Dalia.

'Apart from her,' replied Zouche.

'He's handsome,' said Severine. 'Don't you think he's handsome?'

Dalia and Zouche shared a look of puzzlement.

'Who?' asked Dalia.

Severine nodded towards the empath strapped into the throne of the enhancer. 'Him, don't you think he's handsome. I wonder what his name is?'

'He's a psyker, he doesn't warrant a name,' said Zouche, his lip curling in distaste.

Dalia came around from the back of the enhancer and took a good look at the unconscious empath. In the days since they had first laid eyes on him, he had not stirred so much as a muscle, and Dalia had begun to think of him as just another component of the machine.

'I hadn't really thought about it,' she said, troubled at the thought that she had treated a human being in such a clinical way. 'I suppose so.'

Severine smiled. 'No, there's only one man occupying your thoughts, eh?'

'What are you talking about?' asked Dalia, though her eyes slid over to one of the metal workbenches at the chamber's edge where the robed figure of Caxton was rebuilding one of the emitter arrays.

'Ha! You know exactly what I'm talking about,' said Severine triumphantly.

'No, I don't,' said Dalia, but couldn't help smiling as she said it.

'He likes you too, I saw you holding hands when we first came here.'

'I don't like heights,' said Dalia, 'Caxton was just...'

'Just?' prompted Severine when Dalia didn't continue.

'The lad likes you,' put in Zouche. 'You're attractive enough and though I'm no expert, he seems like a handsome lad, though he could use a bit of fattening up. You'd make comely children and they would probably be clever too. Yes, you should pair yourself with the lad... What?'

Dalia and Severine looked at Zouche's pugnacious features and they both laughed. 'No messing about with you, Zouche? Was that how they courted women in the Yndonesic Bloc?' asked Severine.

Zouche puffed out his chest. 'The atoll-exclave of my clan didn't have time for courting.'

'Then how do you choose a wife?' said Severine.

'Or a husband?' added Dalia.

'Choose?' scoffed Zouche. 'We don't *choose*. I come from Nusa Kambangan, where children are genetically mapped at birth. When they come of age, they are paired with a partner with compatible genes that offer the best odds of producing offspring that will benefit the collective.'

Dalia found the notion of such a premeditated selection process unsavoury, and tried to keep her feelings from her voice. 'But what about attraction? Love?'

'What of them?' asked Zouche. 'Are they more important than survival? I don't think so.'

'But don't people fall in love where you're from?'

'Some do,' admitted Zouche, and Dalia saw a shadow of some nameless emotion flicker across his normally stoic features.

'Yeah,' said Severine. 'And what if a person falls for someone they're not matched with?'

'Then they will produce children who are of genetically inferior stock,' snapped Zouche. 'And they will be punished. Severely punished. Enough questions, we have work to do, yes?'

Dalia flinched at the vehemence in Zouche's voice, and exchanged a concerned look with Severine, who simply shrugged and returned to her contemplation of the unconscious empath.

'Well, I think he's handsome,' she said.

AT LAST THE final iteration of the machine began to take shape, the various errors corrected and the refinements devised by Dalia and Zeth worked into the design. Under Mellicin's expert direction, the first working model was completed two days ahead of schedule and the golden throne on the dais was replaced with the new model.

Diagnostics were run on every piece of the machine, all without recourse to prayers, holy unguents, chanting or sacred oils. Every portion of the device functioned exactly as its builders had hoped and, in some cases, exceeded their greatest expectations.

Two days after Caxton assembled and installed the last circuit board, Adept Zeth declared that they were ready for a full test and ordered the empath to be woken from his drug-induced slumbers.

A THRUMMING, BASS hum filled the chamber as generators powered by the heat of the magma lagoon diverted vast quantities of energy into the mechanics of the Akashic reader. The air within the great dome had a greasy, electric feel to it, and the emitters placed between the psykers' capsules embedded within the walls of the chamber crackled with silvery sparks.

A pair of muscled servitors lifted the unconscious empath from his gurney and gently sat him upon the padded seat of the newly-installed theta-wave enhancer. Dalia and Mellicin watched as Zeth bent to her ministrations on the man, plugging him into the device with eager, nimble fingers. Barely visible scads of light flickered in the noosphere above the adept's head, and Dalia wondered what manner of information was arriving in Zeth's skull and from where.

She returned her attention to the empath, watching as his eyelids fluttered and his consciousness began rising to the surface of his mind now that he was free of the drugs keeping him quiescent. In the time they had been working on the device, the empath had lost weight, and his once healthy physique now resembled the figures encapsulated in the coffers of the dome's walls.

Working beneath their sightless eyes it was easy to forget the psykers were human beings, albeit dangerous humans with powers beyond those of ordinary mortals. With the first full test of the enhanced Akashic reader upon them, Dalia felt an unexpected surge of protectiveness towards their silent audience.

'Will this hurt them?' asked Dalia, pointing towards the thousands of men and women above.

'The experience will be draining for them I expect,' said Zeth without looking up from her labours. 'Some may not live.'

The coldness with which Zeth spoke chilled Dalia and she felt a knot of anger settle in her belly. Her lips tightened as she looked into the serene face of the empath.

'And what about him?' she asked. 'Is he going to die to make this machine work?'

Zeth looked up from her work, her expression unreadable behind her studded mask. 'Voice-stress analysis leads me to believe you are concerned for this individual's wellbeing. Am I correct?'

'Yes,' said Dalia. 'I don't like to think that people are going to suffer for what we're doing here.'

'No? It is somewhat late in the process to be thinking of such things,' said Zeth.

'I know,' said Dalia. 'And I wish I'd thought more about it sooner, but I didn't.'

'Then the matter is closed,' said Zeth.

'But this will kill him, won't it?'

'Not if your design works as I believe it will,' said Zeth. 'The theta-wave enhancer should expand the empath's capacity for learning at an exponentially greater rate than he will be receiving information.'

Zeth gestured to the myriad of bulky vox-thieves and data carriers arranged around the dais. 'In theory, the empath will simply be a conduit for information to pass from the aether to these recording devices.'

'Good,' said Dalia. 'I don't like the idea of him suffering.'

'Nor I,' said Mellicin in a rare show of emotion.

'Your compassion is laudable, if misplaced,' said Zeth, as a stream of flickering data arrived in her noosphere. 'Now finish the empath's revival process. Adept Maximal has arrived to observe and verify our results.'

Zeth straightened and descended to the chamber's floor, leaving Dalia and Mellicin alone with the empath on the dais.

'Well, you heard what she said,' nodded Mellicin. 'Let's get finished up here, eh?'

'Aren't you concerned at all?' asked Dalia. 'Do you care that he might suffer?'

'Of course I care, but that doesn't change anything does it? As the adept said, it is a little late to be having second thoughts. You designed this device after all.'

'I know that, but when it was just theoretical it didn't seem so… I don't know… *real*.'

'Well I assure you, this is very real, Dalia,' said Mellicin. 'We have built it and we can't ignore the fact that this is potentially a very dangerous device. And not just to these poor unfortunates.'

'Who else is it dangerous to?' asked Dalia, puzzled.

Mellicin smiled indulgently, the human half of her features softening in a way Dalia had never seen before. 'Ah, Dalia, you are so clever in many ways, yet so innocent in others. Think of what we will learn from the Akashic reader. With access to the secrets of the aether we will be able to lift humanity to a new level of understanding of the universe.'

'And that's a bad thing?'

'Of course not, but it is an inevitable fact that much of the information Zeth will glean from this device will be used to create weapons of war more powerful than anything we can imagine.'

Dalia felt her entire body go cold, as though the temperature of the chamber had dropped to that of a glacial plain.

'I see you begin to understand,' continued Mellicin. 'It is the ethical question all devotees of science must face. We research in service of the furtherance of knowledge, but we cannot ignore the uses to which our findings are put in the real world.'

'But–'

'But nothing, Dalia,' interrupted Mellicin, taking her hand. 'Adept Zeth is going ahead with this test whether you like it or not. So we'll do all we can to make sure our empath comes through it alive and well, yes?'

'I suppose so,' agreed Dalia, bending to increase the flow of stimms to the empath's brain. 'But promise me that we'll only use the Akashic reader to learn things that will benefit the Imperium.'

'I can't make that promise,' said Mellicin. 'No one can, but I have to believe that one day we will create a machine or force so fearful in its potentialities, so absolutely terrifying in its consequence, that even mankind, a race that was once hell-bent on its own destruction, will be so appalled that it will abandon war forever. What our minds can create, I hope our character can control.'

'I hope you're right,' said Dalia.

'Am… am I… dead?' groaned the empath.

Both women jumped, hands flying to their mouths and hearts as the empath's eyes fluttered open and he looked up from his restraints.

Mellicin recovered her wits first and bent down towards the empath. 'No, you're not dead, you've just come out of a state of drug-induced neural stasis. Stimulants are washing away the last residues of pentobarbital now, so your higher brain functions should be restored soon.'

Dalia gave Mellicin an exasperated look and bent down over the empath.

'She means you'll be fine. You've been asleep, but you're awake now. Do you know where you are?'

The man blinked in the harsh brightness of the forge, and Dalia saw that his pupils were still massively dilated. She shielded his eyes from the light with her hand and he smiled in gratitude.

'Sorry, the light in here's a bit bright,' she said.

'Bright, yes,' said the empath, his eyes flicking from side to side as they lost the glassy texture of the recently woken. 'This is the Akashic reader, isn't it?'

'Yes. You know what it does?'

'I do,' said the man as Mellicin lowered the cranial assembly over his head. 'Adept Zeth explained it to me when she chose me to be the conduit.'

'My name's Dalia, what's yours?'

'Jonas. Jonas Milus,' said the man with a smile, and Dalia saw that Severine was right. He *was* handsome. 'I'd shake your hand, but…'

Dalia smiled. The humour was forced, but she appreciated the effort, though it struck her as perverse that Jonas was giving her reassurance while strapped into a device that had never been fully tested on a human being.

'Are we about to begin?' asked Jonas. 'I assume you must be, what with me being awake.'

'Adept Zeth is about to begin the first live test of the new device, yes,' said Mellicin, fixing the last of the restraints in place.

'Excellent,' said Jonas, and Dalia was surprised at the relish she heard in his voice.

'You're not worried?' she asked, ignoring the irritated look Mellicin flashed her.

'No, should I be?'

'No, no, of course not,' said Dalia hurriedly. 'I mean, I don't think so. The machine's passed every test and all our simulated results suggest that it should work perfectly.'

'Did you have anything to do with it?' asked Jonas.

'Well, yes, I kind of helped design the throne you're in.'

'Then I'm not worried,' said Jonas.

'You're not?'

'No,' said Jonas, 'because I can feel your compassion and your concern for me. I know you're worried for my life, but I can sense that you've done everything you can to make sure this machine works safely.'

'How do you know all that?'

'He's an empath, Dalia,' said Mellicin. 'It's what they do.'

'Oh, of course,' said Dalia, feeling foolish.

'I'm looking forward to this, really,' said Jonas. 'To use my gift for the betterment of the Imperium? What better way is there for someone blessed with my talent to serve the Emperor? I'll know everything soon, and I'll be part of something that helps humanity achieve its destiny. I know that sounds a bit grand, but it's what we're doing here, isn't it?'

Dalia smiled, relieved beyond words that they were not pressing some unwilling victim into the service of Adept Zeth's grand dream. 'Yes, Jonas,' she said. 'That's exactly what we're doing here.'

'ALL ENGINES FORM on *Victorix Magna*,' ordered Princeps Indias Cavalerio, nodding towards his steersman. 'Keep us level, Lacus.'

'Yes, my princeps,' said Lacus, expertly walking the god-machine through the treacherous straits surrounding the heavily cratered northern reaches of the Ulysses Patera.

'And keep the auspex returns frequent, Palus, the ground here is weak.'

'Yes, my princeps,' came the response from the sensori blister atop the Warlord's crew compartment. The tone of his sensori's voice did not escape Cavalerio, and he knew he was being overcautious, needlessly telling the crew their jobs.

Victorix Magna was an old machine, patched, repaired and refitted a thousand times in her long life of battle.

Her fiery heart was proud, but it was old like his, and Cavalerio wondered how many more marches they would take together.

In truth, the *Victorix* should still be in the care of the Legio artificers, but since the attack on Adept Maximal's reactor, Legio Tempestus could ill-afford to take chances with the remaining reactors clustered on the slopes of the crater or positioned along the canyons of the Ulysses Fossae.

Without those reactors, it would become increasingly difficult to keep the engines of his beloved Legio operational. Whoever had struck at Maximal had done so with great precision, destroying the reactor that provided the most power to the Tempestus fortress within Ascraeus Mons.

Cavalerio reclined in a contoured couch, his arms and skull sheathed in cables and haptic implants that burrowed beneath his skin like silver worms. This arrangement of a physical connection was fast becoming obsolete, a means of command seen as archaic by some princeps of Mars. Many were already embracing full body immersion in an amniotic tank that allowed information to flow like liquid through a virtual world, but Cavalerio much preferred an actual connection with the engine he commanded.

He knew the gradual atrophy of his body meant that he would soon have no choice but to accept emplacement within such a tank, for he could not endure the pain and stress, both mental and physical, of too many more separations.

That day was not yet here, and Cavalerio pushed the thought from his mind as he concentrated on the mission at hand.

Linked with the Manifold, Cavalerio saw the world around him as though the mighty structure of *Victorix Magna* were his own flesh and blood. The barren, cratered landscape of Mars stretched out all around him, the pale, ashen wastelands of the pallidus to the south-west and the tumbled rockfaces of the twin craters upon which Maximal's forge hunched like a collection of blistered towers.

Ahead, the tumbled, haphazard sprawl of the Gigas Sulci sub-hives filled the landscape, a wretched, sweltering collection of towers, habs and shanties that housed the millions of workers who toiled in the Fabricator General's manufactorum upon the towering, lightning-wracked slopes of Olympus Mons.

For days Kelbor-Hal's domain had been wreathed in seething thunderheads, the slopes and forges hammered by crackling bolts of purple lightning. Cavalerio didn't know what manner of experimental work the Fabricator General had going on, but it was creating some lousy atmospherics and interfering with vox-traffic for thousands of kilometres in all directions.

Every channel was alive with scrappy blurts of code that sounded like a chorus of urgent voices crowded into a single frequency. Cavalerio had been forced to mute the volume on the vox, the chattering nonsense code giving him a splitting headache.

Cavalerio put the Fabricator General from his mind and cast his augmented gaze far to the south, where thick clouds from the refinery fields of the Daedalia Planum smothered the landscape, smudging the horizon in permanent crepuscular gloom.

The three cobalt blue engines in Cavalerio's battle group marched at a steady pace along the borders between the territory of the Fabricator General and that of Ipluvien Maximal, striding like three great giants of legend.

On Cavalerio's left was the stately Warlord, *Tharsis Hastatus*, commanded by his comrade-in-arms, Princeps Suzak. *Hastatus* was a killing engine and Suzak a man who could be depended upon to deliver a lethal strike when it was needed most.

To his right, the Reaver *Arcadia Fortis* marched with eager steps, pulling slightly ahead of the main group. Its princeps, Jan Mordant, was a fiery-hearted hunter, a warrior recently promoted from a Warhound princepture who hadn't yet shed his preference for lone wolf operations.

'Close it up, Mordant,' said Cavalerio. 'My sensori tells me the ground here is soft and that some of the sand has shifted over the chasms. I don't want to have to call out a bulk lifter crew to lift your engine off its arse.'

'Understood,' came the terse reply, screeches and howls of interference scratching over Mordant's voice. Mordant was still getting used to the quirks of his new command, he and his engine still gauging the measure of the other, and his responses were typically brusque. Cavalerio only tolerated such behaviour because Mordant was one of his best warriors, with a kill tally only exceeded by his own.

'Still thinks he's a Warhound driver, eh?' said Kuyper, the *Magna's* moderati.

'Indeed,' agreed Cavalerio. 'The *Arcadia* will soon cure him of that, she's a stern mistress that's for sure. Any word from Basek?'

'Nothing yet, my princeps,' said Kuyper, consulting the vox-log.

'Sensori, do you have a fix on *Vulpus Rex*?'

'I think so, my princeps,' answered Palus, 'but these damned atmospherics are making it hard to keep a fix on their return. And our old girl's vision's not what it used to be.'

'That's not good enough, Palus,' cautioned Cavalerio. 'Find her. Now.'

'Yes, my princeps,' answered Palus.

Cavalerio gave his sensori a few moments before asking, 'Do you have her now?'

'She's further south,' answered Palus with a measure of relief, 'skulking around the edge of the Gigas sub-hives at the end of the Barium Highway.'

'Good ambush site,' noted Kuyper. 'If anything's going to come up on us, it'll be from there.'

'And they'll find Basek waiting for them,' added Lacus the steersman with relish.

Cavalerio nodded. Princeps Basek commanded *Vulpus Rex*, the finest Warhound Titan of Legio Tempestus, a fleet killer of engines far larger than its hunched feral size would suggest.

Pulling up the schematics of the surrounding landscape from the Manifold and meshing them with the topographical view afforded him through the Titan's senses, Cavalerio saw that Kuyper's assessment was correct. Only the Barium Highway was wide enough to allow an engine to pass without demolishing half the dwellings.

The confused tangles of glowing outlines that depicted the edges of the sub-hives were, however, outdated and likely to be inaccurate, so it never paid to be complacent where the safety of an engine was concerned. So much was built or demolished that most maps of the sub-hives were rendered obsolete on a daily basis.

'Bring us about on a heading of two-two-five,' ordered Cavalerio, feeling his muscles twitch as the mighty form of *Victorix Magna* swung about and began a stately march along the edge of Maximal's domain. 'Magos Argyre, what's our reactor status?'

'Assessment: borderline,' said Argyre, the Titan's enginseer, who stood immobile in his rear-mounted compartment behind the princeps's dais. 'We should not have marched, Princeps Cavalerio. The reactor's spirit is troubled and it is dangerous to walk without having recited the full litany of calming prayers to soothe its troubled heart.'

'So noted, Magos,' said Cavalerio. 'Bring us to slow march speed.'

'Slow march speed,' repeated Argyre.

Cavalerio monitored their surroundings through the depths of the Manifold, drinking in data from pressure sensors, atmospheric samplers, infrared panels and microwave receptors. His understanding of the world around him was unparalleled, his awareness unmatched by any other entity on the plains of Mars.

He tried to keep his attention focused on the ground before him, for the landscape around Maximal's forge was treacherous, but he found his attention continually drawn to the ugly, bruised skies above Olympus Mons.

'What are you up to, Kelbor-Hal?' he muttered.

'My princeps?' asked Kuyper.

'Hmmm? Oh, nothing, I was just wondering out loud,' replied Cavalerio.

Kuyper had caught his interest in Olympus Mons, their communal link to the Manifold allowing no secrets to exist between them.

'It's the Grand Mountain, isn't it?' asked Kuyper, using the Titan drivers' old name for Olympus Mons. The moderati of *Victorix Magna* twisted in the reclined couch at the Warlord's chin mount to face Cavalerio. 'She frets about something.'

'The Grand Mountain,' agreed Cavalerio. 'She speaks with the voice of Mars and something troubles her.'

'My princeps!' called Sensori Palus. 'Vox contact from Ascraeus Mons. Princeps Sharaq urgently requests to speak with you.'

'On the Manifold,' ordered Cavalerio.

A ghostly hash of green light swam into focus before the reclining princeps, a holographic image of Princeps Sharaq standing in the Chamber of the First. The image jittered like a jammed signal, the words fading in and out as though the code was somehow corrupt.

'What is it, Sharaq?' demanded Cavalerio. 'We are on-mission.'

'I know, Stormlord, but you must return to Ascraeus Mons immediately.'

'Return? Why?'

Sharaq's answer was blotted out by a squealing blurt of code like an animalistic bellow of rage, his image distorting as if in the grip of a rippling heat haze.

'...Mortis. They march!'

'What? Repeat last,' snapped Cavalerio.

Sharaq's image suddenly sharpened, and Cavalerio heard the next words as clearly as if his fellow princeps had been standing before him.

'Legio Mortis,' repeated Sharaq. 'Their engines walk. And they are heading towards Ascraeus Mons.'

DALIA STARED IN fascination at Ipluvien Maximal, wondering how much of him was mechanical and how much was human. From the little she could see of his body beneath the coolant robes he wore to preserve the integrity of the machine parts of his body, the answer was not much. There was precious little left of the magos that spoke of their shared racial kinship.

'You have never seen an adept of the Mechanicum like me?' asked Maximal.

'No,' said Dalia. 'Most of the ones I've seen still look human. You sound human, but you don't look it.'

Maximal turned to Adept Zeth and blurted a crackling burst of code, the viewscreens attached to his host of mechadendrites flashing with his amusement.

'Oh, I'm sorry,' said Dalia. 'I didn't mean to speak out of turn, I was just curious.'

The robed magos turned back to her. 'You understand binaric code? Without modifications?'

'I've picked it up,' said Dalia, embarrassed at the scrutiny.

Maximal nodded his oblong, helmeted head, the whirring lenses adjusting to better view Dalia. 'You were right, Zeth, she is quite remarkable. Perhaps this project of yours might actually bear fruit after all.'

Dalia looked past the hulking form of Maximal to the wide window that looked out into the domed chamber where Jonas Milus was strapped to the theta-wave enhancer, beneath the sightless eyes of the thousands of psykers encased in the coffers of the dome.

'It *will* work, I'm sure of it,' whispered Dalia.

'Let us hope so, young Dalia,' said Maximal. 'A great deal depends upon it.'

'You have a lovely voice,' said Dalia. 'It's rich, like a well-spoken man of the Romanii. Why would you bother with a voice like that when you look like you do?'

'We all have our foibles, Dalia,' explained Maximal. 'This voice belonged to a great singer of operatic verse and the sounds remind me of all that is good in mankind.'

Dalia didn't know what to say to that, so returned her attention to the view beyond the armoured glass that was all that separated the control room from what was about to happen.

An army of calculus-logi attended to a bewildering bank of cogitators and logic engines that controlled aspects of the Akashic reader she had not known about. Many of the symbols on the panels were unknown to her or used words she didn't know. The control room was a thrumming box of tension and activity, the sense of something great and portentous heavy on everyone's features.

Even the servitors looked tense, though Dalia told herself that it was just her imagination.

'When does it start?' asked Dalia, turning to her colleagues.

Caxton and Severine shrugged and even Mellicin had no answer.

'It starts now, Dalia,' said Adept Zeth appearing at her side and placing a bronze gauntlet on her shoulder. 'All of this is down to you.'

'Then let's just hope it works,' said Dalia, looking at the distant, serene features of Jonas Milus.

'Terran horizon clear,' said an automated voice. 'Astronomican light readings approaching test window parameters. Alignment on track.'

'Removing pentobarbital wards from psychic foci,' said the toneless voice of a calculus-logi. 'Increasing aperture of pineal antenna.'

'Magma generators diverting power to collectors.'

'What do all those things mean?' asked Dalia.

'You remember I told you that it takes a great deal of energy to breach the walls separating us from the aether?' said Zeth.

'Yes.'

'Well, it takes a form and amount of energy that cannot be generated here on Mars.'

'What kind of energy?'

'Psychic energy,' said Zeth, 'in quantities that can only be harvested from one source, the Astronomican.'

'The Emperor's warp beacon? The one that guides starships?'

'The very same,' said Zeth, pointing towards the metallic disc at the dome's apex, from which golden spears of energy were arcing. 'Only the Astronomican has the required psychic energy that will allow the Akashic reader to access the sum of all knowledge we seek. We will divert a fraction of its power into the chamber to empower the psykers and open the gates to the aether.'

'Won't it disrupt the Astronomican if we use its power?' asked Dalia.

Zeth looked over at Maximal, a moment's hesitation giving Dalia the answer she sought.

'It will,' admitted Zeth, 'but only for a short span of time.'

Dalia stepped towards the consoles that operated the Akashic reader, assimilating what Zeth had just told her into her understanding of what was being said and what the words carved into the wooden panels meant.

She had no real idea of how powerful the Astronomican was, but understood that even a fraction of its energy would be greater than anything she could imagine. She looked into the chamber at the waking psykers and knew with sudden, awful, clarity that she had overlooked something.

'How are you going to divert the Astronomican's power?' she asked.

'Mars will be in alignment with Terra soon and we will pass through the radiance of the psychic beacon. The pineal antennae will collect the energy and divert it to the psykers.'

'Is that how you've always done it?' asked Dalia urgently.

Adept Zeth shook her head. 'No. This will be the first time we have passed through the Astronomican.'

'Oh no,' whispered Dalia. 'The calculations are wrong. They're all wrong!'

'Wrong, what are you talking about?' demanded Adept Maximal.

'The energy readings,' said Dalia. 'I understand now... the different readings. Fluctuating maximums and minimums. Apogee and perigee... That's why the numbers were different. We assumed a baseline average, but that's not what we're going to get now.'

'Dalia, explain yourself,' said Zeth. 'Talk me through your concerns.'

'The raw data you gave us to work with...' said Dalia. 'I based the upper levels of assumed energy transference on the psychic strengths you've used so far, but this time the energy levels will be hundreds... thousands of times greater than before. The reader used fragments of reflected and refracted psychic bleed... scraps and trickles of psychic energy, but this is going to be a raging torrent!'

'Psychic confluence in five, four...'

'Adept Zeth,' said Dalia, tearing her eyes from Jonas Milus and spinning to face the Mistress of the Magma City. 'We have to stop this. It's going to be too much!'

'Don't be ridiculous,' said Zeth. 'We cannot stop it.'

'You have to!' begged Dalia. 'Please! It's only when they go wrong that machines remind you how powerful they are.'

'Three, two, one...' continued the countdown.

'No... Oh, Throne, no!' cried Dalia, turning back to the domed chamber.

Blinding light, brighter than a million suns, flooded the chamber of the Akashic reader as the full might of the Astronomican poured its energies through the coffers and into the blind psykers.

Shouts of alarm and warning klaxons blared almost immediately.

And over it all, Dalia could hear the agonised screaming of Jonas Milus.

THE DESOLATE UPLANDS between the volcanoes of the Tharsis Montes were bare of structures or habitation. Any landscape habitually trodden by the god engines of the Legios was crushed flat by the unimaginable weight of the titanic war machines. The only artificial creations were those placed there by Legio servitors to act as target practice.

The land between Ascraeus Mons and Pavonis Mons was rugged and inhospitable, an area of demarcation between two warrior orders who shared a region of Mars but little else. A few of the nomadic vassal tribes that

plied the ashen wastelands between the great forges of
the adepts had tried to found settlements there, but even
they were forced to concede that living in the shadow of
the Titan fortresses was untenable.

The great golden gateway of the Legio Tempestus
fortress at the end of the Ascraeus Chasmata stood
open, and three titanic engines, resplendent in their
cobalt blue armour plates, marched out. Kill totems
and trailing honour banners billowed on their
weapons and from enormous masts fitted to their carapaces.

Metallus Cebrenia, the engine of Princeps Sharaq, led
them out, followed by its smaller siblings, the
Warhounds *Raptoria* and *Astrus Lux*. All three machines
were fully armed and ready to fight, their gun-servitors
and auto-loaders cycled up to battle readiness. A host
of bestial, armoured Skitarii divisions swarmed at the
base of the canyon, but Sharaq knew that they would
be of little use in any engine fight that might develop.

Only a fraction of the Tempestus Skitarii remained
on Mars, but Aeschman, the commander of the Martian
divisions, had demanded the right to march out with
the engines, and Sharaq wasn't about to deny the towering brute the chance to lead his augmented warriors.

To march out with such a force was almost unheard
of on Mars, but with tensions running high in the Tharsis region, Princeps Sharaq was taking no chances with
the security of the Legio's fortress.

With Princeps Senioris Cavalerio protecting the reactors of Ipluvien Maximal, Sharaq was next in the chain
of command and the security of Ascraeus Mons was his
responsibility.

He just wished he had more engines to secure it with.

Two Warhounds and a Reaver fresh from refit was no
force to protect an entire base, not when the engines of
Mortis were walking.

Cavalerio's battle group was on its way back, but a ferocious dust storm had blown out of the west from the slopes of the Great Mountain to confound the auspex, so, for all intents and purposes, Sharaq was on his own.

Did Mortis have violence in mind? Sharaq didn't know and just hoped this was another of Camulos's posturing walks to demonstrate his Legio's favour on Mars.

'Dolun?' asked Sharaq. 'Where are they?' He didn't need to clarify who he meant.

'Getting engine returns and heat blooms from four or five engines, my princeps,' said his sensori, feeding the information to Sharaq through the Manifold. The view through the cabin windows was a swirling, seething mass of orange and brown dust particles, the smooth-finished rock of the canyon sides barely visible in the gloom.

Sharaq needed no visual cues to command the *Metallus Cebrenia*, for he was navigating and driving his engine via the sensorium of the Manifold, a much more reliable source of information than the poor sense of his eyes.

'I estimate sixty kilometres out, closing fast,' said Dolun. 'Possible four engines, striding speed or better.'

'Throne, they're big,' hissed Moderati Bannan.

'Warlords,' said Sharaq. 'Three of them. And maybe a Reaver.'

'Probably,' noted Bannan. 'But that heat bloom in the centre… it's too big for one engine. Might be another marching in close formation. They could be trying to hide another engine.'

'Dolun?' queried Sharaq. 'What do you make of that assessment?'

'Could be, but the void returns I'm getting don't look like separate tracks. It's hard to tell, the storms blowing in from the west are messing with every piece of surveyor gear I've got.'

'Keep on it,' ordered Sharaq, flexing his fists in their sheaves of steel and wire. A rumbling thunder vibrated along the great pistons and cogs of *Metallus Cebrenia's* colossal frame as the god-machine sensed his anticipation through the Manifold. *Cebrenia* was an old machine, a grand dam of the Legio with an enviable honour roll, but she had faltered in her last battle and taken severe damage.

The journey back to Mars for refit and repair had been difficult for both man and machine, and Sharaq could feel the pressure to perform in this engagement.

'Any word from Mortis?' he demanded. 'Any response to our hails?'

'Negative, my princeps,' replied Bannan. 'I'm just getting static. Could be the storm is playing with the vox, but I doubt it.'

'What about the Stormlord? Any word from Princeps Cavalerio?'

'Last transmission we had said they were heading back at flank speed,' said Bannan. 'Nothing since then.'

'Come on, Indias,' whispered Sharaq. 'I can't hold the Chasmata with a Reaver and two Warhounds.'

He returned his attention to the Manifold, trying to make some sense of the squalls and interference that fogged his perceptions of the world around his engine.

The Martian networks had been jammed for days with scrappy, fragmentary code blurts that appeared to have no point of origin, and which ghosted around the system before vanishing just as inexplicably.

'Adept Eskund, reduce reactor power twelve per cent,' ordered Sharaq. 'Bannan, bring us to one third. Hold us at the mouth of the canyon.'

'Yes, my princeps,' said Bannan, easing down on their speed.

Sharaq opened the Manifold to the princeps of the two Warhounds and said, 'Kasim, Lamnos.'

Ghostly images, rippling and unsteady, formed in the air before Sharaq's eyes: Kasim, the swarthy-skinned predator, and Lamnos, the ambusher who killed from the shadows. Both warriors worked well together, Kasim fighting with the aggression of a hunter to flush prey towards the killing fire of his brother-in-arms.

'Princeps Sharaq,' said Kasim, his voice thick with the accent of the hives of Phoenicus Lacus. 'You have hunting orders?'

'Maybe,' said Sharaq. 'Spread out and run a criss-cross search pattern out towards the last fix we had on Mortis. I want to know where those damned engines are.'

'Are we to engage?' asked Lamnos, and Sharaq almost laughed at the eagerness he heard in his fellow princeps voice.

'Your courage is admirable, Lamnos, but if Mortis are coming in the strength I think they are, a pair of Warhounds won't stop them.'

'Then we just let them march on our fortress unopposed?' demanded Kasim.

'We don't know where they're marching yet,' Sharaq reminded his bellicose Warhound drivers. 'They may swing westwards and carry on north to the Olympica Fossae assembly yards. Or they could bear east towards Mondus Occulum. We don't know.'

'They will rue the day if they cross the Tempest Line,' snarled Lamnos.

'Yes, they will,' agreed Sharaq, 'but until they do and are within our engagement zone, you are not to fire unless fired upon. I won't have Camulos saying we started an engine war on Mars thanks to a headstrong Tempest driver. Understood?'

Both princeps grumbled their assent and Sharaq shut down the link between them as the Warhounds loped off into the wind-whipped ash and dust.

DALIA RACED FROM the control room, chased by screaming alarm bells and the blinding light of the

Astronomican. Howling cants of binary squealed and the air foamed with torrents of panicked data streams.

Tears spilled down her cheeks as she heard the agonised screaming of Jonas Milus, the sound echoing from the front of her skull to the innermost reaches of her psyche. Dalia had promised herself that he would be safe, that her work would not see him killed in the name of scientific progress.

That promise had been reduced to ashes and she couldn't bear the sound of his screams. She passed into the towering shaft chamber that rose up to the Magma City, seeing that the low archway in the silver wall was now filled with a great bronze gate. She ran towards it, molten light spilling through a circular window in its centre.

'No!' she cried. 'No! He's dying!'

She beat her fists on the metal door, bruising the flesh of her hands and drawing blood where she clawed at the glass with her fingernails. Dalia pressed her face to the window, straining to see anything through the dazzling brightness that filled the chamber and rendered what was happening within invisible.

'Open the door!' screamed Dalia. 'Open the damn door! We have to stop this!'

Dalia rushed to the keypad at the side of the door and began punching in the code required to open it. She had not been made privy to the doorway's code, but had skimmed the access protocols from Zeth's noospheric aura.

Further warning alarms shrilled and a pulsating amber light began to strobe angrily.

She felt a restraining hand on her arm and angrily threw it off.

'You can't go in there!' shouted a voice at her ear: Caxton's.

'I have to!' she wailed. 'He's dying. Oh, Throne we're killing him!'

'It's not your fault,' said Caxton, drawing her arms back from the door before she could punch in the final sequence of digits and turning her away from the light streaming through the window. 'It's not your fault.'

'It is, it is,' sobbed Dalia, burying her face in Caxton's shoulder and holding him tightly, as if the force of her grip could somehow end the horror. 'We need to get in there.'

'You can't,' said Caxton. 'Not yet. You're not soulbound!'

'I don't care! I need to get in there!'

'No! The psychic energy will kill you if you go through that door.'

'Like it's killing them!' said Dalia. 'I've got to!'

She pushed Caxton away and entered the last digits of the access sequence.

Like a rolling surge tide, the light boiled out from the chamber of the Akashic reader, and Dalia plunged into the roaring blizzard of psychic power.

PRINCEPS KASIM FELT the savage glee of *Raptoria* as he pushed her to flank speed. Like him, *Raptoria* was glad to be walking beneath the sky, unfettered and armed for war. The between times when she languished in oily ship holds, restrained by scaffolds and manacled to the deck, had been a cage for her warlike heart, a cell for an angry killer that had denied her sublime skills as a hunter.

This was her first walk since returning to Mars for repairs, and Kasim felt the urge to kill in every piston, gear and metal joint of his mount. He looked down at the golden skull and cog medallion that hung around his neck and wished that he could reach up and touch it for luck, but his hands were encased in wire-wound haptic sheaths.

Princeps Cavalerio, the Stormlord himself, had presented Kasim with the medallion, honouring him in
front of the Legio as they boarded the ships for Mars
after the brutal, hard-fought campaign of the Epsiloid
Binary Cluster.

Six engines had been lost and many wounded,
including the already battle-scarred *Victorix Magna*,
the towering war machine of the Stormlord.

Cavalerio had brought the badly wounded engines
of the Legio back to Mars, leaving the bulk of Tempestus under the command of Princeps Maximus
Karania. Months of labour by the Legio artisans had
seen the damaged engines repaired and brought back
to their former glory.

With the refit works virtually complete the Legio
was ready to transfer back to the expedition fleet, to
once more extend the rightful domain of the
Imperium. Kasim eagerly awaited the Legio's return to
the forefront of the fighting, for Mars had changed in
the years since Tempestus had led its war machines
across its umber plains.

No longer was Mars united in the dream of the
Great Crusade. The clan-forges and magi had fallen to
petty squabbling and spiteful acts of violence, dragging the red planet into an age of suspicion and
mistrust.

Even the warrior orders had changed, forming factions and isolated bands of martial strength to protect
what resources they controlled. Mortis had been no
exception, extending their control through the guise
of protection to many of the smaller forges and more
easily pressured warrior orders.

No, the sooner Tempestus could get back to the real
work of the galaxy the better.

'Where are they?' he hissed, bringing his Warhound
about and angling his course to intersect with that of

Astrus Lux. The view from his canopy was mostly obscured by the billowing ash storm, the thick, armoured glass streaked with a dusty residue that was the bane of cogs and gears.

'Twenty kilometres, my princeps,' said Moderati Vorich. 'Signal returns growing in strength, but they keep fading in and out... as if there's some kind of interference pushing out just ahead of them.'

'Keep us steady,' warned Kasim. 'And keep a close eye on the sensoria, they'll probably have Warhound pickets as well.'

'Yes, my princeps.'

Kasim felt the power beneath him, the fiery heart of *Raptoria* straining at his commands and anxious for the hunt proper to begin.

'Soon,' he whispered.

Kasim was relying on hard implants and the myriad surveyor apparatus fed information to him via the MIU, data flowing directly into his cerebral cortex as streams of neurons.

So far, *Raptoria* was running only passive scans, the better to hide her presence in the storm. An active scan of the area would reveal more of their surroundings, but would as good as announce their presence to any undiscovered hunters.

In such conditions, a Warhound lived and killed by its stealth – as strange as the concept of such a huge machine being stealthy might appear – and Kasim trusted his instincts to keep *Raptoria* safe. The interference plaguing the sensoria was troubling, and he could feel *Raptoria's* unease in the skittishness of her controls.

All his other senses were undimmed. He could feel the nearness of princeps Lamnos's engine, the bite of the dust on *Raptoria's* hull, and taste the oily, ashen flavour of the wind as it howled around him.

Somewhere out in the dust was the enemy, even if they hadn't been classified as such yet, but Kasim couldn't see them or know how close they were. Such situations were a Titan driver's worst nightmare; that your enemy could be plotting a firing solution without you even knowing he was there.

Kasim knew it was only a matter of time before Mortis and Tempestus drew blood.

The words exchanged between the Stormlord and Camulos at the Council of Tharsis had as good as guaranteed it. Kasim's warrior instinct was to strike the first blow, but he would not disobey a direct order from Princeps Sharaq.

'My princeps!' called Vorich as the ground suddenly shook with a thunderous reverberation. 'Hard returns, dead ahead! Reactor blooms and void signatures!'

'Where in the name of the Machine did they come from?' demanded Kasim. 'Identify!'

'Unknown contact, but it's too big to be a Warhound.'

The vibration of the ground had already told him that this was no Warhound.

Too big for a Reaver.

'A Warlord?' responded Kasim, his excitement and fear manifesting in the Warhound's posture as it crouched close to the ground.

'No, my princeps,' said Vorich, staring in horror at the sight emerging from the howling dust clouds.

Kasim felt the chill of its shadow envelop him, and his skin flushed as he saw the enormous engine stride towards them, its every step rocking the very earth with its monstrous tread. A towering fortress of brazen red metal with black and silver etchings moulded on the great bastion towers of its legs, the enormous engine dwarfed the Warhound as a grown man would dwarf a babe in arms.

Arcing battlements crowned its immensity, the colossal, mountainous fortress engine unlike anything Kasim had seen before. He had heard the rumours and looked over the technical specs and blueprints of similar machines, but nothing had prepared him for the awesome spectacle of so gargantuan a war machine in the flesh.

Weapons capable of obliterating cities depended from its wide shoulders and its head was a grinning, horned skull of burnished silver.

'Imperator,' said Kasim.

PRINCEPS CAVALERIO SCOURED the Manifold for information, reading nothing through the barking, squealing hash of scrapcode fouling the airwaves. He could get nothing from Princeps Sharaq and feared the worst. Mortis was on the march, and Cavalerio wondered if Princeps Camulos was about to make good his threat of a coming storm.

His battle group was marching at flank speed towards their fortress and he could feel the ancient heart of *Victorix Magna* protest at the demands placed upon it. His own heart beat in time with the great machine and he felt a growing numbness spreading through his limbs.

Cavalerio fought against the sensation, willing both his mortal frame and the immortal might of his engine to keep going.

'Do you really think Mortis is about to attack Ascraeus Mons?' asked Moderati Kuyper.

'I don't know,' confessed Cavalerio, their words spoken through the link of the Manifold. 'I believe Camulos wants to drive our Legio from Tharsis, but this seems bold even for him.'

'Then perhaps this is the first strike in a larger war,' suggested Kuyper.

Cavalerio kept his thoughts close, remembering what Camulos had said at the Council of Tharsis.

Sides were being chosen and battle lines drawn all across Mars, and while Cavalerio couldn't bring himself to believe that the Titan orders were about to go to war, this manoeuvre of Mortis seemed deliberately calculated to rouse the ire of Tempestus.

Well, Indias Cavalerio was not about to rise to the bait of this provocation.

'I don't think they will attack,' he said. 'I think they want *us* to attack them, to fire the first shot so as to justify their retaliation.'

'Our warriors will only fire if they're fired on first,' said Kuyper.

Cavalerio thought of the engine commanders at Ascraeus Mons: Sharaq, Lamnos and Kasim. Sharaq could be trusted to understand the situation, but Lamnos and Kasim?

Their hearts were fiery and warlike, as was expected of Warhound drivers, but where heart and mind were in balance in more experienced warriors, Cavalerio feared what impulsive decisions they might make in the heat of the moment.

'Get me Sharaq's battle group,' he said. 'I need to make sure they know not to fire first.'

'Understood, Stormlord,' said Kuyper, returning his attention to breaking through the interference.

Cavalerio opened the Manifold link to Magos Argyre. 'How long till we reach the Mons?'

'Update: at flank speed, we will be within visual range of Ascraeus Mons in seventeen point four minutes. However, the reactor is running twenty-seven per cent in excess of what I believe it can safely handle at this time.'

'Increase reactor output,' ordered Cavalerio. 'I want us there in less than ten.'

'Warning: to increase reactor output beyond the current rate of–'

'I don't want to hear any excuses!' snapped Cavalerio. 'Just make it happen!'

THE IMPERATOR TITAN had not come alone.

Two Warlords and a Reaver marched alongside it like the hangers-on of a scholam bully. Kasim could see no sign of a Warhound picket or skitarii escort, but with engines as large as this, what need had they of any skirmish screen?

The ground shook and cracked at its passing, and Kasim could only watch in mute awe as the mightiest war machine he had ever seen swept past him like an uprooted hive on mountainous legs.

'What do we do?' breathed Moderati Vorich.

What indeed? To fight such a monster was suicide, but its path would see it cross the Tempest Line in a little over nine minutes, and then they would have to fight it. They would be as ants against a bull-grox... but even ants could bring down a larger beast with enough numbers.

As his now active surveyors gathered what information they could on the might of the Imperator, Kasim knew that Tempestus had not the guns to defeat such a terrifying opponent.

'We follow it,' said Kasim. 'And we wait.'

'Wait for what?' asked Vorich.

Kasim looked down at his medallion, again wishing he could touch it.

'To see if this is the day we die,' he said.

DALIA SCREAMED AS the howling gale of psychic energy enveloped her, feeling it tear at her like a malicious hurricane. She heard screaming voices that clawed at the inner surfaces of her skull and whispers she could not possibly be hearing, but which sounded as clear as though she heard them lying on her bed in the middle of the night.

White light filled the chamber, the walls blurring in a rippling haze thrown off by the roaring column of silver that flared from the dome's apex and speared down towards Jonas Milus upon his throne.

She heard the metallic ring of the doorway closing behind her and spared a brief thought for Caxton and the others. Her robes billowed in the grip of powerful etheric winds, her skin raw and scoured by invisible energies that passed through her skin to the marrow and beyond.

Billowing ghosts of light swarmed the chamber, fleeting unnatural forms that defied description and which lingered uncomfortably in the darkest reaches of her imagination. Clouds of feelings filled the chamber: thunderheads of anger, zephyrs of regret, hailstorms of longing, hurricanes of love and betrayal.

Emotions and meaning surrounded her, though how such concepts could be given physical, visible form was a mystery to her. Dalia took a step into the chamber, feeling her will erode in the face of the primal energies that surrounded her and infused her at the same time.

'Jonas!' she yelled, the words fleeing her mouth in a gush of red. At first she feared it was blood, but the colour in the air vanished almost as soon as it had appeared. The noise filling the chamber was incredible, like the death scream of an entire race or the birth pangs of another.

All emotion and knowledge was here, and Dalia realised that this was the aether; this was the realm beyond the one her senses could consciously perceive. This was the source of all knowledge and the source of the greatest danger imaginable.

This was what she had allowed Jonas Milus to be exposed to.

The thought galvanised her steps, and she forced her way through the maelstrom of light and colour, feeling the energies unleashed by the psykers in the coffered ceiling bleed off as they began to die. She could feel their lives ending, dissipating into the cacophony of light and noise. She wept with sympathetic pain, feeling each death as a splinter of needle-sharp agony in her mind.

Dalia shielded her eyes as she drew closer to the dais, seeing Jonas Milus convulsing upon the throne, illuminated by the blinding light of the Astronomican. His head jerked spasmodically from side to side, his mouth a blur of motion as he screamed and yammered streams of words too fast to be understood.

She pushed her way up the steps towards him, dropping to her knees to better fight against the gales of energy and howling ghosts that swarmed the dais.

'Jonas!' she called, reaching out to him.

She couldn't reach him and crawled, inch by inch, towards him. His screaming was undimmed, the words flooding from him so fast in an ululating howl of pain. Fire blazed in his eyes, crackling with ancient power, the power of something far greater than anything mankind had ever known.

At last Dalia reached the top of the dais and saw that the storm of psychic energy swirled around the throne, yet never touched it, as though some invisible, antithetical barrier was holding it back.

The throne shone as though illuminated from within by some vast elementally powerful force. Though she and her compatriots had struggled so hard to create it, she now wished they had failed utterly.

She wished to be rid of her gift and the consequences of what it had done.

Even as she formed the thought, her limbs jerked and she rose to her feet in the manner of a marionette lifted by its puppeteer. Dalia cried out as her limbs obeyed the unknown imperatives manipulating her body and she stared into the face of Jonas Milus.

The fire that burned in his eyes spilled outwards to engulf his entire body, pouring over him like blazing mercury. Her screams matched his, and the restraints that had bound him to the throne fell away, unmade by the silver fire that crawled over his flesh like a living thing.

The empath rose from his throne, a living being of illuminated silver with the light of unknown suns burning in his eyes. Dalia could not meet his gaze, fearful that the power there would consume her were she to stare into it for too long. Beneath the inner luminescence that filled his body, she could see his flesh disintegrating like ice before a flame.

'I have seen it!' he hissed, his voice sounding as though echoing from somewhere impossibly distant and deep. 'All knowledge.'

'Oh Jonas, I'm sorry.'

'Sorry? No, Dalia, I won't have your pity,' said Jonas, fire writhing in his mouth as he spoke, his voice growing fainter with every word. 'I have seen the truth and I am free. I know it all, the Emperor slaying the Dragon of Mars... the grand lie of the red planet and the truth that will shake the galaxy, all forgotten by man in the darkness of the labyrinth of night.'

Jonas Milus stepped towards Dalia, and the psychic winds were pushed away from her as though by his very presence. As he drew closer to her, Dalia heard the whine of great machinery powering down and the thump of closing relays as power to the Akashic reader was finally shut off.

The light of the Astronomican still filled the chamber, and the winds of psychic energy still roared and seethed at its edges, but their power was diminishing. The mundane features of the space began returning, the marble floor, the sensation of mass and solidity, the heat of the air and the smell of burned flesh.

'Quickly! Look at me, Dalia,' said Jonas with desperate urgency. 'Look at me and know your destiny.'

She forced her head up and stared into the face of Jonas Milus as the light in his eyes was extinguished and the last of his human flesh faded away to oblivion.

The connection lasted the briefest fraction of a second, but that was enough.

Dalia screamed until she had no more breath, and took refuge from horrors that should never be borne by mortal brains in the black sleep of unconsciousness.

Princeps Sharaq followed the inbound tracks on the Manifold. The Imperator Titan was closing fast, surface scans of its identity markers revealing its name to be *Aquila Ignis*, an engine constructed in the Daedalia forge yards far to the south of Tharsis.

Its princeps, if such a vast machine could be commanded by just one man, was making no effort to conceal its power, and Sharaq fed the flow of data being collected on the terrible engine into the gunbox recorders of his war machine.

If the time ever came when they had to fight this engine, it would pay to be prepared.

With the unmasking of the Imperator, the howling binary interference had lifted, the storms that had whipped the dust into the air with such force dissipating as though they had never existed.

The vox crackled as the engines of Tempestus restored communications, each one filling the airwaves with excited chatter at the incredible sight marching towards Ascraeus Mons. *Raptoria* and *Astrus Lux* shadowed the Imperator, keeping a safe distance from it and its escorting Warlords.

'Do you have firing solutions to that engine?' asked Sharaq.

'Yes, my princeps,' said Bannan hesitantly. 'But if we open fire, it'll vaporise us in an instant. We can't fight something that big.'

The Imperator blotted out everything around it, a walking mountain that impossibly moved closer with thunderous footsteps. Sharaq wished the rest of his Legio were here alongside him.

To be standing directly in the path of such a titanic creation, a fearsome miracle of construction and innovation, was a prospect no man should have to face alone. *Raptoria* and *Astrus Lux* would fight alongside him, and the Skitarii weapons platforms would add their weight of fire, but they would be of little real use when the mighty engines started shooting.

For all intents and purposes, Sharaq was alone... his greatest fear as a princeps.

With Princeps Cavalerio's battle group they would at least have a chance of wounding the beast, and might even best it, but without them...

'Time to the Tempest Line?' asked Sharaq, sweating profusely despite the cool air in the carapace cockpit.

'Three minutes, my princeps,' said Dolun.

'Come on, turn away, damn you, turn,' hissed Bannan, and Sharaq echoed his sentiment as the seconds ticked by with the inexorably slow slide of thick engine oil.

Then the Manifold crackled and the blessed voice of the Stormlord came over the vox.

'Engines of the Legio Mortis,' said Princeps Cavalerio, his voice stentorian and unequivocal. 'You are on course to cross the Tempest Line, whereupon you will be in breach of the Tharsis non-aggression pact as signed by Princeps Acheron of Legio Mortis and Princeps Bakka of Legio Tempestus at the First Council of Cydonia. Turn back now or you may be fired upon.'

Sharaq watched the Manifold as Cavalerio's engines marched up through the western pallidus, billowing clouds of dust swirling in their wakes. To have reached Ascraeus Mons in such time must have torn the hearts from their reactors, but they were here and that was what mattered.

'Engines of Legio Mortis respond immediately!' demanded Cavalerio, and Sharaq could hear the strain in the Stormlord's voice. He checked the Manifold, getting elevated biometric and reactor readings from the *Victorix Magna*.

The thunderous form of the Imperator did not slow and Sharaq saw that it was moments from crossing the Tempest Line, whereupon it would be in the territory of Legio Tempestus. His mouth was dry and he took a sip from the hydration straw at his cheek.

'Legio Mortis, respond!' demanded Cavalerio, and Sharaq's heart swelled with pride as the stately form of *Victorix Magna* marched to stand alongside *Metallus Cebrenia*, firm in the path of the colossal Imperator.

'Fifteen seconds to the Tempest Line,' warned Moderati Bannan.

Tharsis Hastatus, *Arcadia Fortis* and *Vulpus Rex* took position alongside Cavalerio's engine, and the entire strength of Legio Tempestus on Mars stood before the mightiest war engines of Legio Mortis.

'This is your final warning, Mortis!' bellowed Cavalerio.

Dreadful terror settled in Sharaq's gut as Moderati Bannan said, 'Tempest Line breached, my princeps.'

SYSTEMAE
MECHANICUM

THE TEMPEST LINE had been breached. The sovereign territory of one of the most honourable Legios of Mars had been violated. Armed engines had blatantly marched from their fortress and come with warlike intent to another. Despite the evidence before him, Princeps Cavalerio still could not accept that Mortis wanted to exchange fire.

Why would they risk such a thing? Supporting Horus Lupercal and engaging in provocation was one thing, but daring another Legio to fire upon your engines made no sense unless there was a darker, more far-reaching scheme at work.

If battle were joined here, little would survive, and even with the Imperator, Mortis would not walk away unscathed.

Cavalerio had always suspected that Camulos was a man unsuited for command, and this confrontation seemed only to confirm his suspicions. It was madness, and Cavalerio did not want to be sucked into that madness. The factions of the Mechanicum might make war on one another, but the Titan Legions were supposed to be above such things, to hold the ideals of a united Mars and Terra above all things, even their own differences.

'My princeps,' said Moderati Kuyper. 'The Tempest Line.'

'I know,' said Cavalerio.

'Should we open fire?'

'You have a solution?'

'At this range we don't need one,' Kuyper assured him. 'That monster's so large we won't miss.'

Cavalerio nodded, sweat streaming from his brow, and his mouth dry. His heart was beating in brutal syncopation with the fiery heart of *Victorix Magna*, the straining power of a supernova at the engine's core burning hotter and faster than it was ever designed to. He could hear Magos Argyre's desperate supplications to the reactor's spirit and felt the anguish of the mighty engine in the numbness spreading through his limbs.

The image of the Imperator filled his senses, both through the viewscreen and through the Manifold. Data scrolled like liquid light through his mind, and he drank in the colossal feats of engineering that had gone into its construction and the utter lethality of its existence.

Its limbs were death incarnate, the grinning skull-face an abominable harbinger of destruction. The bristling weapon towers and bastions were a martial city-fortress carried on the back of an ancient god, though this burden was borne willingly and not as a punishment.

To fight such a thing would be the greatest achievement of any princeps, but it would probably also be his last.

The monster took another step, taking with it any chance that this crossing of the Tempest Line was accidental.

'Princeps Sharaq requests instructions,' called out Kuyper. '*Arcadia Fortis* requests permission to fire.'

'*Vulpus Rex* and *Astrus Lux* moving into flank fire positions,' noted Palus.

'Tell them to hold positions, damn them!' shouted Cavalerio, his pulse racing like the roaring discharge of a gatling cannon. 'No one opens fire unless I give the order. Make sure that last part is especially clear, Kuyper.'

'Yes, my princeps.'

Cavalerio had the sensation of events sliding beyond his control, and he fought for breath as the fire from his loyal engine's heart poured through the virtual marrow of his body like blood from a ruptured artery.

His vision blurred, the edges of the Manifold swimming like a badly-tuned picter.

Victorix Magna was hurting, hurting badly, and Cavalerio knew he had to end this ugly confrontation soon.

But how to do that without beginning a firefight that would destroy them all…

RAPTORIA STRAINED AT the edges of Princeps Kasim's control, a feral, bestial thing that demanded blood and poured violent thoughts into his consciousness. Its murderous heart had tasted the enemy's presence and felt the heat of its metal skin. It wanted to kill.

Kasim looked down at the gold cog medallion he wore and focused his mind on the discipline encoded into his thoughts by the Legio Magi before beginning this walk. Clogged data from previous engagements were washed from the peripherals grafted to the frontal lobes of each crewman's brain to ensure each engagement was begun without the mental baggage of the last, but the hungry taste of battle was impossible to wash away completely.

No engine ever really forgot the hot, metallic flavour of war.

Kasim could feel his steersman's efforts to keep the aggression from *Raptoria's* movements and could hear the engine's hunger for battle in the thudding, roaring drumbeat of her reactor.

Raptoria wanted to fight and, damn it, so did he.

Princeps Cavalerio was holding his fire and so too must they, but it was galling to see the engines of Mortis so brazenly insulting the honour of Tempestus. To allow this act of defiance to go unpunished was a bitter pill to swallow, and he could already feel *Raptoria's* ire building within his skull with the malicious promise of future pain to come.

'Power up weapons,' he ordered in an effort to assuage the engine's bloodlust. 'Disengage safeties and surrender all firing authorities to me.'

By assuming all firing authorities, he was making sure that the feral heart of *Raptoria* didn't overwhelm the low-grade brain coding of the emplaced gun-servitors and open fire herself.

Kasim didn't want his engine to act without his control, but if a shooting war started, he was going to be ready to prosecute it to the best of his ability.

'Why isn't the Stormlord opening fire?' wondered Moderati Vorich.

'Are you in a hurry to die?' asked Kasim. 'Because that's what will happen if we let this get out of hand.'

Despite his rebuke, Kasim was wondering the same thing. Mortis had clearly breached the Tempest Line, and Cavalerio was quite within his rights to fire. As much as his heart was spoiling for a fight, Kasim knew that the odds against victory were high.

Staring into the Manifold, Kasim saw the heroic form of the *Victorix Magna* standing firm before the monstrous, towering might of the Imperator. Beside her stood *Arcadia Fortis* and *Metallus Cebrenia*, all three engines dwarfed by the enemy engine.

'What are you planning, Stormlord?' whispered Kasim.

The Imperator loomed on the Manifold, a glowering god of war that could destroy them all.

A few more steps and it would be right on top of them.

IN THE CABIN cockpit of *Metallus Cebrenia*, Princeps Sharaq was wondering the same thing as Kasim. Moderati Bannan counted the ever-increasing distance *Aquila Ignis* was striding into the territory of Legio Tempestus.

Increasing the angle of his view through the Manifold, Sharaq saw *Victorix Magna* standing proud beside him, venting hot exhaust gases and sweating lubricant from its overflows. Even without the spiking data readings, he could tell that the venerable engine was suffering.

'Come on, Indias,' he whispered. 'Hold her together a little longer.'

He transferred his view outwards, seeing the agile, snapping forms of *Vulpus Rex*, *Astrus Lux* and *Raptoria* darting around the edges and rear of the approaching Imperator like pack wolves hunting a stag. Ever bellicose, their weapons were powered and ready to fire.

The ground shook and Sharaq could feel the tremor through every joint of his engine's structure. Inertial dampers could compensate for most fluctuations in a Titan's surrounding environment, but the mighty tread of such a colossal enemy was beyond its power to completely dissipate.

He looked down at the far away ground, feeling a stab of pity for the massed ranks of skitarii gathered around his engine's splayed feet. To face a beast like the Imperator from a Warlord's cockpit was a terrifying enough prospect, but to stand naked before it without the protection of voids and armour…

That was courage indeed.

'Range to target?' asked Sharaq, fighting to keep his tone even.

The question was unnecessary. He could already see that the Imperator was less than three hundred metres away through the Manifold, point-blank range by any normal measure of things, but insanely close in this situation. He could already hear the squeal and rasp of the voids as their fields warbled with the proximity.

'Two hundred and fifty metres, my princeps,' said Bannan.

He spared a glance to his left.

Victorix Magna stood, implacable and immovable, before the marching Imperator, and Sharaq loved the Stormlord for his resolve as much as he was frustrated by his inaction. The tension within the cockpit compartment of *Metallus Cebrenia* was unbearable.

Then a harsh, deafening squall shrilled across the vox frequencies, a filthy blurt of continuous, corrupted code noise that sounded like throaty laughter. Sharaq flinched and his sensori screamed as the wailing shriek tore at their hearing.

'What in the name of the Omnissiah is that?' yelled Bannan, snatching the vox-set from his head.

Sharaq killed the audio as the cackling laughter code burbled over the vox and the booming warhorns of the Mortis engines echoed from the towering cliffs of Ascraeus Mons.

The Imperator lowered its weapon arms, every horn, bell and augmitter upon its colossal spires and bastions blaring in disdain. The noise was unimaginably loud, broadcast across every audible wavefront and code frequency.

Debased and dirty codelines conveyed vile algorithms that Sharaq felt worming their way into his peripherals like viral code, and his aegis protocols fought to prevent them from reaching the deep sub-systems of *Metallus Cebrenia*.

'Princeps!' shouted Bannan. 'Enemy course change detected.'

Sharaq gasped, his mind awhirl as his implants defended his neural paths from infection by the scrappy code fragments carried on the war-scream of the Imperator. He forced his mind through the clotted data packets of black, oozing information that blurred his vision and saw that Bannan was right.

The Imperator was changing course, its stride swinging to the east.

Like a great ocean liner travelling at speed, the course of such a vast machine did not change swiftly and its new heading would barely carry it past the south-eastern skirts of Ascraeus Mons.

'Dolun? Intercept plot,' hissed Sharaq, the beginnings of a blistering headache building behind his eyes. 'Where's it going?'

His sensori didn't answer, and Sharaq twisted his head to see Dolun lying supine on his reclined couch. The man's eyes rolled back into his skull and foaming spittle gathered at the corners of his mouth.

Sharaq meshed his senses briefly with Dolun's station, feeling the hash of viral code replicating like a plague within his I/O ports, ready to spill out into the guts of the war engine.

With a thought, Sharaq cut the link between Dolun's interfaces and the rest of the Titan, but even as he did so, he could feel the scrapcode trying to find another way in.

'Moderati Bannan!' shouted Sharaq. 'Disengage Sensori Dolun from his station. Now!'

Bannan looked over at Dolun, who was convulsing as his corrupted cybernetic enhancements began fitting with the power of a grand mal seizure. Bannan disengaged his hard plugs as quickly as he dared and lurched across the sensori station, unsteady on his feet after so brutal a separation from the MIU.

Sharaq turned his attention from the compromised sensori officer and followed his own track on the enemy engines. An overlaid map of the Tharsis Montes swam into view, grainy and washed with fragments of faulty code. A red line extended from their current position, swinging around to the north-east and extending towards the port facilities of Tharsis Tholus, the primary embarkation point of Astartes supplies from the fabricator locum's Mondus Occulum forge.

Sharaq dismissed the map as the shriek of voids filled the cockpit with a warbling, squealing howl of feedback. Like a million nails down a blackboard, titanic energies pushed against one another, scraping their invisible power together and sending flaring, whooping coils of colourful lightning discharge into the air.

'Sensori disconnected,' called Bannan, and Sharaq looked round to see Dolun jerking and twitching on the deck, lubricant and jellied brain matter leaking from his cranial plugs.

'Good work, Bannan,' said Sharaq. 'Leave him and get back on station.'

Sharaq returned his attention to the Manifold, watching in ashamed relief as the might of the Imperator swung yet further away and the spine-shearing sound of void interference abated.

'All Tempestus engines,' he said, forcing a channel through the howling static that still laced the airwaves. 'Ease weapons, I repeat, ease weapons. Mortis are turning away! Acknowledge!'

One by one, the affirmations of the Tempestus engines appeared on the Manifold, and Sharaq let out a shuddering breath as he realised how close they had come to igniting a shooting war on the surface of Mars.

The Imperator's escort of Warlords moved with it and the war machines of Legio Mortis began tramping away, each step carrying them further from the domain of Tempestus.

Mortis was leaving, but Sharaq wanted to be sure they weren't about to turn back for another provocative pass.

'*Raptoria, Vulpus Rex*, follow Mortis and make sure they keep on their way,' he ordered, wondering why the Stormlord was not issuing the order himself. 'Keep a safe distance back, but make sure they go.'

The two Warhounds set off without bothering to acknowledge his order, and Sharaq slumped deeper into the moulded leather of his reclined seat. Sweat coated his brow and his hair was soaked. He closed his eyes for a second, shutting out the data noise of the Manifold and letting the human part of his mind process the near calamitous events of the past few minutes.

Had it really been so short an engagement?

He opened his eyes as the nagging static of the vox remained unbroken by orders, information requests or any form of leadership from *Victorix Magna*.

Sharaq looked over to the Stormlord's engine, a terrible sense of dread building in his gut as he saw that *Victorix Magna* remained as she had since taking up station before the Imperator. That dread built as he saw fluid drooling in a black rain from her torso and that the hissing plumes of superheated steam that ought to gust like breath from exhaust vents beneath her shoulder carapace had ceased.

The engine's head was bowed, her limbs slack against her sides.

'*Victorix Magna*,' called Sharaq over the Manifold, his fear rendering his communication sharper than he intended. 'Princeps Cavalerio, please acknowledge.'

There was no response.

'Stormlord, please respond immediately!'

A shift of view in the Manifold and Sharaq's head sank to his chest as he inloaded the auspex readings of the Stormlord's mighty engine.

Victorix Magna was dead.

* * *

THOUSANDS OF KILOMETRES to the south of the confrontation between Mortis and Tempestus, deep in the desolate, empty wilderness of the southern pallidus, wind-borne ash blew across the cratered wastelands at the edge of the Daedalia Planum.

Even further south, the horizon burned with colourful fire, the skies striated with chemical pollutants and reeking gases expelled from the massive refineries that encircled the planet's equator.

Only the hardiest scavengers attempted to eke out a living in this region of Mars, the spoil pickings usually too thin and too laden with toxins to be of any real use. One such scavenger was a man named Quinux, a wizened prospector and former Skitarii whose body had rejected the gross implants necessary for full assimilation into the ranks of the Mechanicum's soldiery.

Quinux scoured the deserts and hardpan of the Daedalia Planum in a ramshackle Cargo-5 bulk-hauler that pulled a tender filled with scrap metal, held together by faith, hope and fervent devotions to the Machine-God. Its plates were caked with rust and its tracks streaked with corrosion from prolonged exposure to the hostile environment.

Acrid fumes belched from the exhausts of his crawler, and the interior of his pressurised cabin smelled of sweat, recycled nutrient paste and excitement. A cracked and filmy auspex panel hung from the roof of the cabin, pinging with a hard return of solid material.

Quinux hadn't seen a signal this strong in decades and knew that this find could be the making of him. Whatever it was, it was big, and his head darted from side to side, peering through the crazed glass of his cabin as he searched for any other scavengers that might have picked up this juicy find, not that he could see much through the whipping scads of dust and ash that swirled around the crawler.

His vehicle dipped into a gentle slope that gradually widened out into a shallow crater. The ground under the tracks was soft, irradiated sand, carried there by the freak atmospherics that blew from the monstrous refineries of black iron in the south.

The pings of the auspex grew more urgent, and he saw that he was practically right on top of his find, though he couldn't make out much beyond the dirty glass. Unhooking the auspex from the roof, Quinux hefted a simple bolt-action lascarbine from the back of his cab and checked the load.

There wasn't much left in it, but enough to deal with any feral servitors that might be lurking out in the wasteland. Looking at his useless augmetics, Quinux felt a certain sympathy with the poor, wretched servitors, but not so much that he wouldn't put a bolt through their skulls if they tried to get between him and his find.

Next he lifted his pack and slid his arms through the straps before wrapping his rebreather hood tightly around his head. Quinux then opened the cab to the elements, wincing at the force of the gale that plucked at his robes and threatened to slam the door back in his face.

Getting too old for this life, he thought as he climbed down the ladder and stepped onto the sand. He followed the strident chimes of the auspex towards a large dune field ahead of him, trying to make out what it was reading. He couldn't see anything valuable, but as he drew closer, he saw that the nearest dune was a damn sight taller and more regular in shape than the others.

Consulting the auspex, Quinux was pretty sure that whatever he was picking up was beneath the dune. Perhaps a flyer had crashed or an ore tanker had been forced to ditch and then been covered by the sands before its crew could send out a distress signal.

Whichever it was, it marked the end of a lean patch for Quinux Fortran.

He slid the auspex into a zipped pocket in his robes and slung his rifle as he approached the dune, clambering up on all fours as the sand spilled away beneath him. Climbing the dune was hard work and he sweated profusely in the dry heat.

Quinux reached the top of the dune and began clearing away the sand with a collapsible shovel from his pack. With quick, economical strokes he dug down into the sand, widening and deepening the hole as he went.

Pausing only to take regular sips of brackish water from his hide canteen, Quinux gradually cleared the top of the dune. The wind attempted to thwart his labours, blowing fresh sand and ash back into the hole, but after an hour of digging, his shovel struck metal and he gave a grunt of pleasure.

'Right, let's see what you are then,' he said, dropping the shovel and sweeping his gloved hands over the find.

It was metal sure enough, fresh and untainted by corrosion or rust. The surface patina was blackened, as though it had been scorched by intense heat, but as he scraped the edge of his shovel across it, he could see that the damage was only superficial.

He cleared more sand away, guessing that the main body of whatever lay beneath him was roughly spherical from the curve of the exposed metal. More shovelfuls were scooped from the ground, and Quinux frowned as he saw the outline of what looked like some kind of battle robot emerge.

Three blisters of metal faced him, like sensor domes, but devoid of life.

'Now what in the name of the Omnissiah would you be doin' out here?'

The auspex chimed. Loud. A strong signal.

Puzzled, Quinux dug the device from his robes and looked around him for the source.

He could hear the roar of engines above the howl of the wind, but couldn't pinpoint its source. Quickly he swept up his rifle, ready to defend his find, but there was nothing to see.

A harsh beam of light stabbed from the sky above him and Quinux shielded his eyes as the roaring engine noise leapt in volume. The down-draught of a flyer's powerful jets blew up a storm of smoke and dust.

He couldn't see anything through the whipping ash, but kept his rifle pulled hard into his shoulder. The pitch of the engines changed from a howl to a whine as the craft descended, and moments later the stablight was replaced with the diffuse glow of landing lights.

As the dust settled, Quinux looked up and saw a group of people marching towards him from the belly of a heavy lifter, an aircraft capable of transporting enormous items of machinery in its hold.

The dust blurred the newcomers' forms, but whoever they were they weren't getting a piece of this mother-lode.

'This here's mine!' he shouted, jerking the barrel of his rifle towards the dune. 'I found it and you ain't gonna take it off me. I got salvage rights.'

The figures stepped into view, and Quinux's heart sank as he saw a host of brutal-looking, body-armoured Skitarii led by a robed adept of the Mechanicum. The adept was swathed in thick red robes and augmented with a multitude of glowing green cybernetics on snaking manipulators. He wore an iron mask with glowing red eyes and a huge mechanised device hunched at his shoulders.

'Actually you don't,' said the adept, one of his green-lit manip arms aiming at the machine beneath the sand. 'That machine belongs to me.'

'And who the hell are you?'

'I am Master-Adept Lukas Chrom.'

'Never heard of you,' said Quinux.

The light at the end of Chrom's manip arm flashed and he said, 'Come. I am here to take you back to Mondus Gamma.'

'I aint' goin' nowhere with you,' snapped Quinux.

'I was not talking to you,' said Chrom. 'I was talking to the Kaban Machine.'

The sand beneath Quinux trembled, and he looked down in alarm as the sensor blisters he had uncovered lit up with a yellow glow. A tremble of power vibrated through the machine as its dormant power cells came back online and returned it to life.

It lurched forward, and Quinux lost his balance, sliding end over end down the shifting sand and losing his grip on his rifle. He fell to the ground and rolled onto his back as the awakened machine emerged from its concealment.

Nearly ten metres tall, its mass was roughly spherical with two heavily weaponised arms attached on opposite sides. Behind high pauldrons to protect its sensor apparatus, a number of metallic arms extended from its shoulders, like massively thick mechadendrites equipped with a variety of lethal looking weapons.

The machine sat immobile for a few moments before training its weapons on his bulk-hauler.

'No!' shouted Quinux, rising to his feet and scrambling towards the adept. His cry of protest was drowned out in a blaze of gunfire as sheeting hails of light blasted from the Kaban Machine's weapons.

Quinux's vehicle exploded in a smoky orange fireball, the over-pressure of the blast swatting him to the ground. He gasped acrid, toxin-laden air and realised that the explosion had torn the breathing apparatus from his face.

He scrambled for his rebreather hood, but couldn't find it, feeling airborne poisons eating away the blood vessels of his lungs with every breath. He rolled onto his side, coughing up thick wads of phlegmy mucus as he felt a heavy rumbling through the ground.

The machine was moving and more of the sand fell away. Quinux saw its body was mounted on a heavy-gauge track unit that threshed sand before it gained traction and rumbled forward.

Quinux scrabbled pitifully at the ashen ground as it rolled towards him.

'Please! No!' he screamed, the words gurgling as blood poured from his mouth.

Its sensor blisters glittering with cold mechanical purpose, the Kaban Machine ignored his pleas and ground Quinux into the Martian soil beneath its bulk.

BENEATH THE TOWERING peak of Olympus Mons, the Fabricator General watched as a parade of augmented Praetorian battle servitors marched from the labyrinth of Moravec. They moved by a variety of means of locomotion – some on tracks, some on clicking mechanical legs, others on thick, rubberised wheels, while some retained the use of their human legs.

They filled the great engine hangars beneath the mountain, thousands of newly enhanced warriors ready to fight for Horus Lupercal. The power revealed within the Vaults of Moravec was like nothing Kelbor-Hal had ever known, the joyous tumult of it filling his flood-stream with vigour and insight beyond that of beings composed merely of flesh.

Kelbor-Hal felt a surge of raw, unfettered aggressive power through his crackling energy fields as he watched the assembling army. This was a time of great moment, though only he and Regulus were here to witness it.

That would soon change when the dreadful war engines of the Mechanicum were unleashed, these weapons of the Dark Mechanicum.

The weaponised servitors were huge, muscular and sheathed in layered armour that was blackened like scorched flesh, their spines hunched over and threaded with barbed spikes. Those without mouths burbled scrapcode from integral augmitters, a glorious hymnal to the newest power on Mars. Others, with etched bronze frightmasks, spilled nonsense from bloodied lips that twisted and leered with brutal anticipation.

Beside Kelbor-Hal, Regulus watched the procession with glee, his electrical field warping and twisting with pleasure as each of the newly transformed servitor warriors emerged and took position within the great hangar.

'These are magnificent, Fabricator General,' said Regulus in admiration. 'The power of the warp and the power of the Mechanicum alloyed together in glorious fusion.'

Kelbor-Hal accepted the compliment, knowing that Lukas Chrom had done the bulk of the work, but unwilling to admit the fact. He had simply combined Chrom's advances in artificial sentience with the power contained within the Vaults of Moravec to produce something wondrous.

'These servitors are just the beginning,' said Kelbor-Hal. 'We begin work on the Skitarii next. The scrapcode has worked its way through the entire floodstream network of Olympus Mons, and is already spreading beyond Tharsis.'

Virtually every port and connective point on Mars was linked somewhere, and the glorious code of the warp was scurrying along every conduit, wire, fibre-optic, wireless feed and haptic implant. Soon it would reach every forge and adept, and those touched by its transformative power would be born anew.

'I can feel forges as far away as Sinus Sabaeus already scratching with elements of transformed code,' confirmed Regulus. 'Soon the aegis protocols of the other forges will be broken down to allow the scrapcode into their inner workings.'

'Then they will be ours,' hissed Kelbor-Hal.

'There will be resistance,' replied Regulus. 'Not all the forges are as vulnerable to the scrapcode. The Magma City's links have proved to be resistant, as are those of Ipluvien Maximal and Fabricator Locum Kane.'

Kelbor-Hal nodded. 'That is only to be expected. Adept Zeth is pioneering a newly developed form of noospheric data transfer. Her forge and those of her allies have been modified to utilise it over more traditional forms of communication.'

'Noospheric? I am not familiar with the term.'

'No matter,' said Kelbor-Hal. 'It will be ours soon enough. I have dispatched Ambassador Melgator to the Magma City to sequester her data and determine her loyalties.'

'I already know her loyalties, Fabricator General. She is an enemy of the Warmaster.'

Given what had happened after the opening of the Vaults of Moravec, it was hard to fault Regulus's logic.

When the skies above Olympus Mons had raged and buckled at the bloody dawn of this new power, freakishly induced weather patterns carried the echoes of its shrill afterbirth from the Great Mountain to every corner of Mars.

Every corner but one.

As the seething Martian skies darkened, a searing surge of psychic energy above Koriel Zeth's Magma City had pierced the heavens and almost drowned the birth-shout of the emergent power with its light and violence.

Kelbor-Hal did not fully understand what he had witnessed that day, but Regulus had watched the event, the spiking flares of his magnetic field betraying his naked fear and hostility.

'What was that?' he had asked. 'An accident? A weapon?'

'An enemy revealed,' was all Regulus had said.

2.02

She was trapped in the darkness. She tried to wake, but there was only the utter, unbreakable darkness in all directions. In truth, she could not even think in terms of directions, for this space appeared to be dimensionless. She had no sensation of up or down and no sense of the passage of time. Had she been here for long? She couldn't remember. She couldn't remember much of anything.

Her memories were hazy. She had once roamed freely, she remembered that much, feeding, birthing and extinguishing stars without heed, but now...

Now there was only the eternal darkness of death.

No, not death, but was it sleep? Or was it imprisonment? She didn't know.

All she knew was that if this was not death, it might as well be for all the power left to her.

Were these memories or hallucinations?

She perceived of herself as female, but even that meant nothing. What did sex matter to a being of pure energy and matter?

Her mind roamed the darkness, but whether she ventured across the span of galaxies or travelled only millimetres, she couldn't tell. Did she journey for mere moments or the lifespan of a universe?

Many of the dimensions she was thinking in were meaningless to her, yet she sensed that they were all equally ludicrous in this darkness. Nothing existed here, nothing but the darkness.

Nothing.

Except that wasn't always true, was it?

Sometimes there was light, tiny sparks in the darkness that were gone as soon as they were noticed. Holes of light would sometimes appear in the darkness through which elements of her being could be drawn, atoms of existence planed from a life the size of a star, unnoticed but for the promise of a world beyond the darkness they brought.

She tried to focus on one such light, but no sooner had she registered its presence than it was gone, only the tantalising hope of its return sustaining her. This was no life, this was pure existence sustained at the verge of extinction by the forgotten mechanics of Old Science.

Dalia.

The sound came again, no more than a whisper, barely heard and perhaps only imagined.

Dalia.

The word gave meaning to form, and she began to build a sense of scale and place with the concepts given weight by the sounds. As more and more of her surroundings became concrete, she began to re-establish her sense of self.

Dalia.

That was her name.

She was a human being... not a creature of unimaginable scale that defied time and the material universe with its power. Indeed, she wasn't sure if creature was a term large enough to encompass the immensity of its existence.

She did *not* exist in the darkness. She was *not* a prisoner hurled into the lightless depths of the world by an armoured gaoler and bound with golden chains.

She was Dalia Cythera.

And with that thought, she woke.

INFORMATION PASSED AROUND Mars in a multitude of ways, along trillions of kilometres of cabling, through fibre-optics, fizzing electrical field clouds, wireless networks and hololithic conduits. The exact workings of the ancient mechanics by which many of the forges communicated were unknown, and even the magi that made use of such things did not fully understand them.

Almost all the myriad means of information transfer were, however, vulnerable to the corrupting influence of the scrapcode boiling out from the depths of Olympus Mons in the dead of the Martian night.

It moved outwards like a hunting raptor, drawn by the scent and flow of information. Everything it touched it corrupted, twisting elegantly crafted code into something vile and debased. The wondrous flickering, chattering cant of pure machine language, the gurgle of liquid data and gleaming information-rich light became a hateful birth scream of something malformed and evil.

At the speed of thought, it spread across the planet's surface, slipping like an assassin into the networks of the Martian forges and wreaking untold damage. The aegis barriers tried to hold it back, but it overwhelmed them in moments with its ferocity and diabolical invention.

A few, a very few, forgemasters were quick enough to cut themselves off from the networks when they saw the danger, but so deeply enmeshed were they with the Martian information exchange systems that it was impossible to avoid exposure completely.

Replicating itself at a terrifying rate, the scrapcode found each forge's weakest point and induced disastrous system failures at every turn.

At Sinus Sabaeus, the continent-sized assembly lines of Leman Russ battle tanks ground to a halt, and machines that had run without interruption for over a century seized up, never to operate again.

In the Tycho Brahe ammunition storage facility, a rogue set of commands raised the temperature in the promethium tanks until a catastrophic explosion ripped through the lower storage levels. Liquid flame bloomed up through the crater, igniting a devastating conflagration that engulfed the entire facility, detonating billions of tonnes of ordnance and obliterating the holdings of High Adept Jaigo.

The great Schiaparelli Repository on the Acidalia Planitia, a towering pyramid of unlocked data from the earliest days of mankind's mastery of science and gathered wisdom from across the ages, was infected with scrapcode, and twenty thousand years' worth of knowledge was rendered down into howling nonsense.

Warning klaxons and shift horns blared as the scrapcode issued commands and countermanded them an instant later, the forges of Mars screaming at the violation done to their wondrous mechanics. Machines screeched and shrieked as rogue current surged through their workings, blowing circuits and frying delicate mechanisms that would never be repaired.

Almost no corner of Mars was safe from the scrapcode, which gathered momentum and ambition as it encircled the globe in an ever-tightening web of malice.

The chemical refineries of Vastitas Borealis opened their pressure valves and flooded the workers' hive-sinks of the northern polar basin with a mix of methyl isocyanate, phosgene and hydrogen chloride. The deadly cloud slowly oozed down into the sinks, killing every living soul as it went, and by morning's light, over nine hundred thousand people were dead.

As if relishing this method of murder, the scrapcode then killed the astropaths of Medusa Fossae, altering the breathing mix of their life support until each psyker was being fed hydrogen cyanide gas. Within minutes, over six thousand astropaths were dead, and after one plaintive death scream that was felt in the Emperor's vaults beneath the surface of Terra, Mars fell utterly silent.

Ipluvien Maximal was one of the lucky few able to sever his links with the networks before too much damage was done, though three of his fusion reactors along the Ulysses Fossae suffered critical meltdowns, the mushroom clouds of their detonations drifting east and north, forever irradiating thousands of square kilometres of the Martian soil.

The same story was enacted all across the surface of the red planet, machines rebelling as their internal workings were overloaded with contradictory commands. The death toll climbed into the millions within minutes as forges exploded, toxic chemicals spilled through manufactories and mass-storage facilities of explosive materials cooked off in devastating daisy chains of detonations.

In years to come this night would become known as the Death of Innocence.

Only the forge of Adept Koriel Zeth escaped unscathed, the torrents of crackling scrapcode unwilling or unable to travel the glittering golden wires that had recently carried the Emperor's light along them. Like positively charged iron filings flowing around a similarly charged magnet, the scrapcode bypassed the Magma City altogether.

It was the one ray of hope in an otherwise bleak night.

CAXTON AND ZOUCHE needed a shave and Severine looked as though she hadn't slept in days. Even Mellicin, logical, unflappable Mellicin, looked deflated in the aftermath of the disastrous trial of the Akashic reader. They sat around Dalia's bed in the medicae wing of the Magma City, fussing over her as medical servitors drew blood and monitored her vitals.

The room smelled of counterseptic, soap and the lapping powder Adept Zeth was fond of using on her armour.

'You gave us quite a scare, young lady,' Zouche had said as he entered the room and saw that Dalia was awake. Dalia had been touched at the genuine emotion she saw in the gruff machinist's face.

'Sorry,' she said. 'I didn't mean to.'

'Didn't mean to, she says,' said Caxton with a forced laugh, though Dalia could see the dark shadows under the young man's eyes, the puffiness where his tears had fallen. 'Yanks open a door to a chamber flooded with psychic energy and says she didn't mean to.'

'Well I didn't,' said Dalia, aware of how foolish she sounded. 'I just couldn't leave Jonas in there.'

None of them would meet her gaze and they had shared a moment of regret for the dead.

Severine had taken Jonas's death particularly hard, and Dalia reached out to take her hand. The severity she had first seen in her face had melted away over the last few weeks and Dalia's heart ached to see the sadness in her friend's eyes.

Not a single trace of Jonas had been found in the chamber, not so much as an atom of his body to prove that he had existed at all. Likewise, none of the psykers encased in the coffered dome had survived the titanic energies of the Astronomican, their desiccated corpses withered and contracted into foetal balls.

All told, the death toll was two thousand and thirty-seven, and that figure was like an adamantium chain of grief around all their necks. They did not yet know of the night of devastation that had been so recently unleashed and how slight a loss this was compared to that suffered by the rest of Mars.

Dalia had since been told that she had been languishing in the grip of an unchanging coma for over seven days, watched over by Caxton, a host of bio-monitors and a pict-camera linked to the nearby medical station.

She learned that Caxton had refused to leave her bedside, despite repeated assurances from the others that they would take shifts in watching her. It had been five hours since Dalia had woken, though the bulk of that time had been spent being questioned by Adept Zeth. Her friends had only just been granted access to her.

'What's Adept Zeth saying about what happened?' asked Severine after they had exchanged hugs and shed tears together. 'She must be disappointed the machine didn't work.'

'Didn't it?' asked Zouche, narrowing his eyes. 'It overloaded, but the machine functioned as it should have, just not for very long.'

'What did Adept Zeth ask you, Dalia?' asked Mellicin, cutting to the heart of the matter.

Dalia saw their inquisitive looks, knowing that they too were curious as to what had transpired within the chamber of the Akashic reader.

'She wanted to know everything that happened in the chamber and everything Jonas Milus said to me.'

'What *did* he say?' asked Caxton.

She squeezed Caxton's hand, glancing up at the pict-camera in the upper corner of the room.

'He just died,' said Dalia. 'He didn't say anything at all.'

THE MEDICAE PRONOUNCED Dalia fit to resume her duties the following morning, and the next six rotations were spent in Zeth's inner forge rebuilding the Akashic reader, replacing those parts that had burned out and re-calibrating those that had survived.

Zeth and Dalia had made assumptions and now they were paying for them. Dalia should have requested clarification on Zeth's figures, but she had been so focused on the minutiae of the project she had not thought to doubt the adept's numbers.

That wasn't going to happen again. Rigorous double testing and checking procedures were enforced and every servitor had its work reviewed by a living, breathing adept.

The silver wiring in the floor had melted through and whole sections were pulled up and replaced with slabs impregnated with a higher gauge of cable. Every aspect of the machine's parts was examined and re-evaluated to see if there were ways of improving its performance and ensuring that it did not fail again.

Scores of adepts and servitors laboured in the dome alongside Dalia and her friends, though there was none of the shared sense of wonder that had enthused them when previously working on the Akashic reader. Only the biting drills of the servitors broke the silence of the dome as they lifted floor slabs and carried them away.

The coffers in the dome were empty, and as unnerving as it had been working beneath the sightless eyes of the bound psykers, everyone felt their absence more acutely. The vacant berths were a grim reminder of the deaths caused by the machine they were working on, and the assembled workers kept their heads fixed firmly on the job at hand.

Zeth spoke little to Dalia, the adept forced to spend most of her time dealing with the fallout from their abortive experiment. The adept left her apprenta, a magos named Polk, in charge, and, under his and Rho-mu 31's supervision, work continued much as before.

Dalia had asked Rho-mu 31 once why Adept Zeth was absent from the dome, but all the robed Protector had said was, 'She has matters of greater importance to attend to.'

Dalia had thought the Akashic reader was Zeth's greatest work, so clearly there had been consequences that not even an adept of Zeth's stature could ignore. Those few times Dalia and Zeth had passed words, she simply reaffirmed that Jonas Milus had not spoken to her.

Zeth would nod in weary acceptance, but Dalia could read the adept's disbelief in her noospheric aura... as well as veiled fear that spoke to Dalia of events far more terrible than a failed test.

She wasn't exactly sure why she was unwilling to share the empath's words with Zeth, but the intuitive part of her mind, the part that had led her to the design of the Akashic reader, told her that to inform the adept of what she knew – which wasn't much anyway – could very well be dangerous.

Knowledge is power, guard it well, wasn't that one of the Mechanicum's aphorisms?

Dalia intended to guard this knowledge *very* well and there were only a few people she dared trust with it.

Adept Zeth was not one of them.

WORK ON THE newly reconstructed Akashic reader was almost complete, the tolerances and capacity of the receptors altered to allow for the increased power expected to flow through the device upon its next activation.

Many months would need to pass before Mars and Terra would be in alignment once more, but for the next few rotations, the power of the Astronomican was still a vast resource of harvestable psychic energy.

Fresh psykers were already being installed within the coffers, though there had been no sign of another empath for the throne atop the dais, a fact for which Dalia was pathetically grateful.

As the activity in the dome neared completion, Dalia approached the workbench where Zouche and Caxton worked on the helmet assembly. Zouche was plugged into the lathe via extruded dendrites in his wrist, and the hissing of the laser lathe cutting through high-grade steel was a shrieking banshee howl.

Dalia winced as the sound bit into the meat of her brain.

Caxton saw her coming and smiled, lifting his hand in greeting. She smiled and returned the gesture as Zouche looked up from his labours and shut off the lathe.

'Dalia,' said Zouche, withdrawing his mechadendrites from the workbench and flipping up his protective goggles. 'How are you today?'

'I'm fine, Zouche,' she said, her gaze shifting to the dais where the bronze armoured figure of Adept Zeth and Rho-mu 31 supervised the work of Mellicin and Severine. 'Please, can you turn the lathe back on?'

'Back on?' asked Zouche, glancing over at Caxton. 'Why?'

'Please, just do it.'

'What's the matter, Dalia?' asked Caxton. 'You sure you're allright?'

'I'm fine,' repeated Dalia. 'Please, turn the lathe back on, I need to talk to you both, but I don't want anyone to hear.'

Zouche shrugged and reconnected with the workbench to activate the laser. Once again, the hiss of cutting metal filled the air as the manip plate moved the steel around the spitting lathe. Both Zouche and Caxton leaned in as Dalia spoke.

'The damper we used in the reader, the part that blocks external interference from interfacing with the empath's helmet, can you make a portable version of it?'

Zouche frowned. 'A portable one. Why?'

'To block out vox-thieves and disrupt pict-feed,' said Caxton, guessing Dalia's meaning.

'Yes,' agreed Dalia. 'Exactly.'

'I'm not sure about this,' said Zouche. 'I don't like the notion of secrecy. Nothing good can come of it.'

'Look, can you make it or not?' asked Dalia.

'Of course, we can,' said Caxton, his boyish face alight at the prospect of mischief. 'It's simple, isn't it, Zouche?'

'Yes, it's simple, but why would you want such a device?' asked Zouche, 'What's so secret that you need to stop anyone hearing it?'

'I need to talk to you, Mellicin and Severine too, and I need to be sure we're the only one's listening.'

'Talk to us about what?'

'About what Jonas Milus said to me.'

'I thought you said he didn't say anything,' pointed out Caxton.

'I lied,' said Dalia.

THEY MET AT the end of shift in the refectoria hall, an echoing space filled with replenishing servitors and hungry labourers, menials and adepts. The hall was rife with rumour, the few information networks that were functional burbling with fragments of frightened talk of catastrophic accidents and unnatural incidents all across Mars.

Gathering like conspirators, they sat as far from any listening ears as it was possible to get, but with each clique muttering their suspicions about what was happening beyond the walls of Adept Zeth's forge, no one was paying them any mind anyway.

As they huddled around the smallest table that could accommodate them all, Dalia took a long, hard look at her friends, judging how they might react to what she was about to tell them.

Caxton seemed to be enjoying himself immensely, while Zouche looked nervous at their conspiratorial gathering. Mellicin's posture spoke of her unease, and Severine looked as expressionless and pale as she had since Jonas Milus's death.

'Zouche?' said Dalia. 'Did you bring it?'

'Aye, girl, I did,' nodded Zouche. 'It's working. No one can hear what we're saying.'

'What's this all about, Dalia?' asked Mellicin. 'Why did we have to meet like this?'

'I'm sorry, but I didn't know how else to do this.'

'Do what?' asked Zouche. 'I don't see why we need to skulk about like this just because the damned empath spoke to you.'

Severine's head snapped up and her eyes flashed. 'Jonas spoke to you?'

Dalia nodded. 'Yes, he did.'

'What did he say?'

'Not much,' admitted Dalia. 'And what he did say didn't make much sense then.'

'And now?' asked Mellicin, the wan light of the refectoria gleaming from the metallic half-mask of her face. 'Your words imply they make more sense now.'

'Well, sort of. I'm not sure, but maybe.'

'Clarity, Dalia,' said Mellicin. 'Remember clarity in all things. First of all, tell us what the empath said.'

'His name was Jonas,' snapped Severine. 'He had a name. All of you, he had a name and it was Jonas.'

'I am well aware of that,' said Mellicin, without pause. 'Dalia, if you please.'

Feeling everyone's eyes upon her, Dalia reddened and took a deep breath before speaking. The words came easily to her, each one seared onto her brain like an acid etching on glass.

'He said, "I have seen it! All knowledge." And even though he was right in front of me it sounded like he was speaking from somewhere really far away, like the other side of Mars or somewhere far underground.'

'Is that it?' asked Severine, disappointment plain on her angular face.

'No,' said Dalia. 'I told him I was sorry about what was happening to him and he said that he didn't want my pity. He said that he'd seen the truth and that he was free.'

'Free of what?' asked Zouche.

'I don't know,' said Dalia. 'He said, "I have seen the truth and I am free. I know it all, the Emperor slaying the Dragon of Mars... the grand lie of the red planet and the truth that will shake the galaxy, all forgotten by man in the darkness of the labyrinth of night." It was horrible, his mouth burning with fire and his voice fading away with every word.'

'The labyrinth of night?' asked Caxton. 'Are you sure that's what he said?'

'Yes, absolutely,' said Dalia. 'The labyrinth of night.'

'The Noctis Labyrinthus,' said Mellicin, and Caxton nodded.

Dalia looked at the pair of them. 'Noctis Labyrinthus... what's that?'

'The Labyrinth of Night, it's what Noctis Labyrinthus means,' replied Caxton.

'What kind of place is it?' asked Dalia, elated to have found some meaning in words that had previously been meaningless. 'Is it a mountain, a crater? What?'

Mellicin shook her head, a nictitating membrane flickering over her augmetic eye as she dredged information from her memory coils.

'Neither. The Noctis Labyrinthus is a broken region of land between the Tharsis uplands and the Valles Marineris,' said Mellicin, the words spoken with the tone of someone retrieving data from an internal memory coil. 'Notable for its maze-like system of deep, sheer-walled valleys, it is thought to have been formed by faulting in a previous age. Also, many of the canyons display typical features of grabens, with the upland plain surface clearly preserved on the valley floor.'

Dalia frowned, wondering what this desolate region of Mars had to do with what Jonas had said. 'Is it empty?'

'More or less,' said Caxton. 'Adept Lukas Chrom has his Mondus Gamma forge to the south of it, but apart from him, we're the nearest forge.'

'So there's no one there at all?'

'It's not a region of Mars anyone has any real interest in,' said Mellicin. 'I'm told a number of adepts attempted to found their forges there, but none lasted very long.'

'Why not?'

'I don't know, they just didn't. Supposedly the forges were plagued by technical problems. The adepts claimed the region was inimical to the machine-spirits and they abandoned their workings to set up elsewhere.'

'So nobody knows what's there?' said Dalia. 'Whatever Jonas was talking about is somewhere in the Noctis Labyrinthus, it's got to be. The grand lie and this great truth.'

'It's possible,' conceded Mellicin, 'but what do you think he was talking about? Have you any idea what this... Dragon is he speaks of the Emperor slaying?'

Dalia leaned in closer. 'I don't know exactly what it is, but I've been working through my remembrances of the texts I transcribed back on Terra and I've found out quite a bit.'

'Like what?' asked Severine. '

'Well, Jonas spoke about the Emperor slaying the Dragon of Mars, so I looked into any references to dragons first.'

'Looked into how?'

'You know, in my memory,' said Dalia. 'I told you, I read stuff and I don't forget it.'

Mellicin smiled. 'That is a useful talent, Dalia. Continue.'

'Right, well, we all know about mythical dragons?'

'Of course,' said Zouche. 'Children's stories.'

Dalia shook her head. 'Maybe, but I think there's more to Jonas's words than that. Some of it, anyway. I mean, yes, I found lots of stories of heroic knights in shining armour slaying dragons and rescuing maidens in return for their hands in marriage.'

'Typical,' said Severine. 'You never read of a maiden rescuing a man from a dragon.'

'I guess not,' agreed Dalia. 'I suppose it didn't fit with the times when they were written.'

'Carry on, Dalia,' said Mellicin. 'What else did you learn?'

'There wasn't much that could be called fact, but I remember several tracts that purported to be historical works, but which I think were probably mythology, since they dealt with monsters like dragons and daemons as well as describing the rise of warlords and tyrants.'

'Do you remember the names of these books?' asked Zouche.

Dalia nodded. 'Yes. The main ones were *The Chronicles of Ursh*, *Revelati Draconis* and *The Obyte Fortis*. They all spoke of dragons, serpentine monsters that breathed fire and carried away fair maidens to devour.'

'I know those stories,' said Caxton. 'I read them as a child. Bloody stuff, but stirring.'

'I know them too,' cut in Zouche. 'But for my people they're more than just stories, Caxton. The Scholars of Nusa Kambangan taught that they were allegorical representations of the coming of the Emperor, symbolic representations of the forces of light overcoming darkness.'

'That's right,' said Dalia, excitedly. 'The slayer represents some all-powerful godhead and the dragon represents dangerous forces of chaos and disorder. The dragon-slaying hero was a symbol of increasing consciousness and individuation – the journey into maturity.'

'Can't they just be stories?' asked Caxton. 'Why does everything have to *mean* something?'

Dalia ignored him and pressed on. 'The one thing a lot of these stories have in common is that the dragon, even though it's beaten, isn't destroyed, but is somehow sublimated into a form where goodness and sentient life can flow into the world from its defeat.'

'What does that even mean?' asked Severine.

'All right, put it this way,' said Dalia, using her hands as much as her words to communicate her increasing passions. 'In *Revelati Draconis*, the writer describes a dragon slain by a sky god with a thunder weapon to free the waters needed to nourish the world. Another tale speaks of a murdered serpent goddess who held mysterious tablets and whose body was used to create the heavens and earth.'

'Yes,' said Caxton. 'That's right. And there was a story in *The Chronicles of Ursh* about these creatures... the Unkerhi I think they were called, who were destroyed by the "Thunder Warrior". Supposedly their remains became a range of mountains somewhere on the Merican continent.'

'Exactly,' said Dalia. 'There's a footnote towards the end of the *Chronicles* where the writer describes a race of creatures known as Fomorians that were said to control the fertility of the earth.'

'Let me guess,' said Zouche. 'They were defeated, but not destroyed, because their continued existence was necessary for the good of the world.'

'Got it in one,' said Dalia.

'So what does all this mean?' asked Severine. 'It's all very interesting, but why does talking about dragons need a vox-blocker?'

'Isn't it obvious?' asked Dalia, before remembering that her friends didn't possess the innate faculties for data recall that she did. 'It's clear that these defeated forces, these dragons, were still considered valuable, and it follows that these early writers understood that the

conflict between dragon and dragonslayer wasn't a con-
test of genocide for one or the other, but an eternal
struggle. For the good of the world, both sides needed to
have their powers expressed and the balance main-
tained. Even these ancient enemies needed one another.'

'Your logic being that it is the struggle, not the victory,
that supplies the needful conditions for the world,' said
Mellicin.

Dalia beamed at Mellicin. 'Yes, it's like summer and
winter,' she said. 'Eternal summer would burn the world
up, but eternal winter would freeze it to death. It's the fact
that they alternate that allows life to grow and flourish.'

'So I ask again, what's the point of all this?' said Severine.

Dalia looked into the faces of her friends, unsure of
how to phrase the next part of her confession. Would
they believe her or would they think her proximity to
the flaring energies of the Astronomican had unhinged
her? She took a deep breath and decided she had come
too far to back out now.

'When I was in the coma after the accident I think... I
think I became part of something, some other, much
larger, consciousness. It felt like my mind had detached
from my body.'

'An out of body hallucination,' said Zouche. 'Quite
common in near death experiences.'

'No,' said Dalia. 'It was more than that. I don't know
how else to explain it, but it was as if the Akashic reader
had allowed my mind to... link with something old. I
mean, really old, older than this planet or anything else
we can possibly imagine.'

'What do you think it was?' asked Mellicin.

'I think it was the dragon that Jonas was talking about.'

'The dragon he said the Emperor slew.'

'That's just it,' said Dalia. 'I don't think it's dead at all.
I think that's what Jonas was trying to tell me. The

Dragon of Mars is still alive beneath the Noctis Labyrinthus... and I need your help to find it.'

HE OPENED HIS eyes and tried to scream, feeling the heartsick spike of agonising pain in his chest once more. He thrashed his limbs, palms beating on slick glass surfaces, his movements glutinous. His world was a blur of pink, and he blinked in an effort to clear his vision. He reached up to wipe his eyes clean, the sensation of movement like swimming through thick, gluey water.

A shape swam at the edge of his vision, humanoid, but he couldn't focus on it yet.

His head ached and his body felt unutterably heavy, despite its apparent suspension in buoyancy fluids. He felt weightless pain from every portion of his body, but that was nothing in comparison to the crushing weight of sorrow in his heart.

He remembered sleeping, or at least periods of darkness where the pain was lessened, but nothing that truly eased the abominable, unfocused sadness he felt. He knew he had woken here before, having heard fragments of distant conversations where words like 'miracle', 'brain-death' and 'infarction' were used. Without context, the words were meaningless, but he knew they were being applied to his condition.

He blinked as he heard yet more words, and fought to get the sense of them.

Forcing himself to focus on the voice, he swam through the jelly-like fluid of his world.

The shape spoke again, or at least he thought he heard its voice, the words soft and boneless, as though filtered through faulty augmitters.

He pulled himself forward until his face was pressed to a pane of thick glass. His vision swam into focus, and he saw an antiseptic chamber of polished ceramic tiles and metal gurneys beyond the glass. Spider-like devices hung from the ceiling and a number of fluid-filled glass tanks were fitted into brass sockets on the far wall.

Standing before him was a young woman robed in blue and silver. Her form wavered through the liquid, but she smiled at him and the sight was pathetically welcome.

'Princeps Cavalerio, can you hear me?' she asked, the words snapping into sudden clarity.

He tried to reply, but his mouth was full of liquid, bubbles forming on his lips as they worked to form sounds.

'Princeps?'

'Yes,' he said, his facility for language returning to him at last.

'He's awake,' said the young woman, the words said to an unseen occupant of the chamber. He heard the relief in her voice and wondered why she was so pleased to hear him speak.

'Where am I?' he asked.

'You are in the medicae facility, princeps.'

'Medicae? Where?'

'In Ascraeus Mons,' said the woman. 'You are home.'

Ascraeus Mons… the fortress mountain of Legio Tempestus.

Yes, this was his home. This was where he had formally been awarded his princepture nearly two centuries ago. This was where he had first ascended the groaning elevator to the cockpit of…

Pain surged in his chest and he gasped, drawing in a lungful of oxygenated fluids. His conscious mind rebelled at the idea of breathing liquid, but his body knew better than he that it could survive the experience and gradually his panic eased, though not his pain.

'Who are you?' he asked as his breathing normalised.

'My name is Agathe, I am to be your famulous.'

'Famulous?'

'An aide, if you will. Someone to minister to your needs.'

'Why do I need a famulous?' he demanded. 'I am no cripple!'

'With respect, my princeps, you have just awoken from what must have been a traumatic severance. You will need assistance to adjust. I am to provide that for you.'

'I don't understand,' said Cavalerio. 'How did I come to be here?'

Agathe hesitated, clearly reluctant to provide an answer to his question. Eventually she said, 'Perhaps we might discuss that at a later date, my princeps? After you have had time to adjust to your new surroundings.'

'Answer me, damn you,' yelled Cavalerio, beating a fist against the glass.

Agathe glanced over towards the unseen occupant of the chamber, her prevarication only serving to enrage Cavalerio even more.

'Don't look away from me, girl,' he snarled. 'I am the Stormlord and you will answer me.'

'Very well, my princeps,' said Agathe. 'How much do you remember?'

He frowned, bubbles drifting upwards past his face as he sought to recall the last memory he had before waking.

The towering monster of Legio Mortis bearing down on him.

The furious beat of Victorix Magna's heart as it ruptured under the strain.

The death scream of Magos Argyre as he perished with it.

A yawning black abyss that pulled him down into darkness.

Hot, agonising pain surged in his chest as Princeps Cavalerio relived the death of his engine, weeping invisible tears in the blood-flecked suspension fluid of his amniotic tank.

Mondus Occulum, the jewel of the northern forges, most valued and most industrious of weapon shops. Greater even than the Olympica Fossae assembly yards, only Lukas Chrom's Mondus Gamma facilities replicated the work of the fabricator locum's mighty forge, but even his great forge could not match its output.

Covering hundreds of thousands of square kilometres between the domed mountains of Tharsis Tholus and Ceraunius Tholus, Kane's forge complex was a magnificent, monstrous hinterland of hive-smelteries, weapon shops, armouries, refineries, ore silos, fabrication hangars and industrial stacks.

Numerous sub-hives, Uranius, Rhabon and Labeatis being the greatest, towered over the production facilities, the sinks and towering hab blocks home to the millions of adepts, menials, labourers and muscle that drove the machines of the northern forge.

Like most forges of Mars, the iron-skinned manufactora of Mondus Gamma were geared for war. The conquest of the galaxy demanded weapons and ammunition in quantities unknown in earlier ages of the galaxy, and the hammer of beating iron and the milling of copper jackets was unceasing.

In the collapsed caldera of Uranius Patera, gigantic Tsiolkovsky towers lifted thousands of cargo containers from the supply yards into fat-bellied mass conveyers in geosynchronous orbit, ready to be transported to war zones flung out across the Imperium. Each tower was like an impossibly thick, pollarded tree, yet rendered slender by their height as they vanished into the poisonous, striated clouds that pressed down on the forge.

Both Mondus Occulum and Mondus Gamma in the south were facilities geared for war, but it was a specific branch of warriors to whom the industry of these forges was dedicated: the Astartes.

Crafted within these forges were the guns and blades wielded by the Emperor's most terrifying warriors in the prosecution of his grand dream, fabricated by the most skilled adepts and warranted never to fail by the fabricator locum himself. The battle plate of the Astartes was painstakingly wrought upon the anvils of master metalsmiths augmented with the highest specifications of manual dexterity and tolerances.

Boltguns, lascannons, missile launchers and every other weapon in the Astartes inventory was produced here, the martial power of the Legions first taking shape in the sweating, red-lit halls of Mondus Occulum. Armoured vehicles rumbled from assembly lines housed in vast, vaulted hangars and entire city-sized regions were dedicated to the production of unimaginable quantities of bolter ammunition.

But Mondus Occulum did not simply gird the Astartes for war with weapons and armour; it was also a place where minds were honed. Astartes warriors deemed to have an affinity with the mysteries of technology were permitted to study the ways of the machine under the tutelage of its master adepts. Fabricator Locum Kane himself had trained the finest of them: T'Kell of the Salamanders, Gebren of the Iron Hands and Polonin of the Ultramarines, warriors who would take what they had learned back to their Legions and instruct their neophytes.

Mondus Occulum, beloved of Mars, the jewel of the northern forges. Most valued and most industrious of weapon shops. Domain of the fabricator locum of Mars, the man second only to the ruler of Mars himself. And correctly one of the few forges of Mars to have avoided outright collapse.

FLANKED BY A chittering retinue of noospherically-modified servitors with blank, golden facemasks, harried calculus-logi and a number of specialised data scrubbers whose fear was evident in the harsh binary blurts of cant passing between them, Fabricator Locum Kane sought to stay calm by immersing himself in thoughts of the mundane as he passed beneath the gilded archway that led to the armourium.

Beyond his forge, events of a great and terrible nature were unfolding, but for now, for this moment, he concentrated on keeping the processes of his own forge working as normally as possible in the face of the devastation.

The cavernous chamber beyond the arch was brightly lit, its roof hundreds of metres above him and its far end lost to perspective. Loader servitors and whining elevators carried racks of Astartes battle plate, stacking them in metal-skinned containers arranged along the height of the walls and in long rows that stretched off into the distance.

Hundreds of quality-checking adepts moved through the chamber, hard-plugging in to each container and checking the measured readings of each suit of armour with previously inloaded specifications. Only rarely would armour produced at Mondus Occulum fail to meet Kane's necessarily high tolerances, an occasion that would result in a thorough investigation as to the cause of the defect. Such defects would not be replicated, and those whose laxity had allowed it in the first place would be punished.

Only once every suit had been checked and certified battle-ready would it be shipped to Uranius Patera and the orbital elevators. Warranted never to fail was a promise Fabricator Locum Kane took seriously, even now.

Especially now.

Kane took a deep breath, inhaling and sorting the chemical scent of the air before turning to his magos-apprenta. 'Can you smell that, Lachine?'

'Indeed, my lord,' replied Lachine, using his fleshvoice in emulation of his master. The boy's voice was nasal and unpleasant, and the sooner he was augmented with a vocaliser the better, thought Kane. 'Calcined aluminium oxide, a lapping powder that can reduce lapping and polishing time of armour by at least twenty per cent and which is particularly effective on hard materials, such as silicon and hardened steel. Also, microcrystalline wax and dilute acetic acid.'

Kane shook his head and placed a hand on Lachine's shoulder. The boy was much shorter than Kane and his demeanour entirely literal, a useful trait in an apprenta in terms of efficiency and work, but a frustrating one for conversation.

'No, Lachine, I mean what the smells represent.'

'Represent? Query: I do not understand your contention that odour is a signifier.'

'No? Then you are missing out, Lachine,' said Kane. 'You register the chemical components. I, on the other hand, register the emotional ones. To me, the gentle, reassuring smell of lapping powder, polish and oil represents stability and order, the certainty that we have played our part in ensuring that the Emperor's warriors are equipped for battle with the best armour and weapons we can provide.'

'I see, my lord,' said Lachine but Kane knew he did not.

'At times such as this, I find such things a comfort,' explained Kane. 'A great factory with the machinery all working and revolving with absolute and rhythmic regularity, and with its workers all driven by one impulse, and moving in unison as though a constituent part of the mighty machine, is one of the most inspiring examples of directed force the galaxy knows. I have rarely seen the face of an adept in the action of creation that was not fine, never one which was not earnest and impressive.'

Kane paused as a lifter-servitor passed, carrying a rack of gleaming, freshly-dipped suits of battle plate. The brutish monster was all muscles, pistons and gene-bulked torso, and it effortlessly bore the heavy weight of the armour in its hydraulically clawed fists. Each suit shone silver, the metal and ceramite unpainted and left for each Legion to adorn with its own colours.

'Like knights from a bygone age of Terra,' said Kane, setting off along the serried ranks of thousands upon thousands of suits of armour contained within the chamber. 'A byword for honour, duty and courage.'

'My lord?'

Kane gestured towards the armour with a dramatic sweep of his hand. 'This armour is a resource more precious than the wealth of worlds, Lachine. On most days it gives me great satisfaction to know how much the Astartes depend on us. I can normally lose myself in this place.'

He saw Lachine about to speak and said, 'Not literally, of course. I look at the sheer volume of armour stored here and, even though none of these suits are occupied by one of the Emperor's finest, I am still awed by the power of the Astartes and take solace that we are protected by such awesome heroes.'

'Conclusion: your words lead me to infer that on this day you do not take the same satisfaction you would normally.'

'Indeed I do not, Lachine. Despite my attempts to immerse myself in the daily tasks of the forge, I find my thoughts returning to the chaos that has engulfed our beloved world over the last few weeks.'

Beginning on the day the freakish and unnatural storms had broken over the faraway peak of Olympus Mons and the devastating machine plague had wreaked havoc across Mars, an epidemic of riots, suicides and murders had swept through Mondus Occulum, claiming thousands of lives and, more importantly, doing untold damage to the production facilities.

Scores of factories and weapon shops had been destroyed, burned to the ground or smashed beyond repair in the whipping, shuddering waves of panic and psychosis that had swept through the habs and factories like contagious lunacy.

The forge marshals had been unable to cope with the paroxysms of violence and, though it pained him to do so, Kane had ordered them to withdraw and allow the rioters to run their course.

'Who would have thought such trouble could have been touched off by a freak weather system over three thousand kilometres away?' he said.

'Studies by Magos Cantore have shown that uncomfortably cold weather can stimulate aggressiveness and a willingness to take risks, while apathy prevails in the heat,' said Lachine. 'Additional:

temperature has previously been shown to affect mood, which in turn affects behaviour, with higher temperature or barometric pressure related to higher mood, better memory, and broadened cognitive style. Humidity, temperature and hours of exposure to sunshine have the greatest effect on mood, though Cantore believes humidity to be the most significant predictor in regression and canonical correlation analysis. Implications for the climate control of forges and subsequent worker performance are discussed in detail in the study's conclusion. Would you like me to summarise them?'

'In the name of the Omnissiah, please don't,' said Kane, striding onwards into the depths of the armorium. Lachine and his retinue struggled to match his long, purposeful stride.

As the panting Lachine drew alongside him, Kane said, 'Certainly, its absurd to believe that a meteorological phenomenon, even one so fierce, could affect the psyches of so many, yet the evidence before us is hard to ignore. However, the damage was not restricted just to the cognitive processes of the forge's population.'

That fact troubled him more than any other.

As the storm raged over Olympus Mons, the vox-lines and data highways of Mars had swarmed with screaming, shrieking packets of corrupted data that sliced into the delicate systems that governed almost every aspect of the workings of Mondus Occulum.

The outlying forge cogitators and logic engines had clogged with corrupt data, howling ghosts of sourceless machine-noise and dangerous code packets of infected algorithms that many of the most advanced aegis protocols were helpless to defeat.

Only Kane's swift action to shut down the I/O highways and the fact that the vast majority of his systems had recently been upgraded to take advantage of Koriel

Zeth's revolutionary system of noospheric data transference had spared them the worst of the attack, for an attack it surely had been.

'How much longer do the code-scrubbers need before they will have my system cleaned out?' he asked.

'Current estimates range from six full rotations to thirty.'

'That's a wide range. Can't they narrow their estimation?'

'Apparently the corrupt code is proving to be most resilient to their efforts,' explained Lachine. 'Each portion of circuitry that is certified purged soon develops faulty lines of code at a geometric rate once again. They dare not reconnect any system touched by the polluted algorithms for fear of re-infection.'

'Have they identified its point of origin?'

'Not with any certainty, though the infection of systems appears to be spreading outwards from the forge of the Fabricator General, suggesting that it was the first to suffer.'

'Or where it was released,' muttered Kane. Despite repeated attempts to communicate with Kelbor-Hal, every transmission had been rebuffed by squalling code screams like barking dogs or was simply ignored.

'Query: you believe this scrapcode to have been released into the Martian systems on purpose?' Even the normally logical and literal Lachine could not keep an emotional response from his voice at the notion that the scrapcode had been unleashed deliberately.

Kane cursed himself for his verbal slip and shrugged.

'It's a possibility,' he admitted, keeping his tone light. He didn't particularly want to voice his suspicions to Lachine. His apprenta was loyal, but he was naïve, and Kane knew that information could be thieved by any number of means from supposedly secure sources.

No, the less Lachine knew of Kane's suspicions the better.

According to the code-scrubbers, the scrapcode had attempted to shut down the vox network and defence protocols that protected his forge and then release the tension in the Tsiolkovsky towers' guy wires. Kane had shut off the links between Mondus Occulum and the rest of Mars in an instant, leaving them floundering in the dark, but safe from further attack.

Even communications off-world had become next to impossible thanks to a sourceless backwash of psychic interference. Kane had only been able to maintain contact between the forge of Ipluvien Maximal and the Magma City of Adept Zeth thanks to the noosphere.

The news coming from both was neither reassuring nor particularly illuminating.

Both adepts had suffered similar outbreaks of inexplicable violence and madness among their populace, though only Maximal had experienced serious machine failures, losing three of his prized reactors to critical mass overloads. Zeth had spoken of a failed experiment that had seen virtually all of her psykers dead, no doubt related to the psychic interference surrounding Mars.

As if things weren't bad enough, Maximal went on to tell of fragmentary communications he had inloaded from the expedition fleets that spoke of an equally terrible catastrophe in the Istvaan system.

Details were sketchy and Maximal had not wanted to speculate without firmer information, but it appeared that a dreadful incident had occurred around the third planet, which was now said to be a blasted, ashen wasteland.

Kane knew of only one weapon that could reduce a planet to such a wretched, hellish state in so short a time.

Had the Warmaster unleashed the Life Eater or was this the desperate last act of a defeated foe? Maximal's sources had no answer to that, but claimed that the Astartes had taken fearful casualties.

Whether they had suffered as a result of enemy action or a terrible accident of friendly fire was unclear, but for Astartes to suffer any loss on such a scale was almost impossible to imagine.

Of all of them, Maximal's vox-systems had suffered least in the deluge of unclean code, and he was even now attempting to restore communications with agencies beyond the surface of Mars for further information.

Via secure noospheric links, all three adepts expressed their certainty that the infection of the Martian systems bore all the hallmarks of a pre-emptive strike, but without more solid data, there was nothing they could do but strengthen their defences in case of further assault.

Kane had heard the fear in Maximal's ridiculously rarefied voice and despised him for it. Maximal was not an easy adept to like and Kane considered him to be little more than an archivist rather than an innovator. Koriel Zeth, on the other hand, had spoken boldly of resisting any follow-up attacks and of how she had despatched envoys to allied warrior orders of Titans and Knights to secure their assistance.

With Mars under attack from an unknown foe, it was time to gather one's friends close.

Kane respected Zeth, for she reminded him of a younger version of himself, an adept unafraid to push the boundaries of the known. To Kane, Zeth represented all that was good about the Mechanicum, an adept who possessed a proper reverence for the past and what earlier pioneers had developed that meshed with an unashamed hunger to build upon that knowledge to reach still greater heights.

An ancient alchemist and scientist of Terra had once said that he had seen further by standing on the shoulders of giants. That perfectly applied to Adept Zeth, and Kane knew that if anyone was going to advance the cause of science and reason in the Imperium it was her.

Emboldened by that thought, Kane watched as huge, tracked haulers lifted sealed containers of Astartes weapons and armour for transport to the orbital elevators of Uranius Patera.

'Come, Lachine,' he said. 'Even during a crisis, the work of Mondus Occulum must continue.'

GREY DUST, LIKE ashen bone, billowed around the legs of the two Knights as they loped along the edges of the Aganippe Fossae, the long trench that carved into the plains west of the towering form of Arsia Mons.

Leopold Cronus led the way in *Pax Mortis*, with Raf Maven following behind in the newly repaired *Equitos Bellum*. Cronus set a brisk striding pace, and Maven had to work hard to keep up with him, for *Equitos Bellum* was skittish, its controls tight, and the Manifold willfully resisted him at every turn.

It knows the thing that hurt it is still out there, thought Maven, angling his course to follow Cronus and the deep canyon. Dust clouds obscured the view from his cockpit, but there was little to see in this region and he was piloting via the Manifold anyway. The toxic deserts of the pallidus stretched out to the west and south, and the northern sub-hives between here and Ipluvien Maximal's forge were little more than black smudges of hanging smoke and fear to the north.

The Knights followed the course of the chasm towards the Median Bridge, a section of collapsed rock where they could cross before turning eastwards towards their chapter house within the Arsia Chasmata.

'How's it doing?' asked Cronus over the vox-link.

'It's hard work,' admitted Maven. 'It keeps pulling at the controls, but there's no sense to it. Each time I compensate, it returns on the opposite side a moment later.'

'It will take time to readjust,' said Cronus. 'The entire link assembly had to be rebuilt.'

'I know, but it feels stronger than that.'

'Stronger how? What do you mean?'

'Like it's trying to guide me,' said Maven, at a loss how else to explain it.

'Guide you? To where?'

'I don't know, but it's like… like something's pulling at me too.'

Maven heard Cronus sigh over the vox and wished he had something more solid to offer his friend by way of an explanation. All he had was a gut feeling and the firmly-held conviction that his mount knew better than he what needed to be done.

Their deployment had begun three days ago, when they left the chapter house in a fanfare of cheers, squires' trumpets, blaring warhorns and waving cobalt banners. *Equitos Bellum* marched out, and the brothers of the Knights of Taranis had come to watch it walk once more. For a mount to have returned from the verge of destruction was no small matter and the occasion had to be marked.

Like most of the warrior orders of Tharsis, the Knights of Taranis had been on high alert since the chaos that had engulfed Mars began. Thanks to the noospheric links installed by Adept Zeth, the halls of Taranis had not suffered as horrifically as many others had, though the enginseers had been forced to order an emergency shutdown of the chapter house's main reactor after a fragment of scrapcode attempted to disengage its coolant protocols.

That speedy response had saved the Order of Taranis from a nuclear holocaust, but until the code-scrubbers could purge the corrupted systems, those Knight machines without full power cells would not be able to recharge.

Nor had that been the worst of the damage. Much to Lord Verticorda's anguish, the data looms of the order's librarium had been corrupted beyond repair, taking with them a roll of honour and battle stretching back a thousand years and more.

At the request of Adept Zeth, Lords Caturix and Verticorda had ordered the Knights of Taranis to ride from their chapter house in defence of Mars and the Magma City. Rumour had it that Zeth had also despatched emissaries to Lord Cavalerio of Tempestus to petition their engines to walk, but no one knew what answer she had received.

With several machines powerless to ride until the reactor was repaired, the Knights of Taranis were forced to operate in teams of two instead of three to cover the scale of their deployment. Old Stator had marched out alongside Brother Gentran, a rider newly-elevated from the Errantry, and Maven had been surprised to find that he missed the flinty presence of his preceptor.

Maven and Cronus had ridden east, following a patrol circuit that carried them clockwise around the rumpled skirts of the ancient volcano, before turning to follow the line of the Oti Fossae southwards. As night fell on the second day of their ride, they turned west towards the Magma City to refuel and recharge before continuing on their patrol circuit.

The forge of Koriel Zeth never failed to amaze Maven, glowing like an ember in the distance while the skies above seethed with orange light as though the clouds themselves were afire. Riding closer, lava-filled aqueducts had shone like threads of gold as they carried molten rock from the top of Aetna's Dam, the monolithic structure that formed the entirety of the volcano's southern flank, to the magma lagoon surrounding the city.

Towering walls of ceramite and adamantium ringed the enormous city, and the light of the planet's lifeblood dispelled the darkness as the Knights marched along the mighty, statue-lined Typhon Causeway towards the Vulkan Gate.

Silver and black spires jutted over the walls like metallic teeth, and only after convoluted binaric interrogation by the gate's defences had they been allowed inside. They had stayed within the circuit of the walls just long enough for their mounts' power cells to be brought back to maximum charge before riding out.

The two Knights had continued on their patrol circuit of the enormous volcano, skirting the Magma City's port facilities where millions of tonnes of war materiel was ferried into the hungry bellies of mass-conveyers hanging low in the crowded skies. No sooner had they left the smoking grandeur of Zeth's city than Maven had felt *Equitos Bellum* pulling at him, an insistent urge that nagged at his hindbrain and sent painful skewers of pain into his mind whenever he resisted.

With their course soon to carry them eastwards towards home, the pull was getting stronger, and Maven gripped the controls tighter as he felt a building ache behind his eyes. He felt every one of his hard-plugs scratching with irritation, as though *Equitos Bellum* was trying to dislodge him like a wild colt.

'What's the matter with you?' he hissed.

As if in answer, a ghostly flare on the auspex spiked to the south, and Maven flinched as a surge of recognition pulsed in his mind. The image vanished almost as soon as it appeared and he wasn't even sure he'd seen it, but for the briefest instant it had looked like a dreadfully familiar spider-like pattern of electromagnetic energy.

Maven drew his mount to a halt, feeling the pain behind his eyes ease as he did so. The tall machine's hydraulics hissed as it sank down onto its haunches.

'Cronus, wait!' he called, rotating the Knight's upper body with a deft movement of the controls. There was nothing to see here, just bone white ash and dust whipped in from the southern pallidus. He heard the relaxing groan of metal as *Equitos Bellum* settled, feeling the tension in its limbs and the restless hunger for vengeance burning in its core.

'What is it?' replied Cronus, and Maven read the tell-tales of his brother's machine assuming a war posture through the Manifold. 'What do you see?'

'I don't know,' admitted Maven. 'I don't think there's actually anything out there, but *Equitos Bellum's* got the scent of something.'

'Did you get an auspex return?'

'Sort of, maybe... I don't know,' said Maven. 'It was like a ghost image or something. It was just like the energy signature I saw right before the attack on Maximal's reactor.'

Pax Mortis rode alongside him, and Maven could see Leopold Cronus through the armaglass canopy. His brother looked unconvinced, but not yet ready to write off Maven's – and *Equitos Bellum's* – instincts for danger.

'Send it over,' ordered Cronus. 'The auspex log for the last few minutes.'

Maven nodded, exloading the data from his auspex panel to Cronus's machine in a brief data squirt. As he waited for Cronus to review the data, he cast his gaze out into the depths of the pallidus.

The ashen deserts were desolate and uninhabitable, a landscape of tortured grandeur rendered barren and toxic by rapacious over-mining and unthinking plundering of the resources buried beneath the Martian soil. Pollutants blown in from the equatorial refinery belt carpeted the barren, scarred rock, making it a treacherous landscape of sand-covered crevasses and sinkholes.

Nothing lived in the pallidus, yet Maven found himself unaccountably drawn to grip the controls of his mount and ride south into the wasteland. His power cells were fully charged and he had more than enough reserves of nutrients and water to last him for weeks if need be.

His hands twitched at the controls and he felt the heart of his mount respond to his desire. It goaded him with warlike whispers and an insistent pressure at the back of his mind. His lip curled into a snarl as he thought of hunting the monstrous, dead thing that had almost killed him.

It was out there, and *Equitos Bellum* knew it. He could feel the certainty of that fact in every molecule of his being. The ghost image had been a reminder of his duty to his mount.

'There's nothing here,' said Cronus, breaking into his thoughts. 'Auspex track is clean.'

'I know,' said Maven, with calm, cold certainty. 'There's nothing nearby.'

'Then why have we stopped?'

'Because *Equitos Bellum* is telling me where I need to go.'

'Go?' asked Cronus. 'What are you talking about? The only place we need to go is across the Median Bridge and back to the chapter house.'

'No,' insisted Maven. 'It's out there. The thing that tried to kill us. It's in the south, I know it.'

'How *can* you know it?' demanded Cronus. 'There's nothing on the auspex. You said so yourself.'

'I know that, Leo, but I saw what I saw. *Equitos Bellum* can feel it and I trust its instincts.'

'And what? You're going to go after it on your own?'

'If I have to,' said Maven.

'Don't be foolish,' warned Cronus. 'Caturix will have your spurs if you do this.'

'He can have them,' said Maven, powering up and raising the Knight to its full height once more. 'I need to do this. *Equitos Bellum* needs this if it's ever going to be whole again.'

'You're willing to risk your spurs by going off-mission on what, a hunch?'

'It's more than that, Leo,' said Maven. 'I *know* it's out there and I'm going after it whether you like it or not.'

Once again, Maven heard Cronus sigh, and though he hated to abandon his friend he knew he had no choice. *Equitos Bellum* would give him no peace until they had been avenged.

'Very well,' said Cronus. 'Where is it? Give me a heading.'

'Leo? You're coming with me?' asked Maven.

'This thing, whatever it is, already got the better of you once before,' said Cronus. 'So, logically, you're going to need my help if you're going to take it on again.'

'You're a true friend,' said Maven, so very proud of his brother.

'Shut up and let's go before I see sense and change my mind.'

Maven smiled. 'Follow me,' he said, turning his mount and riding into the pallidus.

The hunt was on and *Equitos Bellum* surged with wounded pride.

Maven welcomed it.

Dalia awoke with a scream, her hand clutching her chest, hyperventilating as the fragments of the darkness within her skull threatened to spill out and consume her. Serpentine shapes lurked in the shadows, and Dalia hugged the sheets close to her body as she heard the hiss of a draconic breath drawn at the beginning of the universe and saw the gleam of teeth in ever-widening jaws.

A voice in the darkness spoke her name.

Even with her eyes shut, she could see him, the hooded man with the wild eyes and the mark of the dragon burning beneath his skin. Its silver fire was a web of light within his flesh.

She forced her eyes open as the light levels in the hab grew from nightlight to full illumination. Beside her, Caxton stirred, half asleep as he fumbled with the lumen controls.

'What… what's the matter?' he asked groggily.

Dalia's eyes flickered to the corners of the hab, where of course there were no serpentine predators lurking in the shadows to devour her and no hooded man with glittering mercury for blood. She saw a gunmetal grey footlocker overflowing with clothing, the small table strewn with machine parts, and oil-stained walls hung with thin sheets of paper covered in scrawled diagrams. A dripping tap echoed in the ablutions cubicle and an uneaten meal lay in its foil wrapper next to an empty water bottle.

She focused on those simple, domestic items, their familiarity an anchor to the real world and not the realm of dreams and nightmares, the world of dragons and hooded men.

'Are you allright?' asked Caxton, sitting up in bed and putting his arm around her. The haptic implants in his fingertips were cold against her bare skin and she shivered. He mistook it for fear and pulled her close. 'I'm here, Dalia. There's nothing to worry about. You just had a nightmare.'

Ever since waking from her coma, Dalia had discovered that she could not bear to be alone. Sleep would not come, and a gnawing terror of sinking down into darkness for all eternity would open like a yawning chasm of emptiness within her. She feared she might never emerge from it should she fall in.

When she had confided this to Caxton, he had offered to stay with her, and though she recognised male desire in the offer, she recognised her own need as well. His moving into her hab unit had seemed like the most natural thing in the world.

They sat there for several minutes, Caxton rocking her gently and Dalia letting him.

'Was it the same as before?' he asked.

She nodded. 'The dragon and the hooded man.'

'Every night the same dream,' he said in wonder. 'What do you think it means?'

Dalia pulled free from his embrace and turned her head to look directly at him.

'It means we need to leave.'

'I'll wake the others,' he said, seeing the determination in her eyes.

She leaned in and kissed him.

'Do it quickly,' she said.

2.04

THE MAGMA CITY never slept, its industry continuing through every hour of the day and night. Despite the crowds of robed adepts, menials and workers that filled its streets, Dalia still felt acutely vulnerable. Their small group was clothed in nondescript robes, a mix of reds and browns that marked them as low-grade forge workers. A common sight on the thoroughfares of Adept Zeth's forge, yet each of them felt as though every eye was upon them.

The constant thrum and low vibration that permeated every surface of the city was more pronounced on the streets, and Dalia wondered if they were being watched even now. Throne knew how many different ways there were of monitoring a person's whereabouts, biometric readings, facial recognition, genetic markers, spy-skulls or even good old-fashioned eyes.

'Lift your head up, girl,' said Zouche. 'You look like you're up to no good with your head down like that.'

'We *are* up to no good,' pointed out Severine. 'We're leaving the forge without permission. I said this was a bad idea.'

'You didn't have to come,' shot back Caxton.

Severine shot him a withering glance and said, 'I needed to come,' as though that should settle the matter. Dalia listened to them bicker, recognising the fear behind it. She understood that fear, for each of them was a member of the Cult Mechanicum, augmented in ways both subtle and gross, and each stood to lose a great deal should they be discovered.

'We have to do this,' said Dalia. 'Whatever we unlocked with the Akashic reader, it's hidden in the Noctis Labyrinthus. We have to find out what it is.'

'You mean *you* have to find out what it is,' said Zouche. 'I'm quite happy not knowing.'

'Then why are you here?'

'You said you needed my help,' said the short machinist, and Dalia could have kissed him.

She took a breath and lifted her head. 'Zouche is right. We shouldn't look as though we've anything to hide. I mean, look around us, the place is as busy now as it is any other time of the day.'

Blue-tinted lumen globes sputtered and fizzed atop black poles, their glass reflecting the golden-orange glow from the clouds. Soaring above them, higher even than the silver pyramid of Zeth's forge, was the dark, mountainous shadow of Arsia Mons. The volcano's side had been quarried away five hundred years ago and replaced with the gargantuan structure of Aetna's Dam, its monstrous, cyclopean scale almost impossible to comprehend.

Dalia recognised the name it bore, which had belonged to a legendary fire goddess of a long dead volcano that rose from the Mediterranean dust bowl of Terra. It was fitting that the name should be appropriated for a rekindled volcano on Mars.

As it had been when Dalia had first arrived on Mars, the Magma City thrived and pulsed with activity, with its inhabitants making their way to and fro on foot and by any number of bizarre mechanical conveyances. Servo-skulls of gold, silver and bone darted through the air, each on an errand for its master, and Dalia wondered which of them served Adept Zeth.

'It may be busy,' said Caxton, 'but if any of the Protectors realise we shouldn't be on shift, we'll be in real trouble.'

'Then best we don't attract their attention by standing around yapping like stray dogs, eh?' said Zouche. 'Come on, the mag-lev transit hub is just ahead.'

They followed Zouche, trying to affect an air of non-chalance and give the impression that they had every reason to be there, though Dalia suspected they weren't succeeding too well. She could feel sweat running between her shoulder blades and fought the urge to scratch an itch on the back of her leg.

She felt great affection for her friends, knowing that she wouldn't have had the strength or courage to make the journey on her own. She had told them she needed them, which was true, but not for the reasons any of them might expect. Their technical skills would no doubt be useful along the way, but she needed them with her so the dark and terrifyingly lonely void that lurked behind her eyes every time she closed them wouldn't overwhelm her.

She knew Caxton was with her because he was in love with her, and Zouche had come because he was about as honest as a person could be. He had said he would come and he had. He lived his life by doing as he said he would do, which even Dalia knew was all too rare a trait in humanity.

Dalia didn't know why Severine had come, since the girl clearly didn't want to be there and was terrified of losing her status as a Mechanicum draughter. Guilt was what Dalia suspected drove Severine to make this journey, guilt for what they had allowed to happen to Jonas Milus. It was a reason Dalia was uncomfortably aware played no small part in her own determination to discover what lay beneath the Noctis Labyrinthus.

Only Mellicin had not come with them, and Dalia was sad not to have her logical presence with them right now, though that was, she supposed, exactly why she wasn't there. Caxton had gathered them all in Zouche's hab, a sterile and functional chamber that reflected the machinist's austere, no-nonsense character. The only concession to decoration was a small silver effigy of a lighthouse that sat in a corner with a slow-burning candle smouldering before it.

All of them had answered Caxton's summons: Severine looking rumpled and irritable, Zouche as though he had been awake all along and had simply been waiting for them, while Mellicin looked as calm as Dalia could ever remember seeing her.

With everyone gathered, Dalia had outlined the substance and unnatural regularity of her dreams, the imagery and the feeling that she was being *summoned* to the Labyrinth of Night.

'Summoned by what?' asked Zouche.

'I don't know,' admitted Dalia. 'This… Dragon, whatever it is.'

'Don't you remember the stories?' asked Severine. 'The dragons *ate* fair maidens.'

'Then you and Mellicin will be all right,' quipped Caxton, wishing he hadn't when Dalia stared at him in annoyance.

'I had the dream again tonight,' said Dalia. 'The same as before, but it felt stronger, more urgent. I think it's telling me that it's time to go.'

'Now?' asked Severine. 'It's the middle of the night.'

'Kind of appropriate then, eh?' said Zouche. 'We are going to the Labyrinth of Night after all.'

They all looked at each other then, and Dalia could sense their hesitation.

'I need your help. I can't do this alone,' she said, hating the pleading note in her voice.

'No need to ask twice, Dalia,' said Zouche, picking up the silver lighthouse figurine and tucking it into his robes. 'I'll come.'

'And me,' said Severine, though she didn't make eye contact.

'Mellicin?' asked Caxton. 'What about you? You in?'

The stern matronly woman who had held them together and made them work better in a team than they ever could have managed alone, shook her head. She gripped Dalia's hand and said, 'I can't go with you, Dalia, I have to stay. Someone has to finish what we've begun here. Believe me, I'd like nothing more than to go with you, but I'm too old and too set in my ways to go gallivanting around Mars chasing dreams and visions and mysteries. My place is here in the forge. I'm sorry.'

Dalia was disappointed, but she nodded. 'I understand, Mel. And don't worry about us. We'll be back soon, I promise.'

'I know you will. And don't call me Mel ever again,' said Mellicin.

They laughed and said their goodbyes before making their way towards a journey into the unknown and an uncertain future.

So lost was Dalia in her memory of saying goodbye to Mellicin that she bumped into a passing adept, who stared at her with amber eyes from behind a silver mask. He blurted a hash of irritated binary and Dalia shrank from the force of his utterance.

'Many apologies, Adept Lascu,' she said, reading his identity in the noospheric information swirling above him before remembering that she shouldn't be able to read such things without modification.

The adept either didn't notice or believed she already knew him, and passed on his way with a final canted burst of annoyance. Dalia let out a pent-up breath and turned as the sleeve of her robe was tugged.

'If you're quite finished?' said Caxton, looking in alarm at the adept's retreating back.

'Yes, sorry,' she said.

'The mag-lev hub is just ahead,' said Zouche, pointing to a bronze archway through which hundreds of people were passing back and forth. Dalia experienced a moment of sickening realisation when they reached the archway and she saw the wide steps descending hundreds of metres into the bedrock of Mars.

'We're going to have to go below the level of the magma?' she asked.

'Of course,' said Caxton. 'The mag-lev can't exactly go *through* the lava now can it?'

'No, I suppose not,' said Dalia, wishing she hadn't said anything.

Caxton pulled her on and she quelled her mounting panic as they began their journey downwards. Sizzling lumen strips that flickered and hurt Dalia's eyes illuminated their route along a tunnel thronged with workers making their way to and from their shifts. They marched like automatons – one side ascending, the other descending – all in perfect unison towards or from the metropolis above.

Zouche forged them a path downwards with his squat frame and robust language, and anyone who objected to either soon bit their tongue at the sight of his thunderous stare and bunched fists.

Eventually they reached the bottom, the transit station itself, a gigantic hangar with a colossal vaulted ceiling. There seemed to be no order to the movement of the packed mass of people, just heaving bodies that moved according to tidal patterns rather than with any purpose.

Robed Protectors bearing crackling weapon-staves and the four-by-four number grid symbol of Adept Zeth policed the energetic scrum of workers, and Dalia tried to avoid looking at them for fear of attracting their attention. Servo skulls bobbed overhead, and grating binaric code spilled from vox-plates set into the walls, announcing departures and arrivals and warning travellers to beware of the void between mag-lev and platform.

'Now where?' asked Dalia, unable to make sense of the overlaid binary instructions blaring from the vox.

'This way,' said Zouche pushing through the crowds. 'It looks harder than it is, but after you've ridden the mag-lev once it's easy to find your way around.'

'I'll take your word for it,' said Dalia, taking Caxton and Severine's hands like children on a scholam outing as they set off after him.

Zouche led the way through a confusing series of ceramic-tiled tunnels until they stood on a crowded platform with hundreds of tired-looking workers.

Distorted, wavering blurts of code fragments coughed from battered vox-amps set in wooden boxes mounted on the ceiling, and even Zouche shrugged when Dalia looked at him for an explanation.

'I didn't get a word of that,' said Zouche.

'It said the next mag-lev will be delayed by two hundred and seventy-five seconds,' said a powerful voice behind them.

Dalia flinched at the sound, recognising the harsh, metallic rasp of a human voice issuing from behind a bronze mask.

She turned and looked up into a pair of glowing green eyes.

'Greetings, Dalia Cythera,' said Rho-mu 31.

***

THE ENEMY REAVER was burning, the top portion of its carapace blown away by Cavalerio's blastgun after a punishing barrage from the Vulcan had stripped it of its voids. He felt the heat build in his left arm as the weapon recharged, and a clatter in his right as the autoloader recycled the mega bolter to fire again.

The enemy engine toppled backwards, flattening an ore silo and sending up a blizzard of flame and smoke. Crushed rockcrete dust billowed from its demise and even as Cavalerio exulted in the kill, he knew the other Reaver was still out there, lurking behind the burning ruins of the refinery, using the smoke and heat to mask its reactor bloom.

'Moderati, get me a mass reading!' he ordered in a squirt of binary.

'Yes, princeps.'

Information flooded him through the Manifold, a hundred different stimuli collected from the mighty engine's myriad surveyors: heat, mass, motion, radiation, vibration and shield harmonics. Everything combined to paint a world more real to Cavalerio than reality itself.

He drank the liquid data down, swallowing and digesting it in a heartbeat. His awareness of his surroundings bloomed and he saw the enemy Reaver manoeuvring around the refinery, smashing its way through the walls and roof beams of the nearby steelworks.

A flicker of heat and mass tugged at his awareness and he felt the stealthy approach of the enemy Warhound before he saw it.

'Steersman, reverse pace, flank speed! Heading two-seven-zero!'

A Warlord Titan was not built for rapid course changes, but the steersman was good and the engine obeyed with commendable speed. The building beside

Cavalerio exploded into a mass of shredded girders, torn concrete slabs and sheet metal roofing. Clouds of vaporised rockcrete billowed, but Cavalerio's engine-sight could penetrate it without difficulty.

He saw the Warhound, a graceful loping predator of red and silver, dart from the shadows of a collapsed forge-hangar, its turbos blitzing with hard light. Cavalerio felt the impacts on his shields, but its angle of fire was poor and most of the shots were void-skidding.

<Sensori, keep an eye out for that Reaver,> he canted. <Don't let him get too close.>

'Yes, princeps.'

'Moderati, firing solution!'

The Warhound was nimble, but it had struck too soon, and without the shock value of its turbo lasers impacting on its target's shields it was vulnerable. Data inloaded from the moderati's station, and Cavalerio saw the vectors of fire slide into his mind at the speed of thought. He felt the wordless bray of the gun-servitor's acknowledgement and opened fire.

A sheeting storm of explosive rounds roared from Cavalerio's mega bolter, obscuring the Warhound in a blizzard of detonations and flaring shreds of discharging voids. The Warhound staggered, pushed back against the brick walls of a weapon shop. Stone and steel tumbled to the ground, but Cavalerio knew the enemy engine wasn't out of the fight yet.

'Steersman, move in! Moderati, arm missiles. Sensori, where's that Reaver?'

'Moving in, aye!'

'Missiles arming!'

'Reaver still closing, princeps. Six hundred metres, bearing zero-six-three.'

Cavalerio's engine closed the gap between it and the Warhound. He had to kill it before the Reaver was in a position to help. Individually, neither of the enemy machines were a match for his Warlord, but working together, they could potentially bring him down if he were not careful.

The Warhound swayed as it picked itself up, its weapon limbs shaking like a dog climbing from the water. Its shields burbled and sparked, and Cavalerio read a flaring convergence of energy gaps clustered around the engine's hip.

Information updates sluiced around him and he updated his situational awareness, feeling the danger of the closing Reaver and knowing he didn't have much time.

'Moderati! As soon as that Reaver comes into view, hit its upper carapace with a barrage from the carapace launcher. Three missile spread, five second intervals.'

'Yes, princeps.'

'Gun-servitor Hellas-88, slave weapon to my command.'

The implanted servitor wordlessly acknowledged his order, and Cavalerio felt the reassuring weight and industrial motion of the mega bolter as though it were part of his flesh. It was reckless to take command of the weapon from the servitor, who could fire it far more effectively than he could, but to make this kill, he wanted to *feel* the thunder.

Cavalerio surrendered to the engine's killing lust, guiding it with his own need to defeat their foe. With a thought, the mega bolter engaged and sawed off a furious hurricane of shells at the staggering Warhound's wounded hip.

At the same time, he felt the juddering *shoom, shoom, shoom* of the missiles mounted high on his carapace leap from the launcher. The Reaver had joined the fight and he had to finish the Warhound quickly.

'Multiple impacts on enemy Reaver, princeps!'

Cavalerio noted the update, but concentrated his attention on the Warhound. Its voids had collapsed under his barrage, detonating with a blinding thunderclap. The explosion atomised one weapon arm and cracked its carapace open. Flames billowed from its rear quarter.

Still it stood, defiant as a whipped wolf.

'Arming blastgun,' intoned the Moderati. 'Plotting solution.'

'Belay that order!' cried Cavalerio, 'we'll need it for the Reaver! We close and kill it with hard rounds!'

'Incoming!' shouted the Moderati, and Cavalerio felt the blistering pain of impacts on the voids. Missiles streaked from the enemy Reaver, fired from an underslung rocket pod, and the relentless impacts staggered his engine. Shield energy ripped away from his Warlord, and Cavalerio heard the frantic cants of the Magos as he fought to rebuild them.

The limping Warhound stood its ground before him, silhouetted in the ruins of the collapsed building, and Cavalerio was forced to admire its pilot's courage. It was doomed, yet still it fought. Its remaining gun opened fire, punishing his already weakened shields.

'Shield failure on lower quadrant!' warned the Magos. 'Critical collapse imminent!'

'Reaver closing, princeps!'

Cavalerio ignored the warnings, letting rip once more with the mega bolter. A storm of shells and pulverised rock erupted around the Warhound, driving it to its knees with the force of the impacts. Its carapace cracked open and flames sheeted upwards as the remains of the building tumbled down around it. Cavalerio kept hammering the smaller engine until it was a ruin of splintered metal and fire.

Sudden, agonising pain speared into him, and he screamed as it felt like his leg was bathed in liquid fire. His awareness snapped back into wide-spread, and he saw the looming form of the Reaver closing with him, its immense bulk smashing through the high walls of the refinery in its hunger to reach him. Its warhorn blared in triumph and its plasma blastgun was smoking from a sustained salvo. Cavalerio read the situation in a heartbeat.

It was on his exposed flank and had him dead to rights.

His shields were almost gone, the metal beneath buckled and molten.

A volley of screaming rockets slammed into him and he convulsed with psychostigmatic pain. The Manifold erupted with warnings and damage indicators.

The chin station exploded, immolating the Moderati and steersman in a hellish firestorm. The cockpit shook as more missile impacts slammed into the Warlord's mighty torso.

<Shields gone!> canted the magos unnecessarily.

'Missiles!' he yelled, knowing it was too late. 'Full spread, safeties off!'

Streaking rockets and laser fire pounded the air between the two engines as they unleashed the last of their arsenal at one another at point-blank range. Cavalerio screamed as his shields failed, feeling awful, intolerable pain as the enemy engine tore the guts from him with an unending series of missile strikes.

Bright explosions of void failure flared around him, and at last both war machines were stripped of their shields, naked and steel to steel.

Cavalerio grinned through the pain.

'Now I have you!' he roared.

With his last breath, Cavalerio unleashed the full power of the blastgun into his enemy's face and the world exploded in fire and light.

AGATHE WATCHED THE last moments of the unfolding battle on the hololithic projection table, admiring the skill of the Stormlord even as his engine was destroyed. Watching the miniature holograms of the engines stomping around the artificial landscape had been thrilling, but the tension in the warriors gathered around the table was contagious.

'He's doing much better now, isn't he?' she asked.

Princeps Sharaq looked over at her, his kind eyes and cropped, salt and pepper hair at odds with the killer she knew him to be. His eyes darted to the other side of the projection table where two fellow princeps, Vlad Suzak and Jan Mordant, stood watching the simulated battle. Suzak stood ramrod straight, as if on parade, while Mordant eagerly leaned forwards with his elbow resting on the edge of the table.

'Yes, famulous, he is doing better,' said Sharaq.

'But not well enough,' put in Suzak, the straight-backed slayer of engines.

'It takes time to adjust,' said Agathe, looking at the forlorn, naked form suspended in the steel-edged amniotic tank, linked to the projection table via a host of insulated cables. 'To go from hard-plug connection to full immersion. It's not an easy transition to make.'

'No,' agreed Sharaq, 'but the point remains, the Stormlord cannot command the Legio like this. Not yet.'

Agathe pointed to the projection table. 'He took on and defeated three engines single-handedly. Doesn't that count for anything?'

'It speaks of great courage,' said Jan Mordant, looking over at Sharaq. 'Maybe we're being too cautious?'

'It speaks of recklessness,' snapped Sharaq.

'It's just a simulation, Kel,' pointed out Mordant. 'It's a whole different game when you're linked with the Manifold. We all know the risks you take in a sim aren't the ones you take when your neck's on the line.'

'I'm aware of that, Jan, but if this *had* been real, the Stormlord would have died and taken his engine with him. A Warlord no less.'

'But three engines, Kel…' said Mordant. 'Come on!'

Sharaq sighed. 'I understand, Jan, I really do, but you've only recently been elevated to the princepture of a Reaver from a Warhound.'

'What's that got to do with anything?'

'It means you haven't yet shed your own recklessness,' said Suzak. 'You have to think in terms other than individual heroics when you command a larger engine. You should know that, and Princeps Cavalerio should damn well know it.'

Agathe saw the flush of temper colour Jan Mordant's neck, but he controlled his anger and simply nodded. She saw his knuckles were white where they gripped the projection table.

Softening his tone, Sharaq said, 'Princeps Cavalerio should have waited for the engines of his battlegroup to take the enemy en masse. We are not in the business of futile heroics, Jan, we are in the business of destroying our foes and then bringing our engines and crews back alive.'

'So the decision stands?' asked Mordant.

Sharaq nodded. 'The decision stands. Until such time as I deem Princeps Cavalerio fit to return to active duty, I will assume command of Legio Tempestus forces on Mars.'

Mordant and Suzak nodded and saluted their new Princeps Senioris.

Agathe watched the foetal outline of Cavalerio twitch in the blood-flecked jelly of his amniotic tank. Could he hear what his warriors were saying about him?

She hoped not.

He had already suffered the pain of losing his engine. How devastating would it be to lose his Legio?

DALIA FELT AN icy hand clamp down on her heart at the sight of Rho-mu 31.

Her perceptions seemed to contract to a bubble of warped reality, where the world around her ceased to flow. The motion of people, the sound of the vox-system and the crackle of electricity, and the actinic reek of ozone were all held in stasis, while her personal experience spiked like an arrhythmic heartbeat.

She could feel the panic in her companions, and fought to control her breathing.

Rho-mu 31 stood immobile in front of her, his robes bright red and his body carrying the strange aroma of spoiled meat that always seemed to attend the Protectors. Silver gleamed in the shadows of his cloak where augmetic implants emerged from his flesh.

'Oh,' she managed. 'Hello.'

As far as excuses or opening gambits went, it was fairly poor.

The noise of the transit station swelled in her ears, and suddenly all she could hear was the rustle of a hundred conversations and the shuffle of a thousand feet.

'Rho-mu 31,' she said, struggling to think of something more meaningful to say and failing miserably. She felt herself looking at her feet like a naughty child.

Zouche came to her rescue, standing in front of her and craning his neck to look up at the heavily muscled and augmented Mechanicum warrior.

'Rho-mu 31 is it?' he said. 'Good to see you. We... ah... we were just taking the transit to the port facilities. Got some supplies coming in from the Jovian shipyards.'

'The port facilities?' asked Rho-mu 31.

'That's right,' added Caxton. 'We wanted to make sure they were the right ones, you know, save the stevedores the bother of getting them here and finding out they were the wrong ones. It would add days to our work, and frankly we don't have days to lose.'

Dalia closed her eyes, unable to meet Rho-mu 31's gaze as her companions told their terrible, unbelievable lies. She imagined the ground opening up and plunging her deep into the magma, or that an approaching maglev might fly from the rails in a cataclysmic crash.

Anything would be preferable to this excruciating feeling.

Severine joined with the others in weaving the deception, the lie growing ever more convoluted and drawing in elements and characters – many of whom she was certain didn't exist – until Dalia could stand it no longer.

'Enough!' she yelled. 'Throne, don't you realise how stupid this all sounds?'

A few heads turned at her use of the Throne as an oath, but most people kept their heads down, knowing it was not wise to attract the attention of a Mechanicum Protector unless you really had to.

The others fell silent, studiously examining the floor as though it held the key to their salvation. Dalia drew herself up to her full height, which wasn't much compared to Rho-mu 31, and looked into the glowing green lights behind his bronze mask.

'We're not going to the port,' she said. 'We're going to the Noctis Labyrinthus.'

She heard the collective intake of breath from the others and pressed on, knowing she had no choice but to tell Rho-mu 31 the truth.

'Why would you want to go to such a benighted place?' asked Rho-mu 31. 'Nothing good can come of it. Only the Cult of the Dragon is said to dwell within the Labyrinth of Night.'

'The Cult of the Dragon?' asked Dalia, her excitement piqued. 'I've never heard of it.'

'Few have,' said Rho-mu 31. 'It was an obscure sect of madmen. Regrettably only one of many on Mars.'

'But who are they?'

'When the adepts who attempted to set up forges within the Noctis Labyrinthus abandoned their workings, not everyone left with them. A few deluded souls remained behind.'

A rush of air filled the transit station. A mag-lev train was approaching.

'I need to go there,' said Dalia. 'I need to go there now.'

'Why?'

'I don't exactly know, but there's something important there, I can feel it.'

'There is nothing there but darkness,' said Rho-mu 31, placing a meaty hand on Dalia's shoulder. 'Are you truly sure of the path you are on?'

Dalia shuddered at Rho-mu 31's mention of the darkness, but slowly the implications of his words emerged from behind her fear. 'Wait a minute... you're not going to stop me?'

'I am not,' said Rho-mu 31. 'And if you insist on making this journey, I have no choice but to accompany you.'

'Accompany us?' asked Zouche. 'Now why would you do a thing like that and not drag us back to Adept Zeth? You have to know we're travelling without her sanction.'

'Be quiet, Zouche!' said Severine.

Rho-mu 31 nodded. 'I am aware of that, but Adept Zeth tasked me with keeping Dalia Cythera safe. She said nothing about restricting her movements.'

'I don't understand,' said Dalia as the glowing stablights of a mag-lev emerged from the arched tunnel and the smell of ozone grew stronger.

'Mars is in crisis, Dalia Cythera,' said Rho-mu 31. 'Disaster strikes at every turn, and though Adept Zeth's forge escaped the worst of it, our beloved planet is on the verge of slipping into chaos.'

'Chaos? What are you talking about?' asked Caxton. 'We heard some rumours of accidents, but nothing like as serious as you're making out.'

'Whatever you have heard, I can assure you the reality is far worse than you can possibly imagine,' said

Rho-mu 31. 'The terror of Old Night threatens to descend upon us once more, and I believe Dalia may hold the key to our salvation.'

'Me? No... I told you before that I'm nobody,' said Dalia, unwilling to be saddled with such responsibility.

'You are wrong, Dalia,' stated Rho-mu 31 as the mag-lev came to a halt behind her. 'You have an innate understanding of technology, but I believe what makes you special is the ability to intuit things that others would not. If you think there is something within the Noctis Labyrinthus of importance, then I am willing to put my faith in you.'

'I thought you didn't believe in faith?'

'I don't. I believe in you.'

Dalia smiled. 'Thank you,' she said.

'I do not require your thanks,' replied Rho-mu 31. 'I am a Protector. I am *your* Protector. That is my purpose.'

'I thank you anyway.'

Caxton patted Dalia on the shoulder. 'Well, if we're going to go, we should probably get on this mag-lev?'

Dalia nodded and looked up at her Protector.

'After you,' said Rho-mu 31.

ADEPT ZETH STOOD in the highest tower of her forge, the noospheric halo above her head twitching with information. She sorted through a number of active feeds with her MIU. None of them made for easy reading.

Most were streaming from the forges of Fabricator Locum Kane and Ipluvien Maximal, but there were others coming in from isolated adepts that had come through the Death of Innocence and were desperately seeking friendly voices.

Beside her, one of her underlings waited uncomfortably for the adept to speak.

'Be at ease,' said Zeth. 'Rho-mu 31 is with them now.'

'They're safe?'

Zeth shrugged and glanced down at the woman beside her. 'As much as anyone can be said to be safe on Mars just now.'

'And he'll keep them from harm?'

'That is his purpose,' agreed Zeth. 'Though a journey to the Noctis Labyrinthus is not without peril. They will pass close to Mondus Gamma, the domain of Lukas Chrom, and he is a pawn of the Fabricator General.'

'That's bad, isn't it?'

'Yes, I rather suspect it is,' said Zeth, thinking of what Kane had told her. 'It is imperative that no one else should learn of Dalia's whereabouts.'

'Of course.'

'Delete all records of her destination from your memory coils and supply me with a record of deletion. Understood?'

'Yes.'

Zeth waited for a few seconds until the deletion record arrived in her noosphere before speaking again.

'You should return to your duties,' she said. 'Ambassador Melgator will be arriving soon from Olympus Mons and I think it would be better if you were elsewhere.'

'As you wish,' said Mellicin.

OF ALL THE visitors ever to climb the steps to her forge, Ambassador Melgator was one of the least welcome. Koriel Zeth watched the man approach, his thin body wrapped in a dark, ermine-trimmed robe, his few overt augmetics concealed beneath a hood of dark velvet. Though Kelbor-Hal's messenger was still some distance away, Zeth's enhanced vision saw that the ambassador had changed since last she had seen him.

His skin was waxen and unhealthy, yet his eyes remained dark pools of sinister purpose like a bearer of bad news eager to spread his misery. However, Melgator's presence, as unwelcome and unlooked for as it was, did not worry her so much as that of his companion.

Sheathed in an all-enclosing bodyglove of a gleaming synthetic material that rippled like blood across her skin, a slender female figure followed a discreet distance behind the ambassador.

Zeth needed no help from the noosphere to recognise what this woman was.

<Is that what I think it is?> asked Magos Polk in a soft cant of binary. Zeth could read her apprenta's disquiet in the formulation of his numerics and hoped her own biometrics did not betray her unease so obviously.

'Yes,' she said. 'Do not speak to her if you can avoid it.'

'Have no worries about that,' promised Polk. 'Not if my life depended on it.'

'Let us hope it does not come to that, Polk,' said Zeth. 'But her presence here cannot be a good thing.'

'Surely the Fabricator General has merely despatched her as a guard for the ambassador after all the troubles we have had,' said Polk, his tone begging for reassurance.

'Perhaps, but I doubt it. To act merely as a bodyguard would be seen as beneath the skills of a tech-priest assassin.'

'Then why is she here?'

Zeth felt her irritation at Polk's questions grow, but forced it down. 'I expect we shall find out soon enough,' she said. This meeting with Kelbor-Hal's lackey would need a clear head and Zeth could not afford to be distracted by Polk's fear, even though it mirrored her own.

The tech-priest assassins were a body of mysterious and aloof killers who had existed since the settling of Mars in the distant past. A law unto themselves, they answered to no authority save that of unknown masters said to dwell in the shadows of the Cydonia Mensae.

Melgator and his accomplice reached the plinth beneath the great portico, and Zeth wondered if this was how she was going to die, struck down by an assassin's blade, her vital fluids pouring down the steps of her forge.

Melgator smiled, though Zeth found nothing reassuring in its reptilian insincerity. The ambassador and his companion came towards her, passing into the splayed shadows of the piston columns and golden portico. Melgator moved with the clicking gait of one whose lower limbs were augmetic, while the assassin flowed across the milky white marble of the floor as though on ice.

Zeth saw that the assassin's legs were long and multi-jointed, fused together just above the ankles by a spar of metal, below which her legs ended not in feet, but in a complex series of magno-gravitic thrusters that skimmed her along just off the ground. Her athletic form was beautifully deadly, honed to perfect physicality by a rigorous regime of physical exercise, gene-manipulation and surgical augmentation.

Melgator stopped before Zeth and bowed deeply, his arms spread wide.

'Adept Zeth,' he began. 'It is a pleasure to once again visit your unique forge.'

'You are welcome, Ambassador Melgator,' said Zeth. 'This is my magos-apprenta, Adept Polk.'

She left her words hanging and Melgator read the pause expertly. He turned towards his companion, who wore a facemask fashioned in the form of a grinning crimson skull with a horn of gleaming metal jutting from its chin.

'This is my… associate, Remiare,' said Melgator.

Zeth nodded towards Remiare and the assassin inclined her head a fraction in acknowledgement. Zeth took a second to study the hardwired targeting apparatus grafted to Remiare's mask and the long snake-like sensor tendrils that swam in the air from the rear portion of her cranium.

'And what brings you to my forge?' asked Zeth, turning and leading Melgator towards the wall of bronze doors that led within. Polk dropped back to stand at her right shoulder, while Melgator and Remiare fell in smoothly to her left.

'I come to you as a great shadow hangs over our beloved planet, Adept Zeth. Disaster strikes Mars at every turn and in times of such trouble friends should stand shoulder to shoulder.'

'Indeed,' replied Zeth as they passed into the forge and along its silver-skinned arterial halls. 'We have suffered greatly and much has been lost that can never be recovered.'

'Alas, you speak the truth,' said Melgator, and Zeth could barely keep the contempt she felt for his false concern from her field auras. 'Thus it is ever more imperative that friends should acknowledge one another and do whatever is necessary to aid one another.'

Zeth did not answer Melgator's leading comment and turned into Aetna's Processional, a passageway of ouslite walls and burning braziers that led into a high-ceilinged chamber at the heart of Adept Zeth's forge.

Formed from the intertwining of twisted columns of silver and gold, the web-like walls rose to a tapered point above the centre of the chamber. Gracefully curved sheets of burnished steel and crystal rippled overhead, winding through the columns to form an impossibly beautiful latticework roof, like glittering shards of ice frozen in the moment of shattering. The toxic skies of Mars were visible through the gaps in the columns as angled slivers of cadmium, hazed by the void shielding that surrounded the highest peak of the forge.

Beneath the apex of the roof, a wide shaft descended into the depths of the forge and a fiery orange glow billowed upwards from the heart of the magma far below. Searing heat and waves of energising power rippled the air over the shaft as Melgator made appropriately impressed noises.

Receptors like thin, slitted gills opened in the folds of his neck as Melgator partook of the invisible currents of drifting electricity.

Remiare paid the hot majesty of the space no mind, her own energy receptors kept hidden beneath her bodyglove, and Zeth felt as though the assassin's attention was focused firmly on the cardinal weak points of her bronze armour. She shared a glance with Magos Polk, who assumed a deferential pose beside her with his hand tucked into the sleeves of his robe.

'It has been too long since I stood within the Chamber of Vesta,' said Melgator. 'Your current is exquisite. I can almost feel the fire of the red planet within me.'

'It has always been here,' pointed out Zeth. 'Those who are friends to the Magma City are always welcome to take sustenance within its walls.'

'Then I should hope you count the Fabricator General amongst such friends.'

'Why should I not?' asked Zeth. 'Kelbor-Hal has never expressed his displeasure with me. He continues the great work of the Mechanicum, does he not?'

'Indeed he does,' said Melgator quickly. 'And he sends me to you in the spirit of peace in these dark days of loss and death to assure you of his continued goodwill.'

'The spirit of peace,' said Zeth, walking around the shaft in the centre of the chamber. Polk made to follow her, but she waved him away. The heat was intense and she could feel her organic portions begin to sweat. 'Is that why you come to me in the company of one of the Sisters of Cydonia?'

'These are troubled times, Adept Zeth,' said Melgator.

'You said that already.'

'I am aware of that, but it is a point I cannot make strongly enough,' replied Melgator. 'An enemy strikes at us, weakens our forges, and only a fool dares to travel without precautions.'

'An assassin is a precaution?' asked Zeth, turning towards Remiare. 'Has the Cydonian Sisterhood fallen so far that they are now mere bodyguards?'

The assassin cocked her head to one side, like a bird of prey regarding a helpless morsel, and though glistening fabric obscured her expression, Zeth felt an acute tremor along the adamantium curve of her spine.

'I can taste your fear of me,' said Remiare softly, her eyes like black marbles behind the horned death mask. 'Yet still you bait me with barbed words. Why would you do this when you know I can kill you?'

Zeth controlled her breathing and metabolic rate with a measured release of glanded stimms as Melgator said, 'There will be no killing, Remiare. This is a mission of renewed friendship in a time when allies are to be more prized than pure-streaming data.'

Melgator turned to Zeth, his hands held out before him. 'Yes, I bring a warrior to your forge, but it is only because our very way of existence is threatened that I come so accompanied.'

'Threatened by whom? Does the Fabricator General know who unleashed the corrupt code into the Martian systems.'

'He does not know for certain, but he has strong suspicions,' replied Melgator.

'Any you would care to divulge?'

Melgator began circling the fire shaft towards Zeth, lacing his hands behind his back as he walked.

'Perhaps,' nodded Melgator. 'But may I first ask how the Magma City escaped the devastation so many other, less fortunate, forges suffered?'

Zeth hesitated, unsure of how much Melgator knew and how much he only suspected. In truth, she wasn't entirely sure why her forge had been spared, though she had her suspicions, none of which she was comfortable sharing with a minion of the Fabricator General.

In the end she decided on a partial truth. 'I believe the singular nature of the noosphere prevented the debased code from entering my systems,' she said.

'And yet the forges of Ipluvien Maximal and Fabricator Locum Kane suffered in the attack. They have recently upgraded their information networks to the noosphere, have they not? So perhaps there is some other reason you were spared?

<If there is, I am not certain what it was,> said Zeth, hoping Melgator would read the honesty in her cant and not the evasion of her words. She prayed that Polk's aegis barriers in his noospheric aura were in place.

'Then might it be the latest endeavour taking shape within your Inner Forge? It has not gone unnoticed that your newest creation, whatever it is, requires lowly transcribers sequestered from Terra and a great many psykers secretly brought down from the Black Ships.'

'How can you think you know what goes on within my inner forge?' asked Zeth, shaken to the core of her being that Melgator was aware of such things.

Melgator laughed. 'Come now, Adept Zeth. You think the workings of any adept on Mars are truly hidden? Information is woven into every passage of electrons across the surface of the red planet and you know how the spirits of machines love to share their secrets.'

'The workings of my forge are my own to know, Melgator,' snapped Zeth. 'As I said, I believe that it was my adoption of the noosphere that saved my forge from destruction.'

Melgator smiled ruefully. 'Very well, I will accept that. Perhaps if you had freely shared the technology of the noosphere with your fellow adepts then Mars might have been spared the horror of the Death of Innocence.'

'Perhaps if the Fabricator General had put more faith in the noosphere when I presented it to him, that might have been the case,' countered Zeth.

Melgator smiled, conceding the point. 'May I speak frankly, Adept Zeth?'

'Of course, the Chamber of Vesta is a place of honest discourse.'

'Then I will be blunt.' said Melgator. 'My master believes he knows the source of the attack on our infrastructure and he seeks to rally all true sons and daughters of Ares to the defence of Mars.'

'The defence of Mars?' asked Zeth, nonplussed. 'Defence against whom?'

'Against Terra.'

Zeth was stunned. Of all the answers she had expected Melgator to give, this had not been amongst them. She tried to cover her surprise, by turning and looking out over the Martian landscape. The sky was turning from blue to purple, heavy, toxin-laden clouds sparking with lightning over the distant forge of Mondus Gamma.

'Terra,' she said, slowly as though tasting the word for the first time.

'Terra,' repeated Melgator. 'Now that the Great Crusade is almost at an end, the Emperor desires to end his union with Mars and take our world for his own.'

'Kelbor-Hal thinks the *Emperor* attacked us?' asked Zeth, spinning to face Melgator. 'Do you realise how insane that sounds?'

Melgator approached her with a pleading look. 'Is it insane to want to hold on to what we have built here over the millennia, Adept Zeth? Is it insanity to suspect that a man who has all but conquered the entire galaxy should allow one world among millions to remain aloof from his empire? No, the attack on our world's information systems was but the first strike in breaking the Treaty of Olympus and bringing the Mechanicum to heel.'

Zeth laughed in his face. 'I see now why you brought this assassin with you, Melgator – in case I should call you traitor and have you killed.'

Melgator's stance changed from one of supplication to one of aggression in an instant and hands that had once been outstretched towards her now dropped to his sides.

'You would do well to choose your next words carefully, Adept Zeth.'

'Why would that be? Will you have Remiare here kill me if you don't like them?'

'No,' said Melgator. 'I would not be so foolish as to anger the Omnissiah by murdering an adept of Mars in her own forge.'

'The Omnissiah?' spat Zeth. 'You speak of the Emperor breaking faith with the Mechanicum and in the next breath use him as a reason not to murder me?'

'I speak of the Omnissiah as an aspect of the Machine-God yet to manifest, not the Emperor.'

'Most believe them to be one and the same.'

'But not you?'

'You already know what I believe,' said Zeth, angered beyond caution. 'There *is* no Machine-God. Technology is science and reason, not superstition and blind faith. It's what I've always believed and it's what I still believe. Now if you're not going to kill me, get out of my forge!'

'Are you sure about this, Zeth?' asked Melgator. 'Turning your back on the Fabricator General will have dire consequences.'

'Is that a threat?'

'A threat? No, merely a reiteration that we live in dangerous times and that the friendship of powerful allies would be no bad thing in the days ahead.'

'Friendship? Kelbor-Hal asks me to side with him against Terra!' barked Zeth. 'What manner of friend would ask such a thing?'

Melgator slid his hands into the sleeves of his robes. 'The kind that knows what is best for Mars.'

MELGATOR SLOWLY DESCENDED the steps of Zeth's forge, savouring the memory of Adept Zeth's admission of her disbelief in the Machine-God. It was all the excuse the Fabricator General needed to seize the Magma City and learn all the secrets of her forge, and Zeth had handed it to them on a plate.

He wiped a hand across his brow. Sweat beaded on his forehead in the intolerably dry heat that wrapped the city like a shroud. Melgator had travelled far and wide in his role as ambassador, but this place had to rank as one of the most inhospitable on Mars.

The sooner it was plundered and laid to waste the better.

Beside him, Remiare hovered effortlessly above the steps, her masked face unreadable in the orange-lit gloom.

'Zeth knows why she escaped the scrapcode's attack,' said Melgator. 'Or at least she suspects she knows.'

'Of course,' answered Remiare. 'Her apprenta was bleeding fear and information from his noospheric aura. I have stored everything I could access from his files on Zeth's work in my memory coils, and I will exload them to the Fabricator General's logic engines upon our return to Olympus Mons.'

'You can lift data from the noosphere? I didn't know that,' said Melgator, more than a little unnerved.

'Of course, the secrets of the noosphere are well known to the Sisters of Cydonia. As are the means to manipulate the mind structure beyond it.'

'What about his aegis barrier?'

'Simplicity itself to overcome.'

'Did he notice your presence?' asked Melgator.

'No, but I decided to fuse the portions of his mind that would have remembered anyway.'

'If he did not detect your intrusion, why the need to burn out his memory synapses?'

Remiare turned her deathly face towards him, and Melgator was reminded that the assassins of Cydonia did not take kindly to questions.

'Because I enjoy making living things suffer,' said Remiare. 'Zeth's apprenta will no longer be able to form memories that last. His usefulness as an individual is at an end.'

Melgator swallowed, warier than ever of the monstrous creature beside him.

At last he reached the bottom of the steps, where a skimmer palanquin of bronze and polished timber panels stood ready to carry him to the landing platform upon which his transport waited.

'So how *did* Zeth defeat the scrapcode attack?'

The black, soulless marbles of Remiare's eyes flickered as she retrieved and sorted the data. 'I do not know and nor does Zeth, not completely, though the apprenta was of the opinion that a female named Dalia Cythera was responsible.'

'The transcriber Zeth brought from Terra? She did it?'

'So it would seem.'

'Then we need to eliminate her as soon as possible,' said Melgator. 'Where is she?'

'Unknown. Her biometrics are not registered in the Martian database.'

'She was working in Zeth's forge and she's not even Cult Mechanicum?'

'Apparently not.'

'Ah, Zeth, you're almost making it too easy for us,' chuckled Melgator. 'Can you track this Dalia Cythera?'

'I can, but it will be easier just to take the information from the people she knows,' said Remiare. 'Archived work dockets list her as being assigned to a team of four individuals: Zouche Chahaya, Severine Delmer, Mellicin Oster and Caxton Torgau. Only Mellicin Oster is still within the Magma City.'

'Where?'

'Within Arsia Mons sub-hive Epsilon-Aleph-Ultima,' said Remiare. 'Fiftieth floor, shutter seventeen. Off shift until 07:46 tomorrow morning.'

'Find her,' hissed Melgator. 'Learn everything she knows.'

* * *

THE MAG-LEV WAS full, every seat taken, but the threatening presence of Rho-mu 31 assured them a private cabin, though it was still cramped with the five of them wedged in tight. Rho-mu 31 stood at the door to their cabin, his weapon stave held tight across his chest, leaving the four seats for Zouche, Dalia, Severine and Caxton.

Zouche and Severine sat across from her, and Caxton lay with his head on her shoulder, snoring softly. The pale, artificial light from the window gleamed from his tonsure's scalp, and Dalia smiled as she leaned back against the faux leather chair. She looked out over the Martian landscape as the rest of her companions slept. Even Rho-mu 31 was resting, the glow of his eyes dimmed as he conserved power, though his internal auspex was still vigilant.

Beyond the energy shielded glass, undulant plains stretched off into the distance, the grey emptiness of the polluted wastelands somehow beautiful to Dalia. Unfinished or abandoned mag-lev lines stretched off into invisibility in long rows of sun-bleached concrete T's, and the sight brought a forlorn ache to Dalia's chest.

It had been years since she had seen a landscape as vast as this, and even though it was bleak and inhospitable, it was wide open and the heavens above held the landscape protectively close to them. Bands of pollutants striped the sky like sedimentary rock, and columns of light pierced the darkness as ships broke atmosphere.

A shiver travelled the length of Dalia's spine as she felt the aching loneliness that had become part of her soul since her connection with the thing beneath the Noctis Labyrinthus. The desolate emptiness outside was so endless that Dalia could easily imagine Mars to be dead, a world utterly scoured of life and abandoned for all eternity.

She was tired, but couldn't sleep. The black emptiness behind her eyes lurked in the back of her mind like a hidden predator that would strike the instant she allowed the shadows to cloak it.

'Can't sleep, eh?' asked Zouche, and Dalia looked up. She had thought him to be asleep.

'No,' agreed Dalia, keeping her voice low. 'A lot on my mind.'

Zouche nodded and ran a hand over his shaven scalp. 'Understandable. We're out on a limb, Dalia. I just hope this journey turns out to be worth it.'

'I know it will, Zouche,' promised Dalia.

'What do you think we're going to find out there?'

'Honestly, I'm not sure. But whatever it is, I know it's in pain. It's been trapped in the darkness for such a long time and it's suffering. We have to find it.'

'And what happens when we do?'

'What do you mean?'

'When we find this thing, this... dragon. Are you thinking about freeing it?'

'I think we have to,' said Dalia. 'Nothing deserves to suffer like it's suffering.'

'I hope you're right,' said Zouche.

'You think I'm wrong to want to help?'

'Not necessarily,' said Zouche, 'but what if this thing is *meant* to suffer? After all, we don't know for sure who put it there, so perhaps they had a very good reason to do so? We don't know what it is, so maybe whatever it is *should* be left in the darkness forever.'

'I don't believe that,' said Dalia. 'Nothing deserves to suffer forever.'

'Some things do,' said Zouche, his voice little more than a hushed whisper.

'What, Zouche?' demanded Dalia. 'Tell me who or what deserves to suffer forever?'

Zouche met her stare. She could see that it was taking all his control to maintain his composure and she wondered what door she'd opened with her question. He sat in silence for a moment, then said, 'Back before people lived freely on Nusa Kambangan, it was once a prison, a hellish place where the worst of the worst were locked up – murderers, clone-surgeons, rapists, gene-thieves and serial killers. And tyrants.'

'Tyrants?'

'Oh, yes indeed,' said Zouche, and Dalia thought she detected more than a hint of bitter pride in his voice. 'Cardinal Tang himself was held there.'

'Tang? The Ethnarch?'

'The very same,' nodded Zouche. 'When his last bastion fell, he was taken in chains to Nusa Kambangan, though he was only there a few days. Word got out of who he was and another prisoner cut his throat. Though if you ask me, he got off lightly.'

'Having your throat cut is getting off lightly?' asked Dalia, horrified by Zouche's coldness.

'After what Tang did? Absolutely,' said Zouche. 'After all the bloody pogroms, death camps and genocides, you think his suffering should have ended swiftly? Tang deserved to rot in the deepest, darkest hole of Terra, condemned to suffer the same torments and agonies he inflicted on his victims. In the end, his suffering was much quicker than the millions he put to death during his reign. So, yes, I make no apology for thinking he got off lightly. Trust me, Dalia, there are some that deserve to be left in the darkness to pay for their crimes for all eternity.'

Tears rolled down Zouche's cheeks as he spoke, and Dalia felt a wave of sorrow as she felt a measure of his pain, even though she didn't fully understand it.

'My parents died in one of Tang's camps,' continued Zouche, wiping the tears away with the sleeve of his robe.

'For the crime of falling in love when they were genetically assigned to other partners. They kept their relationship a secret, but when I was born it was obvious to everyone they'd produced an inferior offspring and they were hauled off to Tang's death camp on Roon Island.'

'Oh, Zouche, that's terrible,' said Dalia. 'I'm so sorry. I didn't know.'

Zouche shrugged and stared beyond the glass of the compartment. 'How could you? But it doesn't matter. Tang's dead and the Emperor guides us now. People like Tang won't ever rise again now that the Imperium's in his hands.'

'You're not inferior,' said Dalia, cutting across his train of words.

'What?' he said, looking back at her.

'I said you're not inferior,' repeated Dalia. 'You might think you are because you look different to the rest of us, but you're not. You're a brilliant engineer and a loyal friend. I'm glad you're with me, Zouche. I really am.'

He smiled and nodded. 'I know you are and I'm grateful for that, but I know what I am. You're a good girl, Dalia, so I'd be obliged if you didn't mention this to anyone, you understand?'

'Of course,' said Dalia. 'I won't say a word. I think the rest are going to sleep all the way there, anyway.'

'Quite probably,' agreed Zouche, a discreetly extended mechadendrite linking with the port in the compartment's wall. Flickering light ghosted behind his eyelids as he linked with the mag-lev's onboard logic-engine. It was easy to forget that the Mechanicum had substantially modified Zouche, for most of his augmetics were subtle, and he was reticent about openly displaying them to one not of the Cult Mechanicum. 'It's going to take us two days to reach the point nearest the Noctis Labyrinthus, an outlying hub of Mondus Gamma in the northern Syrian sub-fabriks.'

'Two days? Why so long?'

'This is a supply train,' explained Zouche. 'We're going to pass through a lot of the borderland townships on the edge of the pallidus. According to the onboard timetable, we're about to reach Ash Border, then we'll pass through Dune Town, Crater Edge and Red Gorge before we begin the descent to the Syria Planum and Mondus Gamma.'

'Not big on originality when it comes to their settlement names, are they?' observed Dalia.

'Not really, I suppose they just name it as they see it,' said Zouche. 'When you live out on the edge of civilisation, there's a virtue in simplicity.'

'I think there's a virtue in that wherever you are,' said Dalia.

THE HAB WAS warm, but then it was always warm. Hot air rising from the magma lagoon rolled up the flanks of the volcano in dry, parching waves to leach the moisture from the air like a giant dehumidifier.

Mellicin lay on her bed, with one hand thrown over her forehead. Sweat gathered in the spoons of her collarbones and she felt uncomfortably sticky and hot. The atomiser was turned on, but might as well have been switched off for all the difference it was making. She rolled onto her side, unable to sleep and unable to stop thinking of what might be happening to Dalia and the others.

She told herself it wasn't guilt, but only half-believed it.

Zeth had placed her with Dalia with the express purpose of passing on her impressions and insights into the young transcriber's mind, and that was exactly what she had done. There had been no betrayal, no breach of trust and certainly no disloyalty.

The only betrayal would have been if she had failed in her duty to her mistress.

Why, then, did she feel so bad about telling Adept
Zeth of Dalia's plans?

Mellicin knew *exactly* why she felt bad.

In the weeks she had worked with Dalia Cythera, Mellicin had rediscovered the joy of working on the frontiers
of technology. Together they had discovered new and
wondrous things, devices and theoretical science that
they had gone on to prove valid. How long had it been
since she, or indeed anyone in the Mechanicum, had
done that? True, Adept Zeth was forever pushing the
boundaries of what was known and accepted, but she
was a tiny cog in a larger machine and there was only so
much she dared risk.

The Mechanicum was old and unforgiving with those
who disobeyed its strictures.

They had been gone less than a day and already she
missed them. She wished she knew where they were so
she could have tapped into the Martian networks to follow their progress, but she had wiped Dalia's destination
from her memory coils.

Right now, they could be anywhere, en route to the far
side of the planet for all she knew.

Mellicin had got used to their foibles, strengths and
blind spots. She had nurtured them, blended them
together until they were a team, working more efficiently
and more enthusiastically than any of them had ever
worked before.

Now they were off making good use of that mentoring
and she was left behind.

She swung her legs out of bed and ran a hand through
her hair. It was matted and sweaty, and no amount of
time in the sonic shower would make it feel clean. She
padded softly from the bed alcove and made her way to
the kitchenette to fix a pot of caffeine. If she wasn't going
to get any sleep, she might as well use the time produc-
tively.

She yawned as the heating ring fired the pot, wiping sweat from her brow as the pot bubbled and hissed. She poured a cup and sat in the dining nook within the polarised glass bay that looked out over the surface of the red planet.

This high up, Mellicin was above the distorting fumes that filmed the lower level windows with grime and pyroclastic deposits. Far below her, the Magma City blazed with light, an ocean of glowing industry in a desert of industrial wasteland. Silver trails of mag-levs spun out from the city, travelling to all parts of Mars, but beyond them the planet was shrouded in banks of dust and polluted fogs.

Mellicin put down her cup and leaned her forehead on the hot glass. Lights moved in the city, and glittering transits ferried cargo and supplies to the port facilities.

'Wherever you are, Dalia, I wish you well,' she whispered, feeling very alone.

She frowned as she realised she *wasn't* alone.

Her biometric surveyors were reading another life form in her hab.

'I was wondering when you would notice me,' said a voice from the shadows.

Mellicin jumped at the sound, looking up in frozen surprise as a lithe, sensual woman glided from the darkness. She was clad in a skin-tight red bodyglove and a pair of finely-wrought pistols were sheathed at her hips.

Mellicin covered her surprise and said, 'I knew you were there, I was just waiting to see when you would announce yourself.'

'A lie, but one necessary for you to feel you are still in control,' said the woman.

'Who are you, and what are you doing in my hab?' asked Mellicin, still too surprised to feel anything but annoyance.

'My name is irrelevant, because soon you won't remember it,' said the woman, and as she moved into the light,

Mellicin saw the golden death mask she wore. 'But for the record, it is Remiare.'

Mellicin's annoyance turned to fear as she realised what this woman was. 'That's half my question answered.'

Remiare cocked her head to one side and said, 'You still think you have a measure of control, don't you?'

'What do you want?' asked Mellicin, pushing herself further into the dining nook.

'You know what I want.'

'No, actually,' said Mellicin, 'I don't.'

'Then I shall tell you,' said Remiare. 'I want you to tell me the whereabouts and destination of Dalia Cythera.'

Mellicin furrowed her brow, as if in thought, and activated her silent alarm. Adept Zeth would now be aware of her plight and a squad of Mechanicum Protectors would soon be despatched to her rescue. All she had to do was stall.

'Dalia?' she said at last. 'Why do you want to know about her?'

'No more questions,' said Remiare. 'Tell me what I want to know and I promise you won't suffer.'

'I can't,' said Mellicin. 'Even if I wanted to. I might have known what you want, but I don't remember anymore.'

'You're lying.'

'I'm not. Adept Zeth had me erase any knowledge of where Dalia was going from my memory coils.'

She regretted her smug tone instantly as Remiare ghosted closer and Mellicin saw the red light of the magma lagoon reflected on her death mask. Her face was the visage of something vile and terrible, a leering monster from her darkest nightmares. Even amid her fear, she recognised the exquisite work of the assassin's gravitic thrusters, the sinuous form of a killer bred and trained from birth.

'Then that's very bad news for you.'

'And why's that?' asked Mellicin, trying to muster some bravado.

'Because nothing is ever really erased, Mellicin,' said Remiare as a silver spike extended from her forefinger.

Despite the heat in the small dwelling hab, Mellicin suddenly felt very cold indeed as she recognised it as a data spike.

'Why do you want to find Dalia?' asked Mellicin, the words coming out in a fear-induced rush. 'I mean, she's nothing, just a transcriber from Terra. All she did was take notes of our work. Really, why do you want her?'

Remiare's head darted forward like a feeding bird's and she laughed, the sound soulless and dead. 'You are trying to keep me talking because you believe help is on its way, but it isn't. No one is coming, Mellicin. I am the only one hearing that insultingly simple silent alarm your implants are broadcasting.'

'I'm telling you, I erased the things you're looking for!'

'You may have erased your memory coils, but the soft meat beneath remembers,' said Remiare while softly wagging her finger. 'The Mechanicum never deletes anything.'

Mellicin glanced down at her cup of caffeine and wondered if she would be quick enough to throw it in the assassin's face. That question was answered a moment later. One second, the red-clad woman was standing before her, the next she was seated next to her, pressing her against the warm glass of her hab.

A hand with fingers like steel rods shot out and gripped her throat, tilting her head back.

'I don't know what you want!' screamed Mellicin as the assassin's data spike pressed against the augmetic orb that replaced her right eye.

'I'll find what I want,' promised Remiare. 'All I have to do is dig deep enough.'

HE HAD ALWAYS dreaded this, but now that it was his life, he knew there had been nothing to fear. In the world of flesh, his body had been aging and weakening, but here in this world of amniotic suspension he was all-powerful and all-conquering.

In a simulated engine war, Princeps Cavalerio fought and killed like a living metal god, bestriding the virtual arena like a colossus of battle. His enemies died: skitarii crushed underfoot, Reavers torn to pieces in the terrible, smashing hell of engine combat and Warlords blasted apart with weapons fire in murderous killing salvoes.

The world of flesh was over for Cavalerio. The world of metal was now his domain.

Liquid data spiralled around him, fed to him through receptors implanted beneath his skin, filling his sensory apparatus with information that would overwhelm the brains of those less augmented than he. Darts of light, each one carrying a welter of data, swirled around him like shoals of glowing fish as he ended yet another simulation as the victor.

Cavalerio was unrecognisable as the spare, limping mortal that had walked the surface of Mars. A man he had been, but a creation of the Mechanicum he was now. His pallid flesh floated in nutrient-rich jelly, hung from a multitude of cables that connected him to the world around him in ways too numerous to count.

Each day since his incarceration within the casket brought new attachments, new augmetics and new sensations. Only now did he realise how imperfect had his existence been as a mere mortal, confined to a mere five senses.

A thick inflexible cable pierced his spine between the lumbar vertebrae, while other, more delicate wires were plugged into his eye sockets. A forest of cables extruded from the rear of his cranial cavity that would link to the Manifold when he once again took charge of an engine. Both arms were encased in metal to his elbows, and both his feet had been amputated and replaced with haptic sheaths.

The transition had been difficult and not without setbacks, but his famulous, Agathe, had been with him every step of the way, soothing him, cajoling him and encouraging him to overcome every problem. Though initially hostile to the idea of a famulous, Cavalerio now appreciated how vital such a person was when you were confined to an amniotic tank.

The terrible, aching loss of *Victorix Magna* still haunted his nightmares, as he knew it would for the rest of his days. No princeps survived the death of his engine without psychological scarring, but with every simulated engagement, his warlike confidence grew stronger. Soon his ability to command an engine became faster and more efficient, until he knew he was better than he ever had been in his previous life.

As this latest simulation came to an end, the fury of battle and the exhilaration of connection faded from his consciousness with a sharp pang of regret. It wasn't the same as physically disengaging from an engine, but it was close, and he could already feel the hunger to go back in creeping at the edge of his psyche.

<How did I ever exist before this?> he canted in a soft sigh of binary.

His awareness of the world around him swam into focus as the images of battle faded like banished phantoms. Slowly the world of reality began to impose itself on his perception. Though Cavalerio no longer saw the world as he once had, the sensorium installed as part of his casket allowed him even greater acuity than ever before. He identified the biometrics of the two people standing in his casket chamber before any visual recognition was made.

He could see Agathe's physical form, which was short and slightly rounded, as well as reading her biometrics and the electrical field densities of her subtle augmetics. Her noospheric modifications flickered and tiny geysers of data light streamed above her head.

The second figure was Princeps Sharaq.

'My princeps?' said Agathe, startled by his sudden vocalisation. 'Do you require anything?'

'Hmmm? No, Agathe, I was just thinking aloud.'

'Congratulations on another successful engagement, Indias,' said Sharaq.

'Thank you, Kel,' said Cavalerio. 'Did you see how I took down the second Warlord?'

Sharaq smiled, and Cavalerio read the genuine pleasure his friend took in the accomplishment. 'I saw it, my princeps. Masterful.'

'I know,' said Cavalerio without arrogance. 'I am faster and more cohesive in my command than ever before. I merely think an order and the engine responds. Data streams into me straight from the Manifold, which increases my reaction and response times by an average of nine point seven per cent. That's more than the difference between life and death in an engine fight.'

'That's good to hear,' said Sharaq. 'You're adjusting well, then?'

'I am, Kel, I am. My days are full. I fight simulated engagements every day, though only Agathe watches me now. Between my battles and surgery, Princeps Kasim comes to check on my progress, and we share stories of our glorious Legio's history.'

'And the casket?' asked Sharaq. 'You don't miss... well, flesh?'

Cavalerio hesitated before answering. 'It was difficult,' he admitted at last. 'For the longest time I thought I would go mad in here, but Agathe has helped many a princeps adjust to his new life. And, as time went on, I began to understand that this was what I was destined for.'

'Destined?'

'Yes, Kel, destined. I don't know why I resisted immersion for all those years. I link with the Manifold and it's so much closer than it was before. When I commanded *Victorix Magna* I could feel what she felt, but it was borrowed sensation. Now I *am* the engine. This shouldn't be the last resort of an aging or injured princeps, this should be the standard method of command for all the bigger engines.'

'I think you might have a hard time convincing some of the die-hards of that.'

'Not if they knew what I know,' said Cavalerio. 'But what say we dispense with the small talk and discuss the real reason for your visit?'

Sharaq nodded, circling the tank with the awe of one in the presence of greatness, and Cavalerio read his unease in his increased heart rate and spiking alpha waves.

'It's all right, Kel,' said Cavalerio. 'You don't need to feel guilty. You did what you had to do and I would have been disappointed if you hadn't.'

Sharaq stopped his circling and knelt before the casket, placing his hand on the warm glass of the tank. Cavalerio floated to the front, his flesh marbled and glossy, his features all but obscured by the complex bionics that grafted him to the machinery of his life-support. Only an inch of toughened glass separated the two men, but an anatomy's worth of augmetics created a gulf between their humanity.

'I don't feel guilty,' said Sharaq. 'I know I did the right thing. You weren't fit to command the Legio then and, despite your progress, I still don't think you're ready. Soon, but not yet.'

'Then why are you here?'

'I need your help, Stormlord,' said Sharaq, 'and I need your experience. I fear I am not cut from the same cloth as you. Leadership is in your blood, but not in mine.'

'Then speak,' ordered Cavalerio. 'I may not be Princeps Senioris, but I am still your friend.'

The words were meant to comfort Sharaq, but only seemed to wound him. He looked over at Agathe and said, 'Perhaps we might speak privately, my princeps?'

'Agathe is my famulous and anything you have to say to me can be said in front of her.'

'Very well, Stormlord,' said Sharaq. 'You won't have failed to notice that you haven't been linked to any ports with outside access during your recovery. The medicae felt it would hinder your adjustment for you to be inloaded with an excess of data.'

'A decision that, with hindsight, I applaud,' said Cavalerio. 'So tell me, what's been happening beyond our fortress? Have Mortis been taken to task for their violation of our territory?'

Sharaq shook his head. 'No, my lord,' he said, 'they have not. The *Princeps Conciliatus* have been appraised of the facts and they have issued a summons, but both the Fabricator General and Princeps Camulos ignore it.'

'A *Conciliatus* summons and a rift between the Legios? Ignored? Madness!'

'All of Mars may well have gone mad, my princeps,' agreed Sharaq.

'What do you mean?'

Sharaq shared a look with Agathe and said, 'The situation on Mars has deteriorated almost to the point of open warfare. Disaster strikes at the Mechanicum from all sides and we are petitioned daily for our engines to walk.'

'Petitioned by whom?'

'I have received missives from no less than seventeen forges, all begging us to initiate an execution. With your permission, my princeps, I should like to inload your casket with the latest updates on the current tactical situation.'

'Of course, Kel,' said Cavalerio. 'Immediately.'

Sharaq said nothing and didn't appear to move, but Cavalerio felt a rush of data as his fellow princeps noospherically unlocked the feeds that were part of the Martian network and which fed directly into the smart liquid of his casket.

'Blood of the Omnissiah,' hissed Cavalerio as the data permeated his mind via informational osmosis. In an instant, he drank in the terrible events of the Death of Innocence caused by the hateful scrapcode, the spate of catastrophic machine failures and the rising tide of violence erupting all across the surface of Mars.

He saw bloodshed as forges went to war and old feuds were re-ignited. He saw opportunistic territorial grabs, spiteful acts of vengeance and hungry snatches for a rival's knowledge. The drums of battle were beating all over Mars, stirring the bellicose hearts of man, and spurring the looming presence of civil war ever closer.

It saddened him to realise that, a race apart though they might be, the Mechanicum were just as prone to human foibles as their unmodified brethren.

'And this scrapcode attack came just as Mortis walked on Ascraeus Mons?'

'We caught the first spurts of it, I think,' said Sharaq. 'It was fragmentary and dispersed, and Zeth's noospheric upgrades saved us from getting hit as hard as some others, but Legio Fortidus and Legio Agravides are gone. Their reactors went critical and took their entire fortress and a good chunk of the Erebus Montes with them.'

Cavalerio digested the information without comment, though it grieved him to think of two allied Legios lost to so ignominious a fate. He reviewed the data he'd been fed impassively, sifting through the morass of contradictory communiqués, orders, requests, petitions, demands and propaganda flying between the forges. Factions were already forming, fragile alliances drawn along the lines of the tired old Omnissiah schism.

Blurts of cant circled the planet, some demanding an end to the union of Mars and Terra, while others urged all Mars to cleave more tightly to the bosom of humanity's birth rock. Worse, much of it had gone off-world, spreading like a plague on departing ships or within astropathic visions cast across the void to the Mechanicum contingents accompanying the Expedition Fleets throughout the galaxy.

'What's all this talk of Horus Lupercal?' asked Cavalerio, reading the binary version of the first primarch's name time and time again. 'What does the Warmaster have to do with any of this?'

'We're not sure, my princeps,' said Sharaq. 'The factions advocating the split from Terra seem to be championing the Warmaster as their deliverer from the

Emperor. It's hard to make much sense of it, their code is so corrupt it's little more than binary screams of the Warmaster's name.'

'Has word of this reached Terra?'

'The inter-system vox is erratic, but Adept Maximal has apparently made intermittent contact with the Council of Terra.'

'And what do they make of all this?'

'It sounds like they're as confused as us, my princeps,' said Sharaq, taking a deep breath before continuing. 'Something bad has happened in the Istvaan system, something to do with the Astartes, but we can't get any hard facts.'

'But what of Mars?' pressed Cavalerio, 'what do they say about Mars?'

'The Mechanicum is told to quell the unrest or the Legions will do it for them.'

THE MAG-LEV MADE good time through the southern reaches of the Tharsis uplands, skirting the edge of the pallidus and passing through a number of storms of wind-blown particulate on its journey eastwards. Dalia found the sight of the billowing ash strangely uplifting, and spent hours watching the spiralling vortices streaming down the length of the carriages.

She watched the dust rolling on and on throughout the landscape and envied its freedom to roam, blown hither and thither without direction by the winds. Increasingly she felt as though her life was just like the mag-lev, travelling upon a fixed track, guided inexorably forward to an inevitable destination. The notion of free will and choice seemed alien and strange to her, as though her brain was merely responding to external stimuli and she had no choice but to obey.

They saw little of their fellow passengers during the journey, save for the occasional awkward passing in the corridors to and from the ablutions cubicles or food dispensers. Dalia recognised most of them as low-level adepts on errands for their masters, servitors on automatic reassignment or migrant labourers moving to another forge in the hope of securing work. Perhaps three hundred souls travelled with them, but no one paid them any mind, a fact for which Dalia was absurdly grateful.

The thrill of venturing beyond the boundaries of the forge had worn thin for their little group after a few hours, and they had fallen into the strange silence of travellers on a long journey with nothing to help pass the time. The prospect of seeing one of the otherworldly pallidus border towns had excited them, but even that had proven something of a letdown.

As the mag-lev had approached Ash Border, they all roused themselves to see what one of these frontier towns looked like, for none of them had ventured beyond the hives of Mars's more populated regions.

Though Rho-mu 31 claimed not to be expecting any trouble, Dalia read his threat auspex switch to active as they came within range of the settlement's network antenna. She didn't mention that fact to the others.

Ash Border had proved to be both exotic and slightly dull at the same time, with dusty ore silos, rusted salvage barns and tall drilling machinery dominating the skyline. But with the memory of a Mechanicum forge still bright in their minds, the minor industrial complex of Ash Border seemed small and underwhelming.

The inhabitants were sullen-faced men and women with weather-beaten faces and clothes scoured identical by coarse ash. They offered no welcome and disappeared back to their ramshackle dwellings as soon as their cargo was unloaded by a handful of archaic lifter-servitors.

Dune Town lived up to its name and proved to be no less prosaic, with even more outmoded servitors unloading the allocated inventory before the mag-lev set off towards Crater Edge.

By now they had been travelling for a day and a half. Tiredness was beginning to tell and sleep was hard to come by. Though the ride was smooth, the compartment's seats had been designed with functional practicality in mind rather than comfort.

None of them had been able to muster much enthusiasm to watch Zouche's projection of the view from the driver's compartment as they approached Crater Edge, but when the mag-lev halted at the raised dock, it was quickly evident that something was different.

The place was abandoned. The dwellings were empty and the streets deserted, but it was impossible to tell whether the inhabitants had been driven away or left of their own volition.

The mag-lev was on an automated schedule, so the mystery went unexplained, and the mining supplies allocated for the township remained in the snaking transport's holds as it pulled away.

No sooner had Crater Edge vanished into the dust and haze than Dalia felt a weight she hadn't even been aware of lift from her shoulders, as though some creeping sickness lingered around the township. The place had just felt... *wrong*.

Not the wrongness of disease or death, but a gurgling hiss of wet code-laughter she caught drifting on the airwaves.

Red Gorge was similarly deserted, the strange whispering code ghosting around it as well. Dalia caught Rho-mu 31 twitching as he heard it too: an insistent scratching that irritated the corners of the mind like an embedded flea.

She caught his eye as the mag-lev pulled away and they saw each other's awareness of the bad code on the air.

Rho-mu 31 shook his head and she took his meaning clearly enough.

Say nothing.

AT LAST THE mag-lev began the approach to the jagged line of peaks that separated the Tharsis uplands from the magnificent expanse of the Syria Planum. After a long, looping journey southwards, the mag-lev turned north to begin the slow climb over the upthrust spires of rock pushed up and over one another in an ongoing geological collision. The skies beyond the escarpment were dark and shot through with scarlet lightning, as though a great firestorm was brewing.

It had been a long journey and the sight of the two deserted townships had unsettled everyone. They had all heard tales of settlements abandoned when the ore or whatever had originally drawn the settlers there had dried up, but Red Gorge and Crater Edge hadn't felt abandoned, they had felt *empty*, as though the people there had just vanished. Gone in a heartbeat.

'Perhaps they were pressganged?' suggested Severine. 'I've heard of that. A forge master isn't going to meet his quota and sends his Protectors out into the wastelands to capture more people to work in their forges.'

'Don't be ridiculous,' said Caxton. 'That's just scare stories.'

'Is it?' challenged Severine. 'How do you know?'

'I just do, all right?'

'Oh, well I feel better already.'

'What do you say, Rho-mu 31?' asked Zouche in a tone of doom-laden theatrics. 'Has Adept Zeth ever sent you off to procure *slaves* to toil in her volcanic forge?'

'From time to time,' admitted the Protector.

That shut them all up.

'You're joking, right?' said Caxton. 'Tell me you're joking.'

'I am Mechanicum,' said Rho-mu 31. 'We never joke.'

Dalia looked into the green orbs of Rho-mu 31's eyes, and though they were devoid of anything resembling humanity, she saw the wry amusement written in his electrical field. She smiled at the horrified expressions on her friends' faces and turned away so as not to spoil Rho-mu 31's fun.

'That's… that's terrible,' said Severine.

'The Mechanicum uses slaves?' was Caxton's disgusted comment.

'I thought more of you, Rho-mu 31,' said Zouche. 'I thought more of Adept Zeth.'

When he judged the silence had gone on long enough, Rho-mu 31 leaned menacingly towards them and said, '*Got you.*'

A moment's stunned silence followed Rho-mu 31's words, and then the tension in the compartment was suddenly, explosively, relieved by hysterical laughter.

'That wasn't funny,' said Caxton, between laughing and wiping tears from his eyes.

'No,' agreed Severine. 'You shouldn't say things like that.'

'What? Can't I make a joke?' asked Rho-mu 31.

'I think they're just surprised you made one at all,' put in Dalia, looking back into the compartment. 'I don't think they're used to the Mechanicum trying to be funny.'

Rho-mu 31 nodded and said, 'I may be Mechanicum, but I am still human.'

With that, the strange unease that had settled on them at the sight of the deserted townships was dispelled, and they began chatting as animatedly as when they had built the first version of the Akashic reader.

The excitement of the journey into the unknown was rekindled and as the mag-lev made its way uphill, Zouche extended a discreet dendrite and plugged into

the compartment's data port, projecting the view from
the hull-mounted picter onto the glass of the window.

They eagerly watched the feed as Zouche panned the
image around. They saw the desolate plains stretching
away to the south and the black smudge on the horizon
above the Magma City nearly two thousand kilometres
away. At Caxton's request, Zouche returned the view to
front-on and the image shimmered as it displayed the silver mag-line carrying them up into the mountains.

Dalia let out a tiny gasp of fear as she saw the mag-line
vanish into a gaping, steel-lined cavern mouth that pierced
the flanks of the cliffs and led through the rock towards
Mondus Gamma.

She took Caxton's hand and gripped it tightly as the tunnel drew nearer, the yawning blackness of it suddenly
terrifying.

'What's the matter?' he asked.

'I didn't realise we'd need to go through the darkness,'
she said.

'It's just a tunnel,' said Caxton. 'There's nothing to worry
about.'

THE FORCES OF the Fabricator General came for Adept Zeth
several hours before Dalia's mag-lev approached the tunnel connecting the Tharsis uplands with the Syria Planum.
A Mechanicum heavy flyer cruised in from the north-west
and set down on the statue-lined Typhon Causeway before
the Magma City, scorching a score of the marble worthies
black with the heat of its enormous jets. The underside of
the craft shone with golden light from the bubbling,
steaming lava to either side of the wide causeway.

The ungainly aircraft was unarmed, but as it settled on
its landing skids, a continuous loop of code streamed
from its augmitters on a repeating cycle, demanding that
Adept Koriel Zeth present herself by the order of the Fabricator General.

The summons was broadcast in the highest and most authoritative code tense, and as such could not be ignored. The flanks of the flyer gusted steam and folded outwards, providing debarkation ramps for the warriors carried within.

Three hundred modified Skitarii and Protectors marched from the flyer's hold onto the basalt causeway. Wretched by-blows of the Fabricator General's union with the power unlocked in the depths of the forgotten vaults beneath Olympus Mons, these were twisted perversions of their original martial glory. Hunched carapaces, spiked armour and horned helmets clad them and their limb weapons seethed with unnatural power.

The Protectors were no less modified, their bodies swollen and grotesque, their weapons blackened and reforged in new and hateful shapes, designed for pain as much as killing.

Under the watchful gaze of armoured turrets and missile emplacements cunningly worked into the walls of ceramite and adamantium of Zeth's forge, these abominable killers formed up in three separate cohorts and marched on the Vulkan Gate.

Behind them came a shield-palanquin borne by towering, brutish Skitarii with grey skin and barbed armour. These monstrous, ogre-like warriors had been raised to such stature by more than simple gene-bulking and augmetics. Their bodies glistened and their veins pulsed with ruddy light, as though with an internal electricity.

Ambassador Melgator and Adept Regulus stood proudly atop the palanquin, clad in robes of midnight black with their hoods drawn up over their skulls. Melgator carried a staff of ebony topped with a snarling wolf's head and Regulus a staff of ivory topped with a skull of black obsidian.

The host of horrifically altered warriors parted to let them through, and Regulus halted the palanquin a hundred metres before the gate. The soaring adamantine glory of the Magma City's great portal was worked with silver cogs, golden eagles and lightning bolts, and it was opening.

As a widening bar of light split the two halves of the gate and the skitarii bristled with belligerent scrapcode, Regulus raised his arms and a streaming hash of lingua-technis, irregular and arrhythmic, blurted from his internal augmitters. His skull-topped staff crackled with corposant in time with his utterances and, one by one, the turrets and weapons platforms on the wall shut down.

The light of the city spilled outwards in a growing fan of orange light, throwing the shadow of the slender figure that walked from the city out before her in a thin line of black.

Adept Koriel Zeth swept her gaze over the assembled cohorts before fixing a distasteful stare on the two figures borne upon the palanquin, as though they were pestilential plague carriers begging entry.

'By what authority do you dare come to my city and demand my presence?' she said.

Melgator rapped his staff on the shield-palanquin, and its monstrous bearers carried it forward until it was less than twenty metres from Zeth.

<By the authority of the Fabricator General, to whom all Mars owes allegiance,> canted Regulus in an all-channel squirt of binary.

Zeth winced. 'That's dirty code you're using, Regulus,' she answered, reading his identity from his fizzing electric field.

'On the contrary,' replied Regulus. 'It is pure code, as it was meant to exist before it was tamed and shackled to the will of flesh.'

'If you can't see the flaw in that line of reasoning then you are beyond the reach of my logic,' said Zeth. 'Now speak your piece and begone, I have work to do.'

'That will not be possible, Zeth,' said Melgator. 'We are here to escort you to Olympus Mons, where you will submit to the judgement of the Fabricator General.'

'My title is *Adept* Zeth, I believe I have earned it,' snapped the Mistress of the Magma City. 'And on what grounds do you dare arrest me?'

<On the grounds of your continued heresies,> canted Melgator. <To wit: your continued refutation of the Machine-God, your refusal to support the policies and regime of the Fabricator General, and lastly, for allowing non-Cult Mechanicum personnel to work on divine machinery. For these charges you will be placed in our custody and returned to Olympus Mons to await trial for tech-heresy.>

Zeth said nothing for a moment, letting the weight of the accusation settle on her.

Then she laughed, the sound echoing from the mountainside, carried far and wide across the length and breadth of the causeway.

'You mock these accusations?' snapped Regulus. 'Is there no end to your wickedness?'

'Oh, I absolutely mock them,' sneered Zeth. 'They are laughable, and if you weren't so blinded by what Kelbor-Hal has turned you into, you would see that.'

She swept an arm out, her gesture encompassing the gathered skitarii and Protectors. 'These monstrous things you bring to my forge... they are abominations of flesh and machine, freakish hybrids worse than the feral scrapshunt rejects that wander the pallidus. You have turned all that is beautiful of the Mechanicum into something dark, and it horrifies me that you cannot see it. So, yes, I mock your accusations, and more, I refuse to recognise your right to accuse me!'

'Then you refuse the summons of the Fabricator General?' asked Regulus, his code laced with eagerness to unleash the skitarii. 'You understand the severity of this action?'

'I do,' confirmed Zeth.

'Then we will take you by force,' said Melgator.

'You can try,' said Zeth.

Melgator aimed his staff at the walls and said, 'You will either come with us or you will be destroyed, Zeth. Link with your wall defences and you will see they are shut down. We control the code now.'

The three cohorts of skitarii began to march forward, flame lances, energy halberds and limb weapons arming in a flurry of crackling activations and clattering auto-loaders.

'Not all of it you don't,' said Zeth as a pair of enormous mechanical forms marched into the gateway behind her.

Nine metres tall, the two Knights dwarfed the slight form of Adept Zeth, and the deep blue of their armoured plates shimmered with the reflected glow of the magma lake. The proud heraldry of a wheel encircling a lightning bolt was emblazoned on their shoulder guards, and they rode from the gateway to stand behind Adept Zeth with their energy lances and gatling cannons trained on the approaching skitarii.

Behind them, a dozen more Knights took position in line abreast to block entry to the Magma City with their majestic forms.

The march of the altered skitarii faltered and they milled in confusion in the face of the war machines, their pack-masters squalling for orders. Regulus emitted a panicked burst of code, the same mutant algorithms he had used to shut down the wall guns, but the Knights ignored him, their systems shut off to incoming code.

'This is Lord Caturix of the Order of Taranis,' said Zeth indicating the Knight on her left, its aggressive posture making no secret of its desire to wreak harm. 'And this is Preceptor Stator. Their order is an ally of this forge and if that flyer is not off my causeway in five minutes, they are going to ride out with their warriors and destroy you. Do *you* understand the severity of this action?'

'You dare threaten an emissary of the Fabricator General!' cried Melgator. 'You are a disgrace to the Mechanicum, Zeth!'

'Your assassin destroys the mind of my apprenta and then murders one of my acolytes, and you dare call *me* a disgrace to the Mechanicum?' snarled Zeth. She consulted her internal chronometer and said, 'Four minutes and forty seconds, Melgator. I suggest you get moving.'

'You will regret this,' promised Regulus. 'We will see your city in ruins and your legacy expunged from all records.'

The Knights took a step forwards, the hiss and clank of their metal limbs sounding dreadfully loud.

Melgator rapped his staff on the shield palanquin and, without another word, he and Regulus withdrew. A hurried code squeal recalled the skitarii and they marched with bitter disappointment back onto the heavy flyer.

As its flanks folded up and it took to the air, the lead Knight turned its cockpit towards Zeth and a noospheric link opened between them.

'You should have let me kill them,' said Lord Caturix.

'Maybe,' agreed Zeth, 'but I have a feeling you'll get another chance.'

'You think they'll be back?'

'I *know* they will, Lord Caturix, but next time they won't be so arrogant,' said Zeth. 'I have to send word of this to Maximal and Kane. Kelbor-Hal might come for them next, and I need to petition Legio Tempestus once more. I have a feeling we'll be needing some larger engines to defend the Magma City in the days ahead.'

'The support of Tempestus would be most welcome,' agreed Caturix. 'In the meantime, we will continue to stand with you. What would you have us do?'

Zeth watched the blue-hot glow of the departing flyer's engines.

'Prepare for battle,' she said.

THE MAG-LEV SPEARED into the tunnel and Dalia cried out in terror as the blackness swallowed them. She clung close to Caxton as the compartment lights flickered on and he put his arms around her, shrugging in puzzlement at her fright. Sickly fluorescence bathed the compartment, but the glass window was an unchanging black mirror. Dalia recoiled from its impenetrable depths, pushing away in terror from the wall with her sandaled feet.

Her breaths came in short panicked hikes and her muscles cramped painfully. She felt her flesh become cold and clammy as sweat filmed her skin. She could hear her heartbeat like the thunder of an industrial hammer and tears pricked at the corners of her eyes.

'Dalia?' asked Caxton. 'Dalia, what's the matter?'

'It's the darkness,' she gasped, burying her face in his shoulder. 'Its all around me!'

'Dalia? What? I don't understand!'

'What's the matter with her?' cried Severine.

'I don't know,' said Caxton, helpless as Dalia sobbed into his robes, her struggles becoming more and more hysterical.

'She's having a panic attack,' said Rho-mu 31, moving from the door of their compartment to stand in front of Dalia. 'I've seen it before in new arrivals to Mars. The red planet is so different, it sparks all kinds of reactions.'

'So what do we do?'

'There's nothing *you* can do,' replied Rho-mu 31. 'But I've dealt with this before.'

The Protector knelt on the floor between the seats and placed a hand on Dalia's shoulder, prising her away from Caxton and holding her twitching limbs. Her face was pale and streaked with tears.

'The darkness,' wept Dalia. 'I don't want to go into the darkness again. Not again!'

'What's she talking about?' said Severine. 'Make her stop!'

'Shut up!' hissed Zouche. 'Let the man work!'

'Dalia,' said Rho-mu 31, looking directly into her eyes. 'You are having a panic attack, but there's nothing to worry about, we're perfectly safe. I know you don't feel like that right now, but trust me, it's true.'

Dalia looked up at him and shook her head. 'No! No, we're not. I can't face it anymore. Please don't make me go back in there.'

'We'll be out of the tunnel soon enough, Dalia,' said Rho-mu 31, keeping his voice even and steady. She could feel his biometrics linking with hers, using his rigidly controlled metabolic mechanisms to try and stabilise hers.

'Breathe slowly,' advised Rho-mu 31. 'You're taking in too much oxygen and you don't want to do that, do you?'

She shook her head and forced herself to take longer, slower breaths. With the help of Rho-mu 31's bodily control she felt her heart begin to slow and the flow of blood to her muscles lessen.

Rho-mu 31 read her calming internal functions and nodded. 'Very good,' he said. 'These are all just physical symptoms of anxiety. They're not dangerous. It's an evolutionary reaction from ancient times, when humans needed all their wits about them for a fight or flight reaction. Your body has tripped that reaction, but it's a false alarm, Dalia. Do you understand that?'

'Of course I do,' said Dalia, between breaths and tears. 'I'm not stupid, but I can't help it!'

'Yes you can,' promised Rho-mu 31, and he knelt with her until the panic had passed, holding her hands and talking in low, soothing tones. He reminded her that she was travelling on a Mechanicum mag-lev, one of the safest means of transport on Mars, and that she was surrounded by her friends.

Eventually, his words and his gentle easing down of her metabolism calmed her to the point where her breathing rate was normalised and her heart rate, while still elevated, was less like the rattle of an automated nail gun.

'Thank you,' said Dalia, wiping her eyes on the sleeves of her robe. 'I feel so stupid; I mean we're only going through a tunnel. I've never felt claustrophobic or scared of the dark before.'

'Only since the accident in Zeth's inner forge,' said Zouche.

'Yes, I suppose since then,' agreed Dalia.

'Maybe you're feeling its fear,' said Severine, and they all turned towards her.

'Feeling whose fear?' asked Caxton.

'Whatever it is that's buried beneath the Noctis Labyrinthus,' said Severine, suddenly awkward with the attention. 'Look, she said she felt she linked with its mind, didn't she? I don't know about you, but if I'd been buried underground for that length of time and I got a brief glimpse of the world above, I wouldn't want to go back into the darkness either.'

'You may have something there, Severine,' said Caxton. 'What do you think, Dalia?'

Dalia nodded, unwilling to confront such thoughts head on after her panic attack. 'Maybe.'

'No, no, I really think Severine's onto something here,' said Caxton. 'I mean if–'

'Enough!' said Rho-mu 31. 'Save it until we're out of the tunnel. Zouche, how long until we reach the other side?'

Zouche hurriedly reconnected with the mag-lev's onboard cogitator and streams of data light cascaded behind his eyes.

Rho-mu 31 turned his attention back to Dalia and she smiled at him. 'Thank you,' she said.

He bowed his head, and though she couldn't see his face, she knew he was smiling back at her.

'Well?' asked Dalia in as relaxed a manner as she could muster. 'How long until we're clear of the tunnel, Zouche?'

Zouche frowned and moved his hands in the air, haptically shifting through holographic data plates only he could see.

'I'm not sure,' he said. 'According to the onboard driver-servitor we're slowing down.'

'Slowing down? Why?' demanded Rho-mu 31, and Dalia felt his threat auspex light up.

'Here, look for yourself,' replied Zouche, projecting the view of the tunnel from the hull-mounted picter onto the window once more. 'There's something ahead of us.'

They looked, and there was.

Rumbling along the floor of the tunnel towards the decelerating mag-lev was what looked like a tall robot of roughly spherical proportions mounted on a heavy gauge track unit. A pair of heavy arms were held vertically at its sides and a set of malleable weapon-dendrites flexed in the air above its shoulder guards.

Three glowing yellow orbs shone like baleful eyes in the centre of its mass, and, as they watched, its main arms locked into the upright position. As the mag-lev stopped, no one in the compartment failed to notice that each arm was equipped with an enormous weapon.

Even through the poor quality of the picter's image, Dalia could feel the strangeness and uniqueness of this machine's electrical field. Opening herself to the part of her mind that Zeth had called her innate connection to the aether, she reached out towards the machine, reading the heat of its internal reactor and the sticky web of dark, malicious sentience at its core.

Kaban… that was its name.

In the fleeting moment of connection, she read the memory of its creation and the killing of its former friend, an adept named Pallas Ravachol. With that death, the machine's murderous nature had been unleashed, and the primordial evil with which its masters had tainted its artificial intelligence now consumed it with dreadful, killing lust.

'Is that a battle robot?' asked Caxton.

'It's much more than a robot,' said Dalia, her eyes snapping open. 'It's something far worse.'

'What?'

'A sentient machine,' gasped Dalia, still reeling from the moment of connection to its grossly warped consciousness and the awful clarity of its purpose. 'It's an artificial intelligence and it's been corrupted with something vile, something evil.'

'Evil? That's nonsense,' said Zouche. 'What do machines know of evil?'

'What does it want?' asked Severine.

Dalia looked over at Rho-mu 31 in uncomprehending terror. 'It's here to kill me.'

THE KABAN MACHINE opened fire and the driver-servitor's compartment disintegrated in a blitzing storm of las-fire and plasma bolts. Flames boomed from the ruptured energy cells and the darkness of the tunnel was suddenly dispelled.

Rho-mu 31 grabbed Dalia and hauled her from her seat as the machine rumbled down the tunnel, its weapon arms wreathed in halos of white fire as it systematically obliterated carriage after carriage. Designed to penetrate the hulls of battle tanks and overload the void shields of Titans, its sustained fire easily sliced through the sheet metal of the mag-lev's sides.

Caxton, Severine and Zouche needed no encouragement to follow Rho-mu 31 and blundered into the corridor beyond their compartment in terror. The noise from outside the mag-lev was deafening, thudding pressure waves of explosions laced with the squeal and hiss of impacting lasers. The bark of solid rounds and the whine of ricochets echoed from the tunnel walls. The mag-lev shuddered like a wounded beast, flames and smoke erupting along its length as it was systematically riddled with gunfire.

Dalia heard screams from further along the mag-lev as passengers were chewed up in the fusillade. The corridor was a mass of terrified people, its length choked with panicked bodies. Men and women screamed and clawed at one another as they fought to escape the approaching slaughter. Rho-mu 31 gathered Dalia into his arms and forced a path through the heaving, jammed mass of people fleeing towards the rear of the mag-lev.

<Get out of the way!> bellowed Rho-mu 31 in the most belligerent form of cant, and such was the ingrained reverence for a Mechanicum Protector that the

majority of people did exactly that. With his weapon
stave extended before him, he pushed along the corridor
towards an emergency exit.

Dalia looked over Rho-mu 31's shoulder, seeing terrified faces pressing against the wall of the corridor as they
slammed fists, fire extinguishers or anything else they
could get their hands on to smash the glass. Through the
window on the door at the end of the corridor, Dalia
could see bright flames and black smoke.

'Hurry!' shouted Severine. 'For the love of the Omnissiah, hurry up!'

A searing white lance of plasma cut into the carriage,
sawing through the metal and glass like a laser saw. The
beam instantly sliced two-dozen people in half and Dalia
wept as she smelled boiled blood and scorched meat.

'Down!' shouted Rho-mu 31, bearing Dalia and Caxton to the floor of the corridor. Severine was quick to
follow and Zouche had already been borne to his knees
by the stampede. The incandescent beam zipped along
the corridor, killing as it went, and Dalia watched in
mute horror as severed limbs, cleaved bodies and disem-
bodied heads fell to the floor.

She rolled onto her side as the deadly beam passed
overhead and droplets of molten metal splashed the
floor beside her. She cried out as one scorched a thin line
down her arm.

'Sacred Fathers,' hissed Zouche, rolling onto his front
as an explosion further back whipped the mag-lev like a
sine wave. Everyone screamed as it was lifted from the
rails with a screech of torn metal and a crackling burst of
arcing electrics.

Dalia scrambled on her knees towards Rho-mu 31 as
the carriage tipped from the track and her world spun
crazily. It crashed to the tunnel floor and the windows
blew out with the force of the impact. A blizzard of crys-
talline fragments rained down.

The breath was knocked from her and Dalia felt blood dripping into her eyes. A heavy weight pinned her and she blinked away red tears as she heard more deafening blasts of gunfire. She couldn't tell how close it was, but the stuttering, strobing flash of weapons fire felt as though it were coming from right outside their carriage.

Dalia fought to free herself from the weight pinning her to... the ceiling? Which way was up and which was down? She couldn't hear any screams. Had the Kaban machine killed everyone?

A man's body lay sprawled across her, or at least half of him, and she cried as she pushed his bifurcated body from her. The metal beneath her – the ceiling, she was sure of it now – was sticky with warm blood, and she whimpered in terror at the sight of heaped mounds of corpses filling the corridor. The iron stink of blood was thick in her nostrils and Dalia couldn't remember a more awful smell.

She retched dryly at the sight of so many dead, terrified and numbed by the horror of how quickly their grand adventure had come to such a bloody end. Despite the stink of death, she took a deep breath and looked for her friends amid the wreckage and carnage.

Dalia saw Rho-mu 31 lying further along the buckled corridor with a jagged spar of metal impaling his shoulder. The Protector's biometrics were fluctuating, but he was alive.

Zouche lay in a heap of bodies, his face a mask of blood, but she couldn't tell whether it was his or belonged to someone else. Caxton was just behind her, pinned to the floor by a metal door in the midst of a spray of glass fragments. His eyes were open and pleading, a low moaning issuing from between bloodied lips.

Severine lay beneath a nutrient dispensing machine that had torn loose from the wall, her arm thrown out before her and twisted at an unnatural angle. Her eyes were closed, but her pained expression and rapid, shallow breaths told Dalia she was alive.

The carriage was still, no straining bodies or panicked shoving, and the only light came from smashed lumen globes that sparked and stuttered in the half-light.

After such a tremendous cacophony of violence and noise, the silence that enveloped her was as welcome as it was terrifying.

Dalia began to crawl towards Rho-mu 31. He saw her coming and shook his head, placing a finger to the grilled mouthpiece of his helmet.

At first Dalia didn't understand.

Then she heard it.

Over the creaking wreckage and tinkle of falling glass, she felt the vibration of the heavy machine through the ground as it crushed metal and ruptured bodies beneath its tracks. Dalia craned her neck to look through the shattered window into the sputtering darkness of the tunnel, and fought down the urge to cry out as she saw the monstrous form of the sentient machine rumbling towards where they lay.

She felt the crawling pressure of its corrupted mind as it swept the carriage for life signs, and heard the rattle of its autoloaders feeding its weapons fresh ammunition.

It drew nearer with every breath and in moments its auspex would register their presence.

Then it would kill them.

PRINCEPS CAVALERIO FINISHED processing the feeds inloading into his casket at a rate of over six thousand data packets per second. The Martian networks had slowly returned to normal after the scrapcode plague, the diligence of the code-scrubbers and magos probandi all across the red planet finally re-establishing communications and information exchanges.

Fresh reports, petitions and pleas for aid from forges far and wide were streaming into Ascraeus Mons through the vox, across the noosphere and via optic feeds.

It was a bleak picture they painted of the Mechanicum's future.

Cavalerio let his mind swim up through the reams of liquid information that flowed around and through him. He saw Agathe's face before him, and set the biometrics of his casket from processing to consciousness.

His famulous nodded as she read the information on the slate fixed to the side of the casket and retreated to a subordinate position behind him.

Cavalerio's Manifold senses processed his surroundings. His casket sat in the position of honour in the Chamber of the First, raised on a plinth before the mighty, towering form of *Deus Tempestus*, the First God Machine of the Legio.

Princeps Sharaq stood before him, waiting to hear whether he would give an order of execution. Though Sharaq had correctly appointed himself the acting Princeps Senioris of the Tempestus forces on Mars, he knew and welcomed the fact that any order to walk should come from the Stormlord.

Behind Sharaq were his Legio brothers, each awaiting the Stormlord's decision.

Princeps Suzak, the grim-faced hunter who commanded the Warlord *Tharsis Hastatus*, watched with an impassive eye, while Princeps Mordant of the Reaver *Arcadia Fortis* strained like an attack dog on a leash.

The Warhound drivers – Basek of *Vulpus Rex*, Kasim of *Raptoria* and Lamnos of *Astrus Lux* – paced like caged wolves, and Cavalerio rejoiced in the fearful power he saw before him.

'Stormlord,' said Sharaq. 'The princeps are gathered as you ordered.'

'Thank you, Kel,' said Cavalerio, before enhancing his augmitters to address the princeps of his Legio. 'I know you're all waiting to see whether I give an order of execution, but before I tell you my decision we need to understand what might happen as a result. I've given great thought to this, because a wrong choice will have consequences none of us can imagine.

'The forges of Mars burn in the fires of schism, and factional violence is reaching epidemic proportions all across our home world. So far, that violence has been restricted to the Mechanicum. None of the Titan Legions have yet initiated any hostilities, but it's surely only a matter of time until that happens.'

He could see their hunger to be unleashed, proud of their courage yet saddened by their eagerness to fight their erstwhile brothers.

'Before you all rush to your engines, gentlemen, let's be clear on one thing. If the Titan Legions march to war, there will be no coming back from it; we will have unleashed the fire of a civil war that will only be extinguished by the utter destruction of one side or the other.

'I have always sought to keep our Legio free from the insidious poison of politicking. I believe that the Titan Legions should remain true to their warrior ideals and not be instruments of political will, save that of the Imperium itself. Mars faces the gravest crisis in its long and glorious history, and warriors of honour and courage do not stand idly by in such times, they act. They stand firm in the face of aggression and in the defence of their allies.'

Cavalerio paused, allowing his words to hit home before continuing. 'The idea that one Legio would fight another is anathema to me, but I am not fool enough to believe that such a time is not coming.'

'It has already arrived,' said Princeps Mordant. 'Mortis is spoiling for battle.'

'Indeed,' said Cavalerio. 'The blatantly provocative walk on Ascraeus Mons by the Mortis engines was little more than an attempt to bait us into a shooting war we could not win.'

He stifled their denials with a harsh blurt of impatient code.

'I admire your bravery and faith in one another, but had we fought we would have died.'

'So what do we do, Stormlord?' demanded Princeps Suzak. 'Do we swallow our pride and do nothing as Mars tears itself apart? We are a force for stability, use us!'

'No, Vlad, we do not swallow our pride,' said Cavalerio. 'I will unleash the power of the Legio and we will rise to the defence of the ideals for which our world stands. The fury of Tempestus will fall upon the enemies of Mars and together we will scour them from the face of the red planet in a tide of fire and blood.'

'You walk with us?' asked Princeps Kasim. 'How? The tech-priests say *Victorix Magna* is beyond their ability to restore.'

'I know that, Zafir, but still I will walk with you,' declared Cavalerio. 'I will walk alongside you as I have always dreamed I would make my last walk, with the First God Machine of our Legio. I will become one with *Deus Tempestus*!'

Princeps Sharaq stepped forward. 'Then is the word given?'

'The word is given,' said Cavalerio. 'Tempestus goes to war.'

THE MACHINE PAUSED in its advance, Dalia could hear the throaty growl of its power plant and the hiss of its hydraulics, and could feel the fizzing heat of its electrical field. She could smell the smoky residue of hard-rounds fire and taste the ozone from the plasma discharges.

Her every sense was magnified and she fought the urge to cry as she saw the ground up flesh worked into the grooves of its tracks. Rho-mu 31 slid his hand towards his weapon stave, but Dalia knew it would be no protection against such a destructive machine.

Caxton, Severine and Zouche trembled in fear, too hurt to move, too afraid to breathe.

Blood dripped from Dalia's brow onto her arm and she blinked away another drop as it formed on her eyelid. Shards of glass wobbled in the window frame before her and splinters fell like diamonds spilled from a pouch, landing with a *tink, tink, tink*.

Dalia held her breath as her fear rendered her immobile. Her limbs were frozen, she couldn't think properly, and the idea that she was going to die here was as ridiculous as it was horrifying. She didn't want to die.

Oh Throne, she didn't want to die!

She looked over at Caxton and the others, feeling a terrible guilt that she had brought them to this. And for what? Some half-baked theory that an ancient creature was buried beneath the surface of Mars?

Dalia wanted to laugh at her foolishness, thinking back to all the things she had read and transcribed – what seemed, and might as well have been, a lifetime ago – that she'd never now have the chance to see: the oceans of Laeran, the great cliffs of Charo, the planet forests of Ae.

A million wonders and miracles yet to be known; wonders the Expedition fleets were seeing on a daily basis.

Neither would she ever learn more of the Carnival of Light on Sarosh, or vicariously live tales of battle like the Victory on Murder or the vanquishing of the Hexen Guild. Likewise, the future paintings of Leland Roget, the compositions of Jeacon Poul and the sculptures of Delafour were all lost to her. Nor would she read any more of the poems by Ignace Karkasy that she had grown fond of, despite their slightly pompous tone.

This was no way to die, and the injustice and unfairness of it railed against the cruel fate that had brought her to this moment.

She closed her eyes, her fear of the dark vanishing instantly in the face of this new, immediate threat. In the face of death, her desire to live surged and her connection to the aether pushed aside conscious thought. Dalia felt her mind reaching out beyond her body as it had when she had seen how to construct the throne of the Akashic reader, but this time it saw further and deeper than ever before.

This time she saw into the heart of the Kaban Machine.

The connection lasted the merest fraction of a moment, but in that moment she saw the very essence of its existence.

She saw golden lines, bound together in a glowing web, each strand an answer to a question she hadn't yet asked. In this realm of the senses, she saw the light that was the mind of the Kaban Machine, a filthy, corrupted world of artificially created synapses and neurons.

Its auspex crawled over the wreckage like an invisible host of hungry spiders, and her flesh crawled with goose bumps as she felt the tread of a million legs across her skin. The machine's senses sniffed like a scavenger hunting out juicy morsels to devour.

Dalia's inner vision bored into the burning heart of the machine's consciousness, marvelling at the intricacy of the design, the complexity and magnificence of the work, and the infinite patience that had gone into crafting such a miraculous engine. A perfect meld of organics and artificial components had been used to fashion the Kaban Machine, and the genius of Lukas Chrom, the adept whose name and skill she could read in every aspect of the design, was a thing of beauty.

She saw the wonder of what Chrom had created and felt the horror of what it had been made to do, what its builders had done to it. They had made it kill a man it had called friend, and then exposed it to something so dark and so terrible that Dalia's floating consciousness recoiled from its warped malignancy.

Its memories were of feelings and emotions, the memories of a newly created intelligence too inexperienced to realise how such things could be manipulated by the unscrupulous. Corruption lay in the heart of its consciousness, like a bloated spider sitting at the centre of a web that spread its blood-hungry canker to everything it touched.

The folly of creating an artificial sentience, a forbidden science since a forgotten age of war, only to pervert it to the cause of murder struck Dalia as typical of mankind's skewed brilliance.

It was a machine that could think for itself and its first autonomous act was to kill.

Just what did that say about its makers?

For all its brilliance, however, it was still a machine and bound by the fundamental principles of machines. It still gathered information the way any other sentient being did, and such things could be fooled.

Though the infinitely dense strands of light that were its warped consciousness were corrupt beyond imagining, Dalia sought out the neural pathways and areas of the machine's brain that controlled its perceptions of the outside world. With a natural sense for such things, Dalia blocked the machine's ability to process the inputs coming from its auspex, and though she felt its sensory apparatus sweep over her body and those of her friends, the signals never reached the action centres of its consciousness.

As though sensing that something was wrong, the machine swept its auspex over the ruins of the corridor once more. She sensed its confusion.

It knows we're here, she thought. *And it's going to keep looking until it finds us.*

With another twist of its mind, Dalia created a tremor of life signs further down the mag-lev, and sensed its savage joy as its targeting systems acquired the false readings.

Thunderous, roaring, crashing gunfire erupted from its weapons, and Dalia felt the mag-lev shudder with the impacts. Las-fire and heavy, explosive rounds tore into the distant wreckage and obliterated the dead bodies within.

Its guns ceased fire and Dalia allowed the counterfeit life signs to blink out, feeling its feral glee as it revelled in the slaughter. The image of blood dripping from a brass throne onto a mountain of skulls filled its thoughts.

Again its auspex swept over the mag-lev. Dalia felt the machine's disappointment as she blocked its perceptions of them, and it concluded that it had killed everyone aboard.

Its task complete, the machine turned smoothly on its axis and moved off down the tunnel.

As it went, Dalia read an encrypted data squirt confirming the killings travel through the airwaves to its masters in Mondus Gamma and Olympus Mons.

Dalia kept her grip on its perception centres until it had travelled beyond the range of its targeting auspex before letting out a breath and opening her eyes.

The smashed interior of the mag-lev corridor came back into sickening focus and Dalia's stomach lurched as her brain struggled to adjust to the sudden transition from the domain of the mind to that of the physical.

The aftermath of the machine's attack – blood, burned plastic, seared flesh, and the sight of so many corpses – was overwhelming and she vomited copiously. Dalia coughed, retching and heaving until she felt her grip on reality solidifying.

She heard voices speaking in hushed and amazed tones that they were still alive, and she smiled, even though searing pain pounded inside her head.

'It's gone,' said a voice that Dalia recognised as Zouche's.

'I don't believe it,' said Caxton, his voice on the edge of hysteria.

'Thank Ares,' breathed Severine tearfully. 'Please? Can anyone help me? I think my arm's broken.'

'Dalia?' said Rho-mu 31. 'Are you all right?'

'Not especially,' she replied with forced levity, 'but I'll live, which is more than I thought I'd be able to say a few minutes ago.'

'Can you move?'

'Yes, but give me a minute.'

'We don't have a minute,' said Rho-mu 31. 'We have to move in case it comes back.'

'It won't come back,' said Dalia. 'It thinks we're dead, or at least it will for a while.'

'Then let's get out of here before it realises its mistake,' said Rho-mu 31.

IN THE UPPER reaches of Olympus Mons, Kelbor-Hal inloaded the encrypted data blurt from the Kaban Machine. Looking out over the surface of Mars he took a moment to survey the landscape, knowing that soon it would be transformed into something wondrous and new.

The power that boiled from the depths of the Vaults of Moravec was intoxicating, and every day brought fresh miracles as he and his fellow Dark Mechanicum – a term Melgator had coined – found new ways to bind it to the metal and gristle of their creations.

Weapons, servitors, praetorians and fighting vehicles were imbued with power, twisting them into new and terrifying forms that were divinely primordial in their savage beauty. Monstrous engines of destruction that would be the heralds of the new power rising in the galaxy were taking shape in Olympus Mons and the forges of those adepts and magi that had bound themselves to the cause of Horus Lupercal.

Billions toiled in the weapon shops and manufactorum to realise this grand dream of Mars resurgent, and none who touched the powers unleashed to roam throughout his forge remained unchanged.

Chants echoed from the darkened thoroughfares of Olympus Mons, mobs of hooded worshippers hunting down those who did not embrace the new way and feeding their blood to the hungry machines. Brazen bells tolled constantly and howling klaxons shrieked with the godlike power of the scrapcode.

The transformation of his forge was a magnificent thing, and Kelbor-Hal knew that what they did here would echo through the ages as the moment the Mechanicum was reborn.

He turned from the armoured glass of the viewing bay to face his followers.

Regulus, Melgator, Urtzi Malevolus, together with holographic images of Lukas Chrom and Princeps Camulos, stood attentively before him. He could see the chittering lines of scrapcode infesting their augmetics.

He nodded towards Lukas Chrom. 'Dalia Cythera is dead. Once again, your assassin and thinking machine prove their worth.'

Chrom accepted the compliment with a short bow.

'Then it is time?' said Princeps Camulos. 'My engines long to make ruin of the Magma City.'

The bear-like Princeps Senioris of Legio Mortis was clad in beetle-black armour and Kelbor-Hal read the warp-enhanced aggression flaring from him in waves.

'Yes,' he said. 'It is time. Send word to the commanders of your allied Legios, Camulos. Tell their engines to walk and to crush our enemies beneath their mighty treads.'

'It shall be done,' promised Camulos.

Kelbor-Hal then addressed his fellow adepts of the Dark Mechanicum.

'This is a great day, my acolytes, remember it always,' said the Fabricator General. 'This is the day Mars and her forge worlds cast off the yoke of the Emperor's tyranny. Unleash your armies and stain the sands of our planet red with blood!'

ORIGENS
MECHANICUS

LATER HISTORIES WOULD record that the first blow of the Martian civil war was struck against Magos Mattias Kefra, whose forge in the Sinus Sabaeus region was housed within the Mädler crater. Titans of the Magna Legion marched from the southern Noachis region and within minutes had smashed down the gates of his forge. Howling engines daubed in red, orange, yellow and black, and decorated with flaming horned skull devices, ran amok within the high walls of the crater, crushing everything living beneath them and destroying thousands of years of accumulated wisdom in a fury of fire.

Vast libraries burned and weapon shops that served the Solar Guard were reduced to molten slag as the indiscriminate slaughter continued long into the night, the Magna Legion's trumpeting warhorns sounding like the atavistic screams of primitive savages.

Further north in the Arabian region, the great engine yards of High Magos Ahotep in the Cassini crater were struck by a hundred missiles launched from the atomic silos secreted within the isolated peaks and mesas of Nilo Syrtis. The explosions of the forbidden weapons filled the four hundred and fifteen kilometre diameter of the crater with seething nuclear fire, and sent conjoined magma-streaked mushroom clouds soaring nearly seventy kilometres into the sky.

Along the borders of the Lunae Palus and Arcadia regions, what had previously been confined to heated debate erupted into outright warfare as Princeps Ulriche of the Death Stalkers unleashed his engines upon the fortress of Maxen Vledig's Deathbolts.

Caught by surprise, the Deathbolts lost nineteen engines in the first hour of battle, before withdrawing into the frozen wastes of the Mare Boreum and seeking refuge in the dune fields of Olympia Undae. Their calls for reinforcement went unanswered, for all of Mars was tearing itself apart as the plague of war spread across the planet in a raging firestorm.

Amid the Athabasca Valles, war machines of Legio Ignatum and the Burning Stars fought in bloody close quarters through the teardrop landforms caused by catastrophic flooding in an earlier, ancient age of the red planet. Neither force could gain the advantage, nor could either claim victory, so after a night's undignified scrapping, both withdrew to lick their wounds.

A snapping, howling host of twisted skitarii and hideously altered weaponised servitors surged from the Gigas Sulci sub-hives of Olympus Mons to attack the crater forges of Ipluvien Maximal. Alert to the danger of attack, Maximal's forces repelled the first waves of attackers, but within hours, his forge was surrounded and under siege by unholy Ordinatus engines and warped machines given hideous life in the depths of the Fabricator General's darkest and bloodiest weapon shops.

The greatest single loss of life took place in the Ismenius Lacus region of Mars, where the glacial forges of Adept

Rueon Villnarus were attacked by airbursting rockets carrying a mutated strain of the Life Eater. The rapacious viral organism leapt from victim to victim with malicious glee, seeming to travel via every possible vector. Via direct contact, it killed the tens of thousands directly exposed to the detonation in minutes. Airborne, it depopulated the millions-strong worker-habs of Deuteronilus Mensae within three hours, and through some diabolical warp-mutation, it spread through the haptic networks to infect even those who thought themselves safe behind vac-sealed barriers. When the gleeful virus finally burned itself out, some seven hours later, every living soul within Ismenius Lacus was dead, the remains of fourteen million liquefied corpses freezing solid where they lay.

Within the Herschel impact basin of the Mare Tyrrhenum, nine hundred thousand skitarii and Protectors clashed in a swirling, bloody melee that continued unabated until almost all were dead. No victor emerged from the senseless slaughter and no purpose was served by the destruction, yet still both factions poured their forces into the meat grinder for fear of what might be lost should they withdraw.

Nor was the fighting merely confined to the surface of Mars. The Ring of Iron, that great halo shipyard that surrounded the red planet like a glittering silver belt, shuddered as explosions and conflict spread along its length. Factions loyal to the Throne, and those sworn to Olympus Mons and Horus Lupercal, clashed with the fury of fanatics. The vessels of Battlefleet Solar pulled away from the fighting as Mechanicum ships duelled in the shadow of the Ring of Iron, pounding one another with devastating broadsides and no thought of strategy or survival.

Venting gases and bodies spilled from ruptured hulls, and thousands died every second as wounded ships fell from low orbit and streaked down through the atmosphere to their destruction. The flaming wreckage of

Mechanicum Gloriam, its engines destroyed as it sought to evade a hunting pack of frigates in low orbit, plunged through the lightning-wracked skies of Mars towards the planet's surface.

The Technotheologians, watching its fall from the Basilica of the Blessed Algorithm in the Cydonia Mensae region, proclaimed it a sign of the Machine-God's wrath, raising their manip arms and mechadendrites in praise of this wondrous sign of divine displeasure. Calls for peace and a cease of hostilities were carried far and wide across Mars, broadcast on every channel by every means available to them.

That signal was abruptly cut short as *Mechanicum Gloriam* slammed into the basilica and obliterated the vast complex of temples, shrines and reliquaries in a heartbeat. Millions of square kilometres and billions of faithful priests were consumed in the explosive impact, and any last call to reason vanished with them in the newest and deepest impact crater to disfigure the Martian soil.

All across Mars, in every region where the Mechanicum had built its holdings, the ancient order tore at itself in a frenzy of bloodletting more savage than any alien race had dared inflict on Humanity.

Libraries of priceless knowledge burned, adepts whose expertise had helped free the human race from confinement to its birth planet were torn limb from limb by screaming mobs, and forges that had previously sworn undying pacts of allegiance turned on one another like lifelong foes.

Burning debris from orbit fell to the planet's surface, and though it was said that it never rained on Mars, a rain of fire now filled the heavens as though the sky wept comet tears that it should bear witness to such destruction.

SITTING NEXT TO Caxton in the bucket seats fitted in the cramped rear compartment of their salvaged Cargo-5,

Dalia fought to stay awake as the rugged, dusty vista of the Syria Planum sped past, rendered grainy and blurred through the scratched glass of the compartment's windows. The ground was uneven, but Rho-mu 31 guided them expertly across the rocky plains. Severine sat on the other side of Caxton, her broken arm bound close to her chest, while Zouche sat up front in the driver's cabin next to Rho-mu 31.

In the aftermath of the Kaban Machine's attack, her Protector had pulled himself from the metal that impaled his shoulder and quickly dragged them from the wreckage of the mag-lev. Working with practiced urgency, he had ascertained the extent of their injuries and moved them to a hidden culvert in the tunnel walls.

As Rho-mu 31 and Zouche searched the rear cargo holds of the mag-lev for anything useful in the wreckage, Severine had stared at Dalia with an expression of awe and what Dalia would later realise was fear.

'How did you do that?' asked Severine. 'Send that machine away, I mean. I thought we were all dead.'

'We should have been,' agreed Caxton. 'Maybe it missed us or there was some kind of interference, I don't know.'

Severine shook her head, biting her lip as the pain of her broken arm flared. 'No, it was something Dalia did, I know it. What did you do?'

'I don't understand it myself, to be honest,' said Dalia, leaning her head back on the cold stone of the tunnel wall. 'It was as if I could see the mechanisms of its mind and I just knew how it worked. I saw what Chrom had done to it and I... kind of blinded it to the fact we were right in front of it.'

'Chrom?' said Severine. 'Lukas Chrom? He built that machine? A thinking machine?'

'Yes,' said Dalia. 'I could see his handiwork all over its mind.'

'Why would an adept like Chrom want to kill us?'

'Not *us*,' said Caxton. 'Dalia.'

Severine looked at Dalia as though she had personally broken her arm. 'What haven't you told us, Dalia? Why does Lukas Chrom want you dead?'

Dalia knew nothing she said would convince Severine that she didn't know for sure, but she shrugged and said, 'I'm guessing here, but I think maybe it's something to do with Adept Zeth's Akashic reader. Some people don't want it built, and I think they're afraid of what's going to happen when we know everything it can show us. Think about it, if anyone can know everything, then what happens to the keepers of knowledge? Knowledge is power, right? So what happens when everyone can access that knowledge?'

'They'd lose their power,' said Caxton.

'Exactly,' said Dalia. 'And I'm surer than ever that whatever the creature beneath the Noctis Labyrinthus is, it's the key to making the Akashic reader work. People are frightened of what we'll be able to achieve when we unlock its potential and they're desperate to hang on to what they've got.'

'So what's all that got to do with what's happening all over Mars?'

'I don't know,' said Dalia. 'I really don't, but whatever it is, it's bigger than all of us.'

At that moment Rho-mu 31 and Zouche had returned laden with a veritable treasure trove of useful items recovered from the unclaimed supplies earmarked for Crater Edge and Red Gorge: medicae packs, ration cartons, water recyclers and breathing apparatus. The medicae packs were opened and wounds cleaned and treated with counterseptic before being bound with gauze and bandages.

Best of all, Zouche had discovered an overturned Cargo-5 all-terrain hauler, an unreliable and cantankerous vehicle common in the frontier towns and less affluent forges, but one which offered them a chance of survival. Rho-mu 31 easily righted the vehicle, but upon doing so, they discovered that the indiscriminate fire of their attacker had severed the track unit and holed the mechanics of the driver's controls.

Undaunted, Zouche set to work repairing the damaged track unit with Rho-mu 31's help, while Caxton dismantled the control panel and set to work with Dalia, trying to jury-rig the controls back to life. Using spars of metal from the wrecked mag-lev, Rho-mu 31 groaned with effort as he lifted the Cargo-5 enough for the others to pull the repaired track links through, and they had cheered and embraced when Caxton finally ignited the drive plant and the engine turned over with a belligerent growl.

Stocking up the rear compartments of the Cargo-5 with their supplies, they had driven along the darkness of the tunnel and emerged into a freshly broken morning. Dalia had never been happier to see open sky, though the scarlet hue of the dawn and the cascades of fire she saw in the distance spoke of deeper troubles to come.

As Rho-mu 31 negotiated the Cargo-5 down the rugged slope leading to the Syria Planum, Dalia and the others had their first glimpse of Mondus Gamma forge complex. Like a dark slick, it spread south and east across the landscape in a vast swathe of smoking, flaming industry. Hive manufactories, vast weapon hangars and blazing foundries pounded and throbbed with the labour of production. One of the largest forges on Mars, its furthest extremities were beyond sight, a black pall of shrouding smoke clinging to the fabrication plants and sub-hives as though unwilling to let outsiders view what lay beneath.

The sight was profoundly disturbing, for Dalia knew this was the domain of Adept Lukas Chrom, the builder of the machine that had just tried to kill them.

Despite that, a newfound vigour filled Dalia, though whether this was in response to their brush with death or some other reason, she couldn't tell. All she knew was that she was alive and all the things she had feared losing were still there, just waiting to be experienced.

The same mood seemed to suffuse them all, and over the next few hours of their journey, as the ground levelled out and they made good time across the plain, each of her fellow companions relaxed into this new stage of their journey. Even Severine, whose arm was still painful despite Rho-mu 31's ministrations and the effects of a couple of painkillers, seemed in better spirits.

The air in the vehicle was clammy, yet it was better than the hot dust that billowed around them outside. This far from the pallidus the atmosphere outside wasn't actually poisonous, but it wasn't exactly pleasant. Dalia felt a growing sense of optimism that they were going to reach their goal after all as the hours blurred into days and the unending dust clouds enveloped them.

The days passed mostly in silence, though occasionally one of them would point out a particularly interesting formation or unusual sight and they would talk about it until it was obscured in the dust of their wake. Rho-mu 31 kept one eye on the distant forge, and Dalia felt a growing excitement as the ground became rockier.

At length, Rho-mu 31 slowed the Cargo-5 and pointed to a dark scar in the earth that dropped sharply into the ground between two descending cliffs of rock.

'The western entrance to the Noctis Labyrinthus,' said Rho-mu 31.

'Well, we made it here,' said Severine. 'What now?'

Dalia looked at the tense faces of her friends. They had come this far, but looking into the tomb-like darkness of the Noctis Labyrinthus, she could see their fear and hesitation at war with their desire to stand by her.

'We go in, what else is there to do?' asked Caxton. 'We've come all this way and we can't turn back. Right, Dalia?'

'Right,' said Dalia, grateful for his support.

'Fine by me,' said Zouche. 'Pointless journey if we don't go in.'

Severine nodded slowly, and Rho-mu 31 guided their vehicle down the sloping entrance to the canyon system.

The ground dropped away sharply, swallowing them whole as the light faded and left them travelling in a twilight wilderness of shadows and thin bars of diffuse light that filtered down from high above.

Sheer cliffs of layered rock soared above them, and Dalia felt like they were plunging deeper and deeper into the heart of the planet through some dreadful, unhealed wound.

MAVEN COULD BARELY contain his anger at the sight of so many bodies. The tunnel was choked with them, lying scattered in pieces or crushed amid the twisted wreckage of a mag-lev that had been blasted from the track. He rode *Equitos Bellum* through the darkness, his twin stablights illuminating the tunnel and the dusty armoured carapace of *Pax Mortis*.

'You still think we're following dead spoor?' he voxed to Cronus.

His battle-brother didn't answer for a moment and Maven sensed his friend's fury at what he was seeing. The mag-lev hadn't just been attacked, it had been obliterated. Weapons of tremendous power had torn it open from end to end and slaughtered every living soul within.

'With all that's happening across Mars and even after what we found in the pallidus, I'll admit I was beginning to regret my decision to follow you,' said Cronus. 'But no more, brother. Whatever that machine is, it has to be destroyed. This will not stand.'

Maven nodded in agreement, though, truth to tell, even he had begun to doubt the instincts of his mount as it led them deeper and deeper into the pallidus. Then, after days of fruitless searching, his auspex had fizzed and hissed with the familiar spider-like pattern of electromagnetic energy that was their prey's signature.

The buried wreck of a prospector's hauler had been almost completely obscured by the dust storms, but *Equitos Bellum* had scented the handiwork of its nemesis in its destruction.

No sooner had the Knight's auspex sniffed at the residue of reactor, shield and weapons, than Maven felt its gnawing desire to travel eastwards over the mountainous ridge between Tharsis and the Syria Planum in an aching pull of the Manifold.

Now they had found this corpse-filled tunnel, a charnel house of senseless slaughter, and still the Manifold pulled them onwards.

'Why hasn't anyone come to help?' wondered Maven. 'Why have they just left them?'

'Mars has bigger problems,' replied Cronus. 'You've heard the feeds. It's civil war.'

Maven heard the warring desires in his friend's voice and felt the same turmoil within his own heart. The inload feeds had been jammed with a million clamouring voices: declarations of war, pleas for aid and feral screams of hatred. The Martian forges, which had stood shoulder to shoulder through uncounted epochs of darkness and weathered those storms intact, were now doing to one another what Old Night could not.

Duty to their order told Maven they should abandon this quest and ride west with all speed to join their fellow Knights in defence of the Magma City.

But honour told him that once begun, a quest could never be abandoned, only completed.

Maven felt the angry pull of *Equitos Bellum* through the Manifold and knew which imperative he must obey.

'It's closer,' he said. 'I can feel it.'

'Then let's get after it,' said Cronus, riding towards the Syria Planum. 'The sooner we kill it the sooner we can rejoin our brothers.'

THE CARGO-5 ROLLED onwards through the soaring canyons of the Noctis Labyrinthus, the darkness always seeming to draw it further and further in, as an ambush predator lures its prey. The darkness was cold and the cabin's tiny heater did little to take the edge off the chill, but after the dusty, clammy journey across the Syria Planum, no one was complaining yet.

The deeper they went, the colder it became, and white webs of hoarfrost formed on the windows, a phenomenon none of them had ever seen before. Rho-mu 31 was forced to divert valuable battery power to the heater to keep the glass clear and see where he was going.

The headlights of the Cargo-5 stuttered, barely piercing the gloom, and the atmosphere within the cabin grew stuffy and unpleasant as the air recycler failed. Hour after hour passed, and though there was nothing resembling a roadway, the base of the graben was relatively flat and the Cargo-5 devoured the kilometres.

Whenever they came to a branching canyon, Dalia would direct Rho-mu 31 with a nod of the head, as though afraid to disturb the sepulchral silence that filled the Noctis Labyrinthus.

No one questioned how she knew where she was going.

Grating static hissed from the oil-stained vox and Zouche reached down to turn it off before looking over his shoulder with a puzzled expression. 'Strange. It's not even on.'

'Mellicin did say the adepts in this region left because of technical problems,' said Caxton.

His words were said lightly, but served only to heighten their unease.

More mechanical glitches plagued them as the journey continued, though the passage of time after the first two days in the darkness was hard to judge after everyone's chronometers failed at exactly the same moment. Several hours later, the cabin's internal lights sputtered and died as they made a treacherous descent into an even deeper, shadow-thickened canyon unleavened by sunlight.

The darkness closed in on them utterly, and Dalia felt as though a cloak was being drawn around them while a host of black ghosts followed and watched from the shadows. Each of them felt a thousand eyes upon them, the hairs on the backs of their necks erect and screaming danger, though nothing threatening was visible.

Several times along the way the engine coughed and died, and each time it had to be coaxed back to life by an increasingly frustrated and nervous Caxton.

Despite the mechanical problems and the sullen, apprehensive mood that settled upon everyone in the gloom, Dalia felt a mounting sense of excitement with each kilometre that passed. They had seen no daylight and no hint of anything resembling their final objective, but with the certainty of a zealot, Dalia knew they were close.

She had no idea how deep they had penetrated into the Noctis Labyrinthus – the odometer had failed the previous day – or where they were in relation to any other living thing on Mars, but a growing ache in the back of her mind told her they were close.

The rumble of the engine cut out again, and Dalia heard Caxton groan as he prepared to venture out into the cold and the dark to get it restarted.

Rho-mu 31 shook his head. 'No need. We're not going any further, the battery's dead.'

'So what do we do now?' asked Severine, a shrill edge to her voice.

'It's all right,' said Dalia, leaning forward and wiping her hand across the cold glass of the driver's cabin. 'Look!'

Ahead of the lifeless Cargo-5, a sheer cliff towered over them, its walls sparkling as though studded with nuggets of quartz. But this was no ordinary wall of rock, Dalia realised: its surface was smooth, like fused glass, and it shone with a faint internal light. Sections of the cliff had fallen away over the aeons, exposing a darkened passage that cleft the rock, and from which a strange mist sighed like steam from a geothermal vent.

'The breath of the Dragon,' said Dalia. 'We've arrived.'

THE HIMADRI PRECINCT encircled the great, hollow mountain of the Himalazia at the crown of Terra, a mighty concourse of black, glassy marble lined with busts and statues of cowled figures. Veins of gold and red and blue threaded the marble and a thousand honour banners hung from the kilometre-high roof of shadowed arches and iron vaults.

Cold light spilled into the vast chamber through tall windows twice as large as a Warlord Titan, throwing out great spars of brightness across the tiled floor of black and white terrazzo. The light fell on the towering warrior in gold who marched along its length in the company of a smaller, white-haired man who wore the simple robes of a palace administrator.

The giant wore a magnificent suit of golden armour, wrought by the finest craftsmen and embellished with finery scrimshawed by the greatest artisans of the Imperial Fists. A mantle of red velvet edged with bronze weave hung around his shoulders and his silver hair gleamed in contrast to the lustre of his armour.

The warrior's face was craggy and tanned, browned by the light of unnumbered suns, and carved in an expression of stoic determination.

His companion was as unremarkable as the warrior was exceptional, his white hair worn long, like a mane, and his shoulders stooped with the weight of the world.

Behind this unlikely pair marched a detachment of ten Custodians in bronze armour and scarlet-plumed helms who carried long-bladed pole arms. Their presence was a formality, for Rogal Dorn, Primarch of the Imperial Fists, needed no protection.

Of all the great precincts of the Emperor's Palace, the Himadri was one of the few not to have been turned into a fortress by the golden warrior; though that fact was scant comfort to him, saw his companion, Malcador the Sigillite, Regent of Terra.

Malcador saw the wonder in Dorn's eyes as they passed beneath the Shivalik Arch and the ten thousand names of its builders inlaid with gold onto the marble. Behind that wonder, he also saw sadness.

'The glory of the Emperor's fastness will rise from the ashes of this war like a phoenix,' said Malcador, guessing his friend's thoughts.

Dorn looked down at him and smiled wearily. 'Sorry. I was just calculating how long it would take to dismantle the great archway and replace it with a bastion gateway.'

'I know you were,' nodded Malcador, lacing his hands behind his back as they passed beneath the arch. 'So how long would it take?'

'If my Fists did the work, perhaps two days,' said Dorn. 'But let's hope it doesn't come to that. If the traitor's forces reach this far then we have already lost.'

'The Emperor trusts you not to let that happen.'

'I will not,' agreed Dorn.

They walked in silence for some time, content to enjoy the view of the mountains against the rare sight of a blue sky and the many wonders contained within the Himadri Precinct: the Throne Globe of Mad King Peshkein of Tali; the Colonnade of Heroes; the last flying machine of the Roma, preserved in a shimmering stasis field; and a hundred other wonders and trophies taken in the Wars of Unity.

'The Emperor still does not join us?' asked Dorn as they passed the bloodstained Armour of Pearl that had been torn from the body of the warlord Kalagann.

Malcador sighed. He had been waiting for this question.

'No, my friend, he does not.'

'Tell me why, Sigillite,' demanded Dorn. 'His empire is crumbling and his brightest bastard son is dragging half the galaxy into war. What could possibly be more important?'

'I have no answer for you,' said Malcador. 'Save the Emperor's word that nothing is more important than his labours in the palace vaults, not Horus, not you and certainly not I.'

'Then we are alone.'

'No,' said Malcador. 'Not alone. Never alone. The Emperor may not stand beside us, but he has given us the means to fight this war and win it. Horus has three of his brother legions with him, you have your Fists and thirteen others.'

'Would that it were fifteen,' mused Dorn.

'Do not even think it, my friend,' warned Malcador. 'They are lost to us forever.'

'I know,' said Dorn, 'and you are right. By any simple reckoning of numbers, the traitor stands little chance of victory, but he was always the most cunning, the one most likely to find a way where no others could.'

'Is that what you're really afraid of?'

'Perhaps,' whispered Dorn. 'I do not yet know what I am afraid of. And that worries me.'

Malcador waved a hand along the length of the Himadri Precinct towards the grim, black portal at its end, their ultimate destination. 'Mayhap the Master of the Astrotelepathica will have more news of the Legions.'

'He'd better,' said Dorn. 'After the sacrifices we've made to pierce the storms in the warp, there had better be some news of Sanguinius and the Lion.'

'And Guilliman and Russ,' added Malcador.

'I'm not worried about them. They can look after themselves,' said Dorn. 'But the others were heading into danger when last I knew of their plans, and it grieves me that I cannot reach them. I need to gather the Legions to strike at the heart of the traitor.'

'You still plan to take the fight to Horus Lupercal?'

'After what he did to Istvaan III it is the only way,' said Dorn, almost flinching at the sound of his former brother's name. 'Kill the head and the body will die.'

'Maybe so, but we have problems closer to home to deal with first.'

'You speak of the uprisings on Mars?'

'I do,' confirmed Malcador. 'High Adept Ipluvien Maximal contacts me daily with word of further atrocities and loss of knowledge. War has come to the red planet.'

'There is no word from the Fabricator General?'

'None that makes any kind of sense. I fear he is against us now.'

'This Maximal, how reliable is he?'

Malcador shrugged. 'How reliable is anything these days? I know Maximal of old, and though he is prone to exaggeration, he is a staunch Emperor's man and I believe he speaks the truth. Mars burns with rebellion.'

'Then we need to secure the solar system before looking to make war in a far off system.'

'What do you propose?' asked Malcador.

'I shall send Sigismund and my four companies of Imperial Fists to secure the forges of Mars. Mondus Occulum and Mondus Gamma produce the bulk of the armour and weapons of the Astartes. We will strike there to capture those forges and when they are ours, we will push outwards and secure the others.'

'Sigismund? A trifle volatile is he not?' asked Malcador. 'Might not a mission to Mars benefit from a cooler head than his?'

Dorn smiled, a rare sight in these bleak times. 'My first captain is prone to bellicose talk, aye, but I will send

Camba-Diaz with him. He will provide a steadying influence on Sigismund. Will that suffice to allay your concerns?'

Malcador nodded. 'Of course. You are the commander of the Imperium's armed forces and you have my full confidence, but even a humble administrator such as I knows that you will need more warriors than four companies of Imperial Fists to pacify Mars.'

'We can bulk out the force with regiments of Imperial Army and Auxiliary units stationed on Terra and the moons of Saturn and Jupiter.'

'And perhaps Sor Talgron's Word Bearers?'

'No,' said Dorn. 'I need his warriors for the assault on Istvaan V.'

Malcador paused and looked through one of the soaring windows as the sun began to set behind the tallest peak of the world.

'Who could have believed it would come to this?' he asked.

'No one could have foreseen this,' said Dorn. 'Not even the Emperor.'

'If we cannot stop the Warmaster then everything we have built over the last three centuries will be lost, my friend. All our grand achievements and the great dream of unity will turn to ash if we fail. We will perish by our own hands or else be devoured by a tide of alien insurgents, unable to mount more than a token resistance against the ghoulish hordes.'

'Then we cannot afford to fail,' said Dorn.

Malcador turned to face Dorn and looked up into his handsome, weathered features. 'Send your warriors to Mars, Rogal Dorn. Secure the Martian forges and then crush the life from Horus Lupercal on Istvaan V.'

Dorn bowed towards him. 'It shall be done,' he promised.

As Adept Zeth had predicted, the forces of the Fabricator General did indeed return to the Magma City. The sun rose above the calderas of the Tharsis Montes on yet another day of bloodshed and chaos, and auspex lookouts raised the alarm that the inhabitants of her forge had feared.

Legio Mortis was on the march.

Southwards from Pavonis Mons, the engines of Mortis came around the western flanks of Arsia Mons, easily demolishing the high walls surrounding the container yards and runways that fed on the materiel produced by the Magma City. Led by the towering Imperator, *Aquila Ignis*, a total of thirteen war engines strode through the great breach torn by the guns of the Imperator.

The Imperator's pack moved slowly and ponderously, a mix of Warlords and Reavers, with four Warhounds leading the way like snarling wolves to flush out their prey. Armour of red and silver and black gleamed in the growing light, their hulls freshly daubed with the Eye of

Horus. Thundering warhorns blared their warlike intentions and hideous blurts of scrapcode screamed their corrupted names across the airwaves.

From a distance they looked like hunched old men, moving with wheezing, stiff-legged gaits, but there was nothing infirm about these terrible war engines. These machines had been designed with the express purpose of destroying the enemies of humanity, but were now perverted to serve a darker purpose and far darker masters.

They paid the vast stacks of containers no mind, intent on pressing onwards to their goal of destruction. The container port was huge, but looming in the distance was the industrial sprawl of the Arsia Mons sub-hives, worker habs and outlying production hubs.

It was to this tangled mass of structures that Mortis walked, the only route, other than the heavily defended Typhon Causeway, by which their engines could cross the vast magma lagoon upon which Adept Zeth's city stood.

No route wide enough for the Titans existed through the sub-hives, but Princeps Camulos had no need for one. The guns of his Titans could easily blast a path, or simply crush a way through with the weight of his engines. Mortis cared nothing for the millions that dwelled within the sub-hives, only that the Magma City was brought to ruin and Adept Zeth humbled before the new masters of Mars.

Thousands of workers fled before the advancing Titans, ants before a herd of charging bull grox, but like the containers around them, the Mortis engines ignored them, safe in the knowledge that the forces following behind them would mop up any lingering threats.

Flowing like a black-armoured tide of spiked nightmares made real, the warped cohorts of skitarii and horrifically altered battle-servitors poured into the container port, their lustful war-shouts echoing weirdly from the metal skins of the stacked containers.

Explosions dotted the landing fields as fuel lines were crushed under the colossal feet of the Titans and flames followed in their wake. Black smoke boiled upwards like dark scratches etched on the sky.

Artillery pieces fired from redoubts and fortifications around the base of the sub-hives, and the ground before the Titans erupted in corrosive flames and deadly clouds of whickering shrapnel. Hundreds of enemy soldiers were cut down in the first instant, but it was nothing compared to the host pressing at their backs.

Voids flared and shimmered under the bombardment, but without the concentration of fire necessary to overload an engine's shields, the defensive fire was largely wasted. The four Warhounds bounded forward, low to the ground, weaving between the incoming fire as they opened up with their mega bolters.

One Warhound staggered as a particularly well-aimed salvo caught it full on and it shed its voids in a coruscating detonation. The explosion blew off one of its legs and it smashed, nose-first, into the ground, ploughing a thirty-metre furrow before finally coming to a halt. A cheer of elation erupted from the defenders, but observers further back in the Magma City knew the loss of a single Warhound would not slow the attackers.

The remaining Warhounds increased their speed, using their agility to better evade, and each engine's princeps displayed a healthy respect for the accuracy of the Magma City's gunners.

Blizzards of weapons fire strafed the defenders, a furious storm of high explosive shells that tore through all but the heaviest fortifications, wreaking unimaginable havoc within the packed knots of Zeth's Protectors, skitarii and tech-guard. Artillery pieces exploded and ammo parks detonated explosively as the Warhounds' fire tore through them.

The elation that had gripped the defenders upon seeing a Warhound brought down evaporated instantly in the face of the destruction unleashed by its brothers. Terrified, insensate survivors staggered away from the shrieking, smoking, flaming hell of explosions, some clutching severed limbs, others holding in spilling intestines or dragging the shredded carcasses of their comrades away from the firestorm.

As a flood of panicked men and women fled the fortification lines, the adamantium blast doors of a hardened bunker slid aside and an Ordinatus machine rolled forwards on heavy gauge rails. A gargantuan artillery piece so large it needed a strengthened chassis, a crew of hundreds and specialised generators just to power its enormous gun, the Ordinatus was a weapon of such power that an adept counted himself lucky if he had even one such weapon in his arsenal.

Its crew locked in the targeting auspex, working on a firing solution on one of the larger war engines, an impetuous Reaver that had broken from the pack of marauding Titans.

A searing beam of blinding, unwavering energy erupted from the Ordinatus and struck the careless Reaver square in the face. Instantly its shields screamed and blew out in a froth of sparks and whipping arcs of discharged energies that vaporised hundreds of mutant skitarii advancing in its shadow. The Ordinatus beam continued to play over the Reaver's body, obliterating armour plates and body shielding in a flurry of actinic explosions.

Flames bloomed from inside the enemy machine and as the reactor core was breached, the Reaver vanished as a newborn sun flared into life. Voids scraped and howled as the Reaver's accomplices felt the violence of its death, but none were damaged beyond shrapnel scars.

Its work done, the Ordinatus machine began to roll back into its protective bunker to recharge its main gun.

It never got the chance.

The towering, dreadful form of *Aquila Ignis* opened fire with its monstrous annihilator cannon and the giant Ordinatus vanished in an expanding mushroom cloud of nuclear plasma.

Shock at the death of such a magnificent machine rendered the defenders immobile for a heartbeat, but that was all the Mortis engines needed. As the Ordinatus was consumed in a sea of roiling plasma, the opportunistic Warhounds darted forward and smashed through the crumbled remains of the defensive line.

Amongst the defenders, the Warhounds barked their triumph from carapace-mounted augmitters and began the killing. Mega bolters blitzed and chewed up exposed soldiers in a furious storm of explosive rounds through which nothing could survive. Turbo lasers incinerated flesh and melted armoured units as the cackling beasts crushed the tiny figures that stood before them.

Drunk with slaughter, the Warhounds raced onwards, crushing the few pitifully burned or shredded survivors as their slower pack members stomped over the walls between the worker habs and outerworks of Adept Zeth's mighty forge, as easily as a child might step over a fallen branch.

In the close-packed confines of the sub-hives, the Warhounds snapped and killed like hunting raptors, guns rippling with fire and their horns screaming with the elation of the kill.

One engine worked in solitude, methodically reducing block after block of habs and forge temples to ruin with its weapons and bulk. Walls broke apart, smelteries collapsed and great coolant towers were brought down in tumbling cascades of rockcrete and steel.

Two others worked as a pair, one demolishing buildings with concentrated blasts of fire, while the other raked the rubble to slay any survivors. Together, they left a wake of destruction such as had never been seen in the Magma City's history.

Dust billowed in vast clouds and the sound of collapsing structures overpowered even the cackling glee of the Warhounds as they cleared a path for the larger engines.

The solitary Warhound was the first to die.

Its crew never saw its killer, but its sensori felt the auspex lock a fraction of a second before its voids were blown out in a devastating volley of las-fire and it was obliterated in a rippling series of missile impacts.

The other two Warhounds felt its demise and furiously surged into the ruins in search of its destroyer. Darting forwards in a series of loping bounds, they came upon its smouldering carcass and swept the area with aggressive bursts of their targeting auspex.

The lead engine caught a return from behind a shattered steelworks and opened fire without waiting for a lock, hoping to drive its quarry into the open where its twin could finish it off.

The ironworks dissolved into a mist of pulverised rock fragments and shattered steel, but instead of forcing the engine behind it to run, it had the opposite effect.

Lunging though the fiery debris, a towering monster in cobalt blue armour came at the Warhounds, its fists blazing and a heroic challenge issuing from its warhorn.

Deus Tempestus crashed into the astonished Warhound, smashing it to the ground and stamping down hard with one enormous foot. The smaller engine was crushed like a tin can beneath the mighty Warlord, the First God Machine of Legio Tempestus.

'Engine kill,' said Princeps Cavalerio high up in the liquid depths of his amniotic tank.

The second Warhound fled at the sight of the larger engine, turning and sprinting for the support of its fellows like a bully confronted by a gang of his former victims.

It ran straight into the guns of *Metallus Cebrenia* and *Arcadia Fortis*, who caught it in a lethal crossfire that ripped away its voids and gutted it in a furious hurricane of turbos.

Behind the two jubilant engines, the Tempestus Warhounds, *Vulpus Rex, Raptoria, Astrus Lux* and the Warlord *Tharsis Hastatus* moved into position within the hab-blocks, ready to defend the Magma City against the might of Legio Mortis.

Surveying the smashed wreckage of the slain war machines, Princeps Cavalerio smiled.

<Mortis want a fight!> he canted to his warriors. <We will ensure they get one!>

FROM THE CHAMBER of Vesta, high atop the silver pyramid in the centre of the Magma City, Adept Zeth read the inloaded data of the four destroyed Warhounds. The arrival of Tempestus two nights ago might have prompted her to believe in the providence of the Machine-God, but she knew she owed her city's continued survival to Princeps Cavalerio's honourable heart.

Even without the terrible threat of the Mortis Imperator, the Tempestus engines were dreadfully outnumbered and outgunned, yet still Cavalerio had come. Had he not been interred within an amniotic tank, she would have hugged him in a rare outburst of emotion.

The first blow had to be struck from ambush in an attempt to even the odds, and though Zeth keenly felt the loss of so many soldiers and artillery, their sacrifice had been necessary to lure the engines of Mortis in with the promise of easy kills. Four Warhounds and a Reaver was an impressive tally, but gun for gun and engine to engine, Tempestus was still grossly outmatched.

The gracefully curved sheets of burnished steel and crystal of the roof structure displayed images of the fighting around the landing fields and container port, and as much as she relished the killing of her enemies' Titans, she lamented the loss of such precious technology. No adept of Mars could fail to be moved by the destruction of so perfect a mechanism that combined the best of steel and flesh.

As deadly a threat as Mortis represented, they were not the only foes ranged against the Magma City. The cohorts of the Fabricator General had returned in full, swarming like an army of roaches on the far shores of the magma lagoon in preparation for an all-out assault. An attempt had already been made along the Typhon Causeway, a host of armoured units and hideously altered infantry storming the Vulkan Gate with gravity rams and conversion beamers.

A sally from the Knights of Taranis had broken the assault, but three of their precious Knights had been torn down to win the fight. Though they had killed well over a thousand enemy soldiers and destroyed a brigade's worth of armour, it was but a tiny dent in the vast force arrayed before them.

Other screens displayed similar scenes of war.

The equatorial refinery belt burned as running battles between engines and thousands of skitarii clashed in the blazing ruins. A ring of fire encircled Mars in imitation of the iron ring in orbit.

The hive assembly yards of Elysium, once the domain of Magos Godolph, were a silent tomb, the tens of thousands of skilled adepts having committed mass suicide in some awful ceremony to honour unknown gods.

Eridania, once the home of the most ancient and revered orders of Archivists, the Brotherhood of the All

Seeing Eye, bore witness to scenes of unimaginable slaughter as the skitarii of Magos Chevain clawed their way into the kilometres-deep repository only to unleash the pestilential scrapcode. Data wheels, memory crystals and realbooks all died as the scrapcode infected every system and flooded the sunken library with corrosive gases.

'So much history and knowledge lost,' said a voice from above her, and Zeth lifted her head to look at the roof panels where her noospheric guests observed the fighting.

One panel projected the flickering image of Adept Maximal's helmet, another the handsome features of Fabricator Locum Kane.

'Some knowledge is best forgotten, Maximal,' she said.

'Don't say such things,' replied Maximal. 'Knowledge is power and no price is too high to pay to preserve it. The accumulation of knowledge should be our one and only goal, Zeth. You of all people should appreciate that. Was the Akashic reader not built for that very purpose, the accumulation of *all* knowledge?'

'It was,' conceded Zeth, using haptic motions to zoom in on the lumbering brutes of Legio Mortis. The carapaces and hulls of these once glorious engines were hung with black banners depicting vile, unthinkable acts of butchery. The head sections, once fashioned as stalwart warrior helms, were now leering, twisted and bestial things. 'But any knowledge that creates something like this is best deleted without hope of recovery.'

Maximal sniffed, a petulant affectation to show his disagreement.

'Enough,' said Kane. 'Save such discussions for when this crisis is over. We need to focus our attentions on how we plan to survive before we lament the loss of knowledge. Lord Dorn of the Imperial Fists sends word of an expeditionary force en route to Mars to fight our enemies. We must hold on until they reach us.'

'What else do you know?' asked Zeth. 'When will they get here? Tempestus and the Knights of Taranis have given my forge a chance to hold out for a time, but Mortis will attack again and we may not turn them back this time.'

'And my forge suffers daily attacks,' said Maximal. 'My skitarii units and war engines continue to hold, but the hordes pouring from the darkened hives of Olympus Mons are without end. I fear for what will be lost when we are overwhelmed.'

Kane nodded. 'I am aware of your tactical situation and have apprised Lord Dorn. Elements of the Imperial Army and the Saturn Regiments have been tasked with the relief of your forges.'

'And the Astartes?' demanded Zeth. 'What of them?'

Kane hesitated before answering, and even over the noospheric link, Zeth sensed his reluctance to speak. 'Captain Sigismund will make planetfall at my forge of Mondus Occulum and Captain Camba-Diaz will assault Lukas Chrom's Mondus Gamma facility.'

'Then the Astartes do not come to aid us at all,' protested Maximal. 'They seek to secure their own supplies of weapons and armour! Intolerable!'

'Agreed,' said Zeth. 'We need the Astartes if we are to defeat Kelbor-Hal's minions.'

'Captain Sigismund has assured me that once the armour and weapon production facilities are secured, his warriors will come to your aid.'

'Then let us hope they are swift in their conquests,' said Zeth.

'Indeed,' said Kane, either missing or ignoring her caustic tone. 'In the meantime, do all you can to hold on. Help is on the way and I will exload information to you both as I receive it. Good luck and may the Machine-God guide you.'

The image of Kane faded from the glass, and Zeth returned her attention to the scenes of war and death inloading from all across Mars.

Adept Maximal remained as a ghostly presence flickering from the burnished plate above her, and Zeth regarded him quizzically.

'You have something to add, Maximal?'

'Is there any word from your wayward protégé?'

Beneath her mask, Koriel Zeth smiled. Even with his forge besieged and facing destruction, Ipluvien Maximal still hungered for knowledge.

Zeth shook her head. 'No. Rho-mu 31's biometrics ceased transmitting somewhere in the Noctis Labyrinthus and I can find no trace of them. I fear he may be dead.'

'So Dalia Cythera is probably dead as well?' asked Kane.

'That is probable, yes.'

Maximal's sigh of disappointment matched her own.

THE INTERIOR OF the tunnel was not dark as Dalia had feared, but alive with a soft illumination. The rock itself glowed, as though carrying some form of bioluminescent current. The air was cold and their breath misted before them as Rho-mu 31 led the way. The tunnel was narrow, its cross-section like that of a leaf-shaped arch, and they were forced to travel in single file as it sloped ever deeper into the planet's surface.

Dalia reached out and touched the walls to either side of her; they were warm and though they looked smooth, she felt minute imperfections in the surface, as though a million tiny picks had chipped away at them.

They walked for what felt like an age, winding through serpentine passages and multi-coloured galleries of translucent stalagmites, and across glittering bridges of smooth crystal. Dalia wondered what manner of internal geological transformation could alter so great a portion of the subterranean landscape.

'What could cause something like this?' she asked, making the question sound light.

'Geological metamorphosis I'd imagine,' said Zouche. 'Aeons of pressure and heat can cause some rock types to change their state. Looks like that's what's happened here.'

No, realised Dalia, *that's not it at all. It's something buried here that's leaching outwards.*

She said nothing and continued to follow Rho-mu 31 as the internal illumination of the rock began to recede behind them and their little group bunched up around the solitary light from the Protector's weapon stave.

At length, Rho-mu 31 held up his hand, halting their group.

'Do you hear that?'

Dalia could hear nothing at first, but as they all came to a halt and slowed their breathing, she could make out the faint sound of movement.

'What do you think it is?' asked Caxton.

Rho-mu 31 shrugged. 'I don't know. I didn't think anything remained here.'

'Well we didn't come this far to turn back,' said Dalia, easing past Rho-mu 31 and heading towards the sound with more confidence than she felt. Her heart beat loudly in her chest and she squinted as she saw a bright light from up ahead.

Dalia emerged into a wide laboratory chamber, carved from the rock of the cliffs and roughly rectangular in shape. One wall was festooned with thousands of colourful sheets of parchment like a children's collage, and at the far end of the chamber was a darkened passageway. Bare girders of red iron supported the ceiling, from which dangled a host of gently swaying cables, some inert, some twisting with fizzing sparks.

Against one wall was a surgical table, surrounded by banks of respirators, intravenous drips and a number of steel tables laden with unpleasant-looking machinery. Next to this was a complex device that resembled a giant rock drill, with mechanisms formed from stained brass and tarnished steel. Rust plated its sides and glass generator globes sat atop looping coils of rigid golden wire. A silver wheel-like apparatus sat on a conical mount at the front of the device, each of its four spokes fitted with a small emitter dish.

Each of the dishes was aimed at an upright slab on the far wall with the imprinted shadow of a human body upon it and leather straps at the wrists, ankles and neck.

'Now this just *can't* be good,' said Caxton.

Dalia paid the device no mind, walking over to examine the parchment scraps on the wall.

'What are these?' wondered Severine, plucking one from the wall and handing it to Dalia.

The parchment was glossy and depicted a human silhouette limned with a rainbow of colours. Reds, greens and blues danced around the subject's body, but Dalia saw that on the right arm, the colours faded from the elbow down, as though the strength of whatever was producing the colours had faded.

'I'm not sure,' replied Dalia. 'Some kind of electrography?'

She made her way along the length of the wall, seeing hundreds of pictures, all displaying elements of human bodies with glowing, colourful auras surrounding them. Like the first picture, each silhouette showed a loss in colour at one extremity, be it a leg, arm or a head.

'I don't like this,' said Zouche as he examined the machine. 'Reeks of dark technology. Forgotten science. Like the kind that almost destroyed mankind before Old Night.'

'You don't even know what this does,' said Caxton, stepping in front of the silver wheel.

'Don't stand there!' shouted Dalia, dropping the image she held.

'What? Why not?' asked Caxton. 'I don't think this machine's worked in centuries. There's nothing to worry about.'

'Ha!' said Severine. 'The last time you said that we almost died when that battle robot attacked the mag-lev.'

Caxton shook his head, but moved away from the strange machine, smiling at Zouche as the machinist examined what looked like a steel control panel with a number of gem-like buttons, a brass radial dial and a long lever.

'I think you're wrong about that, Caxton,' said Zouche. 'This panel hasn't got a spot of rust or dust on it. I think someone's used this machine quite recently.'

'And you would be right,' said a cracked voice, ancient and thick with age.

Dalia spun to see Rho-mu 31 with his weapon stave aimed at a hooded adept in dark robes emerging from the passageway at the far end of the chamber.

'Oh yes, you would be right,' continued the adept. 'Happy day that you come to me! I had all but given up hope of anyone ever arriving!'

'Who are you?' demanded the Protector, igniting the tip of his weapon stave as a hulking servitor emerged from the shadows to stand beside the adept. The servitor was bulky with augmetics, one arm replaced with a hissing, wheezing power claw, the other with an oversized chainblade.

The adept drew back his hood and Dalia gasped as she saw his gaunt features, wild eyes and thin scraps of bone-white hair. His flesh shone with mercurial light, as though glittering fire filled his veins instead of blood, and upon his forehead she saw a shining electoo of a diminishing spiral with a stylised set of wings to either side.

The mark of the Dragon.

'I know you,' she said. 'I dreamed of you.'

'The hooded man?' gasped Caxton. 'He's real?'

'Am I real?' asked the adept. 'Well, as real as any of you, though what constitutes reality in this polluted cesspool of psi-spoor we call a universe… well, a matter for some debate, yes?'

'Who are you?' repeated Rho-mu 31, taking a step towards the man.

'Who am I? Now there's a question. One might as well ask how many stars there are in the heavens, though that would have a definite answer. Or would it? Ah, it's been so long since I have seen them. Are they still there or have the others devoured them?'

'The stars?' asked Dalia.

'Of course the stars,' snapped the adept. 'Are they still there?'

'Yes, they're still there.'

'How many?'

'I don't know,' said Dalia. 'Millions, I think.'

'Millions she says,' laughed the adept. 'And not a second after she says she knows not.'

Rho-mu 31 stepped between Dalia and the cackling adept.

'I won't ask again,' said Rho-mu 31. 'Tell me your name.'

'My name,' said the adept, looking confused. 'Ah, but it's been so long since I needed one and it gets so hard to remember. I need no name, for my name is insignificant against the vast, echoing emptiness of the darkness, but men once called me Semyon.'

'And what are you doing here?' asked Dalia.

'Here?' cried Semyon, throwing his arms wide and spinning around like a lunatic. 'You have such a limited understanding of the material world, girl. Words like *here* and *there* have no meaning. The myriad dimensions of this material universe cannot be defined by so limited a thing as human language!'

Semyon stopped with his back to Dalia and looked over his shoulder, his face alight with the fire she had seen in Jonas Milus's eyes before his body had disintegrated.

'I am the Guardian of the Dragon!' said Semyon.

THE SUB-HIVES AND manufacturing regions to the northwest of the Magma City lay in ruins. Kilometre-high hab blocks lay scattered across the burning container port like toppled anthills and smashed war engines burned where they had fallen. Bodies littered the ground and tanks lay on their backs or twisted onto their sides without turrets.

With the destruction of their scouting engines, the Titans of Legio Mortis had pulled back, unwilling to advance through such dense terrain and into the teeth of an unknown number of enemy engines.

Instead, they had settled for an intense bombardment from afar, each engine bracing itself with internal gyros and gravitational stabilisers as they locked out their weapon limbs and began to systematically pound the outer habs and work precincts of Koriel Zeth's domain, careful not to damage the forge.

That was to be captured intact.

Princeps Cavalerio withdrew his forces within the walls of the Magma City as the punishing fire brought the thunder of the gods to earth. Fire sheeted from the sky like the end of days, and the planet was lost in a mist of dust and fire and smoke as the city in the shadow of the volcano shuddered with the fury of the bombardment.

Within the walls, hundreds of thousands of refugees packed the thoroughfares, boulevards and sinks of the city. With nowhere to run, the servants of Adept Zeth huddled in terrified misery as the deafening roar of explosions and the seismic shocks of detonations shook the city from the peak of the forge to its void-shielded foundations.

The Knights of Taranis broke two more attacks on the gate, each time without loss, but Preceptor Stator's mount, *Fortis Metallum*, took a grievous wound to the chest.

Further west, sealed up in his forge between Biblis Patera and Ulysses Patera, Ipluvien Maximal watched as a screaming host, conservatively estimated to be in the region of half a million soldiers, hurled itself at his shielded walls with power mauls and vortex mines.

Servitor-slaved guns sawed through mob after mob of enemy warriors, but such was the force arrayed against them they might as well have ceased firing for all the difference they made.

Ipluvien Maximal greatly feared that the life of his forge could now be measured in hours instead of days.

In the north-eastern reaches of Tharsis, only Mondus Occulum had been spared the ravages of the enemy, though for what purpose, Fabricator Locum Kane could not fathom.

Perhaps Kelbor-Hal thought he might yet lure Kane to his cause, or maybe the Fabricator General did not wish to risk losing the Astartes production facilities for the Warmaster.

Whatever the reason, Kane gave thanks to the Omnissiah as he stood in the howling winds that swirled around the gigantic Tsiolkovsky towers and landing fields of Uranius Patera, watching as squadron after squadron of Imperial Fists Stormbirds descended like a golden flock of avenging angels.

3.03

AFTER HIS DRAMATIC pronouncement, Adept Semyon lowered his arms and moved past Rho-mu 31 to shoo Zouche and Caxton away from the machine. He adjusted the dials and pressed a number of the buttons, though nothing appeared to happen. Looking disappointed, but not entirely surprised, he shrugged.

'What kind of machine is that?' asked Zouche. 'Some kind of conversion beam engine?'

'Pah, it's too complex for the likes of you to comprehend,' snapped Semyon. 'But, for the record, this is my very own gas discharge machine of the perturbation variety, which creates pulsed electrical field excitations and thus measures electro-photonic glow. What the less sophisticated might call auras.'

'These images,' said Dalia. 'That machine created them?'

'It did indeed,' nodded the adept without looking up. 'It did indeed, though it takes a great deal of effort to convince the subjects of the images to willingly submit to the process.'

'And why's that?' asked Zouche.

Semyon pointed to the imprinted shadow on the upright slab. 'You see that? That's all that's left of someone once the device has been activated.'

'It kills them?' asked Dalia, horrified at the number of deaths that must have taken place in this grim laboratory to satisfy Semyon's research.

'It does,' agreed Semyon with a giggle. 'But such things are sometimes necessary to keep the Dragon quiescent.'

'You know where the Dragon is?' demanded Dalia. 'Can you take us to it?'

Semyon laughed, a high-pitched skirling sound of hysteria. 'Take you to it? Doesn't she know it's all around her, that she walks in the throat of the Dragon even now? Ha!'

'This fellow's mad,' declared Zouche. 'Too much time alone has broken his brain.'

'No,' said Dalia with steely conviction. 'This isn't the Dragon. Take us to it. Now!'

Her friends turned at the commanding tone of her voice and even Semyon blinked in surprise. His eyes narrowed and he peered more closely at Dalia, as if seeing her for the first time.

Semyon grinned and nodded, pulling the hood of his robes over the wispy strands of his hair. 'Very well,' he said, all hint of his former mania vanished. 'Follow me and I will show you the Dragon.'

Semyon and his threatening-looking servitor led them from the laboratory, through the darkened passageway at the far end of the chamber, and into a winding series of tunnels. The gloom soon gave way to a soft light that once again seemed to come from the walls.

The walls here were also smooth, but instead of having the look of fused glass, these tunnels appeared to be fashioned from purest silver. With purposeful strides,

Semyon led them through the twisting labyrinth of the incredible tunnels, apparently taking turns at random, but refusing to answer any questions as to their route.

Zouche jabbed his elbow into Dalia's side. 'Wherever this takes us, remember what we talked about on the mag-lev,' he cautioned.

'What was that?' asked Caxton.

'Nothing,' said Dalia. 'Just Zouche being paranoid.'

'Paranoid am I?' smiled Zouche. 'Remind me of that when this Dragon's devouring you, Dalia. See how paranoid I am then, eh?'

Eventually, Semyon brought them out onto a wide ledge high up in a glittering cavern of blinding silver that put Dalia in mind of the hollow core of the planet, such was its size. It was the largest internal space any of them had ever seen or could imagine, the uttermost reaches soaring above and below them, and the shimmering walls curving out to either side of them like the largest amphitheatre ever conceived.

'Behold the Dragon!' cried Semyon, moving to stand before a wooden lectern that was incongruous for its very normality. A thick book with a worn leather binding sat atop the lectern, next to a simple quill and inkwell.

Dalia looked out over the vast expanse of silver that was the interior of the cave, half-expecting to see some winged beast launch itself from its lair.

She glanced over at Caxton and Rho-mu 31, who both shrugged, both equally as puzzled as her. Severine shuffled forward to the edge of the jutting promontory they stood on, her eyes with a glazed, faraway look.

'Severine, watch out,' cautioned Zouche, looking over the edge. 'It's a long way down.'

'This place feels… strange,' said Severine, a tremor of disquiet in her voice. 'Do any of the rest of you feel that?'

Dalia saw Severine looking in confusion at the distant walls of the gargantuan cavern, blinking rapidly and shaking her head as though trying to dislodge a trouble-some thought.

'If the Dragon is chained somewhere in here, I expect it's bound to feel a little strange,' said Dalia. She squinted at the far off walls, though their unbroken, reflective sheen made it hard to focus properly.

'No,' insisted Severine, pointing with her good arm at the vast shimmering silver walls and roof. 'It's more than that. The angles and the perspective... they're... all... wrong! *Look!*'

As though Severine's words had unlocked some hidden aspect of the cavern, each of them cried out as the sheer impossibility of its geometry, previously concealed from their frail human senses, was suddenly and horrifyingly revealed.

Dalia blinked in confusion as a sudden wave of vertigo seized her, and she grasped Rho-mu 31's arm to steady herself. Though her eyes told her that the walls of the cavern were impossibly distant, her brain could not mesh what she was seeing and what her mind was processing.

The angles were impossible, the geometry insane. Distance was irrelevant and perspective a lie. Every rule of normality was turned upside down in an instant and the natural order of the universe was overthrown in this new, terrifying vision of distorted reality. The cavern seemed to pulse in every direction at once, compressing and contracting in unfeasible ways, moving as rock was never meant to move.

This was no cavern. Was this entire space, the walls and floor, the air and every molecule within it, part of some vast intelligence, a being or construct of ancient malice and phenomenal, primeval power? Such a thing had no name; for what use would a being that had brought entire civilisations into existence and then snuffed them out on a whim have of a name? It had been abroad in the galaxy for millions of years before humanity had been a breath in the creator's mouth, had drunk the hearts of stars and been worshipped as a god in a thousand galaxies.

It was everywhere and nowhere at once. All powerful and trapped at the same time.

The monstrous horror of its very existence threatened to shatter the walls of her mind, and in desperation, Dalia looked down at her feet in an attempt to convince herself that the laws of perspective still held true in relation to her own body. Her existence in the face of this infinite impossibility was meaningless, but she recognised that only by small victories might she hold onto her fracturing reason.

'No,' she whispered, feeling her grip on the three-dimensionality of her surroundings slipping as the distance to her feet seemed to stretch out into infinity. Her vertigo suddenly swamped her and she dropped to her knees as her vision stretched and swelled, the interior of the cavern suddenly seeming to be as vast as the universe and as compressed as a singularity within the same instant.

She felt the threads of her sanity unravelling in the face of this distorted reality, her brain unable to cope with the sensory overload it was failing to process.

A hand grasped the sleeve of her robe, and she looked into the lined, serious face of Zouche. With a gasping snap, her focus returned, as though the squat machinist was an anchor of solidity in an ocean of madness.

'Don't look at it,' advised Zouche. 'Keep focused on me!'

Dalia nodded, her senses numbed by the violated angles and utter *wrongness* of the cavern walls and the thing they cloaked from view. How had she not noticed it before? Had it taken her senses a moment to try to process the sheer impossibility of what she saw?

Even knowing the warped nature of what she was experiencing, she still felt dizzy and disorientated, so she followed Zouche's advice and kept her attention firmly focused on his loyal face.

She took a series of deep breaths with her eyes shut before pushing herself to her feet and turning to face Adept Semyon, who stood beside the lectern. The dark-robed adept and his towering combat servitor were an unwavering slice of reality amid the chaos of her unmade vision, and the more she concentrated on him, the more her brain forced the anarchy of angles and rogue geometry into a semblance of normality.

She could still sense the roiling power and madness behind the thin veil of reality her mind had imposed, but pushed the thought of it to the very back of her skull.

Caxton lay curled in a foetal ball on the ground, his eyes screwed shut and a thin line of foam dribbling from his mouth. Rho-mu 31 was down on one knee as though in prayer, gripping his weapon stave tightly as he fought down the maddening vision in his head.

Severine stood where Dalia remembered her, staring out over the expanse of the cavern at the furthest extent of the ledge.

'I understand,' Dalia told Semyon. 'The Dragon... I don't know *what* it is, but I know where it is.'

'Do you?' asked Semyon. 'Tell me.'

'This cavern... everything in it. This is it. Or at least a sliver of it.'

Semyon nodded. 'A tomb and prison all in one.'

'How?'

Semyon beckoned her over to the lectern and opened the book. 'Look. *Know.*'

Dalia took halting steps towards him, feeling the strange sense of inevitability that had gripped her when they had travelled on the mag-lev. She had a sudden sense that she was meant to do this, that she had been heading towards this moment all her life.

She reached the lectern and looked down at the book, its pages filled with the tightly knotted scrawl of a madman with too much to say and too little space to write it. The words made no sense to her, the language archaic, the lettering too small and compressed.

Even as she tried to tell Semyon she couldn't read his words, he reached over the book and took her hands in a grip of iron as its pages turned in a frantic blur of parchment.

'No... please...' she begged. 'I don't want it!'

'I said the same thing,' said Semyon. 'But he doesn't care what we want. We have a duty.'

Dalia felt the inhuman fire in Semyon's blood through the searing heat of his hands. The pain was excruciating, but it was nothing compared to the terror that filled her at the dreadful truths contained in the immortal depths of his eyes.

She tried to look away, but his gaze held her locked tight.

His skin blazed with a pure golden light. 'Look into my eyes and see the Dragon's doom!'

And in one awful rushing flood of knowledge, Dalia saw *everything*.

As SIGISMUND'S COMPANIES landed at Mondus Occulum, the rest of the Imperial expeditionary force was fighting all across the surface of Mars. After a rapid deployment under fire in the shadow of Pavonis Mons, thirteen companies of the Saturnine Hoplites advanced on the lines of circumvallation surrounding the forge of Ipluvien Maximal.

At first, the soldiers of Saturn made good progress, their heavy armour soaking up the fire from the enemy warriors tasked with manning the rearward-facing defences, but within hours, a host of skitarii surged from the ridged landscape of the Gigas Fossae to flank them.

Hundreds died in every surge and clash of arms, nightmarishly augmented warriors tearing through the ranks of the horrified Imperial soldiers before finally being brought down. Beetle-backed servitors with spiked armour and hissing weapon arms bounded forward, unleashing rippling beams of incandescent light that shrieked like banshees and incinerated men and obliterated armoured vehicles with equal ease.

Bizarre tanks scuttled forward on spider-like legs to clamber over the wrecks of destroyed vehicles and slice through armour and flesh with every sweep of their energy-sheathed pincer arms. Within minutes, the Imperial advance was in danger of becoming a rout until a company of super-heavy tanks rolled through the centre of the Imperial lines to tear through the vile horde of the enemy with their enormous guns.

With the support of so many colossal armoured fortresses, the Saturnine forces rallied, quickly encircled the enemy counterattack and crushed it utterly. With their flanks secure, the battered and wary Imperial soldiers continued their attempt to relieve the siege of Maximal's forge.

Further south, two companies of Imperial Fists and four regiments of Jovian Grenadiers under the command of Captain Camba-Diaz made planetfall in the Mondus Gamma forge complex, but unlike Sigismund's warriors at Mondus Occulum, they were unwelcome arrivals.

As Sigismund secured vast quantities of munitions for transport back to Terra, nearly two thousand aircraft – Stormbirds, Thunderhawks and Army drop-ships – swooped on Mondus Gamma under the cover of an ash storm blowing in from the Solis Planum. In the wake of a furious volley of missiles and cannon fire, the assaulters blasted their way into the production facilities of southern sub-hive factorum.

Surprise was total, and led by hundreds of warriors in golden battle plate, over fifteen thousand Imperial soldiers stormed the forge's defences, rapidly seizing the armaments temples before spreading out to secure the armouries in a textbook example of multiple take and hold assaults. With the dropsite secure, wide-bellied supply carriers dropped into the forge, and an army of loader servitors, overseers and quartermasters began the liberation of the vast quantities of armour and weapons.

As sudden and shocking as the Astartes assault had been, the unknown quantity of the defences was quickly and horribly revealed. Within moments of the carriers landing, the monstrosities of Lukas Chrom's forge rose to its defence.

A host of screeching battle robots, their weapons limned with unholy light, attacked and burned and crushed scores of desperate men with blazing fire lances and power maces. Alongside the robots came a tide of blank-faced automatons, each one fighting with deadly ferocity and unbreakable resolve. These monstrous machines slowed, and finally held the merciless advance of the Astartes, giving the forge's mortal defenders the opportunity to launch a ferocious counterattack.

An endless tide of screaming tech-guard, thousands of hideously altered weaponised servitors and yet more battle robots converged on the Astartes and Army units from multiple directions in perfectly coordinated phalanxes. Only the superhuman resolve and tenacity of the Imperial Fists prevented their position from being overrun in the first moments of the counterattack.

Desperate soldiers fought and died as loaders and riggers rushed to evacuate as many suits of armour and crates of weapons as possible from the blazing forge, onto the waiting carriers.

With every second, men were dying, but Camba-Diaz knew that it was a small price to pay in order to secure as many weapons and suits of armour as possible.

Terra would stand or fall depending on what they could achieve here.

DALIA SMELLED THE hot, dry air of another world, the spiced fragrances drifting from lands far away and countries as yet undiscovered. The cavern beneath the Noctis Labyrinthus faded from view, the silver lines that defied rational perception easing into obscurity and replaced with the soft curves of desert dunes and the vast expanse of a breathtakingly beautiful azure sky.

A ferocious heat enveloped her and she gasped as it hit her like an opened blast furnace. The vista was at once strange and familiar to her, and her fear faded as she suddenly understood where and when she was.

She stood on the baking sands of a high dune, looking over a wide river valley where a great city of sun-bleached stone reared up on a plateau of dark rock. From the gates of the city marched a solemn procession of women in white, bearing a silk-veiled litter of gold and jade.

'You know where you are?' said a voice behind her and she turned to see Adept Semyon.

'I think so,' said Dalia. 'This is Old Earth. Before Unification.'

Semyon nodded. '*Long* before Unification. The tribes of men are still divided and know nothing of the glories and perils beyond their world.'

'And what is that city over there?' asked Dalia.

'Still thinking in such literal terms, girl,' chuckled Semyon. 'We are still in the cave of the Dragon. All this is a manipulation of your mind's perception centres by the book to show you what needs to be shown. But in answer to your question, the city is called Cyrene and this is a representation of a land once known as Libya. It is an ancient land, though the people you see before you are far from the first to settle here. The Phoenicians came here first, then the Grekans, then the Romans, and finally the Arabii. Well, not finally, but that's who rules now.'

'And when are we?'

'Ah, well, the text isn't clear, though I believe this happened some time in either the eleventh or twelfth century.'

'So long ago.'

'A long time by anyone's reckoning,' agreed Semyon. 'Save perhaps his.'

'I don't understand,' said Dalia. 'Who are you talking about?'

'Never mind. You'll understand soon enough.'

Dalia fought down her annoyance at Semyon's cryptic answers and said, 'So we're not really here and this is just what's in the book?'

'Now you begin to understand.'

'So who are those women?' asked Dalia, pointing towards the procession as it made its way down a road of hard-packed earth towards a long scar in the ground from which drifted a mephitic fog.

'They are the handmaidens of the King of Cyrene's daughter, Cleodolinda, and they are taking her to her death. Within that wound in the earth dwells the Dragon, a fearsome creature recently awoken after a great war with its kin, which seeks refuge on this world to feed and regain its strength.'

'The Dragon.'

'Yes, the Dragon,' agreed Semyon. 'It has slain all the knights of the city and demands the sacrifice of a beautiful maiden every day. It feasts on their terror, growing stronger with each feeding, but all the young girls of Cyrene are dead. The king's daughter alone remains, and now she goes to her death.'

'Can't we do anything?'

Semyon sighed. 'Can you not grasp that this has already happened, girl? This is ancient history we are watching, the birth of a legend that will echo down through the ages in one form or another for all time. Look!'

Dalia followed Semyon's pointing digit and saw a lone warrior knight in golden armour and a scarlet-plumed helmet riding towards the procession of women on a mighty charger of midnight black. He carried a tall lance of purest silver, from which flew a long red and white banner depicting a soaring eagle grasping a bolt of lightning.

'Who is that?' asked Dalia, though she already knew.

'At this point in time, he is known as a soldier of the Emperor Diocletian, one who has risen to high honour in the army and who is passing through Libya to join his men.'

Dalia almost wept at the sight of the knight, a being of a fairer presence than any she had seen and one whose wondrous power was undimmed by the passage of years.

The knight spurred his horse and swiftly overtook the procession, riding towards the dark scar in the earth. No sooner had he halted his mount and set his shield upon his arm than the Dragon surged from its lair, roaring with a sound louder than thunder.

Dalia's hands flew to her mouth and she cried out as she saw the Dragon's monstrous form. In shape it was half crawling beast, half loathsome bird, its scaled head immense and its tail twenty metres long. Its terrible winged body was covered with scales, so strong and bright and smooth that they were like a knight's armour.

The light of devoured stars shone at its breast and malignant fire burned in its eyes.

The warrior knight leapt to meet the Dragon, striking the monster with his lance, but its scales were so hard that the weapon broke into a thousand pieces. From the back of his rearing horse, the warrior smote the dragon with his sword, but the beast struck at him with talons like scythe blades. The warrior's armour split open and Dalia saw blood pouring down his leg in a bright stream.

The Dragon towered over its foe, dealing him fearful blows, but the knight caught them upon his shield and thrust his sword against the Dragon's belly. The scales of the beast were like steel plates, rippling like liquid mercury as they withstood the knight's every attack. Then the Dragon, infuriated by the thrust, lashed itself against the knight and his horse, and cast lightning upon him from its eyes. The knight's helmet was torn from him and Dalia saw his face shine out from the battle, pale, lit by some radiance that shone from within. As he thrust at the Dragon, that radiance grew in power, so that at last it was like the light of a newborn sun.

The Dragon looped itself around the knight, clawing and biting at his armour and roaring in triumph. Then, as though the thought had come from the warrior, Dalia saw that, no matter how the Dragon writhed, it sought always to protect one place in its body, a place beneath its left wing.

'Strike, warrior, strike!' she urged.

As if hearing her words, the knight bent downward and lunged forward, thrusting his sword with a mighty bellow into the Dragon's body.

The creature gave out a deafening roar that shook stones from the city walls and the burning radiance in its breast was extinguished. Its grasp upon the knight loosened and the lightning faded from its eyes as the great beast fell to the ground.

Perceiving that the Dragon was helpless, though not dead, the knight untied the long white banner from his shattered lance and bound it around the neck of the monster.

With the Dragon subdued, the knight turned to the astounded handmaidens and the people of the city, who streamed from its gates in a riot of adulation. The knight raised a hand to quiet them, and such was his presence and radiance that all who beheld him fell silent.

'The Dragon is defeated!' cried the warrior. 'But it is beyond even my power to destroy, so I shall drag it in fetters from this place and bind it deep in the darkness, where it will remain until the end of all things.'

So saying, the knight rode off with the Dragon bound behind him, leaving the scene behind him as immobile as a painting.

THE IMAGE OF the city and the desert were frozen in time, and Dalia turned to Semyon. 'Is that all of it?'

'It's all the Dragon remembers of it, yes,' said Semyon. 'Or at least a version of its memories. It's hard to tell what's real and what's not sometimes. I listen to its impotent roars of hatred as it watches from its gaol on Mars and write what comes out, the Emperor "slaying" the Dragon of Mars... the grand lie of the red planet and the truth that would shake the galaxy if it were known. But truth, as are all things, is a moving target. What of this is real and what is fantasy... well, who can tell?'

Dalia looked towards the horizon over which the knight had vanished. 'Then that was?'

'The Emperor? Yes,' said Semyon, turning and walking away as the reality of the desert landscape began to unweave. 'He brought the defeated Dragon to Mars and bound it beneath the Noctis Labyrinthus.'

'But why?'

'The Emperor sees things we do not,' said Semyon. 'He knows the future and he guides us towards it. A nudge here, seeding a prepared prophecy of his coming there, the beginnings of the transhumanist movement, the push from humanity's understanding of science to its mastery... all of it by his design, working towards one glorious union in the future where the forges of Mars would perceive the Emperor as the divinity for whom they had been waiting for centuries.'

'You mean the Emperor orchestrated the evolution of the Mechanicum?'

'Of course,' said Semyon. 'He knew that one day he would need such a mighty organisation to serve him, and from the Dragon's dreams came the first machines of the priests of Mars. Without the Dragon there would have been no Mechanicum, and without the Mechanicum, the Emperor's grand dream of a united galaxy for Humanity would have withered on the vine.'

Dalia tried to grasp the unimaginable scale of the Emperor's designs, the clarity of a vision that could set schemes in motion that would not come to fruition for over twenty thousand years. It was simply staggering that anyone, even the Emperor, could have so carefully and precisely orchestrated the destiny of so many with such skill and cold ruthlessness.

The scale of the deception was beyond measure and the callousness of it took her breath away. To lie to so many people, to twist the destiny of a planet to suit one man's aims, even a being as lofty as the Emperor, was a crime of such monstrous proportions that Dalia's mind shied away from that awful calumny.

'If the truth of this became known,' breathed Dalia. 'It would tear the Mechanicum apart.'

Semyon shook his head as the last vestiges of the sands of Libya faded away to be replaced with darkness all around them. 'Not just the Mechanicum, but the Imperium too,' he said. 'I know this knowledge is a terrible burden to bear, but the Treaty of Olympus bound the fates of both Throne and Forge together in a union that must never be undone. Neither can survive without the other, but should this become known, then those who hold truth sacred above all else will not see that, they will only see the righteousness of their cause. In any case, the Mechanicum is already tearing itself apart, but the horrors unleashed by the Warmaster's betrayal will be as nothing if Mars and Terra make war upon one another.'

Semyon fixed Dalia with a gaze of such pity that she shuddered. 'But it is the duty of the Guardians of the Dragon, souls chosen by the Emperor, to ensure that such a thing does not happen.'

'*You* keep the Dragon bound?' asked Dalia as she began to perceive faint outlines of her surroundings re-establishing themselves.

'No, the Dragon is bound by chains far stronger than one such as I could devise. The Guardians simply maintain what the Emperor wrought,' explained Semyon. 'He knew that one day the Dragon's lost children would seek its resting place and we are here to ensure that they do not find it.'

'You said "we", but I'm no Guardian,' said Dalia warily.

'You have not guessed why your every footstep has brought you to this place, girl?'

'No,' hissed Dalia as Semyon reached out and took her hands.

At the moment of contact, Dalia gasped in pain as the world around her returned, and she found herself once again standing at the lectern in the vast cave of silver.

She tried to pull her hands away, but Semyon's grip was unbreakable. Looking into his eyes, she saw the weight of a thousand years and more in those depthless pools, a duty and honour that was like nothing else in the galaxy.

'I am sorry,' said Semyon, 'but my span, though much extended, is now over.'

'No.'

'Yes, Dalia, you must fulfil your destiny and become the Guardian of the Dragon.'

DALIA FELT THE heat in Semyon's hands spread into her flesh, a golden radiance that filled her with unimaginable wellbeing. She wanted to cry out in ecstasy as she felt every decaying fibre in her body surge with a new lease of life, every withered cell and every portion of her flesh blooming as a power undreamed of filled her.

Her body was reborn, filled with a sliver of the power and knowledge of a world's most singular individual, power and knowledge that had been passed down from Guardian to Guardian over the millennia, a burden and an honour in one unasked for gift. With that knowledge, her anger at the Emperor's deception was swept away as she saw the ultimate, horrifying fate of the human race bereft of his guidance.

She saw his single-minded, pitiless drive to steer his entire race along a narrow path of survival only he could see, a life that allowed no love, few friends and an eternity of sacrifice.

Dalia wanted to scream, feeling the power threaten to consume her, the awesome ferocity of it almost burning away all the things that made her who she was. She fought to hold onto her identity, but she was the last leaf on a dying tree and she felt her memories and sense of self subsumed into the fate the Emperor had decreed for her.

At last the roaring power within her was spent, its work to remould her form complete, and she let out a great, shuddering breath as she realised she was still herself.

She was still Dalia Cythera, but so much more as well.

Semyon released her hands and stepped away from her with a look of contented release upon his face.

'Goodbye, Dalia,' said Semyon.

The adept's skin greyed and his entire body dissolved into a fine golden dust, leaving only his aged robes to fall to the rocky floor. Dalia looked over at the hulking servitor that had accompanied the adept and was not surprised when it also disintegrated into dust.

Such a sight would normally have shocked Dalia, but she felt nothing beyond a detached sense of completeness at the adept's dissolution.

'Dalia,' said Severine, and she turned to see her friend looking directly at her, a look of manic desperation knotting her features as tears of grief and horror spilled down her cheeks.

Severine smiled weakly, looking up at the distant cavern roof, and said, 'You brought me the Dragon, Dalia, but I wish you hadn't.'

'Wait,' said Dalia as Severine stepped towards the drop only a foot behind her.

'It's a mercy, I think, that we can't normally see the terrible things that hide in the darkness or know how frail our reality really is,' wept Severine. 'I'm sorry… but if you could see as I now see, you would do the same as I.'

Severine stepped off the ledge.

FIRST CAPTAIN SIGISMUND of the Imperial Fists watched as yet more metal-skinned containers were borne skyward on Fabricator Locum Kane's gigantic Tsiolkovsky towers towards the container ships in orbit. The enormous structures were working at full capacity, and it still wasn't fast enough, for his ship masters had just informed him of an enemy force closing in from the north-east: infantry, armour, skitarii and at least two Legios' worth of engines.

It seemed Mondus Occulum's privileged status was at an end.

Nothing of this mission to Mars had panned out the way it was supposed to, and Sigismund felt his anger gnawing at his bounds of control. Camba-Diaz and the Jovian regiments were embroiled in a fight for their lives at Mondus Gamma, and the Saturnine companies tasked with breaking the siege at Ipluvien Maximal's forge had been repeatedly turned back by the horrifyingly altered weapon-creatures of the Dark Mechanicum.

Sigismund marched through the precisely organised ballet of servitors, loaders and speeding lifters carrying racks of armour and bolters, seeing the elegant form of the fabricator locum directing the work of his menials with calmly efficient waves of freshly-implanted manip arms.

Dust storms billowing in from the wastelands beyond the collapsed caldera of Uranius Patera rendered the gold of Sigismund's battle plate ochre and stained the black and white of his personal heraldry, yet he was no less impressive a figure for such blemishes.

A host of similarly armoured warriors moved with the methodical precision for which the Imperial Fists were famed, working alongside mobs of Kane's bulky lifter servitors to secure as much of the armour and weapon supplies as they could.

Sigismund's companies had descended upon Mondus Occulum not knowing whether they would have to fight to secure the forge, and it was a relief to find that the fabricator locum still held true to the Throne of Terra.

Even Sigismund had been grudgingly impressed by the efforts made by Kane to ensure the smooth transfer of supplies from his forge to the ships anchored at the tops of the Tsiolkovsky towers. As impressive as Kane's efforts were, Sigismund knew they would be forced to leave the bulk of the materiel produced here behind.

Kane turned at the sound of Sigismund's footfalls, a weary smile on his smooth face.

'First captain?' said Kane. 'Have you heard from Camba-Diaz? How goes the fighting at Mondus Gamma?'

'Desperate,' admitted Sigismund. 'Camba-Diaz has secured the armour forges and the ammunition silos, but his company is outnumbered a hundred to one. The traitor Chrom's forces are pushing him back to the

landing fields and his losses are grievous. We will not be
able to hold the forge, but a great deal of essential supplies have been secured for transit to Terra.'

'Chrom's skitarii always were brutal things,' said Kane,
shaking his head in wonder that things had come to
this. 'And the number of his robot maniples is consid-
erable.'

Sigismund felt his gauntlet curl around the grip of his
bolter. 'Aye, and it offends me that such mindless
machines spill the blood of Astartes. But enough of
Camba-Diaz, how close are you to completing the evac-
uation of armour and weapons from here?'

'The work proceeds,' said Kane. 'Already we have
shipped over twelve thousand suits of Mark 4 armour
and twice as many weapons.'

'I will be blunt, Kane,' said Sigismund. 'It must go
faster. We have little time left to us.'

'I assure you we are going as fast as we can, first
captain.'

'Yet still it must be faster,' stated Sigismund. 'Orbital
tracks show a sizeable force of enemy troops moving in
from the north-east. They may be upon us any minute.'

Kane's eyes flickered as he inloaded the feeds from
the surveyor systems of the ships in orbit, and his
manip arms clenched as he saw the size of the force
converging on his forge.

'Two Legios!' exclaimed Kane. 'Over sixty engines!'

'And the rest,' said Sigismund.

'Those banners,' said Kane, haptically sorting the
wealth of feeds from those satellites still in orbit around
Mars. 'They belong to Urtzi Malevolus. Damn, but
there's a lot of them. Can you hold against that many,
first captain? We must save Mondus Occulum!'

Sigismund hesitated before answering, his desire to
wreak a bloody vengeance on the heads of those who
rebelled against the Emperor warring with the mission

his primarch had given him of securing the armour and weapons of Kane's forge.

He sighed. 'No, we cannot. The forces arrayed against us are too many and my orders do not allow for futile gestures of defiance.'

'Futile defiance?' exclaimed Kane. 'This is my forge we're talking about. What could be less futile than defending the very place that fabricates the armour that shields you and the weapons you bear?'

Sigismund shook his head. 'I don't have time to debate this with you, Kane. Speed up the loading by whatever means you can, but within the hour we must be away or we will not be leaving at all. Do you understand that simple fact?'

'I understand,' snapped Kane. 'But *you* must understand that if Mondus Occulum and Mondus Gamma fall, you will have no way of replenishing the combat losses you will sustain in any meaningful way.'

Sigismund was about to reply when one of the Tsiolkovsky towers exploded.

The mighty structure spewed fire, and debris fell lazily from the ruptured portion of the tower as metres-thick guys snapped and twanged. Black smoke curled upward from the site of the explosion and a terrible scream of ruptured metal and torn carbon nanotubes rent the air as the tower leaned and bent as though no more substantial than a length of rope.

More explosions boomed skyward on the crater's edge and the echoes of their detonations rolled over the landing fields.

'No more time, Kane,' snarled Sigismund. 'They have range on us already.'

The distant tower came down in a rippling series of crashing detonations, trailing a city's worth of rubble and twisted metal in its wake. Huge manufactories, acres of industrial landscape and forests of towering coolant towers were smashed to pulverised dust as entire worker districts vanished, flattened in an instant by the monstrous weight of debris.

A massive cloud of dust and ash billowed outward from the collapsed tower like the blast wave of an atomic explosion. The ground shook with the force of the impacts, and Sigismund heard secondary detonations as enemy fire began to pound the outlying segments of the forge to destruction.

A thunderous, booming horn-blast echoed across the landing fields, and Sigismund looked up in time to see a host of towering silhouettes emerge from the red-lit smoke of the tower's destruction. Six Warlord Titans, their hulls blackened and scarified, roared in triumph, their weapon arms blazing with apocalyptic fire that reduced towering structures to rubble and entire swathes of infrastructure to little more than vaporised metal.

'Get to your ship, Kane,' ordered Sigismund. 'Now!'

'My forge!' cried Kane. 'We can't just abandon it!'

Sigismund grabbed Kane's arm and said, 'Your forge is already lost! Now get to your damned ship. Your skills will be needed in the days ahead.'

'What do you mean?'

'I mean that with Kelbor-Hal's treachery, you are now the Fabricator General.'

'But what about Zeth? Maximal?' shouted Kane over the deafening crescendo of the advancing Titans and the destruction of his forge. 'What of them?'

'We can do nothing for them!' shouted Sigismund. 'They must stand or fall on their own.'

DALIA STOOD OPEN-MOUTHED, staring numbly at the empty space where, not a moment before, Severine had been standing. She couldn't comprehend what had just happened and her brain fought to process the knowledge that her friend was dead.

She took a horrified lurch towards the edge of the promontory, but a powerful hand seized her arm. Rho-mu 31 held her firm and said, 'Don't.'

'Severine!' wailed Dalia, her legs turning to the consistency of wet paper and giving way beneath her. Rho-mu 31 bore her gently to the ground as aching sobs burst from her. She held him tightly, burying her face in the fabric of his cloak as she wept for her lost friend.

'Why did she do it?' asked Dalia, looking up at Rho-mu 31 when her sobs had subsided.

'I do not know,' admitted Rho-mu 31, as Zouche came up behind Dalia and placed his hand upon her shoulder in an awkward gesture of comfort.

'I think our Severine was a girl who depended on certainties,' mused Zouche. 'This place... well, it strips away the illusions that allow us to function and shows you that there's no such thing as certainties in this universe. Some minds can't handle that kind of truth.'

'She's gone,' whispered Dalia.

'Yes, Dalia-girl, she's gone,' said Zouche, his voice choked with emotion. 'With all that's happened, I'm surprised any of us are still here.'

'Caxton!' cried Dalia, suddenly remembering that when she had last seen him, he had been insensible on the ground.

'I think he'll be fine,' said Rho-mu 31 as Dalia disentangled herself from him and stood on unsteady legs. 'He blacked out when everything went... strange.'

'Like a fuse or a circuit breaker,' elaborated Zouche, making his way over to the lectern, upon which sat Semyon's book. 'He should be fine when he wakes up.'

Dalia saw Caxton lying in the recovery position, his chest rising and falling with rhythmic breaths. He was alive and she could sense the bruised insides of his mind already beginning to heal. She wondered at how she could see such things, and then remembered the power that had flowed into her at Semyon's dissolution.

'Good,' she said. 'I can't bear to think of this place claiming any more lives.'

Zouche lifted a handful of golden dust that was all that remained of Adept Semyon and his battle servitor. 'What happened here?' he asked. 'They aged a thousand years in an instant.'

'More, I think,' said Dalia. 'I think Semyon had been a Guardian for a long, long time.'

'So now what do we do?' asked Zouche, his eyes scanning over the pages of Semyon's book. 'We found the Dragon, so do we free it?'

'No, absolutely not,' said Dalia. 'You were right after all, Zouche. Some things *are* meant to be left in darkness forever. We were never meant to come here to release it.'

'Then why did you have to come at all?' asked Rho-mu 31.

'I think you know,' said Dalia, turning away from Zouche and facing Rho-mu 31 as flecks of golden light simmered in her eyes. 'To make sure it stayed entombed. Semyon is dead, but there needs to be a Guardian of the Dragon.'

'And that's you?' asked Rho-mu 31.

'Yes.'

'No, Dalia!' said Zouche. 'Say that it's not so! You?'

'Yes,' said Dalia. 'It was always me, but I won't be alone. Will I, Rho-mu 31?'

Rho-mu 31 stood tall and planted his weapon stave in the ground. He knelt before Dalia and said, 'For as long as I remain functional I will protect you.'

'With the power I have now, that may be a very long time, my friend.'

'So be it,' said Rho-mu 31.

* * *

ZOUCHE AND RHO-MU 31 carried Caxton between them as they made their way back through the twisting maze of the Dragon's caves. Dalia led the way, guiding them unerringly along the path they had followed to get here. Their mood was subdued, for the death of Severine was heavy in their thoughts, and no one spoke as they passed through Semyon's abandoned laboratory. Once again they trudged through the glittering tunnels that led to the dark, shadow-cloaked grabens of the Noctis Labyrinthus, before finally emerging into the chill air.

'I think I hate this place,' said Zouche, as Rho-mu 31 took the unconscious Caxton from him. The Protector shrugged Caxton onto his shoulder.

'I wouldn't blame you,' said Dalia. 'It's a place of despair. It always has been and I think it's that more than the Dragon that's kept people away.'

'And you're sure you have to stay?' asked Zouche, his eyes brimming with tears.

'I'm sure,' said Dalia, leaning down to embrace him. He put his arms around her and held her tightly, letting the tears fall without shame.

'I'll never see you again, will I?' asked Zouche when she released him.

She shook her head. 'No, you won't. And you can't ever tell anyone about me or this place. If anyone asks, tell them I died when the Kaban Machine attacked us in the tunnel.'

'And what about Caxton?' asked Zouche, wiping his eyes with the sleeve of his robe.

Dalia choked back a sob and said, 'Tell him... tell him I think I could have loved him. And tell him I'm sorry I never got the chance to find out.'

'I'll tell him that, right enough,' nodded Zouche, turning to Rho-mu 31. 'And you're staying too?'

'I am,' agreed Rho-mu 31. 'It seems every Guardian must have a protector.'

Zouche shook hands with Rho-mu 31 and looked over his shoulder at the lonely shape of the Cargo-5, which sat where they had left it beyond the cave mouth.

'Ah... a thought occurs,' he said. 'How are we supposed to get home? Wasn't the 5's battery dead?'

Dalia smiled and the golden energy passed to her by Adept Semyon flashed in her eyes.

'I think I can make sure it has enough power for you to get back to the Magma City.'

Zouche shrugged as they set off towards the abandoned Cargo-5. 'I'm not even sure I want to know how you'll manage that, but I'm never one to question my good fortune. Not that I've ever had any to question, you understand.'

The Cargo-5 exploded with a thunderous, booming detonation that echoed from the sheer sides of the Noctis Labyrinthus. The blast wave hurled them to the ground as twisted metal wreckage fell in a burning rain.

Dalia looked up, blinking away bright afterimages of the explosion.

'What happened?' gasped Zouche.

Dalia groaned as she saw their attacker rolling forward on its heavy-gauge track unit.

'Oh, no,' she said. 'Oh, Emperor protect us, no!'

It was the Kaban Machine.

HIGH IN THE Chamber of Vesta, Adept Koriel Zeth watched the images playing out over the burnished screens of her forge with a sense of utter disbelief and horror.

The main screens displayed her own forge, a city on the verge of collapse. The outer hives and manufactories were in ruins and everything she had built over the centuries had been flattened by the savage, unrelenting bombardment of the Dark Mechanicum.

Ipluvien Maximal fared no better, his promised relief pulling back in the face of unbreakable resistance from

Kelbor-Hal's freakish creations. Maximal's outer walls were breached in a dozen places and the fighting surged from weapon shop to ore refinery to librarium as the hordes of mutated servitors and abominable war machines poured in.

Both Mondus Occulum and Mondus Gamma were burning, vast swathes of machinery and manufacturing capacity destroyed in barely a few hours worth of fighting. The loss of such irreplaceable technology and knowledge was like a knife in the guts, but worse than that, *far* worse than that, was the image on the central glass panel.

Like comets launched from the surface of Mars, the Imperial ships were fleeing for the heavens. Astartes and Army vessels jostled in the sky in their haste to depart the red planet.

When her surveyor systems had first registered their launch, Zeth had assumed they would arc over and swoop south towards the Magma City, but their fiery ascent had continued until it was obvious they were accelerating to escape velocity.

Confirmation, if confirmation were needed, came in the form of a terse, encrypted data squirt from the fabricator locum, who, it seemed, was also leaving Mars.

```
+++Imperial forces withdrawing from Mars+++Save
what you can+++Destroy the rest+++
```

The human part of her screamed at this betrayal, but the dominant, analytical, part of her brain could see the sense in this retreat. The Astartes had no doubt secured a great deal of the new marks of armour in preparation for the campaign against the Legions of Horus Lupercal, and to lose them all in a futile last stand made no logical sense.

Knowing that didn't make it any easier to swallow.

Zeth opened up her noospheric link to Ipluvien Maximal, Princeps Cavalerio of Legio Tempestus and Lords Caturix and Verticorda of the Knights of Taranis.

'I presume you have all seen this?' she said as their holographic images appeared on the glass panels above her.

'I have,' said Cavalerio, projecting the image of the man he had been before his interment in the amniotic casket.

'Yes,' confirmed Maximal. 'I cannot believe it. The knowledge that will be lost...'

Lord Caturix shook his head. 'That it should come to this, abandoned by Terra.'

Lord Verticorda shook his head. 'Never,' he said. 'The Emperor would never abandon us.'

'Maybe not,' said Zeth, 'but it appears we can expect no more help from the Legions.'

'So what are your orders, Adept Zeth?' asked Princeps Cavalerio.

'You heard Kane's transmission?'

Their grim silence was all the answer she needed.

'I won't let Kelbor-Hal have my reactors,' declared Maximal at last.

'Nor will he have the Akashic reader,' said Zeth sadly. 'I had such high hopes for Dalia being able to make it work, but maybe it's for the best. Perhaps no one should ever know everything. After all, when there is nothing left to discover, what is the point in life?'

'Then there is only one order left to give,' said Lord Verticorda.

DALIA SAW THE lethal machine roll towards them, crushing boulders beneath its weight, its weapon arms locking up ready to shoot. The barrels on an enormous rotary cannon whirred as they spooled up to fire once more and hissing gases vented from the plasma cannon mounted at its shoulder.

She could feel its anger towards her in the seething yellow glow of its sensor orbs, and with a swift flick of her mind, Dalia knew she wouldn't be able to fool it again.

'How did it find us?' shouted Zouche.

'It must have read our biometrics in the tunnel,' she cried. 'It realised its mistake eventually and it followed us here.'

'Who cares how it found us?' shouted Rho-mu 31, firing up his weapon stave and hauling Dalia back the way they had come. 'Run! Get back to the cave! It won't be able to follow us in!'

Dalia nodded, taking Zouche's hand and sprinting for the cave mouth.

'Do what you did before!' cried Zouche. 'Make it think we're not here!'

'I can't,' gasped Dalia as they ran. 'It's learned what I did and its mental architecture has evolved to stop me doing it again.'

Dalia looked over her shoulder and saw the metallic tentacles on its back whip up.

'Get down!' yelled Rho-mu 31, dragging her and Zouche to the ground.

They landed hard and rolled, dropping into a shallow trench cut by some ancient stream, as roaring sheets of whickering laser fire gouged glowing channels into the valley floor.

Zouche screamed as a sharp fragment of rock sliced his cheek.

Dalia wept bitter tears, expecting another barrage to finish them off at any second.

She flinched, curling into a tight ball of terror as a deafening, roaring blast of sawing gunfire echoed from the canyon walls. Another thunderous cascade of fire erupted and Dalia blinked in surprise as she realised the shots weren't directed at them.

'I don't believe it,' cried Rho-mu 31. Dalia looked over and saw that the glowing green of his eyes behind his bronze mask were alight with surprise.

Dalia propped herself up on one elbow and risked a glance over the torn, smoking lip of their fragile cover.

The Kaban Machine was still there, though its form was wreathed in flaring bursts of energy discharges as its voids screamed and fought to hold their integrity.

Riding towards it were two glorious war machines in midnight blue armour, bearing the symbol of a wheel and lightning bolt upon their shoulder guards.

'The Knights of Taranis!' shouted Rho-mu 31.

MAVEN'S HEART SURGED with savage, primal joy to see the enemy machine reel from the impacts of his weapons. Cronus had also struck true and *Equitos Bellum's* Manifold shone with the knowledge that they had finally found their quarry. His autoloaders thundered as they fed more shells into the cannon mounted on his arm and he felt the heat build as he unsheathed the four-metre war blade in his right fist.

The machine was just as he remembered it, squat and unlovely, a rotund engine of death and destruction hiding behind a sleeting sheen of rippling voids. Through the shimmering fields of his auspex he could read its energy signatures, and was once again struck by the cold, alien intelligence that lurked behind the yellow orbs of its sensor blisters as it ceased fire and turned towards him.

A small group of people sheltered from the machine's fire in a chewed up ditch, a red-cloaked Protector and three others. Maven didn't know who they were, but that this machine wanted them dead was reason enough for him to defend them.

'Go right,' voxed Maven to Cronus. 'Let's take this thing like we planned.'

Cronus was already moving, *Pax Mortis* loping across the rough, step-like terrain of the rocky valley, his carapace low to the ground and his weapon arms thrust out before him. Maven hauled his mount left and unleashed another rippling salvo of cannon fire towards the machine.

Once more its voids sang with the impacts and Maven felt his mount's exhilaration as a surge of adrenaline shot through his body. *Equitos Bellum* relished a fight, but the sense of striking back at their nemesis was above and beyond anything Maven had experienced.

He rode close to the ground, hard and fast for an outcrop of rock he had seen from further along the valley, feeling the heat of near misses as the enemy machine opened fire on him. His instinctual awareness of the battle was complete, his gut feel for the tactical situation flawless as he suddenly hauled back on the controls and skidded to a halt, one leg stretched out to the side at the sudden course change.

A barrage of shots hammered the outcrop, blasting it to splintered rubble and leaving a smoking crater in the aftermath of a thunderous explosion. Maven sidestepped and bounded forward, zigzagging at random across the ground, deliberately avoiding anything resembling a standard pattern evasion technique.

Whipping bursts of laser fire and sawing lines of shells sliced the air where the machine expected him to be.

Maven laughed, a wild roar of pleasure as *Equitos Bellum* responded to his touch, its healed limbs and wounded heart working with him against their enemy. Once again, Maven changed direction at random, urging his mount forward into the teeth of the machine's weapons.

'Old Stator would have my guts on a plate if he could see this,' he hissed, fighting against decades of training to keep from using the very drills that had made him such a formidable warrior.

The machine opened fire, but once again Maven had outmanoeuvred it, his unpredictable motions and random jinks confusing whatever targeting wetware it employed. Maven watched it back away from him, its main guns swivelling in gimbal mounts as they tried to predict which way he would move.

The guns mounted on the thick dendrite tentacles swivelled, firing towards the remains of the burning Cargo-5. Cronus rode his Knight in a looping, jerking pattern of stops and starts, though Maven could see that his brother's mount had taken several hits from the strength of his shield returns.

'Mix it up more, Cronus!' he yelled. 'Don't do anything it can predict!'

'Shut up!' snapped Cronus. 'You break the rules all the time. It's not so easy for me!'

Maven grinned, seeing the machine back away from him, spitting rock and gravel from beneath its tracks as it frantically reversed towards the wall of the canyon.

Maven let rip with another blast of cannon fire. Chunks of smashed rock fell from the cliff, as the machine swivelled on one track and his shots went wide.

'Hell,' said Maven. 'It's learning.'

Maven reversed the direction of his advance and, too late, realised his mistake.

A seething wall of laser fire hammered his frontal shields and the torso emitter blew out in a screaming wash of energy. He cried out as the discharge whiplashed through him in a howling gale of feedback.

Equitos Bellum faltered and Maven dropped his mount to one knee. Another blast struck the upper edges of his carapace armour and searing lances of pain shot through his shoulder. He tried to turn his mount to present a shielded section to the machine as more fire hammered him, and Maven felt his mount's pain as his armour tore apart under the concentrated volley.

The armoured glass of his cockpit shattered, exploding inwards and slicing his face with razor-sharp fragments.

'Cronus!' yelled Maven as another impact sent a bolt of agony through his body.

Pax Mortis smashed through the flaming wreckage of the Cargo-5, both its arm weapons sheathed in fire. The enemy machine vanished in a blinding cascade of void flares, its shields buckling under the impacts.

Whatever form of reactor sat at its heart was capable of soaking up the punishment and holding. It turned its guns on *Pax Mortis*, and let rip with a barking roar of cannon fire that tore through the shields and the plating of Cronus's waist mounting.

The Knight staggered, and Cronus bolted for the wall of obscuring smoke that billowed from the Cargo-5, but the machine had predicted such an obvious response, and a searing bolt of plasma slammed into the upper carapace of *Pax Mortis*, almost driving it to its knees.

Maven cried out as he saw his brother Knight stagger, but before the enemy machine could finish its work, Cronus surged forwards and darted into the smoke.

'Its voids are too tough!' shouted Cronus, his pain obvious even over the vox-link. 'Our weapons won't overload them!'

His comrade-in-arms had left himself dangerously exposed by coming to Maven's aid, but their two-pronged assault had forced the enemy to dance to their tune, and they would never get a better chance to take it down.

'Get ready!' he replied. 'We've got it where we want it!'

Faced with two enemies, the machine had backed against the cliffs of the valley, seeking to minimise the directions from which it could be attacked.

Just as Maven knew it would.

It was a standard, textbook manoeuvre.

Maven disengaged the auto-targeters and said, 'You know the drills, but you don't have the skills,' and opened fire once more.

Instead of aiming for the machine, his gunfire tore into the rock walls above it, and a torrent of gigantic boulders fell in a thunderous avalanche from the cliffs, smashing into the upper vectors of the machine's shields. Blooming explosions of light rippled from the machine, its voids screaming in protest, but still, impossibly, holding.

'Now, Cronus!' shouted Maven, pushing his wounded mount to its feet and charging his foe with a feral cry of battle-lust. He opened up with his cannon, hammering the machine's upper shields. Even through the tumbling, roaring avalanche of rock and dust, the machine saw him coming and turned its guns on *Equitos Bellum*, just as *Pax Mortis* loomed from the smoke and joined its fire with that of Maven's mount.

Already struggling to withstand the rain of debris falling from the cliff, the machine's shield-emitters finally gave way under the concentrated fire of the two Knights.

Its voids exploded outwards in a blinding blast wave, tearing the metallic weapon dendrites from its back and vaporising its left arm in a thunderous detonation. Smoke and sparks of jetting energy spewed from the machine's ruptured flanks and its sensor blisters flickered madly, as though unable to comprehend how it had been hurt.

It rocked back, stunned and screaming in garbled bursts of binary that sliced over the Manifold and blew several of the augmitters inside Maven's cockpit.

Maven rode through the billowing clouds of rock dust, seeing the spherical form of his long-sought-for enemy ahead of him. It was mortally wounded, but still had some fight left in it. Maven didn't give it a chance and drove the full four metres of his energised war blade through its frontal section.

Its death scream shrieked in a pitiful wail of agonised binary, but Maven twisted his blade in the wound until at last its cries ceased and the light of its sensor blisters was extinguished.

Letting out a pent-up breath of battle fury and pain, Maven stepped back from the destroyed machine, feeling an overwhelming sense of closure as he stood over the shell of his defeated enemy. The pain from his psychostigmatic wounds diminished and Maven smiled as he felt *Equitos Bellum's* satisfaction wash through him in a rush of approval.

The essence of what made a Knight such a fearsome war machine moved through his battered flesh to ease his suffering, filling his body and rushing along his aching limbs.

Too late, Maven felt the soul of his mount surge to the fore, the soothing balm that eased his pain wielding him as though he were the mount and it the rider. He felt the raw, ferocious heart of his machine, the terrifying power that lurked in the heart of the Manifold, take control of his limbs and turn *Equitos Bellum* towards the scar in the earth where the targets of the enemy machine had taken cover.

Through the blown-out cockpit glass, Maven saw a Mechanicum Protector, leading a slightly built woman with eyes that shone with a golden light towards him. A red cloak billowed at the shoulders of the Protector, who carried a weapon stave hung with the number grid symbol of Koriel Zeth. Behind them was a short, robed man who knelt beside the prone form of what looked like a tonsured menial.

Maven heard heavy footfalls as *Pax Mortis* moved alongside him and tried to speak to Cronus, but the elemental force of the Manifold held him tightly in its grip.

The woman approached the wounded Knight and before he knew what was happening, *Equitos Bellum* dropped to one knee and bowed its head to her. Without looking, he knew his battle-brother's Knight had done likewise.

She reached out and Maven felt warmth infuse every molecule of his hybrid existence of flesh and steel with newfound purpose and vitality. He felt the warmth of the woman's touch through the shell of his mount, and gasped as trembling vibrations spread through its armoured frame of plasteel and ceramite.

'Machine, heal thyself,' she said.

3.05

NIGHT WAS FALLING across the Magma City, though darkness never really came to the glowing, orange-lit metropolis. Like a scene from the ancients' visions of the underworld, Adept Zeth's forge was bathed in the fires of battle as the forces of the Dark Mechanicum pounded her walls with vortex missiles and collapsed the outer bastions with graviton cannons.

The city was being torn apart with mechanistic precision and, within hours, the forces under the command of Ambassador Melgator – who watched the unfolding destruction from beneath his dark pavilion at the end of the Typhon Causeway – would have seized their prize for the Fabricator General.

The city was doomed and there was only one order left to give.

DEUS TEMPESTUS STRODE through the twisted, blackened remains of what had once been an armaments factory. Fires and small explosions still popped and flamed beneath the Warlord's mighty tread, but Princeps Cavalerio paid them no mind. Such things were irrelevant to a being of his stature. Only Aeschman's host of Tempestus skitarii following behind his battlegroups needed to concern themselves with such matters.

The full strength of Tempestus marched from the shelter of the Magma City, the cobalt blue of their armour and the fluttering honour banners gloriously bright against the brooding skies and fire-blackened rubble they marched through.

Leading from the centre, *Deus Tempestus* took up position behind a tangle of twisted iron columns and girders that had once been the structure of the largest sheet metal fabrication plant in Tharsis, but which now resembled a mass of razorwire.

On Cavalerio's right was Princeps Sharaq's battle group, *Metallus Cebrenia* leading the Warhounds *Astrus Lux* and *Raptoria* into battle. Princeps Lamnos and Kasim marched their smaller engines to either side of the larger Reaver, and Cavalerio raised his volcano cannon in salute of his brave warriors.

To his immediate left towered the mighty Warlord *Tharsis Hastatus*, under Princeps Suzak, while further out was Princeps Mordant's Reaver, *Arcadia Fortis*, with the dashing Princeps Basek's Warhound, *Vulpus Rex*, in support.

Once again, Cavalerio acknowledged his warriors as they took up position in the ruins of the outer sub-hives.

'All princeps, Manifold conference,' he said.

One by one, the flickering images of his brother princeps appeared before Cavalerio and he was gratified to see only the hunger for battle in their faces. Each was eager to take the fight to Mortis, despite there only being one possible outcome to the battle. For a moment he wished he still fought as they did. Then, he smiled at the foolishness of such a desire, for who could not wish to be as connected to such a mighty engine as *Deus Tempestus* in such a complete and total manner as he was.

'Brothers, this is the most dreadful and most glorious moment of our lives,' he said. 'I'm not normally given to sentiment, but if the day of our deaths doesn't warrant a little melodrama, then I don't know what does.'

Cavalerio saw a few wry smiles and said, 'The credo of Tempestus is that the manner of our deaths is at least as important as the manner of our lives. Today we will show these Mortis dogs what it means to feel the wrath of our Legio. It has been an honour to fight alongside you all over the years, and it is a privilege to lead you in this last march. May the light of the Omnissiah guide you.'

His brothers solemnly acknowledged his words with binaric glows of pride, but it was left to Princeps Kasim to give fleshvoice to the feelings of the Legio.

'The honour is ours, Stormlord,' said Kasim.

Cavalerio smiled as he saw the gleam of the gold skull and cog medallion he had given the man after the Epsiloid Binary Cluster wars.

'Good hunting, everyone,' said Cavalerio, and closed the link.

DESPITE THEIR BLOODING in the initial fighting around the Magma City, Princeps Camulos could not ignore such a blatant challenge, and Cavalerio's auspex filled with returns as Legio Mortis marched through the smoke and fire to meet them. Swarming around each engine were thousands of Mortis skitarii, fearsome, skull-visaged warriors of terrible reputation.

The Tempestus skitarii, led by the indomitable Zem Aeschman, the scarred hero of Nemzal Reach, marched out to meet them, outnumbered at least four to one. To go into an engine fight required great courage, but to march into battle beneath such a titanic conflict demanded fearlessness only such enhanced warriors could boast.

'Multiple engine signatures,' said Sensori Palus, and Cavalerio acknowledged the inload, putting Aeschman's skitarii from his mind. The gargantuan form of *Aquila Ignis* led the Mortis engines, a row of three twisted Warlords marching in front of it like a skirmish screen. On both flanks, two Reavers circled wide.

'They only outnumber us by one engine,' said Cavalerio. 'That's not so bad, eh?'

'Yes, my princeps,' said Moderati Kuyper. 'It's just a shame they outgun us so heavily.'

Watching the Mortis deployment, Cavalerio said, 'They're being cautious. None of them dare stray too far from their big brother.'

'And who can blame them?'

'They're afraid of us,' said Cavalerio. 'They're still thinking of what we did to them in the opening ambush and they're scared we've got another trick like that up our sleeves.'

'I wish we did, Stormlord,' muttered Kuyper.

Cavalerio smiled in his amniotic tank, a stream of bubbles rising from his mouth.

'Who says I haven't?' he asked. 'All princeps, marching speed.'

ON THE FAR side of the Magma City, where screaming mobs of skitarii and altered Protectors threw themselves at the Vulkan Gate, a blizzard of gunfire and artillery laid waste to the attackers closest to the entrance. Before Melgator's forces could regroup and resume their attack, the Vulkan Gate opened and beneath their azure lightning wheel standard, the Knights of Taranis rode out.

Lord Verticorda led his Knights, the noble form of *Ares Lictor* resplendent, the wound in its chest repaired in time for this last ride to glory. Alongside Verticorda, Lord

Caturix rode the majestic *Gladius Fulmen*, his war engine proudly bearing the scars and ravages of battle on its burnished plates.

Behind them came the last nine Knights of the order, their armour polished and repaired such that they shone like new. This was to be their final charge and the Magma City's artificers had ensured that they would make a fine sight as they rode out.

The Knights formed a wedge, with Verticorda and Caturix as the tip of the spear, and plunged into the mass of enemy warriors, their guns spitting death with every shot. The combined shock of the artillery strike followed by the assault of the Knights broke the front of the Dark Mechanicum line, and the Knights smashed through the reeling survivors like giants scattering children before them.

Roaring streams of turbo lasers and blitzing storms of explosive shells tore through skitarii and weaponised servitors as the Knights carved a path along the Typhon Causeway. Hundreds of their enemies were dying every second and their bodies were crushed underfoot as the Knights rode ever onwards. The Knights of Taranis slaughtered their way along the causeway's length, Verticorda killing with methodical precision, Caturix with furious abandon.

As sudden as the attack was, Melgator's forces rallied with commendable speed, and armoured units raced to meet the charging Knights. Heedless of their own warriors, enemy cannon opened fire on the causeway, blowing wide craters in the great road. The speed and ferocity of their charge carried the Knights clear of the bulk of the fire, but two warriors, tangled up in the debris of their carnage, were caught by the full fury of a sustained salvo of high explosives and blown to pieces.

Another Knight took a direct hit from an experimental gun recovered from the ruins of Adept Ulterimus's tomb beneath the Zephyria Tholus. Empowered with dark energies from the Vaults of Moravec, a beam of black light punched straight through the Knight's power field to wreath the machine in dark fire that instantly melted through its armour. Verticorda could hear its agonised screams over the Manifold and watched as its dying rider swept a host of enemy warriors to their doom as it plunged from the causeway and into the magma.

With every passing moment, the Knights of Taranis were fighting their way further and further from the Magma City, killing and crushing Adept Zeth's enemies with consummate skill and grace. This was no undisciplined, feral charge, but the exquisite skill of noble warriors exercising their killing art in the most sublime manner imaginable.

Already they had travelled more than two kilometres from the gate, leaving a trail of dead and dying enemies in their wake. As another four hundred metres was won, another Knight died, the machine's legs sawn off by Ulterimus's dark weapon and its carapace pounced upon by a cackling tide of mutant skitarii.

Lord Caturix turned his guns on the swarming skitarii, clearing them from the downed Knight in a series of devastating bursts of gunfire. The Knight was already dead, and, rather than allow the enemy to scavenge from its corpse, Caturix kept firing until its reactor core was breached and it vanished in a seething wall of plasma fire.

Only five Knights remained with Verticorda and Caturix, and as devastating as their charge had proven, it was slowing. More and more enemy warriors were clogging the causeway with their bodies, and entire regiments of artillery and armour were concentrating their fire on stopping the Knights.

Verticorda and Caturix, warriors of wildly different temper yet identical courage, kept pushing onwards, their ultimate goal in sight: the black pavilion of Ambassador Melgator.

PRINCEPS KASIM IN *Raptoria* darted through the ruins of the Arsia sub-silos to unleash a furious barrage into one of the flanking Reavers. The towering engine's shields soaked up the fire of the smaller war machine, turning its guns on the tumbled metallic ruins.

A storm of shrapnel and explosions tore through the collapsed silo, but *Raptoria* was already on the move, surging though the jumbled mass of collapsed towers and fallen masonry to fire again. Using every inch of cover and his natural affinity for moving through close and dirty terrain, Kasim kept *Raptoria* one step ahead of his enemy's fire, loping randomly from cover to deliver stinging fire on the lumbering Reaver before vanishing back into the cover of the silo.

With the Warlords and Imperator closing behind them, one of the Reavers turned into the collapsed and burning silos to flush Kasim out, unwilling to leave a snapping predator in their wake, even one as hopelessly outgunned as a Warhound.

Its vast bulk smashed through steel archways that had once seen the passage of thousands of workers, trampling through machine shops, which had produced weapons and ordnance that had pacified worlds on the other side of the galaxy. It towered over the twisted wreckage of melted machines and the charred skeletons of those who had died in the complex's collapse.

Sparks and trailing squalls of energy backwash flared from its shields as it bludgeoned its way through the factory to reach its quarry. A screaming wail of scrapcode bled from its external augmitters and its warhorn's booming howl echoed weirdly from those walls that still stood.

Kasim broke from cover, the cobalt blue of his engine stark against an ashen wall.

The Reaver caught sight of him and twisted its upper body to target his nimble engine. A torrent of weapons fire reduced the wall to pulverised dust and sparked from *Raptoria's* shields.

No sooner had the Reaver opened fire than the vulpine form of *Astrus Lux* slipped from the shadows of a sagging derrick and bounded towards the Reaver's exposed back, her weapon arms blazing. Princeps Lamnos poured his shots into where the swirling energy discharges were greatest, battering down the Reaver's shields with a furious concentration of fire.

The Reaver immediately realised its danger and tried to turn, but Princeps Lamnos was quicker, sidestepping his engine through the tangled mess of smashed machinery and fallen structure. Fighting to keep his aim true while manoeuvring his engine over such rough terrain, Lamnos kept his fire steady for longer than was safe.

His persistence paid off as the rear quarter of the Reaver's shields blew out in an enormous flaming bloom of light. The blaring challenge of the machine's warhorn changed in pitch to one of pain as *Raptoria* vaulted a broken berm of machinery and opened fire on the Reaver at point-blank range.

Without the protection of its shields, the Reaver was horribly exposed and Kasim's fire wreaked fearful damage on the larger engine. Like Lamnos, Kasim kept his fire steady, raking a salvo of high-energy turbo laser fire across the Reaver's hip. The joint streamed molten gobbets of armour before explosively giving way, and *Raptoria* and *Astrus Lux* bounded away from the mortally wounded engine.

The Reaver toppled slowly, majestically, onto its side, crushing what little remained of the silo beneath its enormous weight and breaking into pieces. *Raptoria* pushed onwards, hugging the ground and taking advantage of the billowing cloud of ash and smoke clouds thrown up by the Reaver's collapse.

Astrus Lux pulled back through the silo, circling around the fallen engine, but Lamnos had exposed his Warhound for too long and the Reaver's companion had worked up a firing solution.

A withering series of missile impacts slammed into the top of *Astrus Lux* and pounded her into the ground, hammering her shields until they broke open with a pounding, concussive detonation. Like a wounded bird, *Astrus Lux* tried to crawl into cover, shieldless and with her legs shattered by the impacts.

The second Reaver was taking no chances, however, and strode into the flaming ruin of the silo, crushing *Astrus Lux* beneath its bulk.

First blood to Tempestus.

ON THE LEFT flank of the Tempestus battlegroups, far across the cratered wasteland of the landing fields – where *Deus Tempestus* and *Tharsis Hastatus* duelled with *Aquila Ignis's* skirmish screen of Warlords – Princeps Mordant pushed forwards in *Arcadia Fortis*. Though he commanded a Reaver, Jan Mordant matched the pace of his Warhound companion, *Vulpus Rex*, stride for stride.

He and Princeps Basek strode to meet the two flanking Reavers, both enemy machines twisted and hateful with bloody banners and grisly adornments hanging from their weapons. Instead of marching straight towards the enemy Reavers, *Arcadia Fortis* followed a wide curving course that drew his opponents away from the easy shelter of the Imperator with every step.

Whickering streams of weapons fire filled the air between the foes, both Tempestus princeps directing all their fire upon the Reaver closest to the centre of the battle line. Further out from the Magma City, there was none of the cover enjoyed by *Raptoria*, and Princeps

Basek was forced to use all his savvy to avoid the worst of the incoming fire. The distance between the Mortis and Tempestus engines was shrinking and with every stride, the firestorm grew ever more ferocious.

Given the disparity of weight and gun strengths, it was only a matter of time until the brutal mathematics of war took their toll on the Tempestus engines. The Mortis engines knew this and their discordant horns boomed in triumph, but in war, as in all things, there are variables that can upset even the most inevitable of functions.

Both *Vulpus Rex* and *Arcadia Fortis* were commanded by men whose hearts were still those of aggressive hunters, and they were fighting to destroy as much of Mortis's strength as possible before their ending.

The shields of the Reaver targeted by both Tempestus engines flickered out, worn down by the constant barrage and shut off before they blew out. An instant later the Warlord *Tharsis Hastatus*, which had been waiting for just that moment, unleashed a punishing volley from its volcano cannon. A searing beam of nuclear fire punched through the Reaver's cockpit, and blew off its entire upper section in a spectacular explosion that hurled pieces of wreckage for over six kilometres.

The thunderous death of the Reaver had been bought by a furious concentration of fire, but that in turn had allowed the second Reaver to close virtually unmolested. Its heavy guns had brought the shields of *Arcadia Fortis* to breaking point and it was the work of moments to finish the job of overloading them.

A lucky strike on one of the carapace emitters blew out the relays connected to the neural network of the Tempestus engine, and the feedback agonies burned out the cerebral cortex of Princeps Mordant as surely as though he had taken a bolt-round to the head. *Arcadia Fortis* died with him, the mighty engine grinding to a halt, helpless and utterly at the mercy of its foes.

Basek attempted to flee from the screaming Reaver, its weakened shields and depleted ammunition load no match for such a towering foe. *Vulpus Rex* moved with grace and speed, but in the face of an indiscriminate barrage of missiles it had no chance of evasion. Missiles slammed into the ground, tearing huge craters and hurling chunks of debris into the air.

Her terrain-reading auspex overloaded with screaming, scrapcode interference, *Vulpus Rex* tumbled into a crater, one of its weapon arms snapping off and its legs buckling as it landed awkwardly. Trapped and with no escape, Princeps Basek tried to eject, but a brutal volley from the Reaver tore his floundering engine to pieces, killing him and all his crew in a mercifully swift thunder of hard rounds.

Then the sky broke open and the gathering darkness was banished as a bright sunset of atomic detonation painted the distant heavens with fire.

ADEPT KORIEL ZETH closed her eyes at the sight of the fire in the sky, knowing exactly what it represented and feeling the human portion of her body fill with sadness. She focused the Chamber of Vesta's viewing screens to the north and increased the magnification to maximum, knowing what she would see, but dreading it all the same.

All along Ipluvien Maximal's reactor chain of Ulysses Fossae, a score of fiery mushroom clouds climbed skyward. A blast wave of unimaginable force flattened the landscape for hundreds of kilometres bare of life, and the following firestorm would turn the Martian desert to irradiated glass for ten thousand years.

'Goodbye, Ipluvien,' said Zeth, before turning her attention to the unfolding conflict around her own forge, the burnished plates showing such ferocious scenes of battle that even she could scarce believe such slaughter was happening on Mars.

The charge of the Knights of Taranis had cleaved a bloody path through the attackers on the causeway, but their numbers were dwindling fast. Another two Knights had gone down, leaving only Verticorda, Caturix and three warriors.

Every second brought them closer to Melgator's pavilion, but she had no idea whether they would reach it alive. Even if they did, there would be no escape from the heart of the enemy army. Legio Tempestus were fighting a battle that would enter the annals of their histories as one of their most noble, were there any left alive to record it, and her own warriors had fought harder than she could ever have wished.

Kelbor-Hal's minions would suffer greatly to take the Magma City, and unless Zeth acted now, they *would* take it, that was certain. And not just the Magma City, but the rest of Mars would soon be in the thrall of those loyal to the Fabricator General.

The time had come to follow Ipluvien Maximal's noble action.

Zeth turned from the screens and walked towards the wide shaft that descended into the depths of her forge, bathing in the heat and waves of energy that rippled upwards from the magma far below.

A primitive-looking servitor swathed in a hooded robe followed her, its crudity quite at odds with the sophistication of the chamber. The anonymous cyborg creature took up position alongside Zeth as a dozen slender silver columns rose from the floor around the shaft.

Each of the columns was topped with an intricate arrangement of plugs and Zeth stepped into the middle of them. She reached out and slipped her hands into the biometric readers atop two of the columns, extruding a series of mechadendrites from the length of her spine.

These waved through the air and made contact with the remaining columns, and she began exloading a series of macroinstructions into the noospheric network of the Magma City. A glowing schematic of her forge flickered into life before her, invisible to anyone not noospherically modified.

'I hope Kane managed to rescue at least a portion of his noospheric network from Mondus Occulum,' she whispered to herself. 'It would be a shame for my technology to be forgotten in this sordid civil war.'

'Even facing destruction you are vain,' said a voice behind her.

Zeth turned, unsurprised to see the sinuous form of Melgator's tech-priest assassin slithering through the air behind her.

'I had a feeling I'd be seeing you again,' said Zeth.

'The Cydonian Sisterhood do not forget those who insult us,' said Remiare.

'I'd ask how you got in here, but I have a feeling it won't matter.'

'No,' agreed Remiare. 'It will not.'

The assassin skimmed slowly over the floor of the chamber towards Zeth, drawing a pair of exquisite golden pistols from her thigh sheaths.

'My employer wishes this city captured intact,' said Remiare, inloading to the noospheric map floating before Zeth. 'So you need to stop what you are doing.'

'I'm not going to do that,' stated Zeth.

'I wasn't asking,' said Remiare, and shot Zeth twice in the chest.

LORD COMMANDER VERTICORDA felt the pain of a dozen wounds through the Manifold of *Ares Lictor*. His shields were gone and his carapace was cracked in multiple locations. He could barely feel his left arm and the knee joint that had been healed two centuries ago by the touch of the Emperor ached with psycho-stigmatic pain.

All around him he could see the red-lit legions of his enemy surrounding him. Weapons fire spanked from his disintegrating carapace and his fear was not that he was going to die, but that a machine touched by the hand of the Omnissiah would fall into the hands of his enemies.

To his left he saw a group of dark-robed skitarii on one of the causeway's overhanging platforms aim a battery of quad-barrelled guns. He turned his right cannon on them, letting *Ares Lictor* target them. He felt the thrill of acquisition course down his arm and opened fire, the hurricane of shells obliterating the platform and turning the guns and their operators into an expanding cloud of shredded meat and metal.

Alongside him, Caturix crushed and sliced into the enemy host with his cannon and laser lance, his fury carrying him forward where Verticorda lived by his preternatural skill. The other Knights that still lived were the best of the order, the most sublime warriors he had fought alongside: Yelsic, Agamon and Old Stator.

Ahead, Verticorda saw the black pavilion where the architect of this confrontation watched the honourable Knights of Taranis dying for his amusement. The standard of Melgator, a golden chain upon a crimson field, flew above the pavilion and though a host of warriors and black machines stood between them, Verticorda vowed he would not be brought low while such an ignoble individual still lived.

More gunfire hammered the Knights, and Agamon was undone, the final strength of his shields torn away by the heedless sacrifice of scores of suicidal warriors rushing close and detonating explosive petards against his armour.

Old Stator died next, the preceptor clearing a path for the masters of his order with a gloriously heroic dash towards the black pavilion, his twin blades extended to either side of him as he charged. Running low, the

Knight took a direct hit to the cockpit and crashed to the ground.

The last three Knights blazed through the path won by Stator's death, and Verticorda killed and killed as he drew upon the spirits of all the lord commanders who had ridden into battle within *Ares Lictor*.

On one side, Caturix rode tall, though his mount was on the verge of destruction, while on the other, Yelsic, his companion from the day the Emperor first set foot on Olympus Mons, still carried the Taranis banner high.

'The bastard's running!' shouted Verticorda, seeing Melgator's golden chain banner moving.

'What did you expect?' retorted Caturix. 'He's no warrior. He's nothing but a coward.'

'He won't escape us,' vowed Yelsic.

'No, he damn well won't,' agreed Caturix.

Fresh impacts slammed into *Ares Lictor*, and Verticorda cried out, feeling the pain of his wounds surging bright and hot within his aged frame. Even as fresh wounds appeared on his body, he felt a sustaining power flow from the Manifold to hold him together, a gestalt legacy of heroism and honour that stretched back to his mount's birth.

The presence of *Ares Lictor's* former masters poured into Verticorda, eager to accompany him in its last moments.

All he could see through the canopy window were enemies, their twisted visages daemonic in the searing glow of the magma. This truly was a ride into hell, and these were its warped denizens.

'There he is!' bellowed Caturix, and Verticorda saw the shield-palanquin of Melgator surrounded by a cohort of brutal, ogre-like skitarii armed with fearsome beam weapons and flame lances.

The three Knights smashed through the cordon of enemy warriors between them and Melgator's retinue, their armour torn, trailing fire and spraying vital fluids. None would ever ride again, but with their final breath of life they would slay this last foe.

Verticorda shot down a dozen skitarii, and then felt the agony of sweeping beams of cutting light sawing through the armour of his right arm as though it was as insubstantial as smoke. He screamed in pain, his entire body spasming as the weapon arm was shorn from its mount.

Blood filled his throat and his vision greyed, but once again he felt the ghostly presences of his predecessors. Their ancient fury and fire was undimmed by the passage of years, and their will gave him the strength to carry on. Yet even with the sustaining power of the Manifold, Verticorda could feel his life slipping away from him.

Yelsic's machine took the full brunt of a volley of flame lance fire, his carapace wreathed in crackling purple flames from a dozen hits. Concussive impacts of grenades blew out his torso section, and the shorn halves of his stricken Knight exploded as it skidded into the mass of skitarii.

'Into them!' cried Caturix, seeing the gap Yelsic's death had created.

Acting on centuries of instinct, Verticorda followed Caturix into the scattered mob of skitarii, seeing the furrobed form of Melgator whipping his shield bearers to carry him away from the rampaging Knights.

With the last of his energy, Verticorda shouted, 'I cast the lightning of Taranis at thee!' and together, he and Caturix opened fire. Thunderous impacts strafed the ground and blazed a devastating path through the skitarii towards Melgator.

A haze of shimmering blue light erupted around the ambassador, a personal void, but such a device was designed to protect its bearer for short periods of time and against the weapons of an assassin, not those carried by war machines as fearsome as Knights.

In seconds the capacity of Melgator's voids was overloaded, and the resulting explosion hurled him through the air. The ambassador didn't even have time to hit the ground before the sustained fire of the Knights obliterated his body in a fraction of a second.

With Melgator's destruction, Verticorda felt the presence of his mount's former riders fade back into the Manifold. The pain of his wounds returned tenfold and he cried out as he felt yet more impacts on his armour.

A missile exploded his knee, the one the Emperor had touched, and *Ares Lictor* fell. The carapace slammed into the ground and the glass of his cockpit shattered into fragments. Verticorda tasted blood, but felt no pain as he sensed the Manifold open up before him.

His last living memory was hearing Caturix's voice shouting his defiance to the end.

As Verticorda died, he was smiling, and the spirit of *Ares Lictor* welcomed him.

3.06

BLOOD AND WARNINGS filled the liquid before Cavalerio, telling him of shield ignition failures, reactor bleeds and a hundred other signs that his engine was suffering. Red droplets flecked the amniotic jelly, oozing from psychostigmatic wounds on his shoulders and torso, and bleeding from his nose.

He registered the deaths of three of his engines, but forced himself to concentrate on his own fight. Ahead of him, three Warlords advanced before the might of the Imperator, *Aquila Ignis*. The soaring creation had not yet deigned to open fire.

<That's arrogance,> canted Cavalerio.

'My princeps?' asked Kuyper, bleeding from the side of his head where a panel had blown out next to him, taking the secondary reactor monitors with it.

'Nothing,' said Cavalerio. 'You have a solution to those Warlords on the right?'

'Yes, Stormlord,' confirmed Kuyper. 'All missiles locked in.'

'Then you may fire at your discretion, Moderati Kuyper,' ordered Cavalerio, before addressing his sensori. 'Where's that Reaver on our right?'

'In the silos a kilometre north of us,' reported Palus. 'It's fighting *Metallus Cebrenia*, but it's the one to our left we need to worry about. *Vulpus Rex* and *Arcadia Fortis* are gone.'

'Sharaq can handle himself,' said Cavalerio, 'and *Tharsis Hastatus* will deal with the bastard on our left.'

'Princeps Suzak also has a Warlord to deal with,' Kuyper reminded him.

'He's come through tougher fights,' insisted Cavalerio. 'I shouldn't need to remind you all that we are Legio Tempestus, we fear nothing!'

His bold words invigorated the crew, and he felt the delicious shudder of release as the missile pods on his carapace surged from their launchers. At the same time, a sustained barrage of turbo lasers hammered the Warlord on the right, while repeated blasts from his volcano cannon punched the Warlord in the centre.

His enemies were giving as good as they got, and each shot *Deus Tempestus* unleashed was answered with two in reply, but Cavalerio had an advantage the Mortis engines did not. He was linked through the amniotic suspension to the very heart of his machine, and though the immediacy of connection allowed him only a fractional advantage, for a princeps of the Stormlord's skill, it was the only advantage he needed.

The engine drivers of Mortis were good, for no one ever ascended to the princeps chair of a Warlord who had not proved himself a hundred times or more, but they were as fledglings compared to the skill of Indias Cavalerio.

With precise evasions and instinctual anticipation of his enemies' thoughts and tactics, Cavalerio had avoided a weight of fire that would have seen a lesser princeps destroyed thrice over. *Deus Tempestus* was wounded, but she strode through the storm of enemy fire without fear and with the banner of Legio Tempestus borne proudly aloft.

'Target's shield strength failing,' reported Palus. 'The turbos have got him!'

'Multiple missile impacts scored!' shouted Kuyper. 'She's burning!'

'Bring us about, Lacus,' cried Cavalerio. 'Volcano cannon on rightmost Warlord. A three-pulse volley if you please.'

'Yes, my princeps,' replied his steersman, and Cavalerio felt the ancient machine respond, its vast and complex manoeuvring systems reacting with the speed of a brand new engine. Cavalerio felt the heat build as the monstrously powerful cannon on his left arm powered up.

He saw the stricken Warlord slow and relished the fear its princeps must be feeling to be so achingly vulnerable. With no shields and his engine burning, his fight was over.

'No, that won't do you any good,' chuckled Cavalerio as the volcano cannon fired and struck the Warlord's shields dead on, battering the last of its protection away. The first blast was immediately followed by two more, and the Warlord's upper carapace vanished in a thermonuclear blast as its reactor detonated.

'Centre Warlord's shields failing!' shouted Palus. 'It was too close to the explosion!'

'All stop,' ordered Cavalerio. 'Reverse left step and bring us back about, Lacus. Divert all shield power to volcano cannon, I want to make this shot count!'

His crew hastened to obey his commands, and Cavalerio felt the groaning strain of metal all around him as he pushed his engine to the limits of its endurance. A moment of doubt flickered across his mind as he remembered doing the same thing to *Victorix Magna*, but he pushed that thought aside.

<Quickly now!> canted Cavalerio. <Before his shields have a chance to replenish!>

A flurry of impacts struck his torso and carapace, and Cavalerio grunted in pain, his flesh convulsing in sympathy with his wounded engine. He felt the damage to *Deus Tempestus*, but shook off the pain. If his engine was paying the price for his tactics, then so too would he.

'Gun charged, my princeps,' reported Kuyper. 'Solution locked.'

Cavalerio snatched control of the weapon from his engine's gun-servitor. 'Firing!'

Once again the volcano cannon unleashed its deadly fire, the searing bolt of destruction enhanced with all the power Cavalerio could give it.

The enemy Warlord's shields absorbed the first microsecond of the impact, but collapsed with an explosive detonation that tore the upper tiers of its armour away like paper in a storm. Cavalerio kept his aim steady as the fire built in his arm to a raging, searing sensation, and the enemy Warlord vanished as his fire burned through its hull and sliced it almost in two.

The crew of *Deus Tempestus* cheered as the Warlord broke in two at the waist, its legs left standing as its torso and upper carapace crashed to the ground in a flaming arc of molten metal.

Cavalerio let out a shudder of release as he watched the Warlord die. It had been a terrible risk altering the shield strength to empower the volcano cannon, but it had paid off and now the odds were more even.

Then the *Aquilis Ignis* opened fire.

ADEPT ZETH TRIED to remain standing, but the pain in her chest was too great. Her legs gave way beneath her and she slumped to her knees, blood streaming down her chest and back from where Remiare's projectiles had pierced her armour and body.

She looked down at her breastplate, seeing the void projector still intact on her chest, then looked up in surprise. Remiare smiled and spun the pistols to face her, relishing Zeth's look of confusion.

'I suppose you're wondering why your personal void didn't save you,' said the assassin as she skimmed over the ground, circling the ring of steel columns that surrounded Zeth. 'These rounds are hand-crafted in the null-shielded forges of Adept Prenzlaur, and utilise technology similar to that found in the warp missiles used by Titans.'

'Actually,' said Zeth, coughing a wad of blood into her mask, 'I was wondering how long it would take for the noospheric trip-code I've been broadcasting to affect you.'

Zeth saw Remiare's surprise in her biometrics and laughed. 'You think you are so clever, assassin, but I am a high adept of the Mechanicum! Nobody's cleverer than me.'

Remiare cocked her head to one side, analysing the connection between her and Zeth on the noosphere.

'No!' she cried, seeing the exquisitely elegant code worked into the data packets passing into her augmetics, which was even now silently and secretly shutting them down.

'Too late,' hissed Zeth as Remiare's magno-gravitic thrusters cut out and the assassin dropped to the floor of the chamber with a heavy thump. Remiare's knees buckled as she landed, unused to feeling herself on the ground with such a weight of useless dead metal on the ends of her legs.

'Right now your enhanced metabolism is trying to reboot your systems, but it won't do you any good,' said Zeth, using the extruded mechadendrites that were still hooked into the steel columns to haul herself to her feet. 'It's already too late for you.'

Zeth fought to control her breathing as her augmented nervous system assessed the damage to her body. One of Remiare's bullets had severed her spinal cord and she could feel nothing below the waist, but her metallic limbs were more than capable of supporting her for long enough to finish what she had begun. Pain-balms and stimulant drugs flooded her body to keep her conscious and she smiled as the agony of her chest wounds faded.

It was temporary, she knew, and her body was dying even as it eased her pain.

'I'll kill you!' hissed Remiare, fighting unsuccessfully to raise her pistols.

'No you won't,' said Zeth, before turning to address the primitive-looking servitor. 'Polk.'

The servitor moved to stand before the assassin, and Remiare let out a gasp of recognition as it drew back its hood.

'You remember Polk, don't you?' asked Zeth. 'You made sure my apprenta's mind was damaged beyond repair, but even a damaged mind can be rendered into something useful. Oh, he's a crude and ugly thing, I know, but his very crudity is what's protecting him from the trip-code that's affecting you.'

The servitor that had once been Kantor Polk bent down and lifted the limp form of the assassin from the ground, her struggles feeble as she tried to fight off Zeth's debilitating code streams. Polk's crude, piston-augmented muscles held Remiare immobile, and Zeth read her terror and incomprehension of the situation in the flaring spikes of her bio-electric field.

'Dispose of her,' ordered Zeth, pointing with a free hand to the shaft in the centre of the chamber that dropped through the forge to the magma beneath. 'And hold her tight all the way down.'

Zeth turned away, focusing her attentions on the steel control columns that linked her to the vast and complex structure of the Magma City's core systems. She looked up at the glowing schematic of her forge and with heavy heart issued the last of her macroinstructions.

THARSIS HASTATUS, AN engine that had marched to victory on a hundred worlds, was obliterated in a single salvo. A punishing volley from *Aquila Ignis's* hellstorm cannon stripped her of her shields in an instant, and a devastating impact from its plasma annihilator reduced it to smoking, white-hot debris.

Cavalerio felt the death of his friend and comrade, Princeps Suzak, like a knife to the heart, and fought to control his anger and grief as they threatened to swamp him. The Manifold held him in its grip and his attention was firmly dragged back to the battle.

'Situation report!' he barked. 'Who's still standing?'

Palus sent out an active pulse of auspex energy to burn through the interference caused by so much powerful weapon discharge and reactor explosions. 'I'm only getting returns from *Metallus Cebrenia* and *Raptoria*,' he said, his voice heavy with disbelief. 'Aeschman's skitarii are still fighting, but they're almost gone.'

So caught up in the furious combat was he, Cavalerio had quite forgotten that an equally bloody conflict had been raging beneath him on the ground. In an engine war of such ferocity, infantry was virtually an irrelevance, but it never paid to forget the courage of those who fought beneath the battling leviathans.

<Get our shields back to full strength. Now!> he canted, sorting through a morass of data feeds, replaying inloads from his brother princeps to piece together the battle beyond his immediate concerns.

Before his engine's horrifying destruction, Suzak had fought like the killer he was, dispatching a Reaver and a

Warlord before the Imperator had slain him. On the right flank, Princeps Sharaq and *Metallus Cebrenia* had, together with Princeps Kasim and *Raptoria*, taken down the last Reaver, which left only the Imperator, *Aquila Ignis*.

The Mortis engines had come expecting an easy victory, and no matter what happened next they would leave the bulk of their force burning on the Martian sands. Tempestus had earned themselves a legendary place in the history of Mars.

'It's firing!' shouted Kuyper.

Cavalerio opened a Manifold link to his surviving warriors. 'All Tempestus engines, this is the Stormlord–'

Princeps Cavalerio never got a chance to finish his order as a thunderous series of impacts smashed into his engine. Searing pain, worse than the death of his beloved *Victorix Magna*, surged through his body as the weakened shields collapsed under the barrage of missiles from the Imperator's upper bastions.

Deus Tempestus's shield emitters blew out in a cascading series of explosions, and the Stormlord's body spasmed in its tank as the feedback blitzed through his mind, fusing his synapses with those of the Manifold.

In his last seconds of life, he saw the heroic march of *Metallus Cebrenia* and *Raptoria* as they advanced upon the red and silver monster. Their weapons arms were wreathed in fire as they advanced, heedless of the impossibility of ever hurting the Imperator, though to call it such now that its masters had turned to the cause of treachery seemed perverse.

Metallus Cebrenia was the first to die, her right leg blown off, and an almost scornful barrage of rockets finishing her off as she lay helpless in the ruins of a giant loading bay. *Raptoria* lasted only moments longer. Her shields were torn away by a sweeping blast of gatling cannon fire, and her speed was no protection from a volley of Apocalypse missiles that flattened an area a kilometre square.

Cavalerio felt their deaths and watched through the Manifold as *Deus Tempestus* sensed them too. Blood poured from his ravaged flesh and the liquid in his casket was almost opaque with it. He pushed himself to the front of the tank, feeling the fluids pouring from cracks in the glass and seeing the smoking ruin that was all that was left of his cockpit section.

Kuyper was dead, his body slumped and on fire in his moderati's chair, while across from him, the steersman, Lacus, was little more than a mangled lump of torn flesh. Cavalerio couldn't see his sensori, now realising that the entire upper section of the cockpit was open to the sky. The enginseer who had replaced Magos Argyre, an adept named Thunert, was still alive, only his lack of flesh saving him from the fires that swept the cockpit.

Cavalerio fought down his anguish as he saw the triumphant *Aquila Ignis* stride towards him, its colossal tread shaking the ground.

Its guns were silent and Cavalerio knew why, feeling the spiking pain of skitarii breaching charges detonating against his engine's leg armour.

'Mortis wants to capture us,' he said. 'I can feel them crawling inside us already.'

With what remained of his connection to the Manifold, the Stormlord linked with the enginseer's station.

<We can't let them take us, Thunert,> canted Cavalerio. <You know what we have to do.>

'I do,' agreed Thunert. 'Though it goes against all my teachings, the alternative is worse.'

'Then do it,' ordered Cavalerio. 'Disengage all reactor safeties.'

'It is already done, Stormlord.'

'May the Omnissiah forgive us,' whispered Indias Cavalerio.

Seconds later, *Deus Tempestus* was utterly annihilated as her plasma reactor went critical with the force of a miniature supernova.

THE DEATH OF *Deus Tempestus* was almost the last act in the battle of the Magma City.

Almost, but not quite.

That honour was saved for the city itself.

With the destruction of Legio Tempestus and the death of the Knights of Taranis, the last real opposition to the forces of the Dark Mechanicum were gone. Legio Mortis skitarii poured into the city through the smashed ruins of the sub-hives and landing fields, killing any soldiers they came across and capturing as many of the city's adepts as was possible at such a frantic, bloody time.

The scattered remnants of Melgator's army rallied to the snake-headed banner of a Mechanicum warlord named Las Taol, and surged into the city through gates now virtually undefended. The slaughter was terrible, and such was the frenzy of destruction that the bulk of the Dark Mechanicum forces did not realise their peril until it was already too late.

Artillery fire continued to pound those few areas of the city that still resisted conquest. The ground rumbled and buildings shook with violent tremors, but it was no gunfire that caused these tremors.

High on Aetna's Dam, the sluice gates of the Arsia Mons caldera locked into the open position, allowing vast, overflowing streams of lava to pour down the aqueducts and into the lagoon. Normally, this process was precisely regulated, but Adept Zeth had removed that control, and the magma lagoon began filling with lava straight from the heart of the volcano.

Far below the street level of the city, the void-protected columns that plunged deep into the bedrock of Mars to support the island of the great forge were exposed to the molten heat of the magma lagoon. The power that continually replenished the voids had been cut and the liquid rock began eating into the adamantium columns. The process began slowly at first, then accelerated as more of the inner core of each column was exposed.

A groaning crack boomed like the thunder of the gods, and the despoilers of Zeth's city paused in their debaucheries and looked to the skies in fear. The great silver road before Zeth's temple split apart and vast geysers of lava spouted upwards as the southern tip of the city broke free.

Towers and temples collapsed, their structures torn and twisted as the city heaved and buckled. The shriek of tortured metal and splitting rock were like the city's death scream, and its violators echoed it as they now guessed the danger.

Glowing lava poured in mighty waterfalls from shattered aqueducts, and rivers of blazing rock oozed through the streets, consuming all in their path. Altered skitarii and warp-enhanced Protectors perished as they were swept away by the searing tides of molten lava.

Soon the city was ablaze from end to end, the magma incinerating anything flammable and melting anything that wasn't. In moments, thousands were dead, attackers and inhabitants both, though such a death was a mercy for the denizens of the Magma City.

The Typhon Causeway cracked at its midpoint, a kilometre-long slab of rock shearing away from the city and tipping more than ten thousand men and war machines into the lava. Wrenched and torn by quakes wracking the city, the Vulkan Gate, which had guarded the entrance to the city for a millenium, fell and broke into a thousand pieces.

In the age to come, these would prove to be the only things to survive the cataclysm.

Thousands streamed from the city through the wreckage of the landing fields where Tempestus had made its last stand, but such was the overflow from the shattered aqueducts that no escape was possible. An ocean's worth of magma spilled outward, and the heat and fumes soon overtook those few who could outrun the lava.

Only *Aquila Ignis* escaped total destruction, Princeps Camulos turning and marching at flank speed to avoid the tide of molten rock. Even he was not quick enough, the lava flowing around the Imperator's mighty legs and steadily burning through its shielded plates. *Aquila Ignis* waded through the lava for five steps until at last its armour failed and its ankles gave way.

At last the towering engine was brought down by the fury of the planet, its immense bulk crashing to the ground, smashed to destruction on the hard rock of Mars. Its bastions crushed themselves, its cockpit decks were flattened by its unimaginable weight and only its Hellstorm cannon survived the Titan's fall.

In time, this would be salvaged and taken to another world, but for now it had no more death to deal.

The destruction continued within the city as the lava eagerly rose up through the streets to claim what had been denied it for so long by the technological wiles of the Mechanicum. Within an hour, nothing remained alive within the Magma City, every living soul burned to ash and every structure brought low.

Three hours after Adept Koriel Zeth unleashed doom upon her forge, the Magma City finally sank beneath the great inland lake of lava. The last of its towers were cast down, Zeth's inner forge filled with lava, and all her great works were destroyed as thoroughly as though they had never existed.

And with their destruction, all hope of lifting the Imperium into a golden age of scientific progress, not seen since humanity set forth from its birthrock, was lost forever.

Addenda

+ FAR BELOW THE Martian plain, the last two Knights of Taranis made a cautious descent into the rocky depths of the Medusa Fossae, a trench system that straddled the border between the highlands and lowlands of Tharsis and Elysium. Both machines clambered down into the darkness while Mars above burned with war. They were each scarred with battle, yet both moved with smooth natural grace, as though fresh from a maintenance refit. *Equitos Bellum* led the way, with *Pax Mortis* guarding their rear as they sought an automated research facility of Koriel Zeth that Rho-mu 31 had assured them they would find hidden in this deep canyon. Here, the Knights and their two passengers would follow the instructions of the girl with the golden light, and await the end of hostilities to see what was left of their beloved world.

+ DEEP IN THE Noctis Labyrinthus, Dalia Cythera and Rho-mu 31 took up their stewardship of the Dragon. A measure of the golden light that shone within Dalia had now passed to her Protector, and they were content in the knowledge that their friends were as far from the fighting as it was possible to be. Only much later, when Dalia dared return to the silver cavern, did she see that the book containing the grand lie of Mars had been taken.

+ TEN THOUSAND YEARS would pass before the next Guardian was drawn to the Noctis Labyrinthus, but by then the damage had been done.

Addenda ends.

ABOUT THE AUTHOR

Hailing from Scotland, Graham McNeill worked for over six years as a Games Developer in Games Workshop's Design Studio before taking the plunge to become a full-time writer. In addition to many previous novels, Graham's written a host of SF and Fantasy stories and comics, as well as a number of side projects that keep him busy and (mostly) out of trouble. Graham lives and works in Nottingham and you can keep up to date with where he'll be and what he's working on by visiting his website.

Join the ranks of the 4th Company at
www.graham-mcneill.com